FANTÔMAS CAPTURED

A FANTÔMAS DETECTIVE NOVEL

BY MARCEL ALLAIN

Bibliographical Note
This Antipodes edition, first published in 2017, is a republication of the work first published by Stanley Paul & Co, London, in 1926. The original translation has been altered to reflect modern spelling and usage.

ISBN 978-0-9966599-5-6

Contents

FANTÔMAS
CAPTURED

1. A Master's Orders

"Well, François, anything new today?"

"Not a blessed thing!"

"Your chief back?"

"Not yet... Anyway, it's all one to me!"—and stretching himself like a man thoroughly tired out, the usher of the Ministry, the official specially attached to the person of the Minister of the Interior, President of the Council, added:

"The chief, quotha! *I* don't make much account of *him*. A Minister, pooh! A Minister's a chap ain't clever enough even to keep hold of his job. Here today, gone tomorrow! Look at me! Why, it's five and thirty years I've been here—a lease for life, sir! But the chief, why, in another fortnight, the Chambers belike will have chucked him out. But there, you know how it is, my boy!"—and the man, who had long since lost the feeling of admiration generally accorded to the protagonists of the political world, gave a big laugh, then resumed in confidential tones:

"To start with, our President of the moment is no better than a jack-in-office."

"Why so?"

"Why, you know quite well, come! What does the man owe his place as Minister to? To playing the cunning knave, I tell you, to making it his business to challenge his predecessor on the score of Fantômas, to giving a public undertaking in the House to put a stop to 'this intolerable scandal'—his very words, as reported in the *Officiel.*"

"Well?"

"Well, to stop Fantômas, that's the policemen's job. And the police can make no hand of it. And the chief, he won't do any better. So then he'll have to give it up in favor of somebody else... So there you are! there you are, old man!"

To this the clerk in the ministerial offices who was indulg-

ing in this chat with the usher vouchsafed no answer. *He* had
not long been in ministerial employ, and still cherished some
feelings of respect for the masters of a day whom the chances
and changes of parliamentary intrigue and interpellations in
the House installed in temporary power.

Then he began to think things over. It was true, after all, that
Didier Maujean, deputy for the Mid-Rhine, owed his promo-
tion to a cleverly worded interpellation as to the "Fantômas
scandal." A week before this, in fact, when the fresh exploits
of the grim and gruesome Lord of Terror had become known,
when it was reported that once more the scoundrel had escaped
arrest, when it was learned that Juve, who was supposed to be
defunct, had yet again been checkmated by the criminal, "a
raging, tearing" press campaign had been inaugurated. The
newspapers, one and all, had vied with each other in proclaim-
ing—the fact was indeed, undeniable—that it was high time
to have done with this Monster of Wickedness, that France
must be delivered from this Genius of Crime, that in one word,
it was outrageous that, in defiance of all efforts of the police,
Fantômas should still continue the terrible series of his acts of
violence.

Didier Maujean himself had said no more in the Chambers,
albeit three or four broad hints had given the House to understand that the deputy for the Mid-Rhine blamed the Ministry
for not carrying on the struggle with more energy. No doubt
he, no less than others, had been amazed at the result of the
division taken after his speech, a vote that overthrew the government, and pointed so clearly to him as the next President of
the Council that the very next day he had been summoned to
the Elysée by the President of the Republic.

From that moment there could be no mistake about what
was expected of him, whether by the Chambers or by the
Country. Didier Maujean had won his high post because he
had in a way pledged himself to bring about Fantômas' arrest.
But it was a rash promise. Would he succeed in keeping it? Or
was he to prove incapable of gaining the day against the abominable and terrifying scoundrel?

The officials of the Ministry themselves were far from feeling confident on the point. After pondering a while over his fellow-employee's remarks, the clerk asked again:

"Well, anyway, is he in, your Minister?"—and he pointed to the door of the President's private room.

"Don't know."

"But surely…"

"No! don't know… You look surprised? Well, I'll tell you a secret, our gallant friend, ever since he undertook to fight Fantômas, is in a bit of a fright, you must know—very natural too! So he makes a point of behaving with all the mystery he can contrive—goes out without telling anyone, comes back the same, by the private stairs. In a word you think he's here, and he isn't; you suppose he's gone away, and he runs into your arms…"

Suddenly the usher started violently, muttering an oath. Someone had just appeared in the anteroom, striding across the floor with rapid steps. It was Didier Maujean. A man of fifty, or barely fifty, a handsome figure still, tall and strong, with a determined look and energetic bearing, he was a fine representative of the man of action, the leader of men.

"Anything new?" he demanded, as he opened the door of his room.

"Nothing, Monsieur le President."

"My Chief Secretary?"

"Not been here, Monsieur le President."

"And the Office, have they brought the reports?"

"I have put them with the other papers on the desk, Monsieur le President."

"Very good!… Oh! take note, I'm not in for anybody."

"Good, Monsieur le President."

"Not for anybody, d'you hear… I won't see anybody whatsoever. You understand?"

"Certainly, Monsieur le President."

The door of the Minister's room banged shut next moment, while the usher, with a shrug, turned to his colleague.

"There you see!" he said. "Every night it's the same. It's a pose, you must know. 'The Minister is working,' that sounds well. And then, only fair to say, he don't *like* seeing callers. He receives very few people. Orders are to refer all visitors—even deputies and senators—to the Chief Secretary."

Another shrug indicated the underling's private opinion of the politician. Then he continued:

"Say, my boy! a nippy night, eh?"

"Seven below zero, for sure!"

"Luckily the coals cost nothing."

"And the chimneys draw well."

"The chimneys in Ministries, old man, always draw well. A good fire's what all the staff likes,"—and with another stretch and a yawn, the usher planted himself before a stove packed to the throat, and proceeded to warm himself luxuriously, presenting the soles of his boots alternately to the flames.

His companion lit a cigarette.

"On duty till when?" he asked.

"Till he chooses to go."

"The boss?"

"Yes, the Minister… About six, or half-past."

"Goodbye then for the present. I'll be off and take a hand at manille at Paul's."

"First-rate. I'll go too. Unless something unforeseen, of course… But there, with a man like that, there's always a something unforeseen!"—and, left to his own devices, the man went on warming himself.

Little by little, meantime, silence began to reign in the Ministry. Clerks, secretaries, messengers took their departure and the vast edifice in the Place Beauveau little by little assumed the hushed, tranquil aspect of a great house in a provincial town. From beyond the cobbled courtyard that extends in front of the building came the distant sound of the motorcars that roll in a never-ceasing flood along the Rue Saint-Honoré—and that was all.

"Quite true, it *is* cold tonight," grumbled the usher to himself. "But there, it's seasonable weather after all."

Then he gave a start and listened in surprise. "Why, whoever can be coming now?"

Footsteps were audible on the wide white-marble stairs leading to the first floor, where the private office of the Minister is situated.

"Another fellow on the job!" the usher exclaimed disrespectfully. "Another deputy wanting to see the Chief? Very good! I've got my orders: 'Nobody'!"

The steps came nearer. The official straightened his uniform, stood to attention and came forward to meet the individual who appeared in the doorway. It was a man very elegantly dressed and who seemed, to judge by his calm and confident bearing, to be a familiar figure at the Ministry. Wearing a soft hat pulled well down over the brows, his countenance buried in the high stand-up collar of a magnificent fur coat, he had further wound carelessly round his neck and the lower part of his face a white satin scarf. All this, added to the fact that he was provided with a pair of enormous round spectacles made it impossible to make out the man's features.

"Who the devil is it?" the usher asked himself, bowing respectfully. Then, fancying he caught sight of something black— beard or cheek—above the scarf, he thought:

"Ah! the negro deputy, I suppose."

But the newcomer, buttoning the last button of a glove, began to speak:

"Didier Maujean is in, is he not?"

"Did... the Minister... Monsieur le President"... stammered the official for the first time in his life perhaps, taken aback. He was not, for his part, over and above respectful towards the President of the Council; but, to make up, he was well drilled in the ultra-deferential forms of address usual in ministerial circles. The President of the Council was for all men, in the regular course, either "His Excellence," or "Monsieur le Ministre," or else "Monsieur le President." Never, never in all his days had he heard anybody dare to speak so cavalierly by his plain name of the great man of the Place Beauveau.

Absolutely dumbfounded, the usher could only stare the harder when the visitor addressed him once more:

"Well? are you dumb? I am asking if Maujean is in."

Then the usher rose to the occasion. Coldly he replied:

"I do not understand whom Monsieur means… I am attached to the person of His Excellence the Pres…"

"Very well! You are a stickler for forms and ceremonies, I see. You are quite right… But what matter? Announce me…"

"To His Excellence?…"

"Obviously! Don't play the idiot…"

"Play the idiot?… I?… But…"

"Enough! Do what I tell you."

Then suddenly the usher struck his forehead. Yes, he had been behaving like a raw recruit in the service. Of course, this visitor with his impolite, contemptuous ways, why, of course he was just a madman, a poor lunatic at large! Alas, men of the sort are no uncommon visitors at the Ministry. As a rule they never penetrated so far as the anteroom of the President's Office; they were always stopped first. This individual however, had evidently pushed his way past. There was nothing left but to get him out again…

"If Monsieur will go with me?" the usher invited.

"No need. I am in a hurry. I will wait here."

"But, sir, my orders…"

"I know! I know!… There are no orders apply to me."

"Still…"

"My man, I am not patient. When I give an order, I expect it to be obeyed on the instant. Go and announce me!"

"But really…"

"Or I go straight in… And that would be regrettable…"

The stranger had taken a step forward in the direction of the Minister's apartment.

Intrepidly François barred his way. "But, sir, you cannot pass in like that," he stammered. "To begin with, whom am I to announce?"

"True! I have not mentioned my name. I am so much in the habit of being recognized by people."

The visitor gave a little shrug as he spoke. François, later on, was to relate how he had seen him draw himself up sharply, actually turn to stone, it seemed, so stiff, so rigid became the man's attitude.

"Announce me!" he repeated the command. "I am Fantômas."

"Fantômas!"

Hardly were the dread syllables uttered before François sprang back, staggering, swaying on his feet, all but falling…

Fantômas! The grim name, this name that rang out like a death knell, this name that evoked the memory of so many terrifying mysteries, so many appalling tragedies, so many daring atrocities, struck him helpless and speechless. Yet the name, this name of the Lord of Terror, had been spoken in the most natural of tones, in a gentle, perfectly untroubled voice. Nonetheless it had resounded from wall to wall of the apartment, seeming to fill it, seeming to awaken echoes hitherto unsuspected.

"Fantômas! Fantômas!" the usher repeated. A cold sweat beaded his brow. He thought:

"No! no! It is not He! It cannot be He!… It is a madman—yes, a madman!"

But already the other had made a movement, a single movement. Stepping up to the usher, he laid a hand on his shoulder, forcing him to stand up and look him in the face.

"Come, I am waiting!" he said.

Then, docile, beaten, tamed, with chattering teeth, thinking himself the victim of a hideous nightmare, the wretched man obeyed and moved toward the Minister's door. No! all doubt was gone. It was verily and indeed "Fantômas" standing there in the anteroom! It was truly the Lord of Terror who was demanding an audience with the President! No! the usher could doubt no longer. Had he not felt the stranger's blazing eyes fasten upon his with a look whose fierce imperiousness there was no withstanding. Then, as he dropped his eyes, had he not caught a glimpse between the edges of the fur coat of the visitor's costume—a suit of black tights, clinging close to the figure, the dress of legendary horror.

From that moment the unhappy man knew no more what he did, what he wished, what he thought even! It was Fantômas! and Fantômas was ordering him to announce him to the President of the Council! He was in desperation, but he never dreamed of refusing obedience, so utterly astounded his acts henceforth were those of a mere automaton.

"Very good! very good!" he faltered in a choking voice, as with tottering limbs he dragged himself to the door of the Chief's room and opened it with a trembling hand.

"What is it?" demanded a peremptory voice.

"Monsieur le President, a visitor…"

"I am not in for anybody."

"Monsieur le President, your pardon, but…"

"Not for anybody, do you hear?"

"But it is…"

"Come, can't you understand?"

"It is… it is Fantômas!"

Then, at one bound, upsetting his chair behind him, Didier Maujean sprang to his feet. A livid pallor had spread over his features, as in a hoarse voice he demanded:

"What? What do you say?… Speak out, do!"—and with the words he put his hand to his neck with the frantic gesture of a man choking. Then, while the old usher stood motionless, trembling in every limb, tottering on his feet, manifestly fighting to stave off a fit of giddiness, the door behind him opened and a man appeared in the room—Fantômas.

The Arch-Criminal advanced one pace, one pace only at first, into the great room. Well knowing his mere presence sufficed to freeze with horror all who saw him, he made no haste. Once inside the door, he turned around and shut it to after him, locking it carefully; then he stepped forward again.

Neither usher nor Minister moved. Eyes riveted on the terrifying figure, they seemed literally incapable of act or thought of any kind. Then, in the same deliberate fashion, Fantômas spoke.

"Your permission, Maujean?" he asked courteously, and deposited his hat on a chair. He unwound the scarf from his neck; he threw open the heavy fur coat, took it off and tossed on the same seat on which he next threw down carelessly the spectacles he had worn.

And then, then only, it was He, really and truly He, the dread hero of legend and hair-raising story, the monster who was the very embodiment of panic terror. His muscular form clad in the close-fitting suit of black, black gloved and black shod, moving noiselessly, thanks to the felt soles of his shoes, he stood there in the middle of the President's own room, a figure of terror, a shape of darkness and black Night, a portent of Crime—a figure without a face, for he wore a hood whose flowing folds concealed his features.

Then he spoke again:

"I am here, Maujean!" he declared. "I have come to see you. What orders am I to give you...?" But now it seemed the Minister was recovering something of his presence of mind. He was a man of energy, a fighter, was the President. Clenching his fists, shaking with rage from head to foot, he threw himself back towards the wall where a whole battery of electric bell-pushes was installed. The intention was clear enough, but clearer, sharper yet, Fantômas' answer to the gesture:

"What childishness!" he growled. "Come, come, the wires are cut, of course! What did you expect?"

The Minister staggered. But he recovered his balance promptly and strode to his desk, where he fumbled with feverish haste in a drawer. Facing him, Fantômas calmly sat down, while the Minister whipped out a revolver and leveled it.

"Charge drawn!" chanted Fantômas. "What! so simple as all that?"

The Browning dropped from the statesman's hand; he felt himself at his visitor's mercy.

But a fresh access of courage, a new defiance, stirred within him. Was he not in his own Ministry? Was he not guarded by hundreds of police, soldiers, attendants? He had only to cry for help, and they would hear and hurry to the rescue! He opened his mouth, but no sound left his lips.

"Why, no!" Fantômas had warned him coolly. "You will shout in vain! All those about you are fast asleep... No one must overhear the orders I am here to give you... Look you, that servant even is one too many..."—and the unhappy President saw a sight he would never forget.

With lightning rapidity Fantômas was on his feet. In his hand he held a vial, the contents of which he emptied on a wad of cotton wool. Then, turning away his own head, so as not to inhale the vapor rising from the compress, he darted upon the usher François. In the fraction of a second the wad was under the usher's nose—and the man had fallen, a lifeless mass!

"There!" observed Fantômas, "a capital way, you see, Maujean, to rid oneself of interlopers. Chloride of ethyl they call it. It puts a man to sleep before even he has time to realize what they are doing to him. And it is quite harmless… But to proceed to serious matters. You are listening?"

Mechanically the President of the Council nodded. The callous calm of his visitor held him spellbound. Clinging to his desk with both hands, he had ceased even to think of resistance. What orders was Fantômas about to give him? Was the Torturer perhaps on the point of flying at his throat?

"I am not going to put you out for long," resumed the brigand quietly. "I have just two words to say to you… Besides, you must be very busy; you have sworn to have me arrested, have you not?… Hmm! it is a heavy task, do I not say true?"

And as he spoke a smile hovered over the Arch-Criminal's lips.

*   *   *   *   *

Fantômas broke into a laugh, but his mirth ceased suddenly, and it was in a grave, serious voice, just tinged with a note of anger, that he proceeded:

"You wish to have me arrested, my dear Minister. Well, it is a highly praiseworthy aspiration. Let me tell you this: I am greatly interested in your character and admire your courage. For, as a fact, I realize of course that you have declared war upon me, that we two are mortal enemies; one is bound to destroy the other, either you or I must inevitably have the last word…"

As the villain spoke, the Minister could not restrain a shudder. He knew himself entirely at the mercy of the Lord of

Terror. Without hope of succor, alone with him in his room, disarmed, he could not help thinking that, if Fantômas wanted to murder him, nothing could be easier. And what a triumph it would be for the scoundrel, if tomorrow the startled universe heard how the Minister who had been rash enough to promise the defeat of the Arch-Criminal had fallen at his hand in the sanctity of his own ministerial mansion. Was not this a prospect to tempt the Lord of Terror to do the deed? Was he not about to spring up and fly at his victim's throat?

But Fantômas only folded his arms calmly.

"Yes!" he resumed, "your purpose interests me vastly— amuses me even. It adds a spice of novelty to my existence. You will understand, Maujean, I must have adversaries to match my own prowess. Ho, ho! the President of Council my antagonist! An original situation, truly!"

His voice dropped its bantering tone and suddenly grew grave.

"Not altogether a new situation, however!" he declared. "There is a precedent. You remember my struggle with another President of the Council, Désiré Ferrant?... Unhappy man! I had to kill him!..."

Fantômas made a pause. Didier Maujean felt the cold sweat beading his temples. How, alas! was this terrible scene to end? He had the impression that Fantômas was playing with him like a cat with a mouse it has caught between its claws. At first it pretends to spare its prisoner, then suddenly it kills it... Was Fantômas going to kill him?

The brigand continued:

"Désiré Ferrant acted foolishly, however. He was not accommodating. He thought he was stronger than I... Hmm! I hope *we* shall understand each other better... But you do not answer me?..."

There was a silence. The Minister's throat was so stiff and dry he could not have articulated one word. Presently Fantômas shrugged his shoulders.

"My good sir," he began again, in a tone of insulting familiarity, "you give me a poor welcome. I really thought you would be enchanted to make my acquaintance. We are going to join battle. Is it not diverting to see each other first, with no one by, as friends… Why, yes! as friends!"

He gave a short laugh of biting irony, then resumed in a changed voice:

"But I see you do not appreciate my company. Very good. I will not insist. Let us to the point that brought me here…"

He drew himself up. Abandoning the careless attitude he had affected so far, he stood laying his black gloved hands on the edge of the Minister's desk and leaning over it so close the President could almost feel the man's breath on his cheeks. Now a somber fury seemed to prompt the brigand's words:

"I have come to demand a head of you…"

"A head?" gasped Didier Maujean.

"Exactly so… And you are going to give it me…"

"But…"

"Let me finish… You are going to give it me, my dear enemy, because if you do not satisfy my polite request, I shall have to resort to acts which I should deeply regret… Let me tell you this: in case of disobedience on your part, I should revenge myself by attacking Madame Didier Maujean…"

"Attacking my wife?"

"I can only contemplate such a course with great reluctance. Be compliant, and all will be well… Besides, I would have you realize this: I accept your challenge, out of… well, say dilettantism!… because it amuses me. But this by no means implies that I place myself altogether at your disposal. I remain the Master, understand that! It is therefore the orders of a Master you are going to execute."

This time Didier Maujean vouchsafed no answer. Each of the fellow's words added fuel to his anger, increased his fury and bewilderment. What! he was Minister of the Interior, President of the Council! Absolute power was lodged in his hands, and he was to listen to and obey a Master's orders! The unfortunate man felt his brain reeling.

"These," resumed Fantômas, "are the orders in question. My dear Minister, you see before you a chagrined man—a man deeply wounded in his pride, in his self-esteem... Oh! I know such feelings are unworthy of me, but what would you have? I admit their existence frankly... You excuse me, do you not?"

Again he seemed to be bantering his victim. For sure, the Lord of Terror had spoken truthfully when he declared this visit amused him. How fail to find it diverting, to speak in this fashion to the powerful and influential politician?

"I am chagrined," he went on, "because like a simpleton, like a fool—let us give things their right names—I have let myself be checkmated by Juve. Yes, you can see I make no attempt to hide my defeats. Juve has cajoled me—I say so openly. At first I did not believe in his death. Then a doubt assailed me. Then, as I watched the inauguration of the monument erected to his memory, I was convinced he had really perished. In one word Juve has made me feel a fool. Well, that is a chagrin I intend to exact vengeance for... It is Juve's head I have come to demand of you."

The Minister nearly sank through the floor. Doubtless he too nourished something of a personal grievance against Juve, for had he not actually spoken at the dedication of the famous monument Fantômas had referred to? Doubtless he was rather angry with that celebrated police officer, who the better to fight Fantômas had had the effrontery to pass for dead, never hesitating in this way to make a mock of all the authorities. Yet, at the same time, could he fail to agree that Juve was a hero? A hundred times, a thousand times over, had not Juve risked his life to vanquish the Lord of Terror? Juve, Fandor, the two names were on every lip as the symbol of courage, gallantry, an utter contempt for danger, no less than of skill and daring.

And lo! Fantômas was demanding Juve's "head." And he demanded it with threats, presuming to dictate "orders," declaring he would wreak vengeance on Madame Didier Maujean if he was not obeyed! Under the shock of these reflections the politician felt as though just awaking from a bad dream. Fear, consternation more exactly, had held him helpless, incapable of resistance. But suddenly he roused himself. He was ready to defy Fantômas, to do his duty. He was not a very courageous man, no doubt, but he *was* a man of violent temper, capable of those fits of fury that startle and baffle an adversary.

"Enough!" he shouted hoarsely. "Juve is a hero. How dare you order me to become a murderer? I would sooner fall under your blows myself than accept your disgraceful terms."

Suddenly the President of the Council checked himself. Facing him he saw Fantômas lying back in his seat laughing unrestrainedly.

"That is a good one!" he hiccoughed, in the voice of a man tickled in the course of conversation by some totally unexpected repartee.

"A good one?" Didier Maujean repeated the words. "What do you mean?"

"Upon my word! You really suppose I am asking you to kill Juve?"

"You ask me for his head?"

"So you think I employ others to carry out the executions I deem needful? Oh! but such proceedings are worthy of your Judges, Mister President. Yes, *they* must have executioners… *I,* I Fantômas, master of all men and all things, act for myself!"

"I don't understand," bleated the Minister.

"You are going to understand, poor devil… No! I do not ask you to murder Juve. No, no! A thousand times no! Juve shall die by my hand, at my time, when I decide it is to be… What I ask of you is to cashier him; it is his head as a functionary I demand, that is all!"—and as he said the words, it seemed Fantômas had no wish now to laugh and joke. Beneath the folds of his hood his blazing eyes—eyes that seemed of very fire, whose full glare no man had ever dared to confront, flashed fiercer yet.

"Cashier him!" he repeated. "That is all I wish, but that I insist on. Continually I find Juve and Fandor in my path. For Fandor, let him be! He is laughable, diverting, young, little to be feared without Juve… Besides, the necessary steps have been taken in his case. But Juve sets my nerves aquiver. One never knows what he will be at. All means are good in his eyes… See here, shall I make an admission? Well, he is my match! Yes, in his own way, he is capable of the same reckless daring—or almost—that is part of my nature! So, I insist on being rid of him. I thought…"

Fantômas dropped his voice. He resumed, emphasizing his words one by one:

"I thought at first, Didier Maujean, it was best, seeing you have declared war on me, to destroy you without pity, to make an example. Afterwards, I pardoned you. At bottom, your attitude is dictated by political motives. It is neither formidable nor spontaneous. Juve, on the contrary, is a deadly enemy. So I am here to offer you a friendly bargain—and to give you your orders. Dismiss Juve, have him recalled, and I will spare you… Disregard my wish, however, disobey my orders, and I will direct my attack on Madame Maujean… You understand me?"

The President of the Council nodded. Yes, it was quite true, he understood. That Fantômas, indeed, should wish to rid himself of Juve did not surprise, could not surprise him. But how resign himself to this monstrous situation, to the presence of the Lord of Terror in his own private room in his own Ministry, to the fashion in which the scoundrel calmly gave him his instructions. He thought to himself:

"I am bound to say yes, in any case. An oath of this sort binds one to nothing. I must get myself out of the hole for the moment. But tomorrow I shall be free to act as…"

But the President of the Council was not given time to conclude his mental calculation. It seemed as though Fantômas guessed his inmost thoughts.

"Of course," the brigand resumed, "if I pay good heed to your oath, it is only right, my dear Maujean, that you, on your side, pay good heed to my threats. I give you three days to place Juve on the retired list. If in three days it is not an accomplished fact, I give you fair warning to order your mourning. Your obstinacy will have killed your wife. There! You must know that I have never yet uttered such threats in fun and that my plans are always realized. No need to say more, I imagine."

The Minister made no reply. Once more he felt himself helpless. Was it not, in very fact, true that Fantômas' threats were invariably made good? Was it not proved alas! established beyond all doubt that no device, no measure of precaution, no ruse could hinder the villain from striking down whomsoever he chose to strike.

Didier was still without a word when Fantômas rose to go.

"Now I am leaving you," he announced coldly. "I have no further orders to give you… Still, by-the-bye, it may interest you to know that I have a magnificent piece of work in view. Yes, one of those astounding successes that make me famous. So you see that we, you and I, are going to join battle for a prize that is well worth the while. Well, you hear what I say?… What's the matter with you now?"

Fantômas went a step nearer, and broke into a smile. Behind the great desk the President had collapsed in his armchair. He was half fainting.

"A silly fellow, no doubt of it," grunted Fantômas. "Pooh! he must at any rate have secretaries with brains? It will always be a diverting game to play."

Composedly he resumed his fur coat, wrapped his satin scarf round his neck, put on his spectacles again and pulled down his hat over his eyes. He seemed in no way hurried, taking his time about these preparations. Perhaps he was thinking?

Suddenly he exclaimed in a low voice:

"Anyway, the usher will be a good half-hour yet before he wakes up. Come now, I don't like leaving the Minister without someone to look after him. Suppose I give the alarm? He will be opening his eyes in three or four minutes, for sure,"—and the brigand crossed the room and made for the desk. He tore a leaf from a paper block, seized the statesman's fountain pen and wrote two or three lines which he left in a conspicuous place so that Didier Maujean must see them on coming to himself.

This done, Fantômas opened the door and left the room. In the antechamber an usher was on duty, in place of François, whose absence had been noted. The man had no reason for stopping a distinguished visitor who had just enjoyed the honor of an interview with the President of the Council. He bowed obsequiously and Fantômas passed out. Two minutes more and the Lord of Terror was mounting a superb motorcar standing in the Place Beauveau and was borne swiftly away.

Almost at the same instant the President of the Council, recovering from his swoon, caught sight of the lines traced for his benefit by the brigand.

"It is half-past five," Fantômas had written, "and I am forced to leave you, my dear Maujean. I have an appointment with a financier, whom I count upon clearing out forthwith. You will excuse me, I am sure… In case you want anything on waking, I make a point of letting you know you can ring without any difficulty. Your bells are in perfect working order! Your revolver is duly loaded, and nobody in the Ministry is asleep, barring your usher François. I was lying when I told you I had taken these precautions. But there, what would you have? necessity knows no law… In fact, I felt sure, in the panic my visit would have thrown you into, it would never occur to you to doubt my statements!"

"The scoundrel!" groaned the Minister. Then he went on in a broken voice:

"And now, what am *I* going to do? Whatever am I going to do?"

He thought of Juve—the excellent Juve the whole world looked upon and acclaimed as a veritable hero, and he thought too of his wife—his wife whom he adored, and who indeed fully merited this adoration.

2. Fandor Displays a Fine Obstinacy

Half an hour later that same afternoon—at a quarter after four to be precise—Jerome Fandor was alone in the little private office he occupied in the editorial department of *La Capitale*. Overheated by a gas stove, the flame of which the journalist, a dreadfully chilly individual, never turned down, the room was as peaceful as usual, and as usual presented a picturesque scene of disorder. On the walls were nailed anyhow weapons of every sort and kind, trophies of bygone engagements. On the seats, a couch, two or three cane-bottomed chairs and a couple of armchairs, were piled men's clothes of all descriptions, ranging from the workman's blue smock to the smoking coat of the man about town, from a commissionaire's uniform to a peasant's blouse. The floor, again, was littered with whole battalions of boots and shoes, scavengers' knee boots side by side with dancing pumps, soldiers' high-lows cheek by jowl with Basque espadrilles.

And all this conglomeration, which formed the arsenal and wardrobe employed by Fandor in his investigations, revealed how ardently the journalist loved his trade of skilled reporter and criminal recorder, while above all it indicated with what adroitness, with what never-sleeping alertness, he aided and abetted Juve in the unending struggle he maintained against Fantômas.

As for the journalist's table, his writing desk, its condition defied description. To begin with, it all but disappeared under masses of papers heaped together in tumbling avalanches. Further, it was overloaded with numbers of evil-looking instruments whose use a layman would have found it hard to guess— handcuffs, manacles, fetters. The inevitable result was that the young man had only a quite tiny bit of room left available for writing. The utter, incurable confusion of his table forced him in fact to be satisfied with a narrow flap—but little he cared for the inconvenience.

For the moment, indeed, Jerome Fandor had finished his article. He was now engaged in reading over the matter he had written, punctuating the perusal with a series of remarks evidently flattering to his own self-esteem.

"Not bad!" he muttered. "That would soften the heart of a tiger with a raging toothache! It would touch the feelings of a constable just going to be promoted sergeant for excess of zeal! No! honestly, without humbug, I'm sure of my twenty louis!"—and he read out the concluding sentence:

"You know, besides, my dear chief, that everything is 'going hup,' as my concierge puts it. It is only fair then that I should 'go hup' too. *La Capitale,* your paper, possesses in me the best reporter in the world—I say so myself, and you won't call me a liar, I know—so pay him accordingly!"

"Yes, that's vigorously put!" Fandor chuckled. Dupont de l'Eure can't help but take my meaning?… Nothing left but to sign my name,"—and this he proceeded to do with his very best flourish.

"So now to send the chit in"—and Fandor rang his bell for the office boy.

Now this screed he had just read through again and found admirably concocted was a document of some importance. In one word it constituted a petition to the Editor-in-Chief of *La Capitale,* the Senator Dupont de l'Eure, for an increase of salary. At the same time, no anxiety troubled the journalist regarding the reception his demand would meet with. He knew the well-merited esteem in which his chief held him, and his pretensions were in no way exaggerated. In fact he might take it for a certainty that if ever he should have to leave the staff of *La Capitale,* the paper would be bound largely to decrease the number of copies printed…

Presently, at the third ring—the young scamps on the editorial side never come on the first summons—the door half-opened, revealing the merry face of a messenger boy.

"Here y'are, M'sieur Fandor!" the lad announced. "What is

it you want?"

"Take this to the boss…"

"To the boss of bosses, eh?"

"Yes, to the Chief… He's in a good temper today?"

"So he should be. It's quarter-day, and he's got six houses belongs to him…"

"That's true. So, off with you, my lad. Hurry up!"

But the boy had hardly started for the Editor's room when a voice made itself heard from the passage outside.

"M'sieur Fandor!" it was bawling. "Wanted in the Chief's room!"—and hardly was the messenger boy's back turned before a clerk on the staff appeared.

"Hurry up, M'sieur Fandor!" he added. "Certain sure, you're in for a hot dose, you are!… M'sieur Dupont's looking that black!…"

"All right! all right!… Give me back my letter, youngster!"— and Fandor, his letter in his pocket, was three seconds later entering the private office of the Chief of the great and influential journal. It was a vast room, decorously furnished in an antique taste. An imposing desk faced the door. On one side stood a great bookcase, crammed with rare and valuable editions. On the other was a wide, open fireplace of monumental proportions, in which a fire of logs was always burning.

Before the fire stood the Senator Dupont de l'Eure. He was warming the soles of his shoes at the blaze, and his back to the door, merely asked without turning round:

"That you, Fandor?"

"I and no one else, Chief! There can be no mistake, I am unique of my kind…"

"Very good!… But I'm not in a mood for joking…"

"Well, well! May one know why?"

"Because I have something unpleasant to say to you…"

"Better and better!… Now, you know, sir, if you want to give up the idea…"

"No, I am bound to talk to you seriously."

"Oh, well! I'm listening. Only out with it quick, eh? Your looks tell me it's a wigging, and that's a thing I prefer, like castor oil, to swallow at a gulp!"

"Didn't I tell you, Fandor, I was not in a joking mood?"

"Quite true! But, sir, it was you said so, not I!" Jerome Fandor was quite unperturbed. For so many years, in fact, had he been on the staff of *La Capitale,* so many proofs had he had of the sympathy and friendliness his Editor felt for him, that he simply could not regard the latter's words in the light of a tragedy. But next moment his lightheartedness vanished.

"Fandor, my dear fellow," resumed Dupont de l'Eure, "the time is come for us to part."

"For us to part?"

"Yes… at any rate for a while… a longish while…"

"You say?"

"Well, yes… I say… You heard what I said, I imagine?"

"I heard, yes! But I don't understand… You're kicking me out?"

"I am asking you to resign…"

"That's the same thing! For what reason?"

"You want to know?"

"Why, of course."

"Well, here it is. It's difficult to put into words…"

"Out with it, sir!"

"Fandor, your late adventures have caused a scandal…"

"Really?"

"Yes! Knowing that Juve was not dead, you have written, here in this very place, the exact opposite. Over four hundred readers have complained of this fashion of fooling them…"

"Four hundred imbeciles, sir!"

"Granted! But that don't prevent their having insisted on getting rid of you."

"Oh, they? Who?"

As he stood there facing him, Jerome Fandor saw his Chief's face turn pale.

*   *   *   *   *

The journalist, however, was not the man to abandon so readily his efforts to find out a thing he wanted to know.

"Who?" he repeated his question.

"Someone…"

"Well, this someone's name?"

"I have promised not to tell, Fandor."

"Very good! But *I*, I haven't promised not to guess… It was… it was Fantômas?"

Monsieur Dupont de l'Eure never flinched.

"It was Fantômas!" reiterated Fandor emphatically. "It can only be *He* or the President of the Council. Come now, I'm getting on. I can see I'm becoming a personality!"

Juve's friend was now striding up and down the Editor's sanctum with a nervous hurried tread. He seemed to crave movement in order to keep the mastery over his feelings, to hold in check his rising indignation. Suddenly stepping up to the Senator again, he exclaimed:

"Come, let's have straight talk! You are chucking me out?"

"No! no!… Don't say such things!… You know very well, Fandor, I put the highest value on your services."

"Yes, yes! leave it at that!—just the 'comfortable words' they always address to condemned criminals! You deprive yourself of these services of mine? It's the reward for the efforts I have always made to…"

But the journalist stopped. Dupont de l'Eure had given a start. He seemed to be struggling to master his feelings as a man shakes off an overpowering torpor. "Between us two, Fandor," he was saying, "there should be no secrets. Listen to me. I am going to break my word, perhaps, but I think it is my duty to… You must promise me you will never repeat it: to anybody…"

"Not even to Juve?"

"I leave you to judge of that!… Jerome Fandor, if I ask you to leave *La Capitale,* it is because Didier Maujean has begged me to part with you…"

"Well, well!"

"And if Didier Maujean asks this, it is, I think, because he is afraid you will make fun of his efforts…"

"Why, surely!"

"Anyway, you can see how my hand is forced…"

Jerome Fandor burst out laughing:

"My dear Chief," he cried cheerfully, "say no more. You want to pitch me out of doors to please the Minister! Excellent! Only, see here! *I* don't care a hang for your Minister… So, I refuse to go…"

"Eh?"

"Yes, I refuse!… A new battle is beginning Fantômas will inevitably resume hostilities… Well, I will write you reports, and these contributions you will print because they will interest your readers… Oh! I know you, sir!… I wager I'll get you to give me a couple of columns every day. And if the Minister isn't satisfied, you can tell him you hoofed me out of doors… but that I came in again by the window… So there you are! Now, is it goodbye!"

Dupont de l'Eure smiled in spite of himself. The Editor-in-Chief was a journalist to the fingertips. He loved news for news' sake. He prized sensational scoops—and paid handsomely. If he had joined the Senate, this was only an incident like another in a busy life. The politician was of small account in him. And now he was thinking:

"He is quite right, the confounded fellow… I know myself. If he sends me good screeds… I shall take them!… Yet I swore to Didier Maujean at the Senate…"

Then, breaking off his reflections:

"Listen here, Fandor," he said, "it would be best to bow to the storm perhaps?… All said and done, a Ministry don't last forever. You would soon be back again, and a little rest…"

"Thanks for your kind intentions!"

"No, no! Stop joking!… Besides, they have just written me—I don't even know who—offering a job that would fit you like a glove while you are waiting…"

"Really? What is it?"

"I was going to discuss it with you… It's a certain Irene Beauchamp, a woman in the best society and—which makes it all the better—very wealthy. It appears she possesses an admirable library, and she is looking out for a secretary, a man of your sort…"

"Well, tell her she won't find one in me! My particular preference is not to be left 'sitting on the fence.' Very sorry, but I'm on *La Capitale* and there I stay!... Oh! never worry. Tell the Minister you've done the impossible to get rid of me, but that I'm as obstinate as the devil... Good night, sir!"—and without giving Dupont de l'Eure time to get in a single word, Jerome Fandor made a hasty exit. Hurrying to his own office he picked out such of his belongings as he did not care to leave behind and then left the little room, double locking the door after him.

In the vestibule the clerk asked him:

"Well, M'sieur Fandor, what of that summons from the boss?"

"Nothing of any importance, old man!... Only I'm going off on a journey. Don't let 'em make hay of my papers, eh?"

"Never fear, M'sieur Fandor."

"That's all right then... Till we meet again..."—and whistling a tune, Fandor left the building.

Once outside, however, in the crowded Rue Montmartre, the young man lost much of his apparent lightheartedness.

"Very queer!" he muttered to himself. "Dupont de l'Eure footing me out is something quite unexpected. What can there be behind? Ah, well! Juve must give me his opinion... Suppose I went up to see him?"

Fandor hailed a taxi and gave the driver the police officer's address. While the vehicle was on its way there, he sat plunged in thought, an anxious frown on his face. The journalist was too well posted in the terrifying ruses to which Fantômas at times resorted to nourish any doubt about the importance of the interview he had just had with the Editor-in-Chief.

"All this," he repeated to himself, "all this means there's mischief afoot. The President of the Council puts a finger in my pie. By God! it's a great honor! But it's an honor that must have a reason. What can the reason be? I annoy the man by my articles? If so, then there's something to hide... Can Fantômas have been to see him?"

But Jerome Fandor, who by sheer force of logic had come so near the truth, shrugged his shoulders at the mere supposition.

"No! impossible!" he assured himself. "I'm talking nonsense!"—and he pulled a wry face when, on reaching Juve's house, he learned from Jean, the police officer's faithful henchman, that his friend was not at home.

"Monsieur went away a good hour ago," declared the man. "It was M. Havard, I think, summoned him on urgent business to the Criminal Bureau."

"You don't know what for?"

"No, Monsieur Fandor, I haven't an idea… I only know that Monsieur said on the phone: 'Well and good!… If it's about a communication from the President of the Council, I'll come at once…'"

"Very good! That being so, I'll wait for him here,"—and once more the young man put on an air of unconcern that was far removed from his real feeling.

"Oh, ho!" he thought to himself. "So, here we have Didier Maujean making important communications to Juve. Hmm! I don't like the look of it. He's over busy, the Minister is…"

…In M. Havard's room—he had just come back from seeing the President of the Council—Juve, looking a trifle pale, was at that same minute writing a letter, which he signed in a firm clear hand that showed no sign of trembling.

"Here it is, Monsieur Havard," he announced, "here is my resignation… Seeing the President of the Council deems it necessary…"

"Juve, Juve, you say that in a tone…"

"A tone that corresponds with my state of mind!… You don't expect me to be delighted?"

"I wish you would put me outside this… hmm, this adventure, altogether."

"Monsieur Havard, never fear. I know perfectly well it's none of your fault… Anyway, it is of no importance…"

"Of course, Juve, you will come back to us… Between you and me, you know, we may tell ourselves this: Ministers have their day, they don't last forever, eh?"

"Yes, we can say that, Monsieur Havard, certainly we can. But I can tell you another thing: now you have my resignation,

you may be quite sure I shall never come back to ask for my
reappointment till I have arrested Fantômas…"

"But…"

"Because I feel a positive certainty, Monsieur Havard, that it
is not to you, it is not even to the Minister, I have just given in
my resignation… No! it is to Him!"

Juve rose to go. For the twenty minutes he had been in the
Chief's room he had suffered tortures. With compassionate
phrases—very possibly sincere—Monsieur Havard had asked
him to resign, and this in the name of Didier Maujean. A
melancholy end to a glorious, an ever glorious career! He was
turned away! Too dignified even to protest, Juve merely told
himself that this resignation they forced upon him was another
victory for Fantômas… And already he was thinking he would
have his revenge, a revenge that should startle the world.

"Till we meet again, Monsieur Havard," he said simply, and
the telephone bell ringing at that moment. "Don't mind about
me. Answer! answer!"

He was already at the door when a peremptory wave of the
hand from the Chief of the Criminal Bureau stopped him dead.

"Don't go!" the gesture said plainly.

Monsieur Havard was speaking into the instrument.

"Certainly," he was saying, "I understand perfectly… It is a
confidential matter… You would wish, on a private footing, to
have the assistance of a thoroughly competent man… such as
Juve?… Well, as it happens Juve is on leave—hmm! shall we say
retired. What I mean to say is he is free… I will send him to
you, my dear sir!… Why, yes! at once!… He's going now."

Now, from that minute Juve—and Fandor himself—found
themselves fairly started on perhaps the most sinister of all
their adventures.

3. Fantômas' Scheme

The time was about ten o'clock in the evening when, all unwittingly, M. Havard plunged Juve, and Fandor into the bargain, into the most sinister of all the adventures the two heroes had ever known. But assuredly M. Havard would have acted more circumspectly, had he known, had he merely suspected, sundry events that had occurred in Paris during the last hour. Summoned a little before to see the President of the Council, M. Havard, unfortunately, at the time knew only what Didier Maujean had chosen to tell him, and naturally the Minister had not vouchsafed many confidences.

"Sir!" he had merely declared, addressing the Head of the Criminal Department, "the more I dive into the documents relating to the Fantômas incidents, the more I see that many mistakes have been committed. The part played by Juve and Fandor, for instance, leaves a very great deal to be desired. They are heroes no doubt, but they are inconvenient heroes… You hear what I say?…"

"Certainly, Monsieur le President."

"Well, I must tell you I have already taken measures so far as Fandor is concerned. A word on the telephone to my friend Dupont de l'Eure, the Editor of *La Capitale,* gives me the certainty that the journalist in question will cease to interfere—in what is no business of his… As to Juve, you would oblige me by procuring his resignation. His conduct at the time he allowed a monument to be erected to his memory—so making a mock of the Government—would seem to afford a pretext all ready made. May I count on you?"

"Certainly, Monsieur le President." Monsieur Havard made no attempt to save his subordinate's "head." Subject himself to the caprices of the politicians as a functionary peculiarly liable to be superseded, he was far too much afraid of giving offense to show anything but an exemplary docility.

Twenty minutes after this, M. Havard had been closeted with Juve—and it was just the use made by Fantômas of this same twenty minutes that the Chief of the Criminal Bureau did not know and which it would have so much interested him to know.

Once seated in the car waiting for him at the doors of the Ministry of the Interior, Fantomas had issued an order to his chauffeur through the speaking tube:

"The Bois!... an unfrequented road!"—and the car got underway and soon reached a lonely avenue in the Bois de Boulogne.

Fantômas got out. Fantômas? Why, yes! but the brigand, as he now appeared bore no resemblance to the distinguished personage who had interviewed Didier Maujean. Provided no doubt with all toilet requisites in a makeup case, he had practically metamorphosed himself into another man. Taking off his fur coat, he had donned a surtout, comfortable enough but quite unpretending, and put on a round felt, a little the worse for wear. He wore an eyeglass, having discarded the big spectacles. His face, no longer muffled up, showed a bushy white beard and a very heavy reddish mustache. In his hand he carried a cane, which he wielded with so martial an air anyone meeting him could not fail to take him for a retired officer on half pay.

"Upon my word, sir!" muttered the chauffeur under his breath as he looked at him, "damned if I should have known you!"

"All the better!" retorted his master. "But I didn't ask your opinion. Now, drive back to the garage, my lad!"

The Lord of Terror was not much in the habit of joking with his accomplices, and the abashed apache got underway without another word. Then, walking fast like a man in a hurry taking a rapid constitutional, he turned back and made for the Pré Catelan. Before the entrance gates stood a row of taxis, and the villain beckoned one of them.

"Rue d'Auteuil 222," he gave the order.

There he found a house of an unpretending, but comfortable

aspect—one of those little private houses that used to abound in this district remote from the center of the city, nowadays more and more disfigured by huge factories. Fantômas looked it over.

"Excellent!" he told himself. "Madame is at Nice and no doubt has taken most of the servants with her. Remains Monsieur. Well, Monsieur is going to see me,"—and he rang the bell.

Three minutes more and an old manservant appeared at the door.

"Monsieur wishes?…" he inquired.

"I should like to have a word with Monsieur Merandol."

"On particular business, sir?"

"On business connected with the Bank."

"The fact is my master never sees people at his private house… Monsieur has not an appointment?"

"I have something better than an appointment. I am sent here by the Sub-Manager. It is about an urgent and important matter. Will you, please, inform your master?"

"Certainly, sir! Monsieur will excuse me, but I have my orders. But as I see it's important… Will Monsieur follow me,"—and two minutes afterwards Fantômas was ushered into a sort of smoking room, or perhaps working room, evidently the private den of a middle-class business man, well-to-do but of simple tastes.

"Better and better," he said to himself. "A nice quiet retreat! Well, if the information I have received is correct, I think I'm going to…"

He did not finish his sentence. At that moment the door opened and revealed M. Merandol, Acting Manager of the great bank of the Credit International, coming towards him. A man of sixty or thereabouts, but looking less, M. Merandol was what it is agreed to call "well preserved." He was manifestly an active, energetic personage, of a decided temperament, ready for prompt action.

Unaffectedly, with a slight bow, he asked:

"You wish to speak to me, sir?"

"Certainly, and on a matter of the highest importance."

"In that case, I am all attention. To whom have I the honor?…"

"Sir, before even mentioning my name, I should wish to ask you certain questions. Will you allow me to do so. In a few moments you will understand the motives that actuate me."

"Sir, I am at your service."

"Very well, this is the point. Can I be assured that nobody could possibly overhear what I am going to tell you in confidence?"

"I fail to understand you."

"Well, I will explain more plainly. I have a terrible, an alarming secret to tell you. Is this room secure against eavesdropping?"

"Oh! perfectly… but…"

"Your servants?"

"I am alone in Paris with the old manservant you saw… You can hear him moving on the floor above…"

"The members of your family?"

"Traveling… But you make me more and more anxious… Is it a question of…?"

"One moment! We cannot be overheard. Very good! But can we be overlooked?"

"Overlooked?"

"Yes… your neighbors?"

M. Merandol's visitor got up, and stepping up to the window, said softly:

"Would it incommode you to have the curtains drawn?"

"Not the very least… but…"

At this point M. Merandol could not help a feeling of acute discomfort coming over him. The strange language of his unknown visitor caused him shock after shock of amazement. Still, as he was to prove later on, he was not afraid, only anxious. He observed: "But I cannot at all see how it should trouble us, if the neighbors *did* see us."

"The fact is I have something to show you that no one but you must see…"

"Very good! I will close the curtains as you ask,"—and M.

Merandol got up and drew across the windows the heavy velvet hangings that entirely masked them. Then, going back to his seat behind his desk, he half-opened a drawer and slipped in his right hand with a careless air.

"I am listening, sir!" he announced again. "What have you to say to me? What have you to show me?"

Fantômas sprang up, and said simply:

"I have to tell you this, sir—that I am Fantômas! and to show you this…"

In his hand the polished barrel of a Browning suddenly flashed.

*　*　*　*　*

A dramatic moment—and one of a twofold surprise also! Hardly had Fantômas pointed his weapon at the banker before the latter, with a movement scarcely less swift, drew his right hand from the drawer where it had lain concealed and likewise pulled out a revolver.

"A single movement," he stuttered, "and I fire…"

"By all means!" said Fantômas.

Calmer than ever, in fact, the villain seemed as composed and confident as a man can be. Never a quiver could be detected in his voice as he remarked: "I was expecting that!"

Then he proceeded:

"You see I had good reason to shut the window, eh? If our neighbors saw us… well, we couldn't talk at our ease,"—and deliberately, with that nonchalant air that was a characteristic part of his bravado, he moved away, chose an armchair and installed himself comfortably in it.

"You are listening?" he asked.

But the banker was now losing his air of assurance. He had hoped to take his dangerous visitor aback by the rapidity of his defense… Far from that, Fantômas calmly announced how he had foreseen that his adversary would be armed. The scoundrel's coolness was staggering, and more than anything else reduced M. Merandol to helplessness. Nevertheless, forcing himself to speak firmly, the financier repeated:

"One movement from you that I don't like and I open fire. So don't dare to stir!… Now tell me what you expect me to do, what you want?"

"My dear sir, I am going to tell you,"—this without even raising his voice, in a tone testifying to his entire tranquility of mind.

"Yes, my dear sir," he went on, "but first I would point out this: we are armed both of us. Very good!—I expected as much, I repeat. For I never imagined a Bank Manager like you could be so unwise as not to have a revolver always within reach. But to proceed—we are both armed, and that leads you to think I am at your mercy… Is that so?"

"Yes," declared M. Merandol, "only I do not merely think so, I am sure of it…"

"Well, you are mistaken. Come, think!… We can both of us fire, can't we? And the victor will obviously be the one who fires first… You admit that?"

"I fire at your slightest movement!"

"No offense, but you have told me that already… At the slightest movement, eh? Well, I make bold to say I shall nevertheless fire before *you*—if you choose to shoot."

"Why?"

"Why, because, my dear sir, you are an honest man… Now, this is a thing I have often noticed: an honest man never takes aim at a scoundrel without a look in his eyes betraying his intention to shoot… Come now, try, if you want to die!… I am positive your eyes will give me warning—and *I* shall fire before your finger has pressed the trigger… Therefore, I run no risks! You follow me?"

Fantômas broke into a defiant laugh.

A strange thing, but no less undeniable, at this moment M. Merandol began to experience a change of feeling that surprised himself. He was neither a hero nor a coward. He was a man of a cool, calm temper who declined to believe in anything that his reason could not account for. Up to that moment he had not really believed he was face to face with Fantômas. In fact, the latter struck him as being a more or less imaginary being whom there was no chance of his ever knowing or meeting in person. But now, as he noted the mocking nonchalance of his unwelcome guest, he was becoming convinced of his reality. The fire that flashed from those fierce eyes fixed on his seemed to pierce him through and through! He realized, above all, that the man was right—that it would be impossible for him to press the trigger of his revolver without something in his own eyes betraying his intention. And this being so, was not his opponent the stronger? Would it not be he would fire the first?

"I run no risk," repeated the brigand.

M. Merandol protested in a shaking voice:

"A shot may kill me, yes!… But you will be arrested afterwards…"

"No!"

"We are right in the middle of a populous suburb. The shot will be heard."

"It will certainly. But I shall not be captured! They cannot take Fantômas!…"—and the villain laughed as he said the words. He was so sure of himself, his whole bearing was so full of confidence, that M. Merandol said no more.

"What do you want of me?" he asked again. "Your money!" said Fantômas coolly.

"I have not a halfpenny in the house!"

"No, not here… But at your bank?"

"Nor yet at my bank!… And the…"

"Hush! this is idle talking. I do not ask you for your money at a guess. I demand thirty-eight million francs."

"Thirty-eight millions…?"

"Exactly."

"I do not understand you."

"Oh! yes, you do, Monsieur Merandol, I say you do!… But you require details. Here they are then: the Crédit International has received thirty-eight millions on account of the State of Moldo-Slovakia. It is in connection with an issue of scrip. This gold is lodged in your cellars, packed in four strongboxes. Do you say my information is not authentic?"

"I say this specie is not mine!"

"I am not so particular as all that. What difference does it make?"

"Moreover, these millions, you say so yourself, are in the cellars of the bank… Consequently…"

"Consequently, you refuse to go and get them? Obviously, that would hardly be practicable… But I will go there myself…"

"You are joking."

"Do I look like it?"

"Still, you don't realize that…"

But Fantômas was showing signs of impatience. His blazing eyes were still fixed on M. Merandol's, who was really beginning to lose his head a little. The poor man hardly knew what he was saying. Each second as it passed increased his agitation. The hand leveling his revolver was growing numbed. Was he going to drop his weapon? Was that what the brigand was waiting for?

"Monsieur Merandol," resumed the latter suddenly, a sarcastic note appearing in his voice, "let us waste no more time, if you please. Here, in two words, is the understanding I wish to arrive at with you."

"An understanding with me?"

"Certainly. Indeed it is quite a simple matter. I know—I know a great many things, you can see for yourself—I know that the entry of your cellars is guarded by an iron door secured by a secret lock—a lock only one key will open… Well, it is that key I ask you to give me."

"But you are mad! I will never consent… I would rather…"

"Die?"

"Why, yes! I would rather die… I am an honest man…"

"And a foolish one! Nobody, as a fact, would ever know you had handed over this key to me… But I won't press you… Anyway, I know you haven't the key upon you…"

"You know…"

"Why, yes! If you had it, your fear would have betrayed you."

M. Merandol bit his lips in his rage. More than ever he felt the other was playing with him at his pleasure. His complete and perfect coolness was proof enough.

"Nothing here!... I merely wish to inform you of certain facts."

"What facts?"

"This, for instance, that I know where the key I require is always locked up... and I forbid you to change the place."

"So you think that..."

"I think you are going to obey me! By God! yes! See here, I am afraid one of my accomplices, when he was locating the exact place where the key was hidden, may have attracted attention. From that to supposing that tomorrow morning you might be warned, and change the hiding place, is a short step. I have already completed all my preparations and arranged all my plans. You can easily see, then, how such a change would baffle me. Under these circumstances, I have not hesitated to visit *you* to beg you to do nothing of the sort..."

"But this is insanity!"

"Say common prudence..."

"But you know quite well that from tomorrow on the key will no longer be..."

"In your private safe... Oh, yes! it will. It will have to be!"

"Then you think you are going to make me your accomplice?"

"You will be in very good company, Monsieur Merandol! I have only this moment recruited the President of the Council."

"What... You tell me..."

"The truth... I have come here straight from the Place Beauveau."

There was a silence. With what an abominable artfulness Fantômas conducted this interview with his future victim. Surely it was his masterpiece of effrontery! Never had thief or robber dared such a thing before. He was actually warning his intended victims of the thefts he proposed to commit! And what a fine, bold front he showed as he did it!

"By the Lord, yes!... I have just interviewed Didier Maujean... But there, it's next door to a State secret. You will excuse my not telling you more? Anyhow, believe me, you are losing nothing by my reticence. The question we discussed had nothing to do with you personally... To return to what *does* concern you…"

Alas! at that moment M. Merandol could almost have screamed with pain. Just now, in the first shock of surprise, he had leveled his revolver at arm's length at Fantômas. Since then, not to lose his advantage, he had never once shifted his attitude. But now his strength was exhausted. To maintain the same posture any longer was impossible. The weapon seemed to weigh a pound of lead. The wretched man gave a sigh that positively rattled in his throat.

"Oh! I can't bear it anymore!" he groaned. And his arm fell, to rest comfortably on the back of his chair.

Was this perhaps the moment Fantômas was waiting for to spring upon him? The brigand, for his part, all the time seated comfortably in his armchair, held his Browning in an easy attitude. He was evidently not the least tired.

"I am lost!" thought M. Merandol.

But with a smile, Fantômas made instant apologies.

"Ah! forgive me!" he cried. "I had forgotten your constrained posture. It is horribly fatiguing to stay like that without ever moving!… There, look, I am copying you—I lower my weapon myself… Your attention again?"

Subsequently, before the Magistrate, M. Merandol admitted that at this moment a fresh shock of surprise had paralyzed his will.

Fantômas, in fact, suited his action to his words, and did actually lower the muzzle of his Browning! He relaxed, in a sort, his vigilance at the same time that his opponent was forced by exhaustion to abandon his!

"Speak out!" the banker begged.

"Well, here goes. All that is left now is for me to lay down my conditions… I have, as a matter of fact, pointed out what I expected you to do. It is only right to let you know the means I propose to employ to ensure your compliance… Of course, you would refuse a solatium?"

"Of course!" stammered M. Merandol, who had indeed pretty much lost his head by this time.

"A pity! I should have found much pleasure in making you

a sharer in my profits... But there, I should not wish to annoy you by undue persistency... Only, you must see how this largely limits my liberty of action. If I can't say to you: 'Do this, and I will do you such and such a favor,' I am constrained to tell you: 'If you *don't* do this, you will be punished in such and such a way?'"

"You threaten me?"

"Oh! not you!"

"Not me?"

"No! You, you might escape my vengeance... And then, a man is ready to risk his own life, but he does not risk his son's!"

"His son's?"

"Oh! my dear sir, don't play at being surprised!... Come now, you may well suppose I have worked out this scheme in its smallest details. Well, then, I know you have a son—a poor boy of twenty who, after having typhoid, was attacked by mental trouble. Georges Merandol is in an asylum near Chatou, is he not? He *was* there at least."

At these words of the Lord of Terror the unhappy financier was like to faint. His age, indeed, was against him. Up to that moment he had summoned up all the resources of his energy, but at last he felt himself to be incapable of further resistance...

It was true, in fact, that the unfortunate man was wounded to the heart by a grievous domestic calamity. His son—an only son—Georges Merandol, a lad of promise two years before, had been struck down by an attack of typhoid which resulted in the poor fellow being now confined as a patient in an asylum at Rueil. But he would recover! The case was not desperate! Doctors and specialists held out good hopes! And it was on this beloved being, whom his unhappy condition made all the dearer, that Fantômas threatened to wreak vengeance!

The Torturer proceeded, now adopting a tone of pitiless sarcasm:

"Yes, your son *was* confined at Rueil... I say 'was,' for at this present moment he is not there. He has been kidnapped... He is in my hands."

"In your hands!"

"Certainly! And he will only be restored to you if tomorrow you refuse to believe one word of the report your Sub-Manager will make you. You understand, do you not? Do not shift the hiding place of your key, and Georges Merandol will soon be in your arms… Shift it, and you will never see your boy again…"

"Scoundrel! scoundrel!"—and, no longer master of himself, every nerve aquiver, the banker sprang at his enemy. He never so much as thought of his revolver! No, maddened by Fantômas' cowardly threat, the primitive savage awoke in him. What he wanted was to grip the wretch by the collar, to seize him by the throat, to strangle him there and then, without ruth or pity, as a man strangles a mad dog that threatens to fly at him.

But what could the unfortunate man do? Quicker than lightning Fantômas had leapt to one side, at the same instant hurling a chair with all his might and knocking the old man's legs from under him.

The banker fell, and simultaneously a shot rang out with a deafening crash. Instantly the room was plunged in darkness. With marvelous adroitness, incomparable marksmanship, Fantômas had severed the wire that carried the electric current with a well-aimed shot!

Then, in the dark, in the silent room, an abominable scene was enacted. Stunned at first by his fall, fully expecting a second shot would kill him outright, M. Merandol lay still a while.

"Undone! I am undone!" he thought in desperation.

But not a sound was audible anywhere near him. "Had Fantômas gone then?" he asked himself, and instinctively he sprang up with a yell for help.

A hurried step sounded in the garden. A familiar voice was shouting: "Courage, sir! I am here. I am coming!"

The old manservant was hastening to the rescue. But alas! this was precisely what Fantômas was expecting. Motionless as a statue, he stood hidden beside the door, in ambush. The instant the man opened it, he felled him to the ground with a terrific blow. Then, light and active, he dashed out, banging to the door and locking it behind him.

"So there!" he chuckled. "The room is hung with heavy tapestry, the curtains are thick. They'll have heard nothing outside in the street... Not they, by God! I see no crowd gathering..."

Cautiously, from the steps of the little house, Fantômas looked about him. As he said, the Rue d'Auteuil was entirely peaceful, almost deserted in fact. The noise of the explosion had not traveled beyond the garden.

"Now, we must be off!" the brigand ejaculated... "Ah! I hear the telephone bell. My word! it was high time for me to decamp... The visit has kept me longer than I expected,"—and he hurried away towards the railway station, where he knew he should find a cab rank.

At this same moment, inside the house where so abominable a scene had just been enacted, in the private working room in which M. Merandol was still a prisoner with his old manservant, the telephone bell was all the time ringing a peal. Still dizzied by his fall, groping round in a dazed fashion, M. Merandol seized the receiver.

This time the poor man was like to lose the small fraction of presence of mind still left him. The individual, a stranger to him, who was speaking was in fact reporting an amazing piece of news.

"Hello!" he was saying. "This is the Sanatorium at Rueil!... Monsieur Merandol, I am phoning you on behalf of Doctor Sagasse..."

"Yes, yes!" panted the unfortunate banker. Already he was conjecturing the worst tidings—an announcement of his son's having been kidnapped, as Fantômas had just been cruel enough to inform him was the case in a tone of heartless banter.

The voice continued: "Hello! Doctor Sagasse has asked me to inform you of a very fortunate thing: for the first time he has just now noted a decided improvement in your son Georges' condition..."

"But, he is with you then? he is still there?" asked the financier in a choking voice.

"Hello! You're saying...? I don't understand. Of course your son is here." But suddenly at this critical moment, communication was cut off!

Had Fantômas been lying, then? Had the young man never been kidnapped at all?

M. Merandol worked the instrument furiously, but when at last the operator asked him the number he wanted, it was not the Sanatorium at Rueil he demanded to be put through to. It was nothing less than the Criminal Bureau... M. Havard's private room.

4. Juve Intervenes

It was, as the reader will have guessed, M. Merandol's telephone message that reached M. Havard at the very moment the latter was bidding Juve goodbye, after, in a way of speaking, *extorting* his resignation. Thereupon the Chief of the Criminal Bureau had beckoned the hero to wait a few moments, after which, laying down the receiver, he asked him, affecting a sprightly tone:

"You understood what it was about, Juve?"

"Pretty well…"

"But more precisely?"

"Somebody has just telephoned to ask you to send him a detective, services to be paid for… and you thought of me?"

"Just so!"

"Well, it only remains for me to thank you, for I am not a rich man—and to ask you the name and address of the individual."

"Monsieur Merandol, 222 Rue d'Auteuil."

"The Manager of the Crédit International?"

"That's the man."

"Very good! In five minutes I shall be in a taxi, and in half an hour I am at his service,"—and Juve was already making for the door when M. Havard called him back.

"Wait a moment!… Not so fast!"

"You have instructions to give me?"

"Hmm! yes and no! Now, what you have gathered, *I* had also gathered myself. But there's something else that's by no means equally clear. M. Merandol struck me as being in a condition very like panic… *And* he uttered a name…"

"What name?"

"A name of terror! So now I want to make an appeal to your loyalty, Juve. I want it to be understood between us that you will act with the very utmost circumspection, the very greatest discretion… There's no doubt whatever the Minister who told me to 'shelve' you would blame me if he knew I was sending you yonder… You understand?"

"Perfectly. *What* name was spoken?"

"You will learn from M. Merandol… For my part, I don't wish to know it!"

Juve was outside the room almost before M. Havard had finished speaking. As for this name the Chief refused to tell him, this name that sufficed to throw the great man into such perturbation, this name, above all, which a Minister, the President of the Council, seemed to be familiar with, Juve was far too clear-sighted not to have guessed it.

"Fantômas! It is Fantômas again!" he thought to himself—and in the vehicle that carried him to Auteuil he felt the lust of battle reawakening within him. In very fact, if he had ceased to be Chief Inspector of the Criminal Department, if with polite phrases, but nonetheless decidedly, they had given him the sack, forced him against his will to resign, it was to Fantômas, the ever-elusive brigand, he owed this humiliation.

"Oh! to begin the fight! to come to grips with him!" he cried.

He felt almost happy as he sprang from his taxi before M. Merandol's door. An hour later, however, the police officer's enthusiasm, if it had not diminished, was at any rate less exuberant. Possessing as he did in the highest degree the art of making witnesses tell all they knew, the faculty of forcing people to live again in their smallest details the scenes of which they had been the heroes or the victims, Juve quickly learned everything that had happened in the Merandol household.

But if this knowledge more than ever confirmed him in his conviction that it was Fantômas he was going to engage, still he was bound to admit that he possessed only the vaguest inkling of what nature the battle was to be. Half distraught, as he had good reason to be, M. Merandol had contented himself with beseeching him to protect his son.

"I will guard the millions that lie in my bank," he announced. "It is my duty, and I will not shirk it. But, you, Juve, it is for you to save my boy." As he walked away in thoughtful mood from the financier's door, Juve seemed still to hear the agonized prayers of the unhappy father:

"Go to Rueil!" had been his urgent advice. "Georges is still there, thank God! the telephone message assures me of that. Yes! go to Rueil. Warn the doctor! Do not leave my son's side so long as he runs any risk… Or better—see here, remove him from the Asylum, take him somewhere else. I have a small property quite near, in the Ile de Chatou. There you would be in a veritable fortress…"

Yes! Juve could still hear the father's words. The Ile de Chatou! Other people called it the Ile de Croissy—and it was in that very Ile de Croissy his last meeting with Fantômas had taken place… A coincidence doubtless?

But Juve was not stopping to consider such details. Just before, seeing the unhappy father in such trouble and distress, he had been on the point of telephoning afresh to the asylum, then he had thought better of it. Now, on reflection, he congratulated himself on the caution he had exercised.

"For indeed," he told himself, "reckless as Fantômas is, I am bound to allow that he never acts without good and sufficient reasons. Now, what I have just learned, is cram full of improbabilities—stupidities, to speak plainly."

He had taken another taxi, ordering the man to drive his fastest to the terminus of the Rueil trains, promising the fellow a handsome tip—and he was free to think in peace, with closed eyes.

"Yes!" he said to himself, "there are improbabilities without end… To begin with, why warn the banker he was going to be robbed? Then, why declare his son had been kidnapped, if nothing of the sort had happened?… And the odd chance that made the telephone message coincide exactly with the moment when I am all ready to take charge of the matter! Oh, ho! but chance seems to be arranging things mighty opportunely in this adventure!"

But the ironical tone in which Juve uttered the word "chance" showed clearly enough that that officer was very far from admitting that *chance* had anything at all to do with the matter.

No! in police practice chance is never so obliging, so favorable, as all that… Confident no one could hear him in the taxi which was now bumping over the stones of the Avenue de Neuilly, Juve suddenly exclaimed:

"A chance, a coincidence like this bears another name—it is called a plan, a scheme, a plot. It was of set purpose they have brought me into it!… They? If I say 'they,' I mean Fantômas. Yes! not a doubt of it! And, if Fantômas has acted as he has, it is because he is carrying out some sinister purpose known only to himself. *But* what purpose?"

To this question Juve had naturally found no answer yet, when he quitted his taxi in front of the Quartier Guynemer, situated in the very center of the pretty little town of Rueil. Involuntarily, as he looked about him, after paying off his driver, the police official shuddered. Oh! the district was well known to him! Curiously enough, it was also a matter of mad folk that had brought him to the place before—on the occasion of the great fire at the Departmental Insane Asylum. *Chance* again was it?

"Good! We shall soon see," Juve observed. By this time it was almost dark. Nine o'clock had already struck at the old church, and passersby were becoming few and far between.

"Let's take our bearings!" he said to himself. "It is somewhere near here. I know the Sanatorium where the boy is lies contiguous to Malmaison, so I can't be far off. Ah! that's it, I wager!"—and the police officer stood still to examine the place. The Sanatorium was surrounded by a high wall that evidently enclosed grounds of considerable extent, as is generally the case in institutions of the kind. The main entrance was not from the high road to Saint-Germain but opened on a neighboring street. From where he stood could easily be made out the gateway surmounted by a rose-covered trellis, and underneath it two or three attendants enjoying the coolness of the evening air.

"A comfortable, well-to-do, well-looking establishment," Juve reckoned it up in his own mind. "Consequently well guarded and looked after. Well, so much the better! Everything seems quite peaceful. So nothing untoward can have happened. I propose to ask to see the Superintendent, this Doctor Sagasse, and tell him about things…"

Suddenly it occurred to him: "After all, it was doubtless because he was attending specially to the lad that the kidnapping scheme had fallen through,"—and indeed nothing was more likely. Be this as it might, the police officer, putting off till later the inquiries that were obviously necessary, made his way to the gate, searching his pocketbook for the letter he had asked M. Merandol to write for the Physician-in-Chief. His manner was perfectly cool and composed, and it was in a quiet, almost indifferent voice he addressed the Porter:

"I should like to have a few minutes' talk with Doctor Sagasse. I know it is late, but I think he will see me. Will you take him my card and this little note. It is urgent, and…"

But next instant Juve felt himself turn pale, and he had to admit he was greatly alarmed. Without taking the papers, the man had replied:

"Doctor Sagasse? Fact is, he has been away for the last three days, sir; and his Assistant is out…"

"Out, is he?… Hmm! that's unfortunate. You don't know when he will be back?"

"Not before tomorrow morning. He left at two o'clock this afternoon to pay a visit to his relatives in the country… But if Monsieur cares to speak to the Superintendent-in-Chief?"

"Oh, no! Thank you all the same. It's not a medical matter, but a private affair. I believe Doctor Sagasse's Assistant knows about it. But the Superintendent could not give me any information. Thank you! I'll come again one of these days or I'll telephone…"—and with a nod he walked away.

He had given scarce a sign of his consternation on learning Doctor Sagasse's absence. If he started slightly, it seemed only the disappointment of a visitor on finding he cannot be admitted—nothing more than that. Indeed, is it not one of the very first qualifications of a good police officer to possess this outward imperturbability? Those who practice the difficult profession of a detective are bound to constrain themselves to appear always unmoved, to listen, a smile on their lips, to the most startling news.

Not a doubt of it, Juve was surprised—more than surprised, astounded, struck all of a heap. True, he wheeled about and walked away with a careless step. But his heart was beating wildly, and his anger rising to fever heat. This time there could be no doubt about the matter—Fantômas' intervention was undeniable!

At first, indeed, when M. Merandol had declared how he had been visited by the grim Lord of Terror, Juve had asked himself if it was really a fact, so strange did Fantômas' behavior, as he heard it described, appear to him. Now, however, all doubt was removed. Only too clearly he recognized the villain's usual methods in view of these first results of his activity.

Deep in thought, Juve, started to return to Rueil. He was asking himself what he could do, what action he could take? But he quickly found an answer. This King of Detectives, this man who for years had waged desperate war on his formidable adversary, the redoubtable Fantômas, was not one to remain long in uncertainty. He thought:

"Undoubtedly! I am sure of it! A tragic denouement is preparing. Everything goes to prove it. Yes, all we have to do is to recall what has just occurred to realize that,"—and he proceeded to run over the facts again in his mind:

"The Minister demands, nay! insists on my dismissal. Why? Because this extraordinary step was forced upon him. But why was it forced upon him? In order that Havard might communicate the decision to me. But, again, when was Havard to make this communication? No doubt on his return from the Ministry. Therefore, they knew at what hour I should be in his private room. Therefore, they were able to get M. Merandol to telephone to Havard at that same moment. After that, there was every likelihood of my being entrusted with the task of protecting Georges Merandol, and consequently of my coming here..."

At this point in his deductions—simple enough really, but nonetheless testifying to the fine perspicacity that was one of the police officer's prominent characteristics, Juve gave a sigh.

"Yes!" he exclaimed. "They knew I was coming. In fact they have brought me here. I admit the fact. It only remains to discover with what object and in what way my presence can be of advantage to them."

Then he sighed again. More and more problems pressed for solution, and no solution could he discover. A criminal is free, untrammeled in the game he plays. But the police officer! he must guess what the other has decided to do, and this when the evildoer he is tracking down has every motive for deceiving him.

"A heavy job!" Juve told himself. "But after all, my feelings are of no account. I have a duty set me, and this duty I must fulfill. That's all there is to it! For the rest, we must 'wait and see,'"—and as he uttered the words, Juve recovered his wonted serenity of mind. Who better than he could know what patience must be exercised in police work? Who better than he was qualified to practice in pursuit of his investigations the steadfastness of the hunter in ambush, on the watch, with mind ever on the alert? He continued his reflections.

"So therefore, why trouble our heads about the motives that lead the enemy to wish me here? Time enough to find that out later on. Remains another question. What is the meaning of the telephone message to M. Merandol? Obviously it did not come from Doctor Sagasse, for he is not here. I can only conclude therefore, it was sent by an impostor. With what object?"

But to this question Juve quickly found an answer. Indeed a reasonable explanation was not difficult to hit on. "The robber, the man who wants to kidnap Georges Merandol in order to force the boy's father to let himself be exploited, must have failed to carry out his project. Thereupon he telephoned to reassure M. Merandol and dissuade him from coming immediately. Yes! it must be so... Perhaps he even supposed I myself would not come till tomorrow morning?... Hmm!... but then, in that case he had no wish to bring me here—and all my previous conjectures fall to pieces..."

Juve pulled a wry face. He had a vivid presentiment that he

was quite near the truth, but that, nevertheless, he had not yet arrived at it. They had induced him to come for some sufficient reason, but what was that reason? The telephone message had an object? Yes, but what object? Such dilemmas constantly confront the police in their inquiries.

Still Juve was not the man to be easily discouraged.

"Better and better!" he exclaimed suddenly. I am evidently started on an extraordinary and complicated job. Well, no matter! It only remains to see what I can do to checkmate these mysterious plans of my opponent.

Coming to the Saint-Germain high road, he had turned mechanically to the left, making not for Rueil, but in the direction of Malmaison. At the tram terminus he saw two restaurants that seemed to promise well.

"And now for dinner," he said to himself. "I shall have a stiff night of it, I expect. So let's have a good meal… Oh! if only I had Fandor with me!"

Yes, he would fain have had Fandor by his side. He felt, poor man, that he was fighting in the dark, and he well knew, albeit he often laughed at him, how the journalist sometimes gave excellent advice. Then, in the hour of danger, was it not always well to be backed up by a trusty comrade?

Juve entered the little restaurant he had noted and ordered dinner. He quite realized the crisis was a grave one. He was convinced that, from one moment to the next, he was to embark on a formidable enterprise. But he was not the sort of man who gives way to "nerves." "Best eat! and eat heartily!" he advised himself. "Man is a machine. Before working, he must fill up with fuel!"—and he sat down composedly to his dinner. Yet Juve was no gourmand. Always preoccupied with momentous problems, he gave little thought to the pleasures of the table. His reflections pursued their course.

"See here!" he declared presently. "They have brought me here, I don't know why… They have not carried off Georges Merandol, I do not know for what reason… But one thing is certain, that to checkmate Fantômas' schemes, I have only one course to take: to do exactly the opposite of what he must logically have concluded I was going to do."

Forgetting to help himself, the police officer sat still a moment, thinking, the veins swelling on his brow under the intensity of his concentration. Ah! what a battle he felt was coming, and how desperately he longed to win it!—yes, and he meant to win it, if, by the sheer force of his intellect, he could succeed in frustrating Fantômas' machinations. "Yes, he must evidently have thought that… that…"

Then he cried suddenly:

"Not a doubt of it! Fantômas must be saying to himself: 'Juve, finding Georges Merandol at the Sanatorium, is going to take up his station at his side.'" He smiled as he decided: "My plan, therefore, is not to be there at all, where He thinks I *must* be!"

But the problem was far from being solved by this conclusion. Easy enough to resolve to be somewhere else than with Georges Merandol. But *where* was he to go in that case?

"I have sworn to M. Merandol to protect his son," Juve continued his self-communing. "Therefore I cannot do other than keep guard over the unhappy lad. How conciliate the two obligations?"

Juve began to eat at last, almost ravenously, it seemed, muttering savagely to himself between the mouthfuls:

"A lunatic notion!… lunatic!"

Then he went on: "But I'm going to do it all the same! I must do it, it is my duty to do it!"—and, dropping his voice, he added:

"Seeing how on the one hand I must not stay at the Sanatorium, and on the other I am bound not to lose sight of Georges Merandol, well, I have no choice left me—I must take the boy with me… But, as nobody at the Asylum would trust him to me, I can only kidnap him myself. So there you are!"—and he broke into a whimsical smile.

"Only, as I am no longer an accredited agent, I have no legal right to act like this. What I'm going to do means twenty years' hard labor. No matter! to work! The great thing is not to be caught!"

Without even finishing his dinner, he paid his bill and left the restaurant. Outside, it was pitch dark. Juve stepped to the curb to cross the road.

Suddenly a motorcar dashed past him. In the darkness stabbed by the dazzling headlights, he made out the figure of a woman, leaning over and waving her arm.

Then he saw nothing more—for the woman had hurled something at him, something that struck him full in the face, bruising it cruelly!

5. Mad, Poor Fellow!

So far was Juve from expecting the blow he had just received that, at first, he merely clapped his hand to his forehead, rubbing it vigorously, as he growled:

"What an idiot the woman must be! A little more and she would have blinded me!"

He advanced a step, meaning to go on, when he bethought himself:

"And suppose she wanted to blind me?"

An idea had suddenly struck him—a mad notion, or a flash of genius? A coincidence was it, mere chance again, this unlooked-for assault?

"What the devil was it she threw at me?" he asked himself, and began to grope about in the dark road. He could see nothing.

"I can't have dreamt it, can I?"

Then he struck a light, and by the uncertain gleam of the tiny flame flickering in the wind, he caught sight of something like a square of paper that had rolled to a considerable distance. It looked heavy.

"An envelope!" he told himself, and so it was. It was weighted with a stone, no doubt the ballast that had made it possible to throw it.

"Very queer!" Juve muttered. "A letter? A letter meant for me? No, no! I'm going crazy! I'm dreaming with my eyes open!"

But at the same time that he was thinking how his supposition was going beyond all bounds of probability, he was tearing open the cover. Inside he found a sheet of paper, on which he read a line written in pencil in a big, rather trembling handwriting, a woman's handwriting... The message ran: "For pity's sake, in the name of those you love, don't do what you are going to do!"

Juve was smiling now. "No doubt now the letter was meant for me," he decided. "And as little doubt it gives me an important piece of information…"

Suddenly he began to tremble. Yes, it was a fact—in the dark night, in this lonely corner of the Paris outskirts, the letter had confirmed his suspicions. He was right; he had been enticed there! He was no less right in the course he had decided to take. Evidently they expected him to act as logic dictated, that he should mount guard at Georges Merandol's side… In fact, to tell him: "Don't do this—the very thing all probability pointed to his doing—was this not simply to urge him to do it?"

But, tremble as he might, Juve was laughing at the same time—grinning would be the better word… So they thought him a coward? They wanted, by seeming to dissuade him from running into danger, to drive him into confronting that very peril. They were for playing upon his vanity.

"I've found a better way!" he reflected. "I am going to carry out my plan of abduction."

Without a moment's doubt he foresaw that a hideous plot was brewing, and its abominable author was equally obvious. Yes, Fantômas was there, spying out his doings in the darkness, sending this woman and her mysterious warning to him, trying to baffle and confuse him, striving to draw him into the web he was weaving like a monstrous spider lying in wait to do wickedness. Then, still buried in thought, Juve broke into a more cheerful laugh.

"Between us two, Fantômas!" he cried defiantly. "Let us fight it out, till one of us gains the day!"—and he drew himself up gallantly, casting a look of irony about him in the dark night. Where was the monster lurking? Where was he biding his time to attack? What was the trap he had set? Juve could only shrug his shoulder in answer to these questions. Suddenly he muttered:

"All this while, I have never even thought how this unknown woman may be an accomplice, or at any rate a friend, of Fantômas. Pooh! the idea don't hold water. A friend? What sort of friend? Besides, who can possibly know what I have decided to do? Enough of dreaming. To work!"—and the police officer set off again at a good round pace.

The hour was quite late now. Along the high road not a soul was to be seen. When Juve reached the turning where the lane leading to the Sanatorium joined the main road, he could see in the distance the closed gates, and noted that no light now showed in the windows of the Porter's Lodge.

"Capital!" he said to himself. "I have no wish for an audience—very much the contrary!"

Yet anyone who might have seen the detective at that moment pacing, soberly with the air of a harmless gentleman of leisure along the outside of the enclosing wall of the Asylum, would never have suspected the wild projects he was meditating, that this respectable looking individual was contemplating a reckless and perilous enterprise. As a fact, as he went, Juve was spying out the locality, making a careful examination of every detail with those piercing eyes of his, which never failed to note any point that could be of the slightest importance.

"High walls!" he remarked, "and topped with bits of broken bottles at that! A sweet climb!... Anyway, I'm a bit too old for gymnastic stunts... But I'll manage the thing all the same. Let's have a look further on."

Further on, he began whistling—a sign of high satisfaction with Juve. Indeed, he was delighted with what he saw.

"Yes, the Sanatorium is made up of a series of small detached buildings. That suits my plans first-rate... Ah! here we have a block that looks more imposing—the Administrative Headquarters no doubt. But what about dogs?"—and the police officer stopped, listening anxiously. No sound reached him. The patients, confined in their rooms or alas! locked up in their cells, were evidently sleeping. The attendants seemed to be doing the same. Very likely the regulations forbade anybody's going out into the grounds after a certain hour of the evening?

"Yes, yes!" Juve observed, "all that is not only possible, but probable. Only it don't tell me if there are dogs kept,"—adding with a smile:

"The fact is, I adore dogs when I come across them by daylight and have a right to be where I am for the moment. But, at night, after climbing over a wall, I would just as gladly not see them in my road!

Still Juve was not the man to hesitate very long when he wanted to discover something. Continuing along the enclosing walls, he pulled up two or three times in succession and picking up a stone, pitched it over the wall into the grounds. As no barking ensued, "We may conclude," observed Juve, "they don't keep dogs. True they may likely have been afraid they might occasion an accident with the patients."

With a shrug of the shoulders, he went on:

"So, taking that for granted, let's get to work. It is now half-past eleven. The rounds of inspection always take place, by regulation, about midnight. I have time enough…"

But he did not attempt the difficult climb just yet. He was not the sort to leave anything to chance. Far from it. It was his regular custom to foresee everything to the last detail, and this was how he so often succeeded in enterprises where anyone else would have failed.

"Two difficulties," he reflected. "The first: to make no noise. The second: to discover whereabouts Georges Merandol is to be found. The fact is I haven't a notion in which block he is lodged. Well, well, no doubt all this can be arranged."

Two difficulties! Sure the police officer was underestimating the number. Even supposing he managed to get to the unfortunate young man without interruption, was it not obvious that his task would be far from over? He would still have to carry off the patient, and to do that, cheat the watchfulness of the attendants. After that, he would still have to find a way out of the Asylum, for he could not possibly hope to induce the lunatic to climb the wall. And, besides that, in what condition was he going to find the patient. It is frequently the case that the insane instinctively fear and distrust people they have never seen before. Possibly Georges Merandol, on seeing Juve, would start making a scene, screaming, raising an alarm.

For all his habitual coolness, Juve was nervous. He entertained no illusions whatever as to the difficulties of his enterprise.

"If, ten minutes from now, an attendant were to wake up and put a well-aimed revolver shot into me, I should only be getting my deserts. Nay! perhaps that is just what Fantômas wants?"

But the thought of possible, even certain, danger was so far from making him recoil that already he was starting on his preparations. Deliberately he took off his coat, first emptying the pockets.

"We must have something by way of a mattress!" he muttered. "So…"

Then he re-buttoned the coat, laid it on the ground, and slowly and methodically he set about stuffing it with dead leaves and dry grass.

"So far, so good!" he said. "Now the thing is to carry it. Ah! my braces will come in useful…"—and he unfastened them, and then with his knife cut a hole in the collar of his coat transformed now into a sort of scarecrow by the stuffing he had crammed into it.

"So there we are!" he laughed. "Let's pass one end of my braces through the hole, tie a knot on it, take the other end between my teeth and chuck the mannequin on my back… There now, what could be better?"

In this fashion he could conveniently carry his load. Only what purpose was it to serve? But Juve never acted at random. Two minutes afterwards, taking advantage of any tiny footholds and handholds offered by the surface of the wall—cracks due to frost, fragments of stone that had fallen out, Juve was quickly near the summit.

"Now for my mattress!" he panted, and clinging on by one hand to the top, as strong and active as any acrobat—he who had declared he was too old for acrobatic tricks—he gripped the coat stuffed with leaves and grass and threw it on the crest of the wall with its line of broken bottles.

"A good coat ruined!" he grumbled. "But anyhow I shan't cut myself…"

He rested his weight on the improvised mattress, and careless of the now harmless broken glass, leapt down into the grounds.

For some moments he did not stir. Had he been heard? Was some keeper or attendant going to raise an alarm? Was a dog, after all, going to spring at him?

"Not a sound!" he assured himself presently. "Everything quite calm and quiet! Well, I'm getting a first-rate burglar anyhow! As they don't want me any more as a police officer, I might take up this new career? Now, in we go!"—and walking on the grass edges of the flowerbeds, so as not to leave footprints on the gravel of the paths and no less to avoid noise, he set off for the buildings he supposed to be those devoted to the administrative services.

"The charges are high in these private asylums," he reflected. "Consequently there is always an elaborate system of accounts, registration, and so on. The devil's in it if I can't come upon some reference book in which I shall find Georges Merandol's name and see which block he is assigned to!"

Another minute and he had reached the buildings themselves, when a smile of satisfaction rose immediately to his lips. A glass door was before him, bearing an inscription: "Inquiries."

"That's the ticket!" he exclaimed. "I wager it is there visitors apply when they come to visit patients. If only there's nobody about, I couldn't possibly be luckier!"

He fell on all fours, and with the wiliness of a Red Indian tracker, crawled up to the door, and glued his ear to the woodwork.

"Anybody there?" he asked himself. But not a sound could he hear, and perfectly reassured on this point, he laughed: "So, let's hear the 'nightingales' singing, eh?"

For the second time that night, a sigh of regret escaped him: "If only Fandor was here! It would be a fine joke for him, this shameless bit of housebreaking of mine!"

Juve could surely have given points to the most artful of professional thieves. He set "the nightingales singing," as he put it, with such excellent effect that in less than two minutes, as he worked about a little hooked implement in the interior of the lock, the latter gave a small click, almost imperceptible, but entirely characteristic.

"The lever slipped back!" the police officer whispered to himself. "I've nothing to do now but walk in... Ho, ho! but there are bolts too, the door refuses to open. That complicates matters a bit. But never mind; in three minutes..."

He drew from his pocket a miniature "jimmy" consisting of three separate sections that screwed into each other. Putting the implement quickly together, he slipped it in at the bottom of the door between the two leaves, then forcing them apart adroitly, inserted his hand and pulled back the bolt. The same maneuver was repeated at the top and produced the same result.

"Capital!" he said to himself, and the door opened without the smallest difficulty.

Juve crossed the threshold, to find himself in a small room or parlor in which could be seen an unpretending desk and above it a row of shelves supporting heavy ledgers.

"Just what I was looking for," he said, and going straight to the shelves, he took down one of the great books and proceeded to hunt through its pages.

"Alphabetical order! Excellent! I could ask nothing better. Let's see, letter M... Ah! here we have it—Ma... Ma... Me... Merandol... Merandol, Georges; "Pasteur" block; room No. 1, first floor. That's all I want to know... Ah! but what does this 'Refer' mean?" Again searching through the ledger, he found the section that interested him:

"Georges Merandol—Mania of Persecution, with periods of acute Neurasthenia. No visitors without express permission from the Physician-in-Chief."

"Poor young man!" sighed the police officer. "What I am proposing to do will hardly be conducive to his cure. But there, necessity knows no law!"

Putting back the ledger in its place and extinguishing the little electric torch he had kindled, he pulled to the door after him, not wishing to show too evident tokens of his having been there, and stepped outside.

"'Pasteur' block! eh? Well, I must find 'Pasteur' block. Ah! I see the names of the different blocks are written up on their fronts. So, there's no difficulty!"

Still walking on the turf, looking about him the while suspiciously, he set about an exploration of the buildings. First he saw blocks "Chantemesse," "Broca," "Charcot,"—evidently named after famous alienists of the past. Next moment, a smile of satisfaction lighting up his face, he caught sight of block "Pasteur."

"Capital! capital!" Juve chuckled. "Only how does one get in?… Ah! I spy an open window on the first floor—and ivy to help one climb up to it… Yes… But where are the keepers?"

Once again he took to all fours, and crawled round the building. He seemed more than ever well satisfied when he got back to his starting point.

"First-rate!" he chuckled. "By dint of doing the grand and impressing visitors, they are helping the gentle burglar admirably! A charming idea that, of setting up at the door a plan of the interior arrangements! I now know for certain that room No. 1 is the one with the open window. The first time in my life I have had such a fine slice of luck!"—and Juve had indeed good reason to congratulate himself on the good fortune that had so far accompanied him. In his progress round the block he had discovered a second entrance door at which was hung on the wall under a sheet of glass a full and detailed plan of each story—a thing often done in Asylums and Sanatoria.

Greatly encouraged, he listened once more, to find all was silent, not a sound to be heard. Then he set to work deliberately and methodically, and by help of a rain pipe and the ivy that clothed the walls with its tangled branches, he hauled himself up to the level of the open window.

"If there are no attendants about the thing will go on wheels," he told himself.

Then, holding his breath and moving with cautious deliberation, he put in his head, pushing the curtains to either side. At first the room seemed unoccupied, then presently he caught a slight noise, and straining his ears to the utmost, he heard a sound of quiet breathing.

"The patient," thought he. "He is asleep? How comes he to be alone in a room with the window open?"

But this was no time to investigate such questions, concerned as they were with the mode of treatment followed in the case of the unhappy young man.

"It's risky, but I'll do it!" Juve made up his mind. "By God! though, if he calls out, I'm done for!"—and he completed his climb. Gripping hold of the crossbar of the window, he balanced himself on the sill and jumped down into the room. It was indeed lucky there was no attendant there, for lightly as he had fallen, he had made a certain amount of noise. Letting the curtains fall together again behind him, the officer found himself in total darkness. At the same time he could guess, in a way feel, there was a bed near him—a bed on which lay a man asleep.

"Poor Georges Merandol," he thought. "Well, I must wake him, he must not open his mouth, and I must take him away with me..."

He stood a moment hesitating. On his next action depended the whole success of his enterprise. He stammered:

"Light?... Yes, I must strike a light. To throw a light in a sleeper's eyes is the gentlest way of waking him..."

He listened again for a second or two, then flashed on a light. And instantly Juve knew what was going to happen. The brain works fast at such moments! It needed but one look, a single rapid glance, to see everything, to note everything to the smallest details... The police officer saw, by the flickering light, a small room almost devoid of furniture. Yes! he had evidently reached his objective. On the mantelpiece above the fireless grate he saw a photograph, the photograph of Georges Merandol the father.

Reassured on this point, Juve at once went on with his investigation. As he had conjectured he stood close beside a bed, on which was stretched a sleeping figure. And instantly he realized the explanation of a point that had puzzled him. In leaving the window open, the authorities of the Asylum were guilty of no imprudence; the sleeper—the unfortunate Georges Merandol—wore a straitjacket! Bound hand and foot he lay on his bed a helpless bundle. What need of a night watcher beside this patient rendered absolutely incapable of movement?

After that, Juve ceased to think, ceased to see anything but the face of the madman on which his eyes were riveted. Georges Merandol was awake, and instantly a look of amazement had convulsed his countenance—amazement that swiftly changed to anger, fear, frantic terror.

Juve beheld the patient's features contract in a grimace of impotent fury. Above all, he beheld the wretched man's lips open halfway; he foresaw the deep-toned howl of rage that would next moment issue from his throat.

"They will hear him!" he gasped. "They will come! I shall be taken…"

His whole plan was crumbling to pieces! His whole audacious scheme was to go for naught! It meant victory perhaps for Fantômas!

But how impose silence on a madman?…

                    *   *   *   *   *

In a twinkling Juve had realized the danger he ran. Again he told himself how impossible was the attempt to silence this madman he had to deal with. The unhappy young man suffered from the mania of persecution, and was it not inevitable, a natural consequence of his distracted state of mind, that he should look on Juve as an enemy? A sane man in his place would surely have been alarmed; *he* was bound to be the victim of ungovernable terror.

Yet, at the very moment the police officer became conscious of the peril that confronted him, his wonderful presence of mind came instantly to the rescue.

"Madness of persecution!" he exclaimed—and a happy thought, an inspiration of genius, flashed across his brain. Darting to the patient's bedside, before he had time to utter a sound, Juve whispered in his ear:

"Don't cry for help!… I am bringing you a weapon… you are going to kill them!"

"Kill them!" exclaimed the unhappy young man. "Kill

whom?"

"Your persecutors…"

"So you know them?"

"Of course I do… Look, see, here's the revolver I am going to give you…" He had drawn his weapon, and now, without giving it to the madman, he showed it him and watched in his face the impression his words produced. It was a hideous farce he was playing! But in this case the end surely justified the means. With the insane one must never make an open fight of it, never contradict them, or even attempt to coerce their will. Nevertheless, in most instances, you can make them do whatever you wish by pretending to adopt their delusions. Juve had told himself:

"The poor boy thinks he is surrounded by enemies—always the hallucination of victims of the mania of persecution. Well, I am going to offer him my revolver… He will follow me to the end of the world…"

Indeed, the poor creature was growing calmer already. He asked:

"Where are they?"

"The other side of the wall…"

"Then, how do you mean me to punish them?"

"I am going to take you to them…"

"You?"

"Yes, I! See, I am going to take off your straitjacket. They make out you are mad, don't they?"

Juve was handling the case with all the adroitness of an experienced alienist. It is another sovereign method to win the confidence of the insane to tell them people know they are not mad. At the same time, as he spoke, the police officer was unbuckling the straps of the straitjacket, albeit he took good care not to take it off altogether. He was too much afraid the poor fellow might have a sudden access of fury. He was only giving him a little more freedom of movement.

"There!" he said. "You feel more comfortable?"

"Much more!"

"Outside, I will free you altogether. Here, indoors, we must make haste. They might hear us and secure you again…"

"Yes?"

"Certainly they might. Come, get up. But, whatever you do, make no noise…"

But he broke off suddenly, with a shudder of positive horror. The poor young man, having made a movement to rise, Juve had caught sight of an enormous lump disfiguring his skull. Was this the tumor then that caused his affliction.

But the madman was already on his feet. With a grin, he demanded:

"We're not to make any noise?"

"No! no noise at all!"

"And you're going to take me away?"

"At once. I'm going to take your sheets, tie them in a loop under your arms and let you down into the grounds… You won't be afraid?"

It was the most critical moment of all. Would the escape be successful?

"It's not worthwhile!" declared the lunatic, "and I don't want to! You can get down by the ivy… I've got out that way before…"

"But suppose you should fall!"

"I shan't fall… It's no great height… Now, look!"—and before Juve had time to stop the dangerous experiment, the madman was out of the window and hanging suspended from a bough, then he swung lightly from branch to branch to the ground…

"A sleepwalker's cleverness, by God!" muttered the police officer. "No need to have worried my head. He's not going to fall, that's clear!"

So saying, he too mounted the crossbar of the window after the lunatic, and climbed down.

"Now we are in the grounds, though," he reflected, "things are going to get more complicated. How am I to manage?"— and involuntarily, Juve cast questioning looks all about him, interrogating the darkness, endeavoring to force the night to give up its secrets.

The fact is he was far from entirely confident as to the eventual success of the enterprise he was attempting. True, he felt pretty sure Fantômas could not suspect the audacious plan he had conceived. True, he had good hopes, by acting as he did, of frustrating the brigand's schemes. But might he not, after all, have to fear the worst? Was it impossible that Fantômas was there in the darkness, watching his every movement, ready at any moment to appear, dagger in hand, to bar his way?

"Come, come!" he remonstrated with himself. "Sufficient for the moment is the evil thereof! Anyway, we shall see!"

He mastered his nerves, subdued the gnawing anxiety that tortured him. If it was to be a fight, if it came to blows, was he not ready to defend himself? Had he not his faithful Browning in his pocket, a friend he could always rely on?

At the foot of the wall, the madman was crouched, motionless and quite calm now, waiting for his companion. Undoubtedly he looked on Juve as a savior. Undoubtedly it was the notion he was going in pursuit of his imaginary enemies that made him so compliant.

Juve rejoined the lunatic. "Now, no noise!" he warned him. "Hush! They are the other side of the wall… I'm going to climb it, and hoist you up after me. I have a rope."

He had, in fact, unfastened one from a slip-ladder he had noticed leaning against the wall.

But the madman shook his head:

"Rope me?" he demanded. "Hoist me up? Why?"

"Why, to get over the wall…"

"No!"

"No! Why no?… Don't you want to go and punish them?"

"I don't want to get over the wall!"

"But you must!"

"No!… No!… I don't want to!"

Juve trembled for the success of his scheme. And, up to that point, things had been going so well! Was he not, perhaps, at this moment at grips with his worst difficulties? What to do, if, clinging obstinately to one of those unshakeable notions characteristic of the insane, Georges Merandol should refuse point-blank to accompany him? Use force? But to use force was to provoke a struggle that might prove terrific! Madmen, as a

rule, have muscles of steel and fury doubles their strength…
Juve tried to temporize.

"But you must! you must!" he said. "Easy enough to get over
the wall. I am sure you can do it without the smallest difficulty."

"No! no!"

"So you don't want to punish them?"

"I want to go out by the door."

"By the door?… But we should make a noise, don't you see
that?"

"No noise at all!"

"But I say we should! Your enemies will hear you! They'll
run away and escape!"

"We'll go out by the door! I have the key… I stole it… Follow
me!"

The poor lunatic was trembling violently with nervous excitement, and Juve felt a crisis of acute mania was imminent.

"Deuce and all! Whatever happens, we must stave that off,"
he muttered, and added out loud:

"Oh, well! shall we go and see? If it's possible to get out by
the door, we will."

"It *is* possible. Come with me!"—and the young man set
off running. He moved noiselessly, with the light tread of the
sleepwalker, his feet seeming scarcely to touch the ground.
Suddenly Juve started in surprise.

"But, good Lord! he is turning his back to the door. Damnation! the fellow's going to give me the devil of a job!"

The lunatic, in fact, had made a half-turn and was going
away from the entrance gate, scurrying across the grounds.
Running after him, a trifle winded, Juve thought:

"I must do one thing or the other. To go on like this, there's
no sense in it! They may hear us any moment!… Very well! I'm
going to make a dash at him, gag him with a handkerchief and
throw him on my back. A bad job, but there's nothing better I
can try,"—and again he scrutinized the flying figure, wondering what formidable reserves of strength the madman might
possess.

But, next moment, the police officer bit his lips in sheer

amazement. The madman had just reached the enclosing wall, and behold! a small door, a sort of postern, could be made out in it! Oh! the artfulness these madmen are capable of! Georges Merandol stooped, and fished out something from under a stone; it was the key!"

"God-a-mercy!" swore Juve.

"Come," said the madman, "open the door! I, I don't know how."

It was the gap, the sudden break, in the poor creature's lucidity of mind. The unfortunate had found the key and hidden it away. He had not the wits to use it!

"Good! good! first-rate!" cried Juve. "You're a clever fellow! Now we're going to get out quite easily."

It was hardly an exaggeration to say so. Certainly the rusty lock of the postern gave some trouble before it would work, but this difficulty was soon overcome. Moreover it opened, this forgotten door which nobody in the asylum appeared to use, on the open fields. Juve noted the fact at the first glance, and immediately felt full confidence at last in the successful issue of his daring enterprise. Another step and his scheme of kidnapping the banker's son was as good as accomplished.

"Pass out!" he bade his companion.

"You know where we are going?"

"Yes! We're going somewhere quite near, to a house where we shall take ambush…"

"What for?"

"Why, to kill your enemies."

"Then I'll go with you."

"Capital!"—and Juve breathed a sigh of relief. The poor boy was giving proof of the utmost docility. He had only to ply him with lies to get him to do whatever he chose.

"All's going well!" thought the police officer, "perhaps over well! My luck is *too* good!… What devilish revenge does Fate mean to exact from me?"

But really his anxiety seemed misplaced. Everything was working out in the easiest possible fashion. On leaving the Asylum premises, Juve took the precaution of re-closing the door, and even turned the key, which he then pocketed.

"One never knows!" he said to himself. "As things are now, I may surely be forgiven the theft. If ever I should have to come here again, it might prove useful."

But the madman was waiting for him.

"You know the way?" he asked.

"Perfectly!" declared Juve. "We are going straight ahead!"

"As far as the trees?"

"Yes! There we'll take a boat and cross to an island."

"That's where the house is?"

"That's so! Only don't talk. Your enemies might hear us, you understand?"

This time Juve was telling the truth more or less. Midnight had just struck on the Rueil church clock. The night was extraordinarily peaceful and pitch dark. Not a star in the sky, which was veiled in heavy clouds portending storm. Not a ray of moonlight. The cold was severe but still quite bearable, and footsteps rang loud on the frozen ground. Was it not reasonable to fear the unhappy young man's enemies *might* overhear his remarks?

His enemies? No doubt the madman was thinking of the imaginary foes suggested by his sick fancy. Juve, on the contrary, had Fantômas in his mind! Was He keeping watch on the asylum, and was that why all was going so easily, though without his hand being actually visible. Or else, was he crouching in the dark, prowling somewhere at a distance? The dark night, when everything seems mysterious, when every bush and thicket looks unfamiliar, fantastic, terrifying, was of itself enough to account for Juve's ever-increasing agitation! No! he was not afraid; he was above any such ignoble feeling. Yet he felt a strange distress of mind—the distress a man experiences when he knows a vague peril, an unknown, but always possible, danger, near at hand.

"Let's get on!" he suggested.

The madman repeated the words.

"You will lead the way?" he asked.

"Right! But hush!"

Juve increased the pace, making straight before him for the line of trees the tops of which made a yet darker blot on the darkness of the horizon. No doubt they marked the course of the river. Once there, they must look for a boat, a fisherman's dinghy, moored to the bank. It would be easy enough to take possession of it and row across to the Ile de Croissy. Then, disembarking, to lead the madman to the "Romanesque" villa that stood on the island and of which M. Merandol was the owner, would be a matter of a few moments.

"And what a relief to my mind when I am there!" thought Juve. "By the Lord! I shan't ever forget this night!"

But he was wrong to complain. Everything still appeared as quiet and peaceful as possible.

"Come, come!" the police officer rebuked himself. "I'm getting nervous. Certainly, I don't usually have such wonderful luck!"

He laughed at his own fears. Meanwhile the madman, as good as gold, was walking cannily on tiptoe, with an exaggerated effort to make no noise.

"Poor lad!" Juve sighed afresh. "He seems harmless enough. But I wonder if a case like his is ever really curable."

Then, as they reached the riverbank, his thoughts returned to the Ile de Croissy, where he was about to land in such strange and mysterious circumstances… Ah! those terrible hours he had spent there once before. Was it not there he had watched, incapable of interfering, the amazing escape of Fantômas, who had come to fight a duel with Fandor? It was there Fandor and he, in impotent fury, had seen the scoundrel fly off, at the wind's will, in a balloon that had emerged from the sides of a river lighter.

And now he was returned, the villain! ready once more for the vilest atrocities! Was he never to be brought to book?

"Where are we going?" queried his companion, and Juve started violently. In the agitation of the moment, for a few short minutes he had actually forgotten the grim adventure on which he was then embarked!

"Turn to the right!" the police officer replied. "We are going to that house you see yonder. It is a boatmen's eating house. There are sure to be boats moored in front of it. Mind, we must be very, very careful. If they heard us…"

"There is a boat here," said the other unexpectedly. "Why not take that?"

"A boat?… Why, so there is!… But…"—and Juve broke off in doubt and perplexity. The surprising luck that had followed him all through had set him wondering. This last example terrified him. What was the boat doing there? Who had moored it to this lonely shore? With what object?

"I don't like this!" Juve growled. "It's all too easy! Chance alone could never…"

However, it was too late to retreat. And then, all said and done, was it so very extraordinary to come upon a fisherman's dinghy by the riverside here?

"Get in!" ordered the police officer in muffled tones, and he jumped in himself after the madman, who had taken his seat in the dinghy so conveniently found at their disposal at the very spot required.

"Whatever you do, don't move!" he advised his passenger.

"Not I! I'm afraid on the water…"

"Well, there's no danger. Leave it to me!" Over the ink-black waters, in the darkness now growing momentarily deeper under the threat of a coming storm of snow or hail, Juve propelled the frail skiff towards the opposite shore.

Suddenly, with startling rapidity, something loomed through the gloom, like a nightmare vision, a swift hallucination of the senses. Another boat, a light canoe, was noiselessly approaching, to pass close to the dinghy in which Juve and the madman sat.

Juve looked up from his rowing and saw the boat and, to his still greater amazement, saw it carried a woman… "The woman of the motorcar!" he thought as he stopped rowing. "The woman who threw me the letter…"

Then a voice, a voice quivering with passion and pain, a voice of grief and sore distress, sobbed out:

"Juve, Juve! Don't go yonder! Don't go! Don't go!"

"Kill! kill!" vociferated the madman. "Fire, I say!"—and the lunatic threw himself upon his companion, trying to snatch his revolver from his pocket, so that Juve had to fight for his life.

A terrible moment, as the boat swayed wildly, threatening from moment to moment to upset!

"Don't go! In Fandor's name, don't go there!" the voice still echoed across the waste of waters, as the mysterious visitant and her boat disappeared, swallowed up by the darkness, wrapped in the shades of night...

By the time Juve had mastered his companion's struggles, by the time he had drawn tight the straps of the straitjacket and reduced the madman to a state of helplessness, he could see nothing save the lonely darkness, the tossing waves and his own boat, which was slowly drifting down stream.

*   *   *   *   *

So rapid had been this strange scene that Juve was for the moment utterly bewildered. His mind worked swiftly. He was capable—and he had many a time proved as much—of taking instantaneously, or all but instantaneously, the most momentous decisions. Nevertheless for once he felt himself dumbfounded. Without resuming his oars, without stirring hand or foot, Juve let the boat drift down the current.

"The devil's in it!" he cried, as he thought how this was the second time he had received a warning of the sort, a warning so mysteriously given. On the first occasion he had supposed that they advised him: "Don't do this!" for the express purpose of inducing him to do it, knowing as they did his indomitable spirit. That was why, imagining they wanted him to remain with the patient at the Sanatorium, he had resolved on this wild scheme, had determined to kidnap Georges Merandol.

But such a supposition was not now tenable. He was now so far away from the Asylum, well on his way to the "Romanesque" villa, that he could no longer follow the course prescribed by purely logical indications. The woman had urged him: "Don't go yonder!" It followed she knew where he was going. What was her motive in trying to turn him back?

Then, who was she, this mysterious being who seemed to be dogging his footsteps? Despite himself, Juve felt a shudder run down his spine. There was something supernatural, fantastic, uncanny, about this strange creature in the canoe who appeared and disappeared so mysteriously. He admitted to himself:

"I am not a man to be easily scared… and yet she gave me a fright!" It is only people of tried and approved courage who are ready to confess themselves liable to a momentary panic.

Yes! who was this woman? How came she to know where he was going? Why did she persist in giving him such surprising pieces of advice?

As will happen in moments of feverish excitement following on the agitation of startling events, Juve's brain was now working with abnormal swiftness. His overstimulated nerves produced a prodigious activity of thought. He argued:

"To know where I am flying to, to know I am taking away Georges Merandol with me, after all, this needs no wizardry! If the poor boy's father owns this villa on the island, it is doubtless because he wished to have a place where he could stay near the Asylum in which his son was confined. This the people of the Sanatorium are bound to be aware of. They may well have gossiped about it and betrayed the information to anybody who wanted to have it."

Presently he went on again:

"Only remains to guess who the woman is. A friend? Someone who wishes to give a salutary warning. No, no! a thousand times no! A friend would make herself known… A friend would speak more clearly… A friend would not run away and disappear!"—and he drew his conclusion:

"It can only be an enemy… It can only be, very possibly, an accomplice of Fantômas!"

Then suddenly Juve bit his lips, barely stifling a groan of anger and acute distress:

"By the Lord!… If it was Lady…"

He did not finish the sentence. The supposition that had occurred to him left him breathless, panting with excitement and agitation. By the grim brigand's side, companion of the Lord of Terror, ally of Fantômas, had not a strange woman—his wife presumably—often been encountered. Truly this name of "Lady Beltham," which Juve had not dared pronounce, what tragedies it called up! what mysteries! what appalling atrocities!

A very great lady, this Lady Beltham, whose unhappy life held so many strange enigmas. Once welcomed at the English Court, related to the best families of the United Kingdom, by what caprice of Fate had she become the faithful comrade of Fantômas, despite her detestation of his crimes? She loved him. For his sake she was capable of the bitterest sacrifices. Again and again he, that monster of iniquity, had owed his safety only to her intervention.

Yet Lady Beltham—as Juve well knew—was no criminal. She was horrified at the dreadful doings of the man she loved. Her only fault was that she could not tear this unnatural passion from her heart. And Juve, shuddering, a cold sweat beading his brow, pictured the great lady watching over his life, striving at all costs to save him from the traps laid for him. Was not the thing possible after all? With closed eyes, and fists clenched in a spasm of indignant anger, Juve evoked in thought the gracious and fascinating figure of this enigmatic being. Of supreme distinction, a proud woman despite all humiliations, ravishingly beautiful, fair with a complexion of milk and roses, with great dreamy eyes in which ever slumbered the shadow of past griefs, Lady Beltham united in her person the three qualities that make women seductive—beauty, grace and unhappiness...

Alas! could it be she who had just gone by, this furtive figure on the dark waters?

"I did not see her! I could not see her!... And her voice was so broken, so anguished..."

A slight shock at the bow of the boat startled the police officer. Disconcerted by the unexpected encounter, he had clean forgotten for a moment or two where he was. Hardly the time for dreaming, surely! Impelled by wind and current, the boat had all but run aground, striking the overhanging boughs of a pollard willow on the bank.

"There we go! Going to be shipwrecked next! I'm no better

than a fool!"—and he seized the oars again and plied them vigorously.

"Come, come! This is childish!… Lady Beltham or not, my unknown friend—or enemy—can do me no harm. I am only doing what I ought. Once inside the villa, I shall be in a position to stand a siege. Now no more dallying! It's there we must go!"

Juve, indeed, was well acquainted with the property owned by M. Merandol, father of the madman he was bent on guarding against Fantômas' violence. In the Summer, at the time of the last encounter with the scoundrel, the police officer had noticed this quaint-looking house, built of old materials from the demolished Tuileries, all smothered in ivy and almost hidden behind a tangled mass of roses climbing over porch and pergola… He had even admired, in passing, a magnificent mastiff on guard over the premises, a ferocious looking creature despite the kindly gleam in the animal's eyes.

"A fortress! a veritable fortress!" thought Juve. "I can perfectly recall the lie of the ground. The garden is separated from the house by a terrace and steps. The house itself is of solid ashlar. The arched windows are high up in the walls. Yes! I can defy Fantômas and all his gang!"—and this time he pulled deliberately for the bank, where a little creek overhung by tall trees afforded a convenient landing place. Leaping lightly ashore, "Follow me!" he cried in a hearty voice to his companion, who seemed reluctant to set foot on the island.

"Very well, if you want me to," the madman agreed at last. "Is it far we're going now?"

"Not a bit of it—quite close… only a few steps away!"—and, tying up the boat to the trunk of a willow, where no doubt next morning the owner would be greatly surprised to find it moored, Juve turned off to the left across a field washed on both sides by the two branches of the Seine.

"This way!" he said encouragingly. "Look, there's the house…"—and involuntarily Juve heaved a sigh of relief. Only a few more seconds to wait before he might justifiably conclude that he was, he and his convoy, safe from all danger. Hardly a sound to be heard! Far off, on the other bank of the river a dog barked, but in the island itself reigned the deep silence of lonely, unfrequented places.

"The very spot for a quiet sojourn!" muttered Juve. "A hundred yards away the restaurant of La Grenouillère, and no other neighbors at all! Well, let's go in. Tomorrow we can see things better."

He inserted the key M. Merandol had given him in the lock, and the gate opened with the creak and grind indicating a long period of disuse and accumulated rust.

"We're to hide in the garden?" inquired the madman.

"No! in the house."

"There's a bed there!"

"Why, certainly!"

"So much the better! I'm sleepy…"

"Well, you shall have your sleep."

There was a crunching of gravel, as the two advanced along the path leading to the house door, and a nightbird took flight. Juve knew his way perfectly. Mounting the steps before the entrance, he set about opening the door, which was secured by safety locks and was of solid oak. It was really silly to have worried as he had! Had not everything proved childishly easy in this scheme of kidnapping Georges Merandol he had planned? The madman himself was showing quite exemplary docility, far more than he could ever have expected.

"When good luck takes a hand in things, one succeeds, no matter what the difficulties—and without any credit to one's self. All the same, I don't know how it's all going to end. At the Sanatorium, no doubt, the authorities will make a rumpus, send off telegrams, call the police, informing them of the patient's disappearance. And I who promised Havard to act with discretion! I'm letting him in for a pretty business!"—and he broke into a laugh of amused satisfaction. He was at last enjoying the restful feeling that follows a difficult task well accomplished. For all his scheming, Fantômas had not foreseen how he would carry off the unfortunate Georges Merandol to this villa. It was bound to upset all his plans.

"Once the door is open, I'm safe in port!" thought Juve—and at that moment the door came open.

"In you go!" he ordered the madman.

"But I can't see a thing!"

"I'm going to light up. Don't worry your head!"—and following the poor boy, who with the inconsequence that always characterizes the mental processes of the insane, seemed to have forgotten all about the enemies he had set out with the idea of hunting down, Juve stepped into the house.

"So!" he said gleefully. "Let's shut the door and light up..."

Double locking the door behind him as an additional precaution, he struck a light and looked about for a lamp. He soon found one, raised the wick and lit it.

"Fancy using paraffin in this year of grace!" mumbled the police officer, who now felt perfectly secure. "But there, of course electricity is out of the question in this island, to say nothing of the havoc floods are pretty sure to play with the place."

Then, the wick adjusted and the lamp burning brightly, he proceeded to inspect his surroundings. Yes, it was evident enough M. Merandol must have been afraid of floods. Every year, before leaving the villa, he had been careful to remove all articles of value, all breakable ornaments. Juve beheld a large room more than half empty. All that remained was a bed, the mattress of which was gone, a table, two or three chairs. In a corner were ranged garden chairs, empty flowerpots, gardening tools.

"For comfort, it leaves something to be desired," thought Juve. "But one must not ask for impossibilities. Tomorrow I'll see about taking the poor fellow somewhere else."

The "poor fellow," meantime, was still quite calm and quiet. He was strolling up and down the room with unconcealed curiosity, peering about him at its various contents, his mind evidently distracted by the novelty of these unfamiliar quarters. Suddenly he came back to his companion.

"I am sleepy!" he said again.

"Well, you must get to sleep. Go to bed!"

"Where?"

"Why, on the bed of course!"

"And you?"

"*I'm* not sleepy."

"So you don't mean to go to sleep?"

"No! But don't you trouble about that. There now, lie down!"

Juve felt a great pity for the poor young fellow, a man of over twenty with all the simplicity of quite young children. It was heartbreaking!

"I never thought madmen, even mild cases, were so gentle and compliant," he muttered. "What a sad thing to lose one's wits at his age!"

Meantime, without another word Georges Merandol had stretched himself on the bed Juve pointed to.

"You're not going to take this off?" he asked, indicating the straitjacket he still wore.

"No!... You would catch cold."

"It makes me uncomfortable."

"Not a bit of it! Shut your eyes and go to sleep."

Be sure Juve had no notion of relieving the madman of the straitjacket which enabled him, merely by tightening up the straps, to bring his charge instantly to order. Just before, in the boat, when the poor fellow had been terrified by the apparition of the nocturnal visitant, Juve had been only too glad to possess this means of keeping his companion quiet. Afterwards he had loosened his bonds, but he thought to himself:

"I am not an alienist myself. If they have put this apparatus, this straitjacket, on him at the Asylum, it is no doubt because he is liable to fits of acute mania. Best be prudent, and not go against the prescriptions of the Faculty!"

However the madman said no more. Stretched full length on the bed, he shut his eyes and soon lay absolutely still. Thereupon, after shifting the lamp so that the light should not shine in the young man's eyes, Juve threw himself in one of the garden chairs, and taking out and lighting a cigarette, began to smoke with infinite satisfaction to himself.

"So there," he murmured. "A good job successfully accomplished! I defy Fantômas to come here and disturb my night. By God! how good this cigarette tastes! I've well earned it, anyway…"

He had smoked his cigarette to the end and was going to light another, firmly resolved not to close his eye for a single instant, when a groan startled him.

"Halloa!" he exclaimed. "Do you want anything?"

The sound had come from the madman, who now cried out to his companion to listen.

"Listen to what?" demanded Juve.

"I am frightened!"

"Why, what nonsense!"

"But I am! They're prowling about."

"Who are?"

"My enemies…"

"I tell you they are not!" declared the police officer, speaking in the most authoritative tone of voice he could muster. "You're dreaming."

"No, I'm not dreaming! I can hear them! You're not armed, eh?"

"Why, of course I am! I have a gatling gun in my pocket, three daggers and a revolver!…"

"Show me!"

"Look there, you can see the revolver, can't you? I lay it down there on the table, within reach of my hand… Now you can sleep in peace."

The madman said nothing more. Reassured no doubt at sight of the revolver which Juve placed in a conspicuous position on the table, as he had promised, the boy apparently dropped off to sleep again.

"Poor lad!" the police officer thought with renewed pity. "I only hope he won't begin shouting or struggling again."

But, as a matter of fact, the young man's nerves seemed to be getting more and more exasperated. He called out again: "Do you hear me?"

"Yes, yes!" Juve answered. "Go to sleep, do!"

"I can't ! I'm in pain."

"Where is the pain?"

"In my head."

"Well, get to sleep, and you won't feel it."

"Yes, I shall! It's bleeding now..."

"Bleeding? What yarn's this you're telling me?..."

Suddenly Juve sprang to his feet. He had just remembered the great lump, the horrible tumor he had noticed on the unfortunate patient's head. Had he hurt himself by any chance? He went up to the bed, carrying the lamp with him and turning up the wick to see better.

"Where are you bleeding?" he asked.

"My head..."

"Not you! I can't see anything..."

"Yes, you can! You don't look carefully."

"I'm looking very carefully,"—and so indeed he was, staring at the large lump, the tumor, examining it with a curiosity and surprise that grew greater every moment.

"Could it be a tumor, this strange looking excrescence? One might almost have thought it to be, something much more astonishing—much more sinister! One might have sworn it was some sort of pocket or bag of unidentifiable material—goldbeater's skin perhaps? or else rubber? glued on to the unhappy boy's skull.

"Lean over me!" said the madman, "and look close!"

Juve did as suggested and bent over—to his undoing!

At that same instant the madman sprang up with a sudden, violent writhe of the body, dashing the top of his head in the police officer's face, almost knocking him over...

Then Juve realized how the lump that had so moved his curiosity and pity burst apart and an acrid liquid escaped from it, a liquid having the unmistakable smell—of chloroform!...

He felt stifled, suffocated, seized with an irresistible, a hideous lethargy...

Then, through the empty house two words echoed, punctuated by a fiendish laugh:

"Idiot!" sneered a fierce voice—the madman's.

"Fantômas!" stammered Juve with choked utterance... "It is

Fantômas!"

Then came a dull thud, the sound of a body falling. Juve had crashed to the floor, a lifeless bulk!

6. A Lesson in Police Craft

At the moment when Juve fell to the floor unconscious, suffocated by the fumes of chloroform, he had, without an instant's hesitation, recognized the identity of his assailant. Georges Merandol—or to speak more strictly, the individual he had taken to be Georges Merandol—was actually Fantômas! Indeed the audacity and adroitness displayed by the victor were of themselves enough to prove who this assailant was. Who but Fantômas would have thought of such an extraordinary device, at once piteous and cruel, this pretended tumor that actually concealed a bladder filled with chloroform.

Juve, at the same time, on coming to, manifested no surprise. So rapid had been his loss of consciousness under the effects of the powerful anesthetic that fortunately he had inhaled only a small dose. He had been paralyzed, suffocated in an instant, but the sleep thus violently provoked had prevented the resulting insensibility from being very deep or prolonged. The moment he awoke, therefore, he found himself in possession of all his usual clearness of mind. Certainly he had a raging headache and felt a terrible nausea, but that was all. His intellect was bright and active as ever.

"I am done for!" he told himself, and truly he seemed well justified in this belief. On trying to move, he had instantly discovered his entire inability to do so, and at the same moment realized the reason that sufficiently accounted for this state of helplessness. In a word, during his period of helplessness his adversary had strapped him up in the straitjacket he had just himself taken off.

"So!" thought the police officer, "the tables are finely turned… I thought he was the madman… and it was I. I have let myself be tricked like an imbecile!"

Yet in face of the imminent, undeniable danger, Juve, though knowing himself in Fantômas' power, experienced no acute anguish of mind. He was only risking his life! For so long he had vowed the sacrifice of this that he recked little of death! On the other hand, his self-esteem was grievously wounded.

"Beaten!" he groaned. "Shamefully beaten!"

He shut his eyes. He could not bear to look in the victor's face. He wanted first to regain control of his feelings. Fantômas? Was it Fantômas who had just made him his prisoner? On this point he had no illusions. Already, indeed, he perfectly well understood what had occurred.

Georges Merandol, the poor lunatic, the genuine Georges Merandol, had undoubtedly been carried off by the brigand before the police officer had ever gone to Rueil. The "Georges Merandol" whom he had found wearing the straitjacket he now wore himself was therefore Fantômas—Fantômas who had had the audacity to take his prisoner's place, had disguised his features and waited for the detective's arrival. All this Juve more or less divined.

After that, everything that had so much surprised him became clear as crystal. For the time being he had been amazed at the phenomenal good luck that favored his projects? On the contrary, the luck had actually been dead against him. Fantômas had simply guessed the design Juve proposed to carry out, and resolving to play the character of Georges Merandol, he had made it his express business to facilitate the removal of the madman by the police officer. This was why the pretended lunatic had been so ready to climb out of the window to the grounds; this again was why he had led the way to the postern of which he had the key. Then who, if not Fantômas, had arranged to have the boat at the spot where they had so providentially found it on the riverbank?

"Tricked! I have been tricked like a child!" thought Juve, his heart bursting with rage. He had, in fact, thought to frustrate the scheme of the villain Fantômas by doing as he had done. But lo! Fantômas, that was clear, had had the wit to guess his daring plan. How he must have laughed internally, the grim Lord of Terror, the vile Torturer, when, pretending to be

Georges Merandol, he had let himself be lured away by Juve, and had watched him falling, one after the other, into all the traps prepared for him beforehand in his eagerness to bring him to the spot where he now was!

"The low scoundrel!" growled Juve, choking with anger. "The vile artfulness of the way he got me to bend over him just at the moment he found it most convenient to strike me down most effectively! To think how he persuaded me to put down my revolver out of reach… To think how I never suspected a thing!… Why, I am a fool, it seems—the most abject of fools!…"

Another thought set him trembling. The woman who, twice over, had warned him of his danger? Why, it was Lady Beltham, of course! He could doubt this no longer. Guessing at a new crime on the part of Fantômas, she had tried to prevent the imminent catastrophe.

"And I refused to believe her! I saw only an accomplice in her! Oh, I deserve my fate! Let him kill me! It will only be my deserts!"

Then, next moment, he forgot his own peril. His thoughts had suddenly flown to the genuine Georges Merandol. Alas! what had become of the poor half-witted fellow?

"They must have carried him off before the telephone message," Juve calculated. "This had no other object but to entice me to Rueil. It was expressly intended to create a confusion that would inevitably bring me to the scene of action. Yes! it all fits in together!"

But as he uttered the words, Juve could not check a shudder. It all fitted in together, did it? No indeed! not quite that! With what ulterior purpose had Fantômas, as a matter of fact, arranged all this series of events? Great as was his hatred of the police officer, it would be folly to suppose he had had no other object in view save his capture!

"No, no!" Juve concluded. "There is something more behind. It all forms part of a definite plan. Well, I know all the details of its execution—I ought therefore to be able to divine what is preparing. Yes, I ought, I certainly ought!"

But he could make no guess whatever. What a fine thing, anyway, that the poor man should even now be striving to solve the problem at the very time he was a prisoner in Fantômas' hands.

Suddenly a cry escaped him. A jug of cold water had been pitched full in his face. He opened his eyes, to see "Georges Merandol" standing before him, a grin on his lips.

"You've woke up then? I was really getting a bit anxious. Accidents so often happen with chloroform…"

"Thank you!" Juve replied in the same ironical tone, wishing to show himself equal to the occasion and give back scorn for sarcasm. "Don't put yourself about. I am very well, I thank you, Fantômas!"

"Fantômas?… But I am the madman, mind you, Georges Merandol!"

"Say rather you are admirably disguised. Please accept my congratulations!"

"My turn to thank you, Juve! You are too kind! But really, without flattering, you think I have made myself up successfully?"

"Like a first-class actor!"—and now the police officer was more than half in earnest. He fixed his keen eyes on Fantômas' face. Never yet had he seen the man's real countenance, never for so much as one second beheld his true features. Well, even now, he was bound to admit that beneath the paint and all the tricks of "getup," Fantômas presented absolutely the appearance he had chosen to adopt, now he had the opportunity of examining him at leisure. Yes, even were he to escape, even were he—a very improbable contingency—to avoid death, he would fail to recognize him when he had ceased to be Georges Merandol.

But now the brigand again broke in on the detective's reflections.

"A truce to silly compliments!" he exclaimed. "Juve, I have something to show you. Is it well done?"—and Fantômas flourished a sheet of letter paper before his prisoner's eyes, a sheet covered with writing.

Juve started and trembled. It was *his own* writing, it was *his own* signature, he saw. So perfect was the imitation he would have been taken in himself!

"You are an accomplished forger," he declared.

"I love to hear you say so… Now will you excuse me, Juve? I must leave you for a couple of minutes, the time to send off this little missive. Then I'm with you again."

Fantômas left the room, and the police officer heard voices whispering below in the garden. Was an accomplice there? Next minute Fantômas returned. Truly, what a fund of refined irony he had at command, this man of blood, this man—this monster, whom his atrocious crimes put outside the pale of humanity! He now asked:

"Well, Juve, shall we have a talk? The time must seem long to you, eh? Anyway, it is only an hour after midnight, and I cannot kill you right away…"

"Really? Well then, let's talk"—this without a sign of perturbation. He asked:

"What is it you wish me to tell you, Fantômas?"

But the brigand gave a shrug. "Excuse me," he countered, "but I think it is for you to question me."

"Oh? Why, pray?"

"You're not asking yourself what it is I am preparing?"

"Perhaps I am. But you wouldn't tell me!"

"Oh! yes, I would… seeing you will be dead before you have a chance to reveal my secrets…"

"True!" said Juve calmly. "My word! I never thought of that."

A weird conversation! Juve seemed just as cool and unmoved as his executioner!

"Well, I'm listening!" he added in an indifferent tone.

"No! I can see this does not interest you anymore. In fact, it is only natural you should feel an aloofness from the things of this world. Besides, time is passing. Just now you congratulated me, did you not? Let me tell you I appreciate your cleverness too highly—yes! I really do, Juve—not to feel convinced that before an hour is past you will know everything I could tell you…"

"You are expecting something then?"

"No! Someone."

"So? Who is it?"

"Oh, Juve! What a question to ask! Quite unworthy of you, Juve, not to guess who it is I'm likely to be expecting!"

"Indeed?"

"Unless you're playing the innocent on purpose?"

"A plausible hypothesis, Fantômas!" remarked Juve, his eyes flashing.

"I am expecting M. Merandol," resumed the brigand coolly. "A car has carried him the letter I showed you and which is ostensibly written by you. It is bound to make him decide to come here instantly. It is an urgent summons. The car will be at his disposal… Oh! of course I need not tell you I have taken my precautions to inspire him with confidence, this financier friend of yours."

"I may know how?"

"Why not?… Frankly, Juve, while you were still asleep, I borrowed the use of your thumb to put an impress of it on my letter. Besides which, I make you say in that document, 'so that you may have no doubt it is really I, Juve, who beseech you to come without losing a second, I print the mark of my thumb on the paper. If you feel any hesitation, call at the Criminal Bureau. The slip with my fingerprints is there. They will tell you a signature of this kind is impossible to imitate. Perhaps, even, M. Havard will come with you.'"

Fantômas interrupted himself to laugh, then continued:

"Eh? What do you say to that? *I* think he will come. What do *you* suppose?"

Juve could only make a wry face. Rage was choking him, for all his outward calm. What cleverness, what ingenuity, even to the smallest details, in all this monstrous villain did! If M. Merandol did call at the Department, was it not quite certain they would acknowledge the imprint of his thumb? Was it not equally sure that M. Havard would wish to accompany the Banker? Juve thought:

"Yes! that's it. *I* am in the net—and I am to serve as bait! Fantômas means to use me to entice M. Merandol senior and

Havard to come here. He wants to win a complete, a wholesale victory!"

Then he went on with his monologue:

"And yet, no! I understand how, by demanding my dismissal, by arranging to have Merandol telephone to Havard just when I was at the Department, then afterwards by telephoning a lying message himself, he enticed me here... I can guess too how he exploits me to get M. Merandol and M. Havard into his power... But I do *not* understand why he committed the imprudence of going to tell Merandol how he was proposing to steal the thirty-eight millions! Devil take it! Thieves don't give the alert before beginning operations—even when they are called Fantômas!"

However Juve was not to be left long in peace to his reflections. Fantômas got up and resumed his remarks:

"Why, yes! Time flies. These gentlemen cannot be far off now. They will come by the road along the riverbank, quitting their car in the middle of the Pont de Chatou, which crosses the island. Excuse me, Juve, I must be getting ready to receive them..."—and the brigand actually started on his sinister preparations. Nor was the detective long in gathering what it was he was contriving. On the floor he spread a carpet or rug, to the four corners of which were fastened four long, slender ropes. These ropes Fantômas, mounting on a ladder, passed through four pulleys fixed in the ceiling. He explained:

"A haphazard contrivance, you see, Juve, but it will serve its purpose. Indeed, it was the conveniences on the spot that suggested the idea to me. The pulleys belong to M. Merandol. No doubt they used them for hoisting up his furniture in case of floods. *I* am going to make them serve another purpose. Soon as our good friend enters this room to join you, I shall haul on the ropes. The carpet will immediately lift, and M. Merandol will topple over. The thing can't fail! Once on the ground, I shall know how to deal with him... But you say nothing, Juve?"

"I beg your pardon!... I was a bit absentminded..."

What more could Juve do but make a show of scorning the villain who had him at his mercy? Suddenly Fantômas came up to him again. "Hush!" he said. "They are coming… No, I hear only one. Merandol has not been for Havard… A pity, but no matter!"

The brigand laid his hand on the police officer's shoulder, who still of course wore the straitjacket.

"And now one last word, Juve! You might very well, even with my dagger at your throat, yell a warning to M. Merandol: 'Don't come in!' See, I am gagging you…"

Juve gnashed his teeth with rage. Cry out to Merandol to fly! Why that was the very thing he had been meditating—and lo! Fantômas had foreseen the act of self-devotion he was ready to perform!"

Unable to resist, condemned by the straitjacket he wore to utter helplessness, willy-nilly he had to submit… Never, never would he forget the intolerable torture of that moment! A crime was about to be committed before his very eyes. With hideous cruelty Fantômas had told him as much—and he could do nothing, absolutely nothing, to prevent the horrid deed. Lying helpless on the bed where the brigand had thrown him, Juve could hear the financier's footsteps coming nearer and nearer. He noted his momentary hesitation at the gate of the garden. He heard the creaking of the gate as it opened. Then the steps sounded on the flight of stairs leading to the front door. The victim had arrived.

In the dark room Fantômas stood waiting, never stirring. At last the front door opened.

"Juve? Are you there?" questioned M. Merandol, and the unhappy man took another step—only one… Oh! Fantômas had said true, the trap was infallible. The brigand hauled on the ropes, the carpet lifted… Staggering, crying out in horror and surprise, M. Merandol fell… Then the cry was stifled instantly. With a stunning blow, delivered with all his strength, Fantômas had struck him down, killed him perhaps.

Juve shut his eyes. All the blood in his body flooded back to the heart. He would gladly have died that minute rather than see more. Yet he looked again, as Fantômas' voice mocked:

"Look, Juve! Here's what you did not understand… what

I was waiting for! Do you see that?"—and he held up a key he had snatched from the Banker's bosom, hanging by a little chain round his neck.

"The key of the iron door of the bank cellars, Juve! Just that! Ah, ha! Never say I'm not giving you a fine lesson in police craft… But you don't understand yet? Come, Juve! Follow me carefully!… The truth is, I had no notion whatever where the key was hidden. A fact, I hadn't! That was why I went to see M. Merandol. Why, naturally, when I told him the contrary, saying I knew where the key was, I was pretty sure to put him in a quandary. From that to guessing he would be so imprudent as to carry the key about with him, was a short step. All I had to do then was to entice him here—and the day was mine! Oh, ho! Simple as A B C, wasn't it? A pity, eh? You won't have an opportunity to repeat the story!…"

Juve lay with closed eyes, biting his lips till the blood came not to scream out in fury. Yes! How simple it was! And yet, he had never guessed! Fantômas resumed:

"Why, you're asleep, dear boy—or pretending to be. Very good—as you please! In fact, I propose here and now to devote you to a long sleep…"

The wretch fell silent. Taking a whistle from his pocket, he blew a shrill blast. Next instant an accomplice hailed from outside the door:

"You called me, master?"

"Yes!" said Fantômas. "Go fetch the winding sheets!"

Juve was still shuddering at sound of the dreadful word, realizing how these winding sheets were for Merandol and himself when a fresh surprise set him wondering. Fantômas had gone on to add in a reflective tone:

"Surely, the beeves should be at the bridge end by now!"

What could the strange words mean?

7. Fandor Is Patient!

"Now tell me, Jean, do you understand anything of this?"

"No, Monsieur Fandor…"

"And that is all you have to say?…"

"Yes, Monsieur Fandor…"

"Your master disappears, vanishes, fades into thin air… and you take it all as a matter of course?"

"I didn't say that, Monsieur Fandor…"

"Obviously! You don't say anything,"—and turning away, Fandor left Juve's old servant and went back to lean out of window. He did not stay there long. In two minutes Jerome Fandor was back at old Jean's side.

"You are sure," he asked, "that day before yesterday he went off to the Criminal Bureau?"

"Perfectly sure, Monsieur Fandor…"

"It was really Monsieur Havard who phoned him?"

"I think so…"

"Then it's to see him he must have gone… So, I'm going to telephone…"

Jerome Fandor unhooked the instrument on Juve's desk, then replaced it—an action he had repeated a hundred times over already.

"On second thought," he muttered, "better not! Juve made me swear not to worry the Chief. He told me he knew Havard was upset, and prejudiced against him. I can't really risk making more mischief."

For thirty-six hours the young man had been there in the little flat Juve occupied in the Rue Tardieu, and he had never been still for one minute all the time. He had come to see his friend to tell him about the extraordinary conversation he had had with his Editor, to let Juve know of the threat of dismissal he had received. The latter had not been there to welcome him for the very good reason that he had left home, "summoned by M. Havard," as old Jean stated. At first, Fandor had been merely annoyed at the disappointment, but now, after all these hours, his annoyance was succeeded by a very real anxiety. The police officer had not come back, and never even telephoned to warn his servant of his prolonged absence.

"Why, yes!" growled Fandor, "I know very well Juve is quite the man to disappear for a matter of official duty without telling a soul, but, all said and done, this has gone on too long… What the devil is he after?"

Leaving the sitting room, Fandor went back once again to find the old servant, who was busily employed cleaning up the silver.

"Jean!" he called.

"Sir?"

"You can bear witness I have been patient?"

"Patient?"

"Yes, patient!… That I have waited for news as long as it was right I should?…"

"Oh?"

"Why, certainly, man! What makes you say: 'Oh?' That means nothing, that doesn't!"

"No, sir!"

"Then, I repeat: You can bear witness I have been patient."

"Yes, sir!"

"Very well! It follows I need have no scruples now, doesn't it? That's your opinion, eh?"

"My opinion, sir?"

"Yes! Your opinion I say! One would think I was talking Chinese… Come now, don't you think it's alarming to the last degree, this long absence of your master?"

"Yes, I do, sir!"

"At last!… Well, I am a patient man—up to the point when I'm impatient. So then, as that moment happens to be the present moment…"

"Then, sir?"

"Then, I'm off, I'm going…"

"Monsieur Fandor is going?…"

"Yes, and right away. I'm off right away…"

"Monsieur can do as he likes…"

"By God! you're enough to drive a man crazy!"

"And Monsieur is going?"

"To the Department. If Juve comes in meantime, you'll tell him…"

"Monsieur can rely on me."

"Very good!… Oh! but I'm sick of being patient… Still I *am* patient! I really am!"

Like a whirlwind Fandor dashed out of the place, banging shut the doors behind him, then tearing down the stairs four steps at a time. Patient or not, the police officer's faithful comrade knew Juve—"his" Juve as he used to call him. Better than anybody he knew the furious impetuosity with which Juve would rush into the most hazardous adventures, when he believed it to be his duty to confront danger. Better than anybody Fandor knew that Juve never faltered in the campaign he was engaged in against Fantômas. Was he not justified then in the acute anxiety he felt at his friend's prolonged absence, an absence that might well be accounted for by the opening of a new battle with the "Lord of Terror"?

In the cab that carried him to the headquarters of the Criminal Bureau, Fandor thought:

"In my case, Dupont de l'Eure wanted to sack me from his paper. True, that don't matter, because I don't allow myself to be sacked. But all the same, the Chief didn't get this idea out of his own head. It was by someone else's orders… Who is this 'someone'?… Fantômas! Oh! I could swear by all the gods it is!… So, Fantômas is at work at this moment. So, is it unreasonable I should feel anxious?"—and strong in this conviction, which he firmly held, on however slight grounds, the young man declared out loud:

"I must be patient, by the Lord! of course I must… and I have been… Still, I mustn't, neither, show the energy of a jellyfish!"

The journalist, who delighted in the daring colloquialisms of modern slang, need have had no fear of ever being credited with energy of that flabby sort.

When eventually his taxi pulled up at the door of the Department, he shot out—"got out" would be too mild a way of putting it, his excitement being by this time at fever heat. Four steps at a time he sprang up a broad staircase leading to an antechamber where a stout usher was dozing.

"What! you, M'sieur Fandor?" cried the man, stretching himself.

"Juve?" was all the journalist's answer.

"Monsieur Juve?"

"Yes!"

"Well?"

"Well, have you seen him?"

"When?"

"Why, today... yesterday, anyway?... You can see very well I'm anxious about him."

For once the usher shook off the apathetic phlegm of a functionary whom nothing ever disturbs. He said:

"Wait a moment!... Why, yes! I saw Monsieur Juve... Yes! was it yesterday?... No! day before yesterday... the Chief was expecting him..."

"The Chief?... Havard?"

"Of course... Who do you suppose?"

"Take in my name..."

"But, he's at work... No one to be admitted... He told me..."

"Then... don't take in my name,"—and leaving the usher dumbfounded, and amazed into the bargain, Fandor dashed forward, and flung wide open the door of the working room sacred to the Head of the Criminal Department. The latter, absorbed in important work, gave a start of surprise.

"What! you!" he exclaimed.

"Yes! I won't deny it! I apologize, but I am anxious about Juve."

"Well, what about Juve?"

"You didn't see him day before yesterday?"

"As a matter of fact..."

"Was it on police business?"

M. Havard scratched his head and looked embarrassed. He was far from finding pleasure in the prospect of informing Fandor of his friend's dismissal!

"Why do you ask me that?" he inquired.

"Because… what *is* the secret?"

"Juve has handed me his resignation."

"Eh?… You tell me?… Say it again!"

"The Minister…"

"Oh, well! no matter! A political dodge!… Hmm! the plot thickens. I chucked out at *La Capitale*—and Juve dismissed from the Police!… A fine beginning truly!"—and the young man mopped his brow angrily.

"To proceed!" he said. "So! they've given Juve the boot. After all, that's of no importance. They're bound to be offering him their apologies one day or another. It's only a question of waiting, a matter of patience!… That fits me like a glove!… Now another thing, he has never been back home. You know the reason?"

Involuntarily M. Havard knit his brow.

"Well?" he began. Then he spoke out:

"He is away on business…"

"Private business?"

"Entirely so. M. Merandol demanded his help…"

"The financier?"

"Yes, the financier. And in fact… by the Lord!"—and suddenly he sprang to his feet. For thirty-six hours, having had no news of Juve, not hearing a word from M. Merandol, he had not given a thought to the police officer. But Fandor's manifest anxiety was infectious… M. Havard suddenly remembered: "Fact is, Fantômas' name was mentioned, I imagine…"

Then he said aloud:

"See here, Fandor! It's idiotic what I'm going to say… But here it is!… You ought to see Merandol. He was afraid… I don't know what of… He spoke of… It was on the phone and no doubt I misunderstood… He spoke of Fantômas, it seems to me…"

"By the Lord!" cried Fandor. "I was sure of it… Poor old

Juve!"—and all the gamut of human pain sounded in the journalist's voice. Oh! he had felt a presentiment of evil in his heart
without any positive reason, and lo! a single word had confirmed it… Juve was away on some business, and vouchsafed
no news of his doings—and Fantômas was mixed up in it!

The journalist did not waste one second. Wheeling round on
his heels, he hurried to the door. His duty was plain before him.
Juve, his best friend, was he knew not where. He was resolved
to find out! Like a bloodhound he threw himself on the scent…
He was not called Jerome Fandor for nothing! The ex-reporter
of *La Capitale* dashed down the stairs of the Department like
a bombshell.

"Merandol… Manager of the Crédit International… Rue
d'Auteuil… Lucky I know my Paris Directory by heart! The
number I can't remember, but I shall discover it all right,"—and
find it he did.

Three-quarters of an hour later Fandor was ringing with a
trembling hand at the financier's door.

"Monsieur Merandol?" he asked the manservant who
appeared.

"He is not in, sir!"

"Not come back?… Gone out?… Still at the Bank?"

"Monsieur has not come back, sir. I can't say if he is at the
Bank. But he is long behind his time…"

"I can telephone?… It is about a serious matter…"

The servant's face fell, a look of anxiety and alarm appeared
on his countenance.

"Monsieur is of course at liberty to use the phone!" he
agreed, and softly closed the door.

At that moment a queer look crossed the young man's face.
"Ho, ho!" he grunted, and then in a reflective tone: "Well,
well?"—and in strong contrast to his previous headlong haste,
he went slowly back to his conveyance, thinking to himself:

"That servant had a pestilent look about him!… By God!
a financier whose whereabouts they don't dare specify… A
failure perhaps?… A bankruptcy? A tragedy of sorts brought
about by Fantômas? I must look into this!…"

He got into his conveyance again, giving the address of the Boulevard Haussmann where the offices occupied by the Crédit International were situated. But the taxi had hardly reached its destination when Fandor felt his face turn pale. Before the imposing entrance of the huge bank a crowd was gathered. Yet the gates were shut. Police were pushing back the inquisitive throng.

"Damnation!" swore Fandor, and leapt to the ground, shouting to his driver: "Wait for me!"

Then, plying his elbows vigorously to force a passage through the crowd, he reached the first row of curious onlookers.

"Hi, there! you! keep back!" yelled a policeman, darting forward to bar his way.

But Fandor stopped the man in full career. "Press!" he cried. *La Capitale!* I can pass?" And so he did without further demur. In front of him, half a dozen yards away, he saw a group of grave-looking individuals standing before the closed doors, apparently waiting. At the first glance he made out M. Havard, and running up to him:

"Well? Merandol?" he asked.

"I know nothing!" gasped M. Havard, throwing up his hands in a gesture of horror. "You had hardly gone when a telephone message from the Commissary of the District informed me of the scandal."

"What scandal?"

"Why, have you no eyes? The gates are shut... And it's not four o'clock in the afternoon! The thing's unheard-of! The Bank never closes so early."

"Then?" panted Fandor.

"Then, that's all... We're waiting for a locksmith. Ring as we may, peal after peal, nobody answers! One would think every soul was dead in the building..."

M. Havard seemed half beside himself. Fandor, on the contrary, the more he learned of the fantastic events happening, seemed the more completely to recover his coolness.

"They've telephoned?" he inquired.

"Why, of course!... Without result."

"So no employee gives any sign of life?"

"None,"—and pointing dramatically to the facade of the bank, to which formidable iron gates forbade nearer approach, M. Havard added:

"It's very certain something is up inside!... But what? No way to find out!... No way to get in! I don't even know if a locksmith will be able..."

"Good! Just wait a moment... I undertake to open the gates!"

By many years' practice Fandor had acquired the dexterity of the professional burglar. There was hardly a lock in existence could foil him. Only Juve might boast of equal skill.

"I have my tools with me!" he announced, and the journalist dived into the pocket of his jacket and brought out a slim canvas case, from which he extracted two or three implements of steel.

"Come, Monsieur Havard, never gape at my little collection!" he laughed. "It's a souvenir was given me by a housebreaker your constables never caught! They're first-rate tools, as you'll soon see..."

And Fandor was not exaggerating. Under the eyes of the amazed police officers—the whole staff was by now on the spot—he knelt down, introduced a picklock into the keyhole, and worked it about slowly. A sharp click was heard, and:

"There!" said the journalist getting up. "It's a 'nightingale,' and I can tell you it sings beautifully... The way is practically open now..."

The iron gates, in fact, stood ajar. In two steps the young man was before the solid mahogany doors that guarded the entrance to the great hall of the Bank.

"A matter of half a second!" he declared. "This second lock, a child could pick it!... There!... Forward!... Devil take it! What a queer smell..."

Scarcely had Fandor pushed open the door he had just unlocked before an extraordinary odor, a sour, acrid perfume, spread in all directions.

"Forward!" cried the journalist again, and at M. Havard's side, followed by the whole force of police present, he dashed in. But progress was almost instantly arrested. With a simultaneous cry of horror, amazement and terror, one and all came to a stand, petrified by the sight that met their eyes. The great hall of the Crédit International—one of the sights of Paris—was crowded with people. The clerks were at their desks. Customers filled the rotunda. A whole nation seemed gathered in the vast building…

But this nation, these customers and employees, were motionless every one, some bending over their writing, others standing at the pay-desks, leaning against the pillars of this temple of mammon, sitting at tables, on chairs and benches… A mysterious, an appalling cataclysm seemed to have overwhelmed every soul in the Crédit International. Livid with horror, staggering back at the dreadful sight, M. Havard stammered in a voice hoarse with emotion:

"Dead! They are dead?"

But Fandor had already run to the nearest of the victims. Putting his ear to the chest of a bank clerk, he cried:

"Dead! Not a bit of it! Not a man Jack of them! Asleep! Nothing worse than that!… And ourselves… Great God! Air, that's what we want."

The journalist felt an indescribable torpor creeping over him, gaining upon him. His thoughts were confused, his eyes grew dim—a result, no doubt, of the overpowering odor he was inhaling. He looked round, to see M. Havard staggering, on the point of falling. The Chief of the Municipal Police was in the same plight, while his subordinates were beating the air with their arms like drunken men who feel the ground reeling under them.

"Asleep!" repeated Fandor… "Yes, yes! asleep!… And ourselves. My God! my God!"

He had no strength left. Yet never, perhaps, had the journalist done anything much more heroic than what he started to do at this supreme moment. His limbs were like lead; his muscles seemed unstrung; a clash of bells made a maddening uproar in his brain.

But now he felt in his pocket, drew out his revolver, panting:

"Air! We must have air! I want… I want…"

Four shots rang out one after the other. The young man, leveling his weapon at the colored glasswork of the magnificent dome that roofed the great hall of the Bank, had shattered it without the smallest compunction. Then, as fragments of broken glass fell rattling to the ground, life-giving currents of air flooded the vast space.

And Jerome Fandor rubbed his eyes in sudden amazement. He beheld littering the floor shining gold pieces, that had rolled hither and thither, napoleons, half-napoleons. They seemed to have been scattered about in handfuls.

8. Juve's Thumb

For some seconds, despite his enormous energy, Jerome Fandor still stood motionless, as it were dumbfounded. He could see the gold that littered the floor, he gaped at it with staring eyes of amazement, but he seemed incapable of understanding what it meant, unable to draw any reasonable conclusion.

Meantime the fresh air continued to flood the great hall, and the strange, nauseous smell grew less overpowering. Suddenly Jerome Fandor came to life.

"By the Lord!" he exclaimed. "…Why, yes! of course!…"— and he looked about for M. Havard, who at the moment was mopping his forehead in a mechanical sort of way.

"You understand?" Fandor asked him.

"An abominable robbery!" stammered M. Havard. "Fantômas!" declared Fandor, his voice quivering with rage.

But at this moment the pair were interrupted. Shouts resounded, shouts of fear and fury. Revived by the refreshing currents of air, the employees and customers of the bank were awaking from the strange sleep in which they had been buried. And now, one and all, as if struck with sudden insanity, they began to beat the air with their arms and run hither and thither in a panic such as follows on some terrific cataclysm of nature.

"Fine work!" growled a voice. Fandor looked round to see the man who had spoken. It was Inspector Henri.

"True for you! Fine work!" declared the journalist… "And it's going to be finer still in three minutes, if nothing's done. M. Havard, what the devil are you waiting for?"

"Waiting to do what?" asked the Chief of the Criminal Bureau in a faltering voice.

"Why, to bolt the doors, by God! Aren't you awake yet?"

No! M. Havard seemed far from being in full possession of

his faculties! Fandor lost no more time.

"Everybody gather to the right of the Hall!" he shouted in a stentorian voice. "And nobody is to go out!... Six constables, revolver in fist, to guard the gates!... And call up the Police Reserves!..."

Then he went back to M. Havard.

"Better now?"

"I... I feel... Very queer..."

"Well, well! That'll pass..."

"But, tell me, you seem to understand, *you* do?"

"Why, yes! Easy enough to see now!"

"But..."

"No *but* about it! It's as simple as A B C... If Jules Verne were still alive, we'd have to hold him partly responsible. The sudden sleep of all these people amazes you? This sleep was deliberately provoked, M. Havard, provoked by the gas protoxide of azote! Fantômas simply saturated the atmosphere with the stuff at a moment's notice—and every soul in the place found himself fast asleep without knowing a thing about it... Read your 'Adventures of Doctor Ox' again."

"But... but... how?"

"How did he set about obtaining this result?"

"Oh! you ask me too much. There are a score of ways... But, there, look! Of course they have electric lighting here. But, besides, there's a complete installation of gas, in case of emergency. All he had to do was to fix tubes of compressed protoxyde of azote gas on the ordinary gas pipes, and turn on a tap..."

"Mad work! it's mad work!" panted M. Havard. "Or mighty clever work! Oh! Science has not said her last word! A genius like Fantômas knows how to utilize her secrets... That's the whole explanation!"

Fandor spoke with a touch of ill-humor he hardly tried to conceal. He proceeded:

"And this is the time they choose to put Juve on the retired list! That's what I call doing things reasonably!"

Then, with a shrug, Fandor stepped away, as if to leave the

Chief. But the latter called him back.

"And the shutting of the gates and doors? How do you suppose?..."

"My good sir!" retorted Fandor coldly, "I have certain ideas of my own on that point, I admit... Yes, I might keep them for the readers of my paper... but there, I'm quite ready to share them with you... Anyway, first turn your head—do you see that?"—and he pointed to an object lying on the floor under a bench.

"A mask!"—and M. Havard gave a start—"a gas mask!..."

"Like what the 'Poilus' had in the War!... Come, you're coming quite awake! You understand the stunt now? Fantômas made his preparations for his general poisoning of the air. To start with, he posts two or three accomplices at the entrance who shut the gates of the bank; at that moment he turns on the gas taps. Then, with other accomplices, protected like himself by masks that safeguard them against the stupefying vapors, he forces the doors of the cellars, grabs the millions he covets, and loads them up, I conjecture, on a truck waiting in an inside courtyard—and disappears!... You take me? You understand?"

Yes! M. Havard understood. Now the strange torpor that for some minutes had kept him practically helpless was all but gone. At Fandor's last words he recovered his self-possession and wringing his hands with rage, he panted:

"Fantômas! Fantômas. But the villain will stop at nothing then? There is no limit to his boundless audacity?"

"Yes! that strikes me as likely enough!" laughed Fandor, and M. Havard threw a venomous glance at the young man.

"You think it funny, eh?" he demanded. "And, to begin with, what is there to prove it *is* Fantômas?"

"Nothing at all, M. Havard! Nothing at all!... No! I have no proof to give you on that point... Only find me another criminal capable of such a daring attempt?"—and Fandor pointed dramatically to the signs of pillage and panic in the great hall of the bank, where the police reserves, called up in hot haste on the telephone, were trying in vain to restore order.

Thereupon a silence fell between the two. With downcast

eyes M. Havard was thinking. Once again he found in his path, this time the successful perpetrator of the greatest of all his enormities, the ever-elusive Fantômas. Once again the "Lord of Terror," the sinister hero of so many villainies, had carried out another of those monstrous deeds of audacity that mark an epoch in the annals of Crime! Once again, to crown his exploit, he had disappeared, vanished into thin air. Where, indeed, was he? Where look for him? Where attempt his arrest? M. Havard felt a sense of profound discouragement growing on him.

Meantime, Jerome Fandor's face had paled, then reddened. Though he had bravely, more bravely than M. Havard, fought against the poisonous vapors, he had likewise felt their debilitating effects. But this sense of weakness was now passing to be succeeded by his normal activity.

"Come, to work!" he said to himself—and turning to M. Havard:

"You hear Paris?" he cried "…We must avenge its wrongs…"

Through the open doors of the Bank, in fact, a loud, confused, angry clamor was now audible. The city had just learned the fresh villainy perpetrated by the Arch-Criminal. And Paris was shouting forth its indignation. Paris, sick with disgust was raging in impotent fury. Black with people, the Boulevard Haussmann might have been in the throes of a revolution. The police detailed to curb the violence of the crowd seemed powerless and were beginning to lose their heads. M. Havard struck his forehead with an air of bewilderment.

"I must take measures!" he exclaimed. "Fandor, *you* will pursue inquiries here?"

But the journalist shook his head.

"My word! No!" he said. "I think I have done enough for you. Now each for himself… Juve is no longer one of your staff… I don't see why I should undertake to do your business!… 'Your servant, sir!'"—and the young man swung round on his heels and walked away. Truly, to dare to speak in this fashion to the puissant Chief of the Criminal Department, Fandor must have been in full possession of his faculties, and more than that, must needs have been very angry—as indeed he was!

By this time the first confusion was merging into some sort of order. A body of Inspectors had arrived hotfoot from the Prefecture of Police—men who had not inhaled the poison gas and were now busy questioning the employees, visiting the cellars and generally carrying out an investigation with the utmost energy. In a very short while the Police would be in possession, if not of the key to the mystery, at any rate of a more or less satisfactory explanation of what had occurred.

But little recked Fandor of all this.

"Juve has been dismissed the force," he told himself. "Juve has been turned out, in one word! Very good! It is my business to find out a way to avenge the slight, to see him vindicated and reappointed with the honors he deserves. M. Havard must fight his own battles!"

Juve! Yes, it was only of Juve he was thinking. It was only his lifelong friend's interests the gallant journalist cared for. Strangely enough, ever since he had known of these fantastic happenings—the bank pillaged in broad daylight, the crowd gassed by Fantômas, the millions so easily carried off by the audacious scoundrel, Fandor had felt much less anxiety about Juve than before... True, the police officer had disappeared; none knew what had become of him. But, strong in the blind confidence he reposed in his old friend's abilities, Fandor was now relieved of a great deal of his earlier suspense. For how could he suspect the terrible trap into which the detective had but now fallen? He reflected:

"Juve is bound to be on Fantômas' track. Dismissed or not, he is not the man to abandon the fight. So, he must evidently have lighted on an important clue. All that concerns me now is to discover traces that will enable me to join company with him."

Accordingly, without troubling his head further about the official activities of the police, Fandor began a personal investigation. He went down to the cellars of the Crédit International, where, as he had foreseen, he discovered without the least surprise that they had been robbed. Sacks of gold had been cut open, and it was from their sides had poured the flood of napoleons that still littered the great hall of the Bank. From the cellars he next proceeded to the rooms forming the basement of the premises. He examined the heating apparatus, found nothing out of the ordinary there, then went on till he reached a kind of storehouse in which were stacked printed forms packed in heavy bales.

"Hello!" he said suddenly, "what have we here?"

He had caught sight of a door communicating with another little room, a sort of narrow cave.

"Ah, ha!" he exclaimed. "The gas meter and a score or so of tubes containing or having contained compressed gases. So, that proves I was not mistaken. Good! have the police seen this, I wonder? Anyway, let's shut the door! So much the worse for them! They have got rid of Juve; let 'em play out the game themselves; let 'em muddle round on their own account!" Laughing to himself at the trick he was playing M. Havard, whom he could not forgive for not having retained Juve in his service, at any cost, he went up again to the main hall.

"Yes!" he muttered. "All this is very fine and large, but I'm no better off than before. Where to go to find Juve? whereabouts to look for him? That's what I want to know!"

Suddenly the journalist stopped dead. So noteworthy had been the part he had played at the moment of the first discovery of the crime that they had let him come and go unhindered about the building. Now the course of his investigations had by mere chance brought him to a door over which was a brass plate lettered "Manager."

"Good God!" swore the young man, "I'm just crazy." This is where I ought to have been an hour ago! M. Merandol's private office? Why, it's here I may come upon a clue!"—and he dashed into the room.

A man was there already, who, on seeing the journalist, held out his hand in a gesture of sympathy that was quite genuine.

"You!" he cried. "I have been asking for you for the last half-hour!"

"I didn't know that, Monsieur Fuselier!" replied Jerome Fandor. "Else I should have come at once," and he spoke no more than the truth.

Germain Fuselier, now Procureur de la Republique, had long held the office of Examining Magistrate in Paris. How often had he not, with Juve no less than with Fandor, studied the mass of documents relating to the Fantômas case! A trifle meticulous, a trifle timorous, often afraid of compromising himself, dreading like the plague any abuse of the powers entrusted to him, hesitating to break, even in the most insignificant degree, with established rules and regulations, for which he professed an almost religious veneration, Germain Fuselier was, nevertheless, a magistrate of the best type. For Juve and Fandor he cherished a boundless admiration, while the two heroes felt a sincere affection for him. Suddenly M. Fuselier demanded:

"Have you discovered anything fresh, Fandor?"

"No! Nothing you don't know already, for sure. You have seen M. Havard?"

"Yes! But he has lost his head! If I durst…"

"Speak out, M. Fuselier!"

"I should propose you and I join forces. The post of Procureur-Général will soon be vacant…"

"And you covet it?… It's a fine opportunity. This business will make it yours. For me, *I* want to see Juve righted…"

M. Fuselier smiled. "The Ministry is fallen!" he said simply.

"Already?"

"Five minutes after the news of all this was reported to the Chambers."

"*De profundis!*" chanted Fandor. "I feel better… To go on, *you* have news to tell, M. Fuselier?"

"Not I! I have searched all the papers… I thought to find a threatening letter… some clue or other… but no! nothing! Yet you are well convinced that M. Merandol is with Juve?"

"Why, yes!… It's a matter of some special duty… But what is it?… Havard can say nothing definite."

"Ah, well! there's nothing in the Manager's precious documents to tell us. I have searched even the secret drawers!"

"Good Lord!" Fandor suddenly broke in, "look here!"

He had that moment noticed a sheet of paper on the floor

which the wind was blowing about in all directions. He stooped and picked it up, and his eyes, round with amazement, proceeded to read the document.

"A letter from Juve!" he stammered.

"You're crazy!"

"No! I'm not… Listen here… There are words missing…"

"But it cannot be from him."

"But it is!… No doubt about it! Oh! I know his writing… But better than that! There's the print of his thumb!"

"His thumb?"

"Why, certainly! Look!"—and Fandor held up the paper he had just retrieved before the Magistrate's eyes. The imprint of a man's thumb was plainly visible on it.

"And you must know, I should recognize that imprint among a thousand. You see that mark, left side, in the central furrow. *That* cannot be imitated…"

Fandor was trembling as he spoke, and it was in a hoarse voice he went on:

"But the thing's unintelligible! There are words missing… whole lines. The ink is almost faded away… Listen here!"

He had run to the window, and in the good light proceeded to spell out, hesitatingly, what was left of the police officer's message:

"the business… successful… had to carry off… son… We… safety… come… ly you receive… Fantômas… here…"

"No sense at all!" groaned Fuselier.

"Wait a bit… Now come two lines that are complete:

"Will recognize my writing. If needful, call at the Department. I put the print of my thumb. They will tell you there it is proof positive of my identity. If M. Havard wishes…"

"And that's all!" concluded Fandor.

"And that means nothing!" Germain Fuselier said once more. But the Magistrate had not finished speaking before Jerome Fandor, with a contemptuous shrug:

"On the contrary, the thing's as clear as daylight!" he declared. The fact is the journalist was so well used to the elucidation of such enigmas that this one could hardly offer much difficulty to him.

"The meaning is quite clear!" he announced, and he expounded:

"The business has proved successful. Meantime I have had to carry off 'your' or 'his' son… or 'their' son. We are in safety. Come, as soon as you receive this message. Fantômas 'knows' or 'does not know' we are here."

Jerome Fandor had hardly finished speaking when Germain Fuselier sprang up eagerly, exclaiming:

"Mercy on us, you're a wizard, Fandor!… See here! here's a paper showing that M. Merandol had a son—a son confined as a lunatic at Rueil…"

"Eh, what?"

"More than that, Havard has told me that Juve had, so he believed, been commissioned to protect this son."

"Then all's going swimmingly. Here's our clue!"

But Germain Fuselier had now taken the document and was examining it with a thoughtful air.

"No!" he observed, "there are two objections…"

"What objections?"

"How came this precious paper to be lying about on the floor? Is it a snare? Is it not meant to start us on a false scent?"

Then, more excitedly, Fuselier added:

"And besides, why the devil are there words missing?"

But the journalist found a reply without a second's hesitation. He was wildly excited. He felt that the clue so long sought was found. In his mind's eye he could see Juve waiting for his coming, in need of his help…

"Your two objections amount to nothing," he declared. "The paper was lying about because M. Merandol was so upset he dropped it after reading it. He was in a hurry to set off… As a fact, he did go away last night…"

"Go away last night? How do you know?"

"Look at his watch, there on the desk. It has stopped. He never thought of winding it up, he clean forgot in his hurry… M. Merandol went off that night from this room. He was here to keep an eye on his millions. Anyway, the employees will tell us if they saw him last night or this morning..."

"Good!... But the missing words?..."

"Monsieur Fuselier, that's simpler still! The letter was written in sympathetic ink. Juve expected the writing would fade out altogether. If certain words are still legible, if certain lines are intact, that's because M. Merandol wept as he read the message. His tears fixed the writing, made it permanent."

Verily, at this moment, Fandor had no inkling, could have none, that he was laboring under a twofold mistake, a fatal mistake! He was close on the truth! He was giving proof of a professional acumen that Juve himself, as a detective, might have been proud of! But all the time, he was the victim of one of Fantômas' ruses!

This letter, this precious letter, alas! it was not Juve who had written it! It was Fantômas and no one else! The message, indeed written in sympathetic ink, actually intended to fade away, but partly preserved by the financier's tears, had no other object save to entice M. Merandol to the Romanesque villa... It was without knowledge of what he was doing that Juve had put the print of his thumb on the paper, as a seal of indisputable authenticity.

"You are a genius, Fandor!" declared Germain Fuselier. "M. Merandol's son was at Rueil. Rueil is where we must begin our inquiries..."

"Evidently!" Fandor agreed.

"To Rueil, then! You are coming, Fandor?"

"Certainly, I am going there..."

M. Fuselier left the Banker's office. Walking fast, delighted at having Jerome Fandor at his side, counting already on an investigation that should cover him with glory, he almost broke into a run, outstripping his companion.

"I have engaged a first-class car at the Opera," he explained. "This way! It's waiting for me close by. Let's leave by this door... Eh? what? why? Fandor? Fandor, I say!"

The Magistrate had looked behind him, and now stood stock-still in surprise and utter bewilderment.

Jerome Fandor was no longer at his heels! Jerome Fandor

was nowhere to be seen! Jerome Fandor had vanished!

*   *   *   *   *

Strange as Fandor's sudden disappearance may have appeared to M. Fuselier, there was, however, nothing really tragic or mysterious about it. It was simply that, at the corner of a corridor, the young man had turned off to the right, while the Magistrate turned to the left. Not, however, that this was due to any mistake or absentmindedness, for the journalist was acting quite deliberately.

"No!" he admonished himself, "don't let us start off in the dark on a business that looks like being serious! It's never wise to mix up together table napkins and kitchen clouts!"—and with this homely phrase, Fandor made up his mind to leave the Procureur there and then.

"I know my man," he reflected further. "He is too much enamored of his rules and regulations not to act with perfect propriety!… Yes, he's going, this worthy official, to pay a polite visit to the Rueil Home… where they'll tell him just what they choose to say. Then he will draw up a carefully written Report, which he will communicate to M. Havard… and Havard will come and pursue further investigations—when he can find the time. For my part I prefer more expeditious methods!"

Still laughing to think of the bewilderment he felt sure M. Fuselier was experiencing on finding himself left in the lurch, the journalist quitted the Bank and made for a neighboring cafe.

"So, now to set about things expeditiously and judiciously too!" he said with his customary cheerful optimism. First of all, to let Juve know I'm on his track. No very great difficulty about that…"

But it may well be Fandor was exaggerating a bit. Not having the faintest notion where Juve was, how could he hope to communicate with him?

"Waiter, a black coffee, black as they make 'em," he ordered. "And writing materials…"

While his wants were being supplied—one by one, as usual,

with long waits between—first writing pad... then the ink-stand... then paper... then a pen—Fandor was indulging in another soliloquy:

"Wherever Juve may be, no doubt he is thinking of me. With me in his thoughts and not knowing that *La Capitale* has given me my congé, no doubt again he is laying out his three sous to purchase that excellent sheet and read the article which I should, under normal circumstances, be devoting to current events. Well! now's the time to write the said article,"—and Jerome Fandor dipped his pen in the ink, but did not start writing just at once. The fact was he was no longer on the staff of *La Capitale*. How then be sure that his contribution would be printed?

"Good and well!" he grunted. "I know the boss. The whole point is to get him interested. If I can do that, if I can get him to scent a fine 'scoop,' he'll pass my stuff. He is too good a journalist to do anything else,"—and this time he began writing at top speed.

"A headline's the first thing—a headline that'll make him bite! 'Mea culpa,' there you are! A correction—I stick in a note of interrogation. Yes! it looks better like that, 'Mea Culpa?'... Now we go on!"—and he wrote crisply and concisely:

"We have already advised our readers that as a result of disagreements that have occurred between Jerome Fandor and our Board, we have been compelled to dispense with the service of our very estimable collaborator, whose only fault—we say so frankly—was that of excessive zeal."

"There you are!" exclaimed the young man parenthetically, "when a man is talking about himself, well! he's bound to speak up for that individual!"—and he resumed his task.

"Today we are about to say our Mea Culpa for the... 'vivacity' shall we say? we have perhaps exhibited in his case... Did not Jerome Fandor deserve a little more indulgence?

"Our readers have perused the article we devote to the fearful scandal that has just occurred at the Crédit International. They have read of the robbery, and they have noted the part played in it by Jerome Fandor.

"Within the last hour, just as we are going to press, we have been informed from another quarter that Jerome Fandor has since made certain sensational discoveries.

"It appears he has found out that Juve and M. Merandol, both of whom have disappeared, are together! It would seem that he has found out where the two—the police officer and the financier—have met! Yet another piece of news—to the effect that Juve, more ardently than ever, was still on Fantômas' track…

"Yes! let us proclaim our Mea Culpa with all sincerity. Jerome Fandor could never turn his back on our paper. If his investigations enable him to throw some little light on this fresh crime of its terrible and still unpunished perpetrator, Fantômas, we may regard it as certain that it is to our columns he will first contribute an account of his revelations."

"So there we are!" Fandor resumed his monologue. "I send this up to Dupont. He will understand the hint. In fact, he will be only too delighted to have me back again. Thus I work my own restoration to office!… So far so good! And now to the work in hand. I must catch up with M. Fuselier and get out of him whatever he has discovered in my absence… and then discover a bit more myself…"

The young man paid for his refreshment, tossed into a pneumatic letterbox the short half-column he meant for *La Capitale,* then hurried off to find a taxi.

"Rueil, my lad! and go your hardest. To put your engine on its best behavior, here's fifty francs for yourself!"—and the driver he had just hailed and to whom he addressed this persuasive discourse, smiled broadly and promptly got underway…

9. "Monsieur" or "Madame"?

It was close on eight o'clock at night when M. Germain Fuse-lier quitted the Rueil Home after carrying out an investigation at once tactful and adroit. The Magistrate was smiling like a man who is well satisfied with the course of events and, in par-ticular, feels a pleasant sense of confidence in a successful issue.

"Fandor acted foolishly in leaving me!" he told himself, as he made for a roadside tavern before which his conveyance was standing. "He does not know what I know!"

Then he gave a sudden start. A young roadman, his shirt flying half-open over his naked chest, a red sash bound tightly round the waist of his velveteen breeches, stood in front of him, holding out a cigarette.

"A light, M'sieur, if it's not troubling you," he begged.

"Here you are, my lad!" said Germain Fuselier, offering his cigar.

"And now," went on the roadman, "a bit of information—does the alliance still hold good?"

"Eh? What?" exclaimed the Procureur. But he added next instant:

"I'm not dreaming, come? It is… it is…"

"Don't trouble to give me a name, sir!… Yes! it's I all right!"

The roadman was… Jerome Fandor! Marvelously disguised, so perfectly made up his very features seemed altered, the jour-nalist was entirely unrecognizable. Experienced as he was in such fakes, Germain Fuselier confessed himself utterly amazed.

"You're an astonishing fellow!" he declared. "Where do you spring from now?"

"Out of the ditch."

"I saw that much… but…"

"Ever since I have been here, I've never left it…"

"But why not have come with me?"

"Why two people to go to the same place?" retorted the young man phlegmatically. "You were making your inquiries here, and I just left the job to you. That's all there is to it. You have discovered something?"

"Yes! There's news!"

"Tell me!"

Fandor, like Juve, had a wonderful knack of extracting from others whatever of interest they had to tell. M. Fuselier spoke succinctly.

"In three words, here's the story," he began. "Georges Merandol, the lunatic, has disappeared, has been kidnapped. The attendants found his room in good order, but the window open… So it was by the window he was carried off. Moreover, the ivy shows traces of someone having climbed it."

"Capital! capital! And then…"

"Then… Hmm… Well, I have taken prints…"

"Prints?"

"Yes! Highly important ones. On a pane of the window was the mark of Juve's thumb… So, so it was Juve who had carried off the poor madman…"

"Better and better!… Afterwards…"

"I'm coming to that. It's a fine tale as it stands! Naturally, I draw certain conclusions…"

"Well, may I hear them?"

"They are self-evident, Fandor. It was Juve who carried off the madman—and he did it secretly. Therefore, he feared some danger—therefore, he dreaded Fantômas… And that's why he gives us no news of himself. But I regard all this as reassuring. Juve, M. Merandol, and Georges Merandol are together. They are in hiding. There! you agree with me?"

"Certainly!"

"And you are coming back with me to Paris?"

"No!" Fandor refused gently, but firmly.

"But…"

"You are going to inform M. Havard, are you not?"

"Surely I am!"

"Well, I prefer to wait till he comes…"

"But nothing tells us he'll come right away…"

"I'm in no hurry."

"Well, please yourself!" retorted M. Fuselier dryly. "Good evening, in that case!"

"Good evening, my dear sir!" said Fandor, and next minute saw the Magistrate drive off.

We may be very sure the latter was far from suspecting that at that same moment Jerome Fandor, once more ensconced in his ditch, was weeping scalding tears.

"Juve! my poor, dear Juve!" he sighed. "Is he still alive, I wonder?"

The truth was, if Germain Fuselier was well satisfied with his own discoveries, Fandor too might have been justifiably proud of the results of his personal inquiries. He had not been speaking quite accurately when he explained to M. Fuselier the reason for his not accompanying him, saying it was because he saw no use in two pursuing their inquiries in one and the same place. The real reason was that he had been detained by a personal investigation of his own, which had resulted in the discovery of sundry highly disconcerting and alarming facts.

Proceeding with all the activity and enterprise of a professional detective—as the Magistrate had not done and indeed could not well do—the young man, on arriving at the Asylum, had not presented himself at the entrance gate till he had taken time to examine the surroundings. Slowly and with extreme care, trying to see without being seen—not always such an easy thing, as many a police officer has found—Fandor had made a circuit of the premises, precisely as Juve had done.

The result was not long to seek. In two minutes: "By the Lord!" cried Fandor with a start, "Juve has been this way!"

In the mud of the roadway, dried by the hot afternoon sun, the reporter to *La Capitale* had seen the imprint of a boot he would have known among a thousand. Long ago, in fact, Juve and Fandor had come to a mutual agreement in the interests of their respective investigations, to put certain recognizable marks on their boot soles. Bending down to examine more closely the device imprinted on the mud, Fandor knew for certain that his old friend had been there.

"Yes! Juve has passed this way!" he said again. "He has been prowling about the place, like myself. This time I have undoubtedly found a clue."

But, unfortunately, the clue was soon broken off. To the young man's experienced eye the traces of Juve's scramble over the wall were evident enough. Only, obvious as the fact was that Juve had climbed the wall at this particular point, there was nothing to show whether he had done this in order to get into the grounds or to leave them.

"Best go on," the journalist had decided, "and see what's to be found farther on,"—and then it was that Jerome Fandor had lighted upon the most important of his discoveries. On the opposite face of the surrounding wall, the side that looked on the open fields, Fandor came to a dead stop, like a pointer dog, before the little door or postern by which Juve and the pretended Georges Merandol had made their escape. True, Juve had been careful to re-close the door on that occasion, but for all that, it did not take Fandor two minutes' examination to arrive at a definite conclusion.

"Juve left the place by this door," he told himself with absolute assurance. It was evident, in fact, that the door had recently been opened. Spiders' webs were torn and hung round the framework. Elsewhere the dust had been disturbed.

"Yes! Juve went out this way!" Fandor repeated, "and he was not alone. Now, who was with him?"

Again, stamped in the mud of a neighboring roadway—a narrow path running alongside a sort of sewer—appeared at intervals the marks of two pairs of boots, that had followed the same track, and followed it in company, for they looked as fresh one as the other.

"This," decided Fandor, "was Juve's boot. There, quite distinct, is the cut in the heel that forms the identifying sign. As for the other, whose can it be? M. Merandol, senior's, or M. Merandol's son's. There was good cause indeed why Fandor should hesitate between these two alternatives. However, one of these was soon to be found untenable.

"Well, let's remember what we know about the boot-making trade!" he laughed, hiding from himself the poignant anxiety he felt. "Let's measure this mark,"—and he proceeded to do so, using a penny for the purpose. This done, he said to himself:

"Size 9! That's something definite to go upon. The man with Juve wore No. 9 boots. Well, I can find out at the house in the Rue d'Auteuil if M. Merandol, senior, wears a bigger or smaller size. At the Asylum, on the other hand, I'll get them to show me an old pair of Georges Merandol's and so find out what *he* wears,"—and excited at the thought that he had at last found a clue, Fandor had hurried on to follow up his investigation. Walking fast, but stooping from time to time to make sure of the footprints impressed on the mud of the roadway, he congratulated himself on his lucky find.

But alas! a disappointment awaited him. The marks had now led him to the bank of the Seine. There the grass was so thick that no further trace was visible.

"Right?… left?… which way did he turn?" the journalist asked himself. "Confound the man! Can Juve have swum across the river to break off the scent—just like a stag that knows the dogs are close on his haunches?"

Curiously enough, Fandor at that moment had all but guessed the literal truth. Juve, at the point where Fandor was now arrived, *had* actually tried to break the scent! It was just there that the police officer had taken boat along with the supposed madman, who not many minutes after was to master him under such tragic circumstances.

Unable, however, to reconstruct the incident exactly, as it really occurred, Fandor had now lost time in a painstaking search, this way and that, to right and left, for the vanished footprints. Naturally he had found nothing, and night coming on, further investigation could lead to no result.

"Best go back to the Asylum," the young man had decided. "Fuselier too is bound to have discovered something, and he will tell me the result. Then I will act as circumstances dictate."

But now Fandor was more perplexed than ever. No doubt, by his finding of Juve's thumbprint on a windowpane in Georges

Merandol's room, M. Fuselier had confirmed his own previous discoveries. But he had thrown no further light on them. Thinking things out where he still lay crouching in his ditch by the roadside, Fandor told himself:

"So, here's one fact established: Juve has been here; another fact: he has gone off with someone who wears No. 9 boots. But the mystery remains unsolved who was this companion of his? and where Juve has taken him?..."

But by this time night had fully fallen, and, wearying of his inaction—for nothing was more distressing to Fandor than sitting still and doing nothing—he left his hiding place without further delay.

"Suppose I too risked a little tour of inspection?" he muttered. A sudden thought had struck the young journalist, always attracted by any daring project. Why should he not try, in his turn, to get into the Asylum? Why not, without showing himself—for he realized the necessity of acting furtively so as not to give the alert to Fantômas—make an attempt to ascertain if Georges Merandol wore number nines.

"Juve climbed the wall," he smiled. "*I* will do as much!"

Nor was he the man to hesitate for long. Juve had surmounted the difficulty, why should not he? But he never stopped to consider that, when his friend performed the feat, no one in the asylum knew anything as yet of the events that had occurred, whereas now, after Georges Merandol's disappearance and M. Fuselier's visit, it was very certain a strict surveillance was being exercised that must prove highly dangerous to his designs!

"Now for it!" he cried. "Two o'clock is striking. Everybody is bound to be asleep in a 'Home' of this sort," and he advanced to the surrounding wall at the precise point where Juve had climbed it, and, younger and more active than the police officer, he did not take two minutes to reach the top.

Then: "Confound and damn it all!" swore Fandor, "broken bottles! I'm going to get my hands and knees in a pretty state!"

But he was not to be stopped by such an obstacle. Where Juve had taken proper precaution, Fandor gave fresh proof of dash and daring as a journalist. Indeed, was not this his first and foremost characteristic, the possession of what is appropriately enough known as "go"? Never stopping to think of the risk of cutting himself, he gripped the crest of the wall, put the toe of his boot between two shards of glass, then, with a heave and lift of the body, wriggled to the other side. Thus he hung suspended, as it were, looking down into the grounds. The wall was a high one, but he cared nothing for that.

"Here we are!" he panted. "We've only got to jump down!"— and he let go. Luckily the grass was long, and he alighted without noise.

"Capital! First-rate!" he chuckled again. "Now to take our bearings!"

But next moment he thought differently.

"Why, no! it's not *capital* after all! What are those lights yonder?"

Near by, in fact, in the different blocks, he could see the windows lighted up.

"So, nobody's gone to bed yet?… Hmm! I must wait a bit…"

Making the best of a bad job—what else was there to do?— Fandor started creeping towards a clump of thick bushes.

"Let's slip in there and wait!" he muttered with a sigh. "But, damn! it's not common sense to go sitting up so late in an asylum!"

The journalist found waiting a tedious business. He dared not smoke, and this increased his ill humor. At long last, one by one, he saw the vexatious lights extinguished. When the last had disappeared, he got to his feet.

"So there!" he growled. "Forward! Objective of the expedition to procure one of Georges Merandol's old boots!" He took a step—and stopped dead. Suddenly, at the turning of a path, moving with the utmost precaution, evidently using every effort to make no noise, Fandor had caught sight of a shadowy figure creeping towards the asylum buildings.

"Oh, ho" was all the journalist said, as with a determined effort of will, he checked the violent beating of his heart.

A question, meantime, was clamoring insistently for an answer:

"This nocturnal prowler, this furtive intruder, who could he be?"

Jerome Fandor pronounced two names in a questioning tone of agonized suspense:

"Juve?… Juve, or Fantômas?…"

*   *   *   *   *

The night unfortunately was very dark, and Fandor was forced to admit the impossibility of answering his own question. All he saw was "a shadow." The behavior of this shadow, the precautions taken to make no noise, to keep hidden, showed plainly enough that no denizen of the "Home" was in question. But there was no means of ascertaining more. Juve, no doubt, might be lurking about in this fashion… But might not the same be said of Fantômas? Fandor reflected:

"What the devil, though, should Juve be doing on the premises? He has been here already, and he is not the man to have forgotten to spy out every single detail. I could swear his investigation here is complete and done with!"

Then he thought further:

"But Fantômas, neither has he any motive to haunt the place. *He* has got what he wanted. The thirty-eight millions are in his pockets—so to speak. Why then should he venture in the asylum grounds, where he knows quite well he runs a thousand risks?"

Finding himself thus compelled by circumstances to remain in doubt, Fandor adopted the only course of action open to him.

"Well, let's shadow the fellow!" he growled. "By finding out what he's up to I shall doubtless discover who he is,"—and in the silence and darkness he set about his perilous task. From one moment to the next the journalist might be confronted with the most terrible of antagonists. If it was Fantômas he was tracking down, he well knew he could expect no pity, if the brigand saw him.

"Yes! That's a fine prospect!" he laughed to himself. "But then, I have my chance too of arresting the scoundrel at last,"—

and he took his revolver from his pocket and pulled off the safety catch. "Fantômas! Well, if Fantômas, Fantômas the Lord of Terror, did stand face to face with him, he would never blench. Blood for blood! A life for a life! It would be a desperate battle, a war to the knife!"

But suddenly the journalist stifled an exclamation of surprise:

"By the Lord! A woman! It's a woman!"—and an instant after:

"An old woman... A poor woman..."

Between two clouds the moon had shone out for one second. The mysterious figure had darted into hiding in a thicket of shrubs, but still Fandor had had time to see its outlines... Yes, it was a woman—a poor woman apparently, walking bent double under the weight of years...

"I'm all at sea!" grumbled the young man in a vexed tone. "Who the devil can this old dame be?"

Meantime, the woman, evidently quite unsuspicious of being watched, moved on again, always choosing the darkest corners. Keeping away from the main buildings, she was making for a low shed of sorts, the nature of which Fandor soon guessed...

"A greenhouse!" he exclaimed. "She's going to the green-house! What, ho!"—and he broke into a short laugh—a laugh of self-mockery:

"My good little man, I like you very much," he told himself, "but I'm going to speak to you quite frankly: you're nothing more nor less than an idiot!"

Then, after abusing himself in this uncompromising fashion, he went on:

"Juve or Fantômas, you were asking? Not they! The leaders don't go patrolling the ground themselves. This mysterious in-dividual is of course a spy, someone instructed to watch what's going on here!"—and he concluded with an angry shrug:

"Only, it may be a spy of Juve's, or just as likely, a spy of Fantômas'. I'd give twopence to know which, but I wager nobody will take my offer and let me know..."

At that moment he saw the night prowler go into the conservatory. To follow her into that confined space was clearly not to be thought of. Then, what to do?…"

"Nobody will tell me anything," muttered the young man…" Yes! Nobody, except the person chiefly concerned. Very good! It is to the person chiefly concerned I'm going to address myself."

He smiled to himself, and ended:

"But I'm going to ask my question so politely she won't know which side I belong to… Now, if the woman was sent by Fantômas, she won't own up to anything, unless she thinks I'm an accomplice of her master's!… And if, on the other hand, she is acting for Juve, I can easily explain away the mistake…"

Now, at that moment Fandor was laying his plans to afford yet another proof of his talents as a first-rate police officer. He told himself:

"I make arrangements to be captured—then, changing parts, I make a capture myself! Good! If anyone heard what I'm saying, he'd not find it over and above clear! But no matter for that, *I* understand!"

As he spoke, the journalist was searching his pockets, and in a couple of minutes extracted a pair of handcuffs from one of them.

"We'll clap these bracelets on my wrists—without fastening the padlocks. He proceeded deliberately to handcuff himself, but took good care not to lock the implements, which left it in his power to throw them off at a moment's notice.

"So there!" he proceeded. "And now, on with the play! Someone escaping from the asylum, handcuffs on wrists, that can't be anything else but a prisoner making off—in the eyes of an accomplice of Fantômas… So much the better for us!"—and he took no further pains to tread softly, made no attempt to avoid noise. On the contrary, walking very fast and making the graveled paths rattle under his footsteps, Fandor made for the greenhouse and went in.

"Curses on it!" he groaned in a muffled voice, as if convinced there was no one there, no woman hidden inside, listening and spying on his doings. "Oh! that confounded Juve! To have put the handcuffs on me… But I'll surely find a file, or a cold chisel…"

And next minute he felt sure the woman was going to tumble into the trap he had laid. A noise, a rustle, became audible. The woman was leaving her hiding place.

"To climb the wall with handcuffs on, impossible!" went on Fandor. "Anyway, in three minutes they'll be after me… Damnation!"

The journalist was stooping down, pretending he was trying to break the handcuffs against a spade he had found in a corner and which he held under his foot. Suddenly a voice whispered in his ear:

"Hush! Don't kick up such a racket! I'm going to set you free—more by token I've got my cutter with me, and it's as sharp as sharp!… So, Fantômas has sent you along too? Who are you? It was M'sieur Juve nabbed you, eh?"

Fandor needed no more enlightenment. The woman's words had given her away absolutely. She spoke of Fantômas, acknowledged she was sent by the Lord of Terror! Yes! her capture might be well worthwhile. The journalist sprang up suddenly, and the thing was done in half a second. *His* hands were free, while his companion was hard and fast, the handcuffs he had worn locked on her wrists. But not a sound! All this was done so quickly, with such a surprising sleight of hand, the unknown had only just time to swear:

"God A'mighty! What's up now? I'm a goner that's what I be!"

"A goner, if ever there was one!" grinned Fandor, resuming his natural voice.

But a fresh and even more startling surprise was in store for the young man. His prisoner's voice had a strange ring for a woman's, and in the twilight of the conservatory the features had an odd look.

"Bless my soul!" cried the journalist, "can I be making a mistake on an important point: Ought I to say *Monsieur* or *Madame?*"

In other words he was asking himself if he had not clapped the bracelets on a man dressed up as a woman…

He had not long to wait for his answer.

"Oh, ho! Why, here's a good'un!" ejaculated at that moment the individual—man or woman—he held prisoner. "How small the world is!… Hello! M'sieur Fandor! But I'm downright glad as how it's you as is here!"…

At the words, Fandor came near toppling over with sheer amazement, as he stammered brokenly: "Bouzille! It's Bouzille, by the Lord!"

10. The Plot Thickens

For the moment so dumbfounded was Jerome Fandor he could not so much as think of a word to say. Had he been asked to mention the most unlikely person he could have come upon in the Rueil "Home," he would unhesitatingly have named Bouzille. Yet it was Bouzille and no other who stood before him, wearing that look of sham satisfaction a man puts on who is asking himself how everything is going to end, but at the same time insists on affecting an air of complete confidence.

At last the journalist spoke in a hoarse voice of anger:

"Why! what are you doing here, in God's name?"

"And *you,* M'sieur Fandor?"

Then, apparently unruffled, the old tramp tried to turn it off with a joke:

"Can't be, surely, all the cracks you've had in the noddle have made you silly-like? You're not gone 'dingo,' eh?"

Fandor was not even listening to the old fellow. His mind was busy recalling strange memories. Did he not remember how Bouzille, honest man as he was in his own particular fashion, had for years, turn and turn about, aided and abetted Fantômas and joined in the campaign against him? Was he not, with his utter absence of moral sense, always ready to help whoever paid him, or at any rate, whoever inspired him with salutary fear?

"The very last time I saw him," Fandor told himself, "the confounded old scamp had just saved Juve's life by affording me the chance of finding him in Fantômas' hands! At that time he feigned a mortal terror of Fantômas... He pretended he was leaving France... He wanted to disappear in order to escape the vengeance of the Torturer... I engaged a place for him in the airbus that leaves Le Bourget for Brussels... I swore I would not tell a soul, not even Juve, what had become of him... And lo! here he turns up again!"

Bouzille, for his part, had fallen silent. The dread of being forced to make some compromising admission checked his usual loquacity. Fandor noted the old fellow's unaccustomed reticence, and demanded:

"Bouzille, you haven't answered my question. What are you after here?"

"And what about you, M'sieur Fandor?"

"You're trying to lie low, eh? and not tell me."

"No offense meant, M'sieur Fandor, but I might return the compliment…"

"Very good!… That being so, I'm *going* to tell you. I'm here to arrest Fantômas' accomplices…"

"Lordy! Are there some here then?"

"Bouzille, you're making a big mistake in playing cunning!… Come! Off you go! This time you're fairly caught…"

"Oh! M'sieur Fandor, you can't mean it. You'd never have the heart to take me to quod."

"Oh! yes I would!"

"For sixpence worth of stuff I'm a-pinching of?"

"So you're after pinching something here, are you?"

"As if you didn't know, M'sieur Fandor?…"

"As if I didn't know what, Bouzille? Yes or no, will you speak out?"

"Hmm!… At the pub then?"

"No! Here, and now!"

"But I'm a-dying of thirst, M'sieur Fandor!… The pleasure of seeing you's made me feverish-like… So, it's only just and fair…"

"Come on, to jail!" Fandor interrupted ruthlessly, gripping the old vagabond by the arm.

But Bouzille shook himself free:

"M'sieur Fandor! Old friends like us!… Comrades!… Colleagues in a way o' speaking!…"

"To prison, Bouzille! to prison!"

"For a sixpence worth o' flowers?"

"What's that you're gassing me about flowers?"

"Why, the truth, M'sieur Fandor! the plain truth! I'm a flower girl, I am!"

"A flower girl?"

"Why, yes! a florist."

"A florist, eh?"—and in a savage voice Fandor demanded:

"Are you making a fool of me?"

The effect was electrical. Calling on all the gods to witness, Bouzille broke into a torrent of indignant protestations:

"Me make a fool o' you, M'sieur Fandor? By the tomb of my father and mother—I never knew 'em and they may be alive yet for all I know—I'd never dare to!… Make a fool o' you? Good Lord! When I've proved my honesty times and times again!… Oh! It's mean to suspect me o' such things… It's like as I told the constable the other day—come now, no games o' that sort betwixt pals! It cuts all confidence, it do!… I'm a flower girl. Well, is that forbidden?… True enough, I'm taking flowers as don't belong to me. But they're perishing here! If I pick what's being wasted, is that any harm?… But there, you're not a man o' prejudices, you ain't, M'sieur Fandor. For M'sieur Juve, no! I wouldn't say as much… But you?… Is M'sieur Juve well and hearty, by-the-bye?"

The old man could easily have run on like this for a couple of hours without ever uttering one useful word, but Fandor cut him short again:

"You're a flower girl, you say? Prove it!"

"That's easy enough!… Yes! That's what I call talking!… Proofs you want, eh? Just one step, and you can see my flowers!"

And, as a fact, a yard away, in a lean-to adjoining the conservatory, Fandor beheld two enormous bouquets that were doubtless Bouzille's work. Was he then to accept the old vagabond's statement that he had turned flower girl, and that his sole object in coming to the greenhouse was to steal flowers? For a moment Fandor was tempted to think so. But next instant he changed his mind, suddenly convinced that the tramp was laughing at him. When first Bouzille approached him, had he not spoken of Fantômas? Was not that proof positive he was acting a part? Now the journalist spoke severely:

"A truce to useless lies, Bouzille! You have said too much. You know what's afoot here?"

"Oh! no, I don't…"

"And you also know why *I* am here…"

"And I'll take my oath I don't…"

"Enough said!… You come with me! You shall tell your tale to the judges at the Assizes. I'm not laughing now!"—and he seized the tramp by the arm in a way that admitted of no gainsaying. At last Bouzille was beginning to lose his air of assurance. Too clever not to guess that Fandor was proof against his wiles, the old fellow resigned himself to the inevitable.

"Come, M'sieur Fandor, you're not angry?" he whined. "Stand me a pint, just one pint, and you shall hear every blessed thing I can tell you…"

"I'll stand you a drink when you've spoken up…"

"Very well! On tick then, eh? Righto!… But I may bring my flowers along? Fact is, I'm behind time… I might get some more stuff somewhere else, you know… I might miss my market…"

"Bouzille, I tell you…"

"I twig, M'sieur Fandor! I know you! There, I'm not angry… You know what business is!… So, there's my two bunches under my arm. Now I'm ready… You know the way out?"

In spite of himself Fandor gave an embarrassed smile. "Hmm! That's as may be," he said. To admit the fact that he was in the Asylum without any right to be there was evidently inadvisable. But how hide the truth from this clear-sighted individual? To convey the old man outside by climbing the enclosing wall and making him do the like was simply to confess how things stood, or pretty much so.

"M'sieur Fandor," the tramp began again, "if so be you think I don't know the dodge, just follow me. I'll go first… Anyway, we've got to bunk it, along of the patrol that's just coming,"—and going on ahead of his companion, the old man, still handcuffed and greatly hindered thereby in his movements, slipped out of the greenhouse.

"Follow me, will you?" he proposed. "For sure, the water's precious cold, but there's stones one can step on, if only a chap don't slip…"

The old fellow started off across the grass at a run, and presently came to a little watercourse that was carried through the grounds in an artificial channel and found its way out by a culvert under the boundary wall. Evidently it emerged from underground some distance away, for neither Fandor nor Juve had seen it when they were making the circuit of the Asylum premises.

"There, M'sieur Fandor!" announced Bouzille. "That's the road your humble servant gets in and out by. The water's low, along of the hot weather. So, by jumping from stone to stone and stooping double where it goes under the wall… The brook, as you might say, runs under a sort of tunnel it dives into… We do the same, and same as it, we comes out again fifty yards away… You can see now I knows a thing or two, eh?"

So saying, Bouzille proceeded to suit his action to his words. Springing onto a big stone in the bed of the brook, he leapt from that to another, and quickly disappeared underground.

"A funny way to go!" thought Fandor, following his leader. "How is it all going to end? Pooh! I'll force the fellow to speak, never fear!…"

But his reflections soon came to an end. Lighting a tallow dip he drew from his pocket, Bouzille fared on his way. Suddenly he stooped and picked up an object from a hole in the rock.

"Praise the pigs!" he cried gleefully. "That's the other! the second one! And I've been looking for it everywhere… That makes the pair,"—and he flourished a boot in the air.

Fandor felt his face blanch. "The other?" he asked. "So you've got the first?"

"Hmm!… yes!… It had dropped…"

"Off his feet?" queried Fandor, who had no notion whose feet he was talking about, but was fishing to get at the truth.

"Off of his feet, yes!" declared Bouzille. "More by token, it was just when I said: 'Look here, I don't half like to see him head downwards, I don't!' You see, I was speaking up for him, eh, M'sieur Fandor?"

"Maybe," said the journalist dryly, and suddenly he put the question that was burning his lips:

"But, do you know who it was you were speaking up for?" he demanded.

"Damn!" snapped Bouzille. "D'you think I'm quite a fool?… Georges Merandol, o' course!"—and then he stopped dead with a choking cry of pain, for losing all control of his temper, Fandor had sprung at the old scoundrel and gripped him by the throat.

"Blackguard!" he yelled. "So you own you were a party in kidnapping the poor fellow…"

Then he snatched the boot from the old man's hand and hastily examined it. It was quite a small, slender boot. The size would be 6 or 7—certainly not 9. So it was *not* Georges Merandol who had been Juve's companion!

"Mercy!" whined Bouzille, who was staggering, half suffocated.

"Mercy, no!" growled Fandor in a voice of fury. "Speak out! Tell me all you know! Tell me now, instantly!… Or else…"

No need to complete his threat. Entangled in his woman's clothes, distraught with fear, the old villain was ready to confess anything and everything!

"M'sieur Fandor, let me go!" he begged. "God's truth! I'll tell you everything!… Only loose hold of me!"

They were still under the tunnel or culvert by which the brook found issue. In the distance, however, a vague diffused gleam of light showed the spot where the stream emerged into daylight. Fandor acted at once. Pointing to a stone, he ordered Bouzille:

"Sit down there—and tell your story! No lies! If you start lying…"

But the old man was obviously frightened to death, and his terror had robbed him of all wish to palter with the truth. He stammered:

"M'sieur Fandor… here's what I knows… But, God A'mighty! what a terrible man you be!"

*   *   *   *   *

Bouzille had lost all inclination to laugh. Many a time before had Fandor and Juve, as he well knew, shown themselves indulgent to his faults. But no less often had the old scamp's native sagacity led him to realize how he had got himself into serious trouble by his attempts to hoodwink his benefactors. He had no wish, therefore, to repeat an experiment that might easily prove disastrous.

"M'sieur Fandor," he now resumed, "it's no 'stories' I'm telling you, but a true story. Gospel truth it is! Only, listen carefully. When so be you've heard it all, you'll see plain it was more ill luck, it was, than ill-doing with me,"—and this exordium ended, a preface specially calculated to excite the pity of his auditor, Bouzille started off on the most prolix of narratives.

He had actually been to Belgium by air, being desperately anxious to avoid all chance of encountering Fantômas, who could hardly be anything but ill-disposed to him after the old villain's repeated acts of treachery.

"Of course, at Brussels, you may bet your life, I didn't put up at no palace," he explained. "It was more like a hovel, the place was. And that's, likely, what was my undoing. There were mates o' mine there. I stands a glass, and they stands another. One thing leads to another, and there weren't no end to it. I'm not an unneighborly chap…"

"Get on with your story," Fandor cut him short. "You got drunk. So, then?"

"Then, I gets talking…"

"That's likely enough…"

"And it's true, M'sieur Fandor! I talk, and after that I drops off fast asleep. Talk of a shop, my word! D'you know what I saw when I woke up?"

"Fantômas?"

"No!… I should a-died o' fright. I saw another chap what was holding salts under my nose… And then he says to me: 'You're sausaged. Don't you try to move!'"

"You were what, Bouzille?"

"'Sausaged,' I tell you… Oh! you don't twig! 'Sausaged'—tied up. You understand, don't you?"

"Very good! You were tied up then?"

"Then they claps me in a car, and off we go... By God! I didn't half like the jaunt—Fantômas was at the far end!"

"Well? He hasn't punished you?"

"Hmm! Don't know about that!... So, the car whips me off, and I couldn't stir a finger!... We pulls up at a house at the Glacière, and down they pops me in the cellar."

"For how long?"

"Oh! I don't know that! I didn't have no almanac... I was in a sore bate. I said to myself..."

"No matter! Get on!... Afterwards?..."

"M'sieur Fandor, you do spoil my story like... Never mind! I know you're in a hurry... Well, after that, one fine day, comes two chaps and takes me away."

"Chaps? What chaps?"

"Fantômas' chaps, bless you! Fantômas' accomplices!... And rough devils they was too! No joking about *them!* 'Get up!' says they, 'you're wanted. You've got to keep watch!' 'Keep watch! where?' I asks 'em... 'If anybody questions you, you're to say you don't know nothing!' That's all the answer I got. So there, M'sieur Fandor, what more could I do?"

"To the point, Bouzille, come to the point!"

"I'm coming to it, M'sieur Fandor. Don't you muddle my wits... Next comes another car, and they brings me along here... There was one chap stands at the mouth of the tunnel, and the rest of 'em hands me inside. 'You bide there!' they orders me. 'If it's aught serious, you'll give a whistle... If there's tees come along, you'll whistle!' There, you see how it was. I was to whistle for everything..."

"Go on, Bouzille!"

"I'm a-going on. But mark this, M'sieur Fandor, there wasn't nothing I *could* do but obey... Seeing as how, M'sieur Fandor, I've been treated that bad..."

"Stop it! Bouzille! That's useless talk... So, there you are, keeping watch. What next?"

"Next? There's no next. Naught happened. O' course I don't whistle, why should I?"

"Granted, Bouzille!... And later on?"

"Oh! later on, oh! Something did happen! A bit after, the other fellows they come along quiet-like, carrying the boy with 'em. 'Have a care!' says Fantômas—I tell you I knew his voice—'Have a care!' says he, 'he's dingo, is Georges Merandol, but he might start calling out.' That's how I came to know the young fellow's name."

"Really and truly?"

"O' course, seeing as how I'm a-telling you!... Then he drops his boot—and I picks it up. It was a new 'un. With the other I reckon as how that makes the pair. Ain't I got the other here?... Say, wasn't I doing right to collar it? What good to anybody to leave it to lie and rot?"

But Fandor was lending only half an ear to the old chap's explanations. He was not stopping to gauge just how much truth and how much falsehood there was in his statements. Had the part he played been precisely what he made out? What mattered that, after all?

"One thing *is* important," reflected the journalist. "He saw the young man carried off. So, it was really Fantômas who kidnapped Georges Merandol. So it was probably Merandol senior who was Juve's companion. Where have they been to, the pair of them?"

Aloud, he asked:

"Finish what you're saying, Bouzille. What has Fantômas done with his prisoner?"

But the tramp sprang up protesting:

"Oh! as to that, M'sieur Fandor, I can't tell you! I don't know!... They plumped him in the car, and off they go again. That's all I know..."

"But you?"

"I?"

"Yes! what did they do with you?"

"They did nothing, M'sieur Fandor! They just left me where I was."

"Without orders?"

"Oh! a ridiculous order!"

"Well, but what was it?"

"Well! hmm!… I was free to do what I chose. And if I saw anything, so to say, interesting, well, I was free to mention it!"

"Who to?… Where?… When?…"

"M'sieur Fandor, I'll tell you no lies. It was Fantômas I was to tell about it… seeing as how he suspected M'sieur Juve and you were a-going to get busy… But as to an appointment to meet him anywheres, no, honor bright, there wasn't none… Fantômas, he said to me: 'I'll find you again when I want you'… See here! just now, when you come into the greenhouse, I thought first thing as how it was him…"

—And Bouzille ended up:

"There, I've told you everything, M'sieur Fandor…"

"Everything—except about the flowers…"

"The flowers, eh?"

"Yes! Who do you sell them to? Why do you come to the Asylum to get them? Oh! that strikes you as funny, does it?"

Bouzille, in fact, had burst out laughing. His conscience now at ease, for he had really told Fandor what he knew, the tramp slapped his thigh gleefully.

"About the flowers, M'sieur Fandor," he went on, "why, that's another rummy thing, that is!… But I reckon it's naught to do…"

"Still, tell me!"

"As you will, M'sieur Fandor!… Well then, here's Fantômas and his loony and the fellows, they drives off. Now, d'you suppose I was a-going to stay hanging about the place?… I thought to myself, I did, things'll be getting hot presently at this here Asylum… So, off I goes…"

"Off you go! Where to?"

"Not far, for sure! I was a-padding the hoof on the high road, M'sieur Fandor, when, all of a sudden, a woman, she rushes up to me…"

"A woman?"

"Yes! and a real woman this time!… a dark woman… and a pretty 'un… with a soft voice of her own… 'Bouzille,' she says to me…"

"She knew you then?"

"Most like!… But *I* didn't know her… 'Bouzille,' says she, 'it's a girl they've been and kidnapped'… Say, M'sieur Fandor, you can fancy my face when I hears that. But there, I'd got to answer something. So, I says right out: 'No! it was a boy.'"

Bouzille broke off for a moment, then went on gravely:

"Then, M'sieur Fandor, when she heard that, the lady, she started crying… 'If that's true,' says she, 'then she's dead. The flowers I'm taking her are really for her grave!'—and, I tell you, she seemed clean to forget *I* was there at all."

"Then, Bouzille, after that?…"

An insufferable spasm of pain and regret swept over the journalist. Up to that point he fully understood what Bouzille had related, but now a fresh mystery, he felt, was brewing. Who was this unknown woman? How had she been able to address the old man by his name? Why, at the very time Fantômas had just carried off Georges Merandol, did she know, so it seemed, that such a crime had been committed, yet was laboring under a mistake, supposing it not to be a young man but a young girl the villain had kidnapped?

"After that," Bouzille replied in his wheedling voice, "after that, M'sieur Fandor, when I heard her a-talking about flowers, why, o' course, I pricks up my ears… Flowers, God bless you! I'd seen enough and to spare o' them in the greenhouse…"

"So, you had been in the greenhouse, Bouzille?… You told me…"

"Hmm! You must a' misunderstood, M'sieur Fandor! It was in the greenhouse I'd been keeping watch…"

"You said it was in the tunnel…"

"M'sieur Fandor, don't go badgering me about that, eh? It was in one or the other, I tell you… I'd given a hand, to help carry Georges… if you like…"

"Well, go on, Bouzille! You said to the lady?"

"I said to her, o' course: 'If it's flowers you're wanting for a grave, give me the order! I'll get 'em for you!'"

"And she agreed?"

"Right off the reel, she did, M'sieur Fandor. A nosegay a day.

142 THE LORD OF TERROR

God's truth! but that was doing business, eh? Bound I was to
stay here to see to it and all. Might as well take my opportunity to pinch some flowers when I knew I could sell 'em… You,
M'sieur Fandor, you'd have done the same?"

"No, Bouzille, I shouldn't. But that's not the question! About
this lady, where are you to take her flowers?"

"Why, to a grave, o' course!"

"What grave?"

"Oh! I couldn't tell you that. I'd have to take you there…"

"To have me tumble into a trap?"

"Oh! M'sieur Fandor, M'sieur Fandor, how *can* you say such
a thing?"—and the old scamp put on an off ended air.

But once more the young man stood buried in his reflections. That there was some tie between the mysterious lady
and Fantômas he could not fail to see. The mere fact that she
had called Bouzille by his name, indeed, proved it. But who
could this "dark, pretty lady" be? What bond could attach her
to Fantômas? And suddenly, as Juve had done at the same
thought, Fandor shuddered.

"Lady Beltham?" he muttered.

Could it be Lady Beltham?…

Then he turned paler yet. If it was really Lady Beltham who
had stopped Bouzille on the high road, who could the young
girl be whose fate interested her so keenly? Another name
sprang to the young man's lips—the name of Helene, the gentle,
innocent girl he had loved, who had been his fiancée and who
alas! proved to be the daughter of Fantômas, the child of the
vile and terrible Lord of Terror…

But Fandor dared not pronounce the syllables of this
name—Helene, that had it in their power to stir such profound
emotions in his bosom. There are memories so painful, memories that revive such wounds in the inmost heart, that a man
dreads to evoke them as one fears to look down into a fathom-
less abyss.

Helene! The daughter of Fantômas! Never once, since his
coming to life again at Marseilles had Fandor allowed himself
to make the smallest allusion to the matter! Never once had he

spoken of it to Juve, nor had Juve ever named it to his friend, surely suspecting the young man was not cured of this passion, so tender and so pure, so confident in its assurance—and no doubt forever hopeless! Alas! was the lover now to learn that it was to deck Helene's grave that Lady Beltham was having a daily offering of flowers brought?

Fortunately the journalist's silence was beginning to get on Bouzille's nerves. His tongue, as he put it to himself, was itching to speak:

"So now," he said at a venture, "suppose we hook it?"

Waking with a start from his dreams, Fandor replied:

"As a fact, I'm just going..."

"Let's be off then, M'sieur Fandor."

"No! Not you! You stay here, Bouzille..."

"Eh? What? You're saying?..."

"Would you rather have me take you to jail?"

"But, all the same..."

"Bouzille, it's no good protesting!" the journalist cut him short. "You've given me a certain amount of useful information. But I must verify your statements. Till then, you will stay where you are... I'm going to 'sausage' you, as you call it, tie you up... You'll be quite all right, waiting for me..."

"M'sieur Fandor, you can't mean it, God's truth! you *can't!*"

"Yes! I can. Anyway, if you haven't been telling me lies, I'll come back for you—and pack you off to get hanged somewhere else... If, on the contrary..."

"M'sieur Fandor, I give you my oath..."

"Hold your tongue. I'm in no humor for joking. You're precious lucky already I'm not hauling you off to the Criminal Bureau!"

The threat was bound to produce its effect, and Bouzille's loquacity instantly dried up. An appearance at the Department was anything but an agreeable prospect. Better trust to Fandor's good will, who the tramp was well aware cherished a certain liking for him.

"Very good, M'sieur Fandor," the old man therefore assented. "You're the master, so I'll stop my gab... But what is it you want to verify?"

"I'll tell you later on…"

"Anyhow, be quick about it. Look you, I'm like to have a weary time waiting for you."

"Have a nap; then the time won't seem so long,"—and tying up the tramp, leaving the handcuffs still on and tightening them up a hole, Fandor was preparing to take his departure when suddenly the old fellow called him back: "M'sieur Fandor!"

"What now?"

"It's about the lady you're put out?"

"Of course it is."

"Well, I'm going to tell you a thing…"

"Good! out with it!"

"It's this ways—to get you to come back quicker…"

"All right! All right! Speak out!"

"M'sieur Fandor, I followed the lady… She was going to Auteuil…"

"To Auteuil?… to Auteuil, eh?"

Mechanically the journalist pronounced the words:

"Rue d'Auteuil, I wager, No. 222."

Involuntarily his thoughts turned to M. Merandol's house. But Bouzille, quite unconcerned, corrected him:

"Not a bit of it!… It's Rue Michel-Ange… No. 106."

"So she lives there?"

"Oh! I don't know! I saw her go in there!… You'll let me go after that…"

But Fandor was already hurrying off. At last his quest was making giant strides… His conversation with Bouzille might well afford him some useful hints. To begin with, it was now clear that Juve had not carried off Georges Merandol—seeing Georges Merandol had been kidnapped by Fantômas before the police officer had even arrived at Rueil. It was no less certain that Juve's companion, the person wearing No. 9 boots, could not be the lunatic. Furthermore it was proved that a woman was concerned in the drama that had culminated in the pillage of the Crédit International.

But who was this woman? And for what grave was she

sending flowers by so strange a messenger—this old scamp of a Bouzille who, without a qualm, was betraying one side as much as the other?

"I mean to find out. I take my oath I *will* find it," Fandor answered himself. So agitated was the young man, so tortured by grief and suspense, he never so much as heard the groans and lamentations with which Bouzille greeted his departure.

"To go and leave me here!… a place that's good for naught but growing mushrooms! God's truth! M'sieur Fandor, it ain't kind o' you! To plump me down like a blessed package—me, a flower girl! Fact is, you haven't got no heart, no lights nor liver, you haven't, nor bowels neither!…"

No! he was not listening to Bouzille, was Fandor. He was hearkening to the echo of two names, names at the sound of which he trembled as he said them over, in a voice of horror and in a voice of hope:

"Lady Beltham!… Helene!…"

11. Fandor Contracts a Deplorably Bad Habit

The dawn was just breaking in an overclouded sky as Fandor left Bouzille, greatly perplexed by the old tramp's revelations, which awoke such poignant memories. At that moment the journalist had every reason to feel exhausted with fatigue: for four-and-twenty hours without intermission he had been engaged in the most trying of duties, that of a police officer, where mind and body alike are strained to the uttermost. But Fandor was not the fellow to stop even for one second when following up an important clue, when he realized that the truth, elusive, but sure, was within his reach.

Accordingly the young man took the first Saint-Germain train for Paris. Then, after telephoning to old Jean at the Rue Tardieu and being informed that Juve had still vouchsafed no sign of life, he made for his own lodging. Every nerve on edge, his mind revolving blackest thoughts, convinced that once again he must face the terrible Lord of Terror in a struggle that could be nothing else but ruthless, Fandor resorted to his usual method of regaining calmness and reinvigorating mind and body. He proceeded to fill his bath with ice-cold water and plunged in, to leave it two minutes later feeling fit and well.

"Now to have a change of clothes," he decided. "A roadman's getup is hardly the thing in town. Besides, I'm going to change trades—everything seems to point that way."

Two hours later, a young man took his seat in front of an unpretending cafe in the Place d'Auteuil, wearing a cap, a soft striped collar, a gray, ill-fitting lounge suit and clumsy boots with thick soles. It was no other than Jerome Fandor, and in this rig the journalist might easily pass for a small clerk, an ill-paid official or some city worker out of a job.

"Monsieur would like?" the waiter asked.

"A shoehorn!" said the customer.

Then, at the astounded look on the man's face, he pretended to give a start as if realizing the silly thing he had said.

"Beg pardon!" he explained, "but I've just been sacked from my job for a little game about a shoehorn. It was still running in my head… It's a cup of coffee with milk I want."

This want supplied, Fandor treated himself to a roll and butter, and while enjoying this frugal feast, was burying himself again in his reflections when the waiter came back and sat down opposite him, resting his elbows familiarly on the table.

"You've lost your job," he began. "Perhaps you're a chauffeur?"

"Manservant!" declared Fandor.

"So?… You were in this district?"

"Boulevard Beauséjour," the journalist never hesitated at the falsehood, not boggling about such a trifle. "At Comte Borovine's…"

"An Italian?"

"A Pole… By-the-bye, the bootmaker just now told me of a job vacant… You don't know the place by any chance?… At a house—Rue Michel-Ange, No. 106…"

"No! don't know it."

"A pity that!… You might have managed to get me this crib…"

A fresh customer appeared at this moment and Fandor was left alone. Manservant? Why, of course! For the past hour the young man had been persuading himself that was just his line.

In the first instance, he had started by scouring Auteuil, looking out for shoemakers' shops and cobblers' stalls, mostly near the railway station, in other words near M. Merandol's.

"Folks always have a pair of boots want resoling," he told himself with a fine optimism, "and almost inevitably they apply to a cobbler in the neighborhood… I'm going to dig out the disciple of St. Crispin who works for M. Merandol…"

And he had actually found the shoemaker in question. Giving himself out as a newly engaged servant, he had asked the man straight out:

"Say, are you the fellow has a pair of 'high-lows' to 'vamp up' for M. Merandol?"

"Yes!" replied the shoemaker, "but they ain't ready..."

"Oh! I thought so... I've only been at his place since yesterday."

"Well, you've gone there at a fine time, that's all I can say! Say, there's a mighty kick-up there, eh? over this Crédit International business?"

"Yes! yes!... So, you're sure they're not ready, those boots?"

"Don't I tell you so?... Ah, look, there they are..."

Fandor followed the shoemaker's glance, which had turned quite naturally to the pair belonging to M. Merandol senior. This was all the journalist needed. Long accustomed to measure with a glance the most heterogeneous objects, possessing, as he put it, "a pair of compasses in his eyes," Jerome Fandor was instantly certain of his fact.

"Very certainly," he thought to himself, "those boots are not number nines. Our friend M. Merandol must have a small foot. No! they're not nines—and that proves it was not he who accompanied Juve when the latter left the asylum by the postern door."

But the shoemaker was still talking.

"There you are, my lad!" he was saying. "Well, you're in luck's way. You've got into a good place!... Oh! it ain't like some houses where the servants can't ever stop... *I* know some cribs!"

"So do I, my word!" said Fandor with a knowing smile. "There's plenty of that sort about!... Now, at 106 Rue Michel-Ange, eh?"

"At Madame Rosemonde's, you mean?"

Fandor had named the address supplied by Bouzille at a venture, thinking it quite likely he might obtain some useful information from a shopkeeper of the neighborhood. So, when he heard the name "Rosemonde" mentioned, he declared—it was the purest guesswork.

"Yes! at Madame Rosemonde's."

"Well, that's just the sort of crib I was talking about!" asseverated the cobbler, as he rolled a cigarette. "Nobody ever stays on there!"

"Nobody?"

"But, anyway, that's no fault of the mistress."

"Really?"

"It's along of the major-domo, the house-steward. A skunk, that fellow! By what folks say, too, Madame Rosemonde's never to be seen. She never looks after a thing. A great lady, she is; an Englishwoman, they tell me—and eccentric…"

Now, indeed, Fandor was all ears. How fortune had befriended him! How many of the shoemaker's remarks seemed to fit in with Lady Beltham's personality. She was an Englishwoman, this unhappy woman, Fantômas' wife, and she was assuredly constrained to lead a life that could hardly fail to be deemed eccentric; and was it not very natural she should pay no heed to her house-steward's doings and the care of her establishment, she who had once, in her palace as a great Court lady, had about her ushers and chamberlains whose very business it was to relieve her of all the duties incumbent on the mistress of a house. Wishing to prompt the shoemaker to further revelations, Fandor remarked:

"Really? So it's a rummy crib, eh?"

"Yes, it's just 'come today, go tomorrow' there. Why! I suppose a round score of menservants have been in and out of the place in the last six months."

"Quite likely!"

"Louis was the last, the chap you knew…"

"Hmm! No!… I don't even know his name… We had a game or two of cards together, certainly…"

"Ah! yes! that must have been Louis. He was a great player… He left yesterday. The major-domo sent him packing."

"Really?… Well, anyhow, it's eight o'clock? So, when'll my boots be done, eh?"

"Afternoon—will that do?"

"That'll do! I'll tell the boss then"—and he turned away, just managing to hide a great laugh. Truly, M. Merandol little suspected that moment how his shoemaker was being cross-questioned.

"Poor man, anyway!" Fandor thought to himself, sobering down again. "If only one knew where he was! With Juve? It seems likely, but there's no proof of it... Besides, *where* is Juve?"

Every time he remembered his dear friend and comrade, the young man felt a pang of grievous distress. Juve had disappeared. Alas! what perils might he not be facing perhaps, while Fandor could not so much as make a guess as to his whereabouts or share his danger?

"But I mean to find him!" the journalist had sworn.

Next moment found him seated in the little cafe in the Place d'Auteuil, where, delivered from the waiter's inquisitiveness, the journalist rapidly reviewed the situation in his own mind.

"My investigations go on," he summed up, "without making headway! All I've learned is that there is a Madame Rosemonde lives at 106 Rue Michel-Ange, that is at the house where Bouzille saw the mysterious lady he encountered on the high road go in. Hmm! That don't come to much!"

Then, smiling:

"It isn't much," he went on, "but it may lead to much! Anyhow, there's no other way of getting to work..."

It was clear that Fandor had just definitely made up his mind for some decisive course of action. To find Juve, to hasten to his friend's help, was he not bound to continue his investigations, elucidating one by one each of the mysterious points he had so far discovered? Juve had gone to Rueil. At Rueil he had followed up his traces actually to the bank of the Seine. He had discovered that the police officer was accompanied by a man who wore No. 9 shoes. Now this man was neither M. Merandol the father, nor M. Merandol the son. So much was proved. But the Rueil clue carried him no further.

Bouzille, on the other hand, had indicated the existence of a lady who greatly exercised the young man's curiosity, a lady who "seemed" to be acquainted with Fantômas, who "appeared" to be interested in a certain young girl, who "might" be Lady Beltham. Was it not his very next duty, postponing his immediate effort to find Juve, to follow up the clue afforded by this enigmatic personality? In police investigations it is a standing rule, which must never be forgotten and should govern the conduct of all detectives, that no detail ought ever to be neglected, no point left unregarded, that everything, however unimportant to all appearance, deserves examination.

"Come then!" Fandor decided, as he got to his feet. "It is nine o'clock—a suitable hour to call at the house. So, let's try our luck!"—and he paid his score and left the cafe. A few minutes more and, after climbing a feebly lighted backstairs, the young man found himself standing, cap in hand, at the door of a very handsomely appointed kitchen.

"What do you want, young fellow?" demanded the woman in charge, who had answered his ring.

"I've come to seek employment," replied the journalist. "There's a job to be had here, is there not?"

"Why, yes! as manservant. Who sent you?"

"I heard talk of it at the grocer's."

"Good!… Well, I'll go tell the house-steward."

"So, there's a house-steward kept, is there?" questioned Fandor, playing the simpleton to perfection.

The woman shrugged. "Why! of course there is!" she exclaimed. "More by token, it's he is the real boss! Madame—you never catch sight of Madame! I've been here a fortnight, and I don't so much as know if she's fair or dark!"

"Say, that's a funny thing!"

"There's a many other funny things into the bargain!" grumbled the woman. "But you'll see for yourself… Come with me, and I'll take you to the house-steward."

Twisting his cap between his hands and assuming the most timid air he could compass, the young man followed the good woman who had admitted him into this "Madame Rosemonde's" house, whom he half hoped to find identical with Lady Beltham. Be sure, as he traversed the different corridors of the flat, Fandor took careful note, without appearing to, of all he saw, only too eager to mark anything out of the way, any detail that seemed worthy of attention. But as a matter of fact, everything seemed quite ordinary. A refined, unpretentious luxury was the keynote of appointments and decorations, without ostentation or any sign of bad taste. All he specially remarked was sundry pieces of furniture of unmistakably English origin. But did that warrant the conclusion that this was really Lady Beltham's? Was she the only Englishwoman in Paris?

"Stay here!" the woman bade him. "I'll go and tell the house-steward you're here."

"He's a great man then, this house-steward of yours, eh?"

"I have my orders!" returned the other. "Whatever you do here, you must do just as you're told,"—and leaving Fandor in a dimly-lit anteroom, she knocked at a door, with the words:

"Monsieur Felix, a young man come about a place."

"Very good! tell him to wait."

The applicant had to wait a good quarter of an hour, which he employed, sitting there by himself on a wooden bench, in looking about him curiously in all directions.

"Queer!" he reflected. "This flat is divided up in a funny way—all holes and corners everywhere. Must be the tenant who has had these partitions fixed up all over the place. It can't be the same as this on the other floors. But after all, what of it? Whether Madame Rosemonde was Lady Beltham or not, obviously she had a perfect right to modify the internal arrangements of her flat as she chose."

But at this point Fandor felt himself tremble, and frowned with a sudden exclamation of dismay. Then with a rapid change of mood, he broke into a laugh, quickly stifled.

"Ah, well!" he grinned, "I suppose I shall always be the same. What sort of a story would Juve tell, if he could see me here!"

Nevertheless, the thought that for the moment had moved the journalist's laughter was far from specially mirth-provoking. He had just reflected:

"After all, if I am really and truly at Lady Beltham's, I might very well find myself all of a sudden face to face with Fantômas. Hmm! a contingency that might surely prove highly unpleasant and lead to unexpected developments!" Indeed there was no denying the danger Fandor ran in presenting himself at the house of this unknown lady whom he believed himself in a position to identify. Yet the young man felt no sort of fear at the prospect. To meet Fantômas face to face, to fight the villain to the death, why! that was his fondest hope.

"Still there's one thing that worries me," he observed to himself. *"He* will know me while *I* cannot possibly be sure I actually have my man before my eyes. Maybe he comes here under a disguise it is impossible for me to foresee."

He had reached this point in his reflections when a door was roughly shoved open, and:

"Come in!" said a voice.

The journalist rose respectfully, darting a questioning look from under his dropped eyelids. Could this be the house-steward? Quite an old man, with bent shoulders, supporting his tottering steps with a rubber-tipped stick, met the journalist's view. Speaking in a harsh voice, he asked:

"You offer yourself as manservant, do you? We pay 300 francs and perquisites. I want only sober and serious persons, not given to talking. The work is not hard... You do the rooms, open the door and so on. Of course you know the usual duties?"

"I have been in service in the provinces, sir."

"Your references?"

"I have left them at the registry office, but I can go and get them."

"You are free now immediately?"

"Certainly."

"Very well, I engage you on trial. The work is behindhand, as a fact... Come and put on your apron."

A quarter of an hour afterwards Fandor found himself in a sitting room, feeling very much embarrassed what exactly to do. He carried a feather-brush, a broom and under his arm a duster.

"Devil take me!" he muttered, "if I know which I ought to start off with. Does one begin with the brush, the duster or the broom, I wonder."

Finally he chose the broom, an implement that struck him as the easiest to manage.

"Now to work!" he said to himself encouragingly. "The great thing is to stay on here for twenty-four hours and find means to see the lady of the house. If it's Lady Beltham I cannot fail to recognize her,"—and expending a great deal more energy than was strictly necessary, Fandor fell to sweeping out the room. But, being very clumsy at the job, he did not fail to administer sundry hard knocks to furniture and walls. Indeed he banged them with such goodwill that suddenly he stopped dead, startled and surprised in the highest degree.

"Impossible!" he muttered. "I'm crazy…"

The fact was, he had just struck one wall that sounded hollow!… Was it a cupboard perhaps opening from an adjoining room?

"I must find out!" the journalist told himself.

In two strides he was across the apartment. Then opening a door, he examined carefully the new room he saw. It was a working room or study of sorts, furnished in rustic style with an oak writing desk, chairs of oak and a bookcase of the same wood. A large bench or settee, the back of which was formed of a heavy bar of wood, occupied a whole section of wall.

"And no cupboard at all!" Fandor noted. "Why, then the wall ought to sound solid everywhere!"—and filled with a momentarily growing curiosity, he went back to the sitting room.

"I may be mistaken. Anyway, I'm going to find out!" he growled. "By God! I *know* I'm not mad!—and kneeling on the floor, he took a penknife from his pocket and began to sound the partition wall. No doubt for anybody but the journalist quite a number of hypotheses would have seemed plausible enough. The wall sounded hollow, that was certain. But was that such an extraordinary thing? Might it not be simply explained by some architectural arrangement of an entirely ordinary nature? A chimney perhaps was carried through it. But Fandor shook his head, in his own mind answering this objection:

"No! It's not a chimney. It's a question of a party wall and not a main wall. Consequently…"

But at that moment his deductions came to a sudden end. He had just caught a slight sound behind him, and turning round, the journalist saw the major-domo darting a look of acute suspicion at him.

*   *   *   *   *

Some looks are so expressive, some silences are so signifi-
cant, as to render words entirely superfluous to indicate their
meaning. The instant Jerome Fandor saw the house-steward at
his back and observed the way the man was regarding him, he
lost all hope. He told himself plainly:

"It's all up! all up with my plan!"—and he jumped to his feet.
No use assuming an air of smiling nonchalance.

"Why! I never heard you come," he remarked casually, but it
was too late to put the old man off the scent. In a voice shaking
with ill-concealed fury, the house-steward demanded:

"What were you doing?"

"I was straightening the carpet," Fandor lied shamelessly.

"You were knocking on the wall! I saw you!"

"Oh, yes, that's quite likely."

"Why?"

"Why? Upon my word, because I was finely surprised…"

"What at?"

"Seemed to me the wall sounded hollow."

Without another moment's hesitation Fandor had un-
masked his batteries. Further pretense was useless. He foresaw,
possibly without sufficient reason, that a desperate encounter
was imminent between himself and the old man. So be it. He
was going to startle him by the brusque straightforwardness of
his replies. He proceeded:

"And as it's a party-wall, where there can't be any chimney, I
was asking myself what was hidden inside…"

"That doesn't concern you!"

"Evidently, sir, but all the same…"

"It's just a partition they have had put up—double planking
with a space between. In any case, I repeat it's no business of
yours! Moreover, as I don't like inquisitive fellows…"

"Inquisitive fellows? But come…"

"Enough! No excuses! I turn you off."

"Now, at once?"

"This very moment!… Out you go!…"

It was a hard struggle for Fandor to keep himself in hand
at the moment. The hollow party-wall he had discovered, the

furious behavior of the old man, it was all very strange. But so far there was certainly no definite deduction to be drawn. None of the observations he had made since entering the flat bore any precise significance... But, all the same, he conjectured some mystery, he felt there was something sinister underneath. And inevitably, with his eager, impetuous temperament, Fandor was at this moment sorely tempted to throw himself on the man who was turning him out of the house, hurl him to the ground, render him helpless and at his leisure make sure of what this strange partition concealed. But on second thoughts, he quickly changed his mind. After all he could not be sure, he might be mistaken. And then, what if, by any chance, the other found time to parry his attack and shout for help, if the police rushed in and arrested him in the act of assailing this old man?

"No scandal!" Fandor warned himself, mastering his anger. "The Law is not on my side. Once they arrested me, I should have the deuce of a job to secure my release... As for claiming a police investigation, I have no plausible reason to allege for demanding it." In any case, it was now too late to act. Striding up to him with a vigor quite unexpected in a man of his age, the house-steward had gripped him by the arm and was pushing him out of the room.

"Your cap?" he cried. "Take it and be gone! My advice to you is: never set foot in this place again. Madame Rosemonde would make a complaint to the authorities. Clear out, I tell you!"

Hustled out on the landing of the backstairs, Fandor had recovered his wits before the door of the flat banged to behind him. Left to himself on the steps outside, the journalist could not help pulling a wry face.

"Oh, ho!" he muttered, "I've been shown the door pretty often these last few days. At *La Capitale!* And now here!... Hmm! I'm contracting very bad habits,"—and suddenly he broke into a smothered laugh, a nervous laugh that meant more than any cry of menace. Two minutes later he was making off, still thinking hard.

"They chuck me out o' doors, eh?... Very good! But that

don't prevent the wall being hollow; that don't hinder the house being full of mystery… What a pity I couldn't so much as set eyes on this Madame Rosemonde!"

Still thinking, he reached the entrance hall of the mansion.

"Yes! a pity!" he repeated. "But this may only mean a postponement, after all!… When a man's kicked out of the door, why, he's always at liberty to come back by the window, I take it?"

He had just emerged into the street, and now wheeled about to scrutinize the front of this house that now presented for him a problem of such absorbing interest.

12. Double or Nothing

Two hours afterwards—a neighboring church clock had just struck twelve—Fandor was seated at table at an unpretending little wineshop very conveniently situated at the corner of the Rue Michel-Ange and the Rue d'Auteuil. Still wearing the same humble, not to say shabby clothes, his cap pulled down over his eyes, the famous reporter of *La Capitale* was enjoying a hearty breakfast, while pretending to scan with the deepest interest a racing paper spread open before his eyes and resting against a water bottle, thus hiding his face more or less from the glances of any curious passerby. As a fact, the young man was paying mighty little heed to the news he was supposed to be devouring, the only object of its perusal being to keep himself in countenance. Turning over in his mind the recent series of events, Fandor had never, from the first moment of leaving Madame Rosemonde's, ceased to keep an eye on a second door giving access to No. 106. He reflected:

"No! I am perfectly right! The sitting room where I was is the last room in the flat, and therefore adjoins the next house in the row. To conclude from that fact that the hollow party-wall might likely mark a secret passage connecting the flat in No. 106 with the corresponding flat in 108 is no great stretch of imagination. Well! It's an interesting problem…"—and ordering a new dish, Fandor went on quietly with his meal—and with his lucubrations:

"Supposing now this Madame Rosemonde to be really Lady Beltham, would it be anything strange if, in that case, there were a secret passage between her flat and the flat in the adjacent house? No! Clearly not!"

And now the young man's wits wandered far afield, indulging in the wildest hypotheses.

"Why, no! If this Madame Rosemonde—who knew Bouzille

and appeared to know Fantômas—was really Lady Beltham, it was not surprising that her dwelling should be in some sort 'faked.' Was she not bound, in fact, to receive frequent visits from her husband, the Lord of Terror? Was it not reasonable, in that case, to conclude that Fantômas, with his usual foresight and artfulness, had actually contrived in his wife's apartments a way of escape for himself, a safe place of concealment, enabling him easily to baffle any perquisition by the police.

"Yes!" the journalist pursued his reflections, "the thing begins to take shape. Madame Rosemonde must be Lady Beltham, and the hollow party-wall no doubt marks a secret issue, an emergency exit."

Then he brought his deductions to a sudden, definite conclusion:

"Well, anyhow, I shall know tonight…"

Yet how *could* he hope to attain any certainty as to facts it was now impossible for him to check? Was he proposing to appeal to the official Police? Had he decided to inform M. Havard or M. Fuselier of the result of his investigations? As a matter of fact the truth was the exact opposite; not for one instant had so foolish, so idiotic a notion crossed his mind. The Police could not have helped him in the least; they would never have paid the smallest attention even to his statements. So vague, so indefinite were the particulars he had noted, so startling seemed the revelations made by Bouzille, that very surely no magistrate, no official detective—Juve excepted—could possibly take them into consideration.

Turning his thoughts, therefore, in quite another direction, Fandor resumed as he went on with his dessert:

"I shall know tonight, yes!… Unless, indeed, between now and then, I have had the luck to see Lady Beltham leave the house. Disguised or not, made up or not, I shall know her, I swear I shall!…"

Such, in fact, was the journalist's first hope… If he had taken post in this little restaurant, if he was still there, it was simply because from that point of vantage he had every opportunity to watch the comings and goings of the occupants of No. 106 Rue

Michel-Ange.

"Granting that it *is* Lady Beltham who commanded my services, without knowing it and for five minutes, as her man-servant, there can be little doubt her house-steward will have informed her of what occurred. From that it is a short step to conclude she will be anxious, that she will wish to warn Fantômas, to ask his advice, possibly to take to flight—and this being so, I have a very good chance of seeing her leave the place." But, as an actual fact, nobody had left the building of a sort to merit Fandor's attention. If Lady Beltham did live there and if she had been advised of the incidents of the morning, there was nothing whatever to indicate that she was proposing to desert her home.

"Well and good!" resumed the journalist to himself. "In that case I shall play my big stake tonight…"

At that moment the landlord appeared again.

"Capital stuff, my beef *réchauffé,* eh?" he asked his customer.

"Why, yes!" agreed Fandor, who had not a notion what he had been swallowing, "Delicious!"

"It's my strong point!" the man went on boastfully. "But, say, you've had no luck?"

"Had no luck? What d'you mean?"

"Your friend?… He ain't come?"

In spite of himself the young man felt tempted to laugh. He had clean forgotten how he had told the landlord he was there to wait for a comrade in the regiment, knowing as he did that the friend in question passed by the house every day, though he was unaware of the exact hour. He had concocted the story as offering a good pretext for making a long stay in the restaurant.

"Why, no!" he replied in a tone of vexation. "It's quite true, he has never turned up… It may be he only comes this way evenings, returning from his work?"

"And you mean to wait for him?"

"Certainly! I *must* see him…"

"My notion, in that case, is he owes you some tin! That's the only thing to account for so much patience, eh?"

"Right you are. That's how it is," agreed Fandor.

Presently, rid of the man and his tiresome inquisitiveness, the journalist once more buried himself in his private reflections, absorbing the while a glass of liqueur unmistakably adulterated.

"Yes!" he told himself, "it is simply a question of patience. I must just wait for tonight. I must stop here all day—unless of course I catch a sight of Lady Beltham..."

Then he went on reflectively:

"My word! There's no reason I shouldn't work out my plan of action. After all, the game I'm going to play is so serious I'm bound to study my cards well. It's surely 'double or nothing' I'm going for. If I get myself caught, I'm certain to spend three or four days in jail, till my case has been cleared up. Then, into the bargain, I'm pretty sure to give the alert to the parties I'm going for, and so put them to flight."

Nor was the journalist mistaken in his conclusions. More daring even than usual, he had resolved on a course of action that undoubtedly exposed him to the direst perils. Possibly he was too imprudent, too reckless? Excited to the last degree by his discoveries in Madame Rosemonde's flat, he had positively made up his mind to burgle the premises, to force a way in at night and so find out what mystery underlay the hollow party-wall. The risk of getting himself clapped in prison, the further risk of giving the alarm to Lady Beltham—if Madame Rosemonde was really the notorious Lady Beltham—even this did not sum up all the dangers Fandor was preparing to confront.

There was a third peril of which the journalist said nothing, but which nonetheless was obviously to be reckoned with. Did he not run a great chance of being murdered, and that without his murderers having to fear any risk of discovery or prosecution. If Fandor, as he thought possible, was surprised in the flat he proposed to break into, anyone who should discover him would be fully justified in opening fire and shooting him down—precisely as a man has the right in legitimate self-defense to fire on a burglar he surprises at night in his house. This risk, however, the young man never thought of taking into account. To die in the performance of duty, to die for Juve's sake and while devoting all his energies to the task of ridding the world of Fantômas, this, in Fandor's eyes, was so simple a matter it never occurred to him to give it a thought. So, still sipping his abominable tipple, the journalist proceeded to turn over in his mind the details of the nocturnal visit he intended to pay.

"In short," he quickly decided, "to make a stealthy entrance into this Mme. Rosemonde's premises is an easy enough job. All I need do is to find a way after nightfall into the house numbered 104. The building is a trifle higher than its neighbor, No. 106, and I shall hide on the roof. Once there, I shall wait till it's quite dark. Then, to get from the roof of 104 to the roof of 106, to crawl along the eaves and down a drainpipe and so on to Mme. Rosemonde's balcony, well that is a bit more complicated—but it's not impossible for anybody but a cripple or a one-armed man, and thank goodness! I'm neither one nor the other."

As for finding a way from the balcony into the actual interior of the flat, this seemed to Fandor so easy he never so much as gave this detail a thought.

"And your friend? Not come yet?" questioned the landlord towards six o'clock in the evening, when his customer, after ordering one after the other beer and a succession of soft drinks, was getting somewhat weary of his long and fruitless vigil.

"No! not here yet!"

"Perhaps he has heard from a mate that you were on the lookout for him?"

"My word! Quite likely!"

"It's a big lot he owes you?"

"Big enough…"

"Well, you're quite right then to hang on… You'll dine here?"

"At seven, to the minute."

"And till then, you don't want anything?"

"Yes! yes! I do… a glass of Vichy water."

It was the last drink Fandor allowed himself. In the excited state he was now reduced to, he was consumed by a burning thirst which only pure water could alleviate. Yet, strangely enough, when the time for action drew near, his agitation was succeeded by a feeling of entire calm. To face a known danger, to fight a battle, even a desperate one, is for truly energetic natures infinitely less torturing than to wait, perhaps to wait in vain.

"Nobody has left the building," Fandor reflected, as he paid his shot. "It follows Mme. Rosemonde is within. Well! I am going to pay her a visit. It's the least I can do!..."

Walking with a deliberate, confident gait, as if he had indeed been about to make a call on a lady of his acquaintance, the young man left the wineshop where he had spent the day and made for the house bearing the number 104—the house from which he proposed to take the leap that was to land him in Lady Beltham's apartments.

Was he destined to carry through his audacious project?

*   *   *   *   *

A moment or two later, with the mien of a casual visitor, a man perfectly sure of himself, Jerome Fandor walked into the entrance hall. But luck was against him—the concierge emerged from her lodge and confronted him.

"You want to see...?" she demanded. Fandor burst out laughing.

"Oh, ho! but that's a good one!" he protested.

"You don't know me, Madame? Yet I'm constantly in and out..."

"Gracious me!" the woman exclaimed. "I didn't recognize you. You're Monsieur Henri's friend, o' course, eh?"

"Why, certainly!" declared the journalist—who knew nothing whatever of this M. Henri. "Is he upstairs?"

"I think so. I haven't seen him go by... He's likely in his bedroom just now. They dine early, his family do..."

"Then I'll go up right away,"—and he passed hurriedly into the courtyard to escape other embarrassing questions. In fact, what the good woman had told him was all the enlightenment he needed. She had mistaken him for the pal of some servant, so he could now mount to the sixth floor without fear of attracting undue attention.

"A good beginning!" he chuckled. "The only trouble is that the good dame won't see me pass out again."

But with his habitual optimism, Fandor ignored such a trifling detail. He proceeded to climb the stairs and soon arrived at the sixth floor, where at the first glance he perceived a skylight over the landing opening onto the roof.

"I couldn't wish for anything better!" he muttered below his breath. "The great thing is to get to work quickly and noiselessly."

Defying giddiness—a weakness he had never known indeed—and congratulating himself on the fact that the passage in which he stood was quite deserted, the young man mounted on the banisters, and from there, gripping hold of an iron clamp fixed below the skylight to rest a ladder against, hoisted himself up by his hands. He ran the risk of a highly unpleasant surprise, for if any servant belonging to the house had come out of his room at that moment, he would infallibly have been taken for a thief. But fortune often smiles on the bold adventurer. Not only did nobody see him, but he actually succeeded, without having made the very smallest noise, in opening the skylight, pushing it up with one hand while holding on to the iron clamp with the other, and finally crawling out on to the roof.

"There," he observed with unfeigned satisfaction, "that's the first stage completed. Now to shut the skylight to again—and wait developments." He did as he said, and after carefully re-closing the skylight, crept along the roof and gained the shelter of a chimney stack, then keeping close to the brickwork, remained absolutely still.

"It's not much fun this waiting, by God!" he sighed. "Still I'm not here for amusement. Damn! the cold bites shrewdly at this height." It was rapidly getting dark and as the night advanced, the cold increased—so much so, indeed, that when, after three hours had gone by, he resolved to stand up, he found his limbs quite benumbed, almost paralyzed in fact.

"A bad business!" he groaned. "A pretty thing truly, just

when I'm to attempt a venture on a tricky bit of gymnastics. But as I can't help it…"—and he shrugged his shoulders, firmly resolved to make the attempt at all costs. Crawling along the roof, always taking care to make no noise, he reached the eaves which overhung the house No. 106. From there to jump down on to the lower roof was a simple matter, and this he did without any difficulty.

"So far, so good!… But this is just where things get a bit more complicated… Devil take it! one can't see one's hand before one's face this side!"

It was no exaggeration. This face of the building was plunged in absolute darkness.

"If I let go the drainpipe I'm going to claw down, if I miss my hold, I shall break my neck!… Pooh! no matter! Nothing ventured, say I, nothing gained!"

But surely the risk was too great. Leaning out over empty space, he scrutinized—so far as the heavy darkness allowed— the drainpipe that fell vertically to the ground below. It was by sliding down this fragile support he hoped to reach Mme. Rosemonde's balcony. But was the feat practicable?

"I can only know that when I've tried!" he suddenly exclaimed. "Anyway, I am wrong to complain of the darkness. If it were lighter, I should risk being seen. That wouldn't be pleasant either… But come, no more gassing! To work! It's close on midnight. I've no time for loitering…"

The risk was terrible, the feat one to make the bravest tremble. Letting himself slip from the roof, clinging to the rain gutter, which he could feel bending under his weight, the young man lowered himself towards the drainpipe. Below him was empty space, dark and threatening.

"Capital! capital!" he told himself. "But the pipe, where the devil is it?"—and he groped for it with his feet, scraping along the stonework.

"Ah! I've found it. Nothing could be better. All I've got to do now is to clip it between my knees… to let go of the eaves with my hands, and grip the new support. If I can do that, I'm safe— or as good as safe." In very truth there were twenty chances to one he would not manage it. Numbed with the cold, his hands felt stiff and bruised. Then, could he grip the drainpipe tight enough with his knees not to slip? Would he be in time to loose the gutter and then cling on to the drainpipe?

"Double or nothing!" he thought… "Away we go!"—and next second he had done the trick.

But he was not out of the wood yet. Under his weight the pipe, made in sections merely fitting one into the other, threatened every moment to break up. He could feel it shaking.

"Quick time now!" he thought. "Must be moving on! But, by the Lord! What a height a house is!"

Then he started to swarm down slowly and carefully towards the ground. Never was the journalist to forget what ages it took him to slide down like this from the roof to the balcony he meant to land on. Nor was he ever likely to forget the agony he had endured during the last few yards of this terrible climb. His strength was exhausted. His bleeding fingers refused to support him longer. To let go, to plunge into the abyss that seemed to be dragging him down, to tempt him to give up the struggle from sheer exhaustion, would have been an infinite relief, a positive pleasure.

Nevertheless he made good. Doing the impossible, accomplishing one of those prodigies of endurance the mind refuses to credit and yet the will brings to pass, he reached Mme. Rosemonde's balcony and found his footing there.

"At last!" panted the journalist… "It was high time!"

For a while he did nothing, so exhausted that he felt incapable of the smallest effort, unable to frame a lucid thought. However, it was never Fandor's way to give in even to the most pronounced weakness. In five minutes he was on his feet again, courageous as ever.

"Yes!" he cried, "I'll still play the game!… Double or nothing! Is it to be victory or defeat?"

The shutters were shut, but this obstacle troubled him very little. To insert a hook in the crack and so lift the catch was the work of a moment. Nor did he find any greater difficulty in opening the window itself. For him, to use a diamond and cut out a hole in a pane, then pass his hand through and work the catch was child's play. But would he not be heard? Besides, might he not be attacking a window opening on a room where somebody was? He glued his ear to the shutters, listened with all his might, then gave a smile of satisfaction.

"No! I'm positive there's no one there. If there had been anybody, the alarm would surely have been given before now... Forward!"—and he set to work. In less than three minutes the shutters were open, and the window forced.

"The critical moment!" thought the intruder. "Have I made a mistake or no? Is it really the window of the sitting room where I was this morning?"

The window now wide open, he crept through onto a thick carpet, and listened again, still without hearing a sound.

"One step forward," he calculated, "and I shall touch the piano. If I find it there, I am right!"—and groping with out-stretched arms in the pitch-darkness of the room, he risked this decisive movement. He was acting, in fact, the part of a burglar, a criminal, and was actually in the most compromising of positions. If he were wrong in his suppositions, if he were not really in Lady Beltham's apartments, he had earned a term of penal servitude! If, on the other hand, he was actually in the flat owned by the great lady, he might expect from one moment to the next, to see Fantômas appear.

Suddenly Fandor bit his lips. He had just upset something in the room with a resounding crash...

"Done for!" he thought. "I'm done for this time!"

He supposed they *must* have heard him. But nobody came. Then he took another step forward, and all but gave a cry of delight.

"The piano!" he muttered. "Yes! It is really the piano blocks my road."

All hesitation was now at an end. The piano once located, he knew where he was and could, without risk of caroming against any other piece of furniture, make for the partition that had attracted his attention.

"About five steps," thought Fandor, "and I ought to come

upon it. But no! five steps is not enough... six... seven. Well! this is funny... I'm positive the room is not so big as that... Can the piano have been shifted to a different place?"

Bewildered by his failure to reach the wall, the journalist came to a halt. Again he found it needful to master his nerves, to calm his agitation. Besides, he felt he must listen once more to make sure nobody was coming. But hearing nothing to alarm him, Fandor was ready next minute to hazard a most perilous step.

"Let's throw a light on the subject," he resolved. "Without a light I'm simply wasting time. So here goes—double or nothing. That's the game nowadays!"—and striking a match, he kindled the tiny wick of a spirit cigarette lighter which as a smoker he always carried with him.

Hardly had the feeble gleam in some degree dissipated the gloom when Jerome Fandor barely checked a cry of rage and utter amazement. What he saw baffled all possible anticipation, so absolutely unexpected was the sight that met his eyes. He was certainly in Mme. Rosemonde's salon, the room where that very morning he had been doing duty as a house-servant. But the room was completely transmogrified. Fully furnished a few hours ago with a number of chairs, glass cabinets of bric-a-brac, valuable pictures, it was now empty—or all but empty! All that was left was a few articles too heavy to be quickly removed— among the number being the piano. A large sofa still stood in the middle of the room.

"By the Lord!" growled the young man. How had the removal been effected? How had they contrived, without his having seen anything brought out of the house door, to clear out the flat—for the whole place appeared to have been stripped bare.

"This proves it is Lady Beltham lives here," Fandor reflected. "Yes! It's proof positive! But it comes too late. She has taken to flight!... It is Fantômas has sprung this surprise upon me!"

Then, next instant, his reflections came to an abrupt end. There, on the very same partition he had come to examine, he had caught sight of the most astounding thing. Fixed on the wall with four pins was an envelope—an envelope that bore his own name "For Jerome Fandor."

The journalist had to bite his lips to check a yell of rage and fury. What he saw, was it not indisputable evidence that once again he had been made a fool of? If this envelope bearing his name was there waiting for him, it meant his enemy had made sure he would come there. And was it not equally self-evident that now his investigations were foredoomed to failure?

"I've acted like an ass," thought the young man. "This morning I was spotted! My God! I've only got my deserts."

Then he sprang forward. Recovering from his first amazement, he felt a burning curiosity to know the contents of this letter that had been written for him to read. Wounding as it was for his self-esteem, he felt bound to find out what it said, as perhaps affording him some useful piece of information. In feverish haste Fandor snatched the envelope from the wall and more eagerly still tore it open… Inside was just a single sheet of letter paper on which were inscribed in typescript some half-dozen lines. Astounded, the journalist read a sort of warning conceived as follows:

"If Jerome Fandor finds this note—and he will find it—he is requested seriously to weigh its contents. He has no call to persist in police investigations which will not, and cannot be of any advantage to him. He is a journalist, let him stick to his trade and not go out of his way to enter the lists against—he knows whom! Out of sheer good nature, indeed, he is warned that, if he hopes in this way to come to the rescue of his friend Juve, he is simply wasting his time. Juve needs no man's help now. He is dead, as all will die who choose to get in my way." There was no signature.

Hardly had Fandor glanced through the missive ere the portentous document fell from his hands. Little he heeded now the insulting irony of the threat! No! it was no longer of himself he was thinking—it was of Juve, and what a flood of bitter grief overwhelmed him. So, Juve, the good, the brave Juve, was dead! So, Fantômas had had the last word in the long-drawn struggle between the great detective and the Lord of Terror! It was Fantômas, of course, who had concocted the outrageous message. Not for one instant could Fandor doubt the fact. Overwhelmed, staggering under the weight of crushing sorrow the young man stood motionless with downcast eyes.

"Juve is dead!… dead!" he kept repeating. "It is no use my trying to come to his help!"

He was in despair, sick of unavailing effort. If Juve was dead, why! what had he to do there? But such weakness could only be short-lived. Suddenly he raised his head.

"I'm going crazy," he stammered. "Is it not up to me to avenge him? And punish his murderer? And deliver the world of Fantômas? Is all that nothing?"

A flash of self-contempt made him wince. What! was he going to forswear the battle, just because a soldier who was dear to him had paid forfeit for his gallantry with his life?

"Come, come!" he chided himself, "I am not one to desert the colors. Juve himself would have told me…"

He broke off suddenly, while his eyes, in which the tears were welling, grew keener, fiercer, more determined.

"Juve would have told me…" he said again in doubtful tones.

Then next instant, he concluded:

"But, there, it's fatigue, exhaustion makes me so silly. By God! what is there to prove Juve is really dead? Am I to believe whatever Fantômas says? Am I to credit every lie he chooses to tell?"

Fandor shrugged his shoulders. Once more he fell to examining the mysterious partition. Once again he was ready for the fray.

Suddenly he stood motionless, his ears strained to listen.

"I'm not dreaming?" he muttered. "Someone is speaking?… Someone is coming?…"

He listened harder, his face paling.

"This way, constables… this way!"

No need to go on listening. "The police!" he told himself. "No mistake about it, it's the police!"

This was perhaps the most formidable danger that could threaten him. How, indeed, came the myrmidons of the law to be in the flat? Had they been watching his descent by way of the drainpipe? Or else, perhaps, had Fantômas given the alarm by telephone, warning a police station that his house was being raided by burglars?

"Anything is possible!" thought Fandor. "But no matter for that, the only thing of importance is for me to get away—and in double quick time!..."

Turning the key in the lock, the journalist returned to the balcony. Leaning over, he peered down into the street, but could see no one.

"There you have it!" he laughed to himself. "Always the same thing! The detectives must have roused out the concierge and discussed the situation at length with her. Then, the whole lot, one after the other, gallantly marched upstairs. Never one of them has had the gumption to post a sentinel to keep an eye on the house... So much the better for me!"

But it needed a man like Fandor to dare the risk of another descent like the one he had already faced. Yet, without a moment's hesitation, the young man climbed the railing of the balcony, and once more gripped the drainpipe and hung suspended in mid air.

"If nobody goes by in the street, I shall manage all right," he calculated, "but can I hope for such luck?"

Again he had to fight against the agonizing cramp in arms and legs, and his bleeding fingers had to hook themselves round the shaky drainpipe. But the journalist was not the sort to be balked by any obstacle, no matter how terrifying. He was resolved to reach the ground, and reach the ground he did. As his feet touched the pavement, he could hear from above his head an uproar that sufficiently told its tale.

"So far, so good!" he chuckled, as he made off hurriedly, though with tottering steps. "The constables are in the room. They can see for themselves I've bolted. Let them enjoy the joke."

Almost laughing out loud, albeit so exhausted he had to support himself by the walls of the houses not to fall, Fandor managed to stagger some little distance away.

"But where to now?" he was asking himself. "What to do

next? Fact is, I have no clue left to follow up... At Rueil, all seems at a standstill... Here, Fantômas won't turn up again just yet awhile in all likelihood... As for Lady Beltham—if it *was* Lady Beltham..."

He broke off, and looked up with a start. Turning out of the Rue d'Auteuil, driving slowly and keeping close to the sidewalk, a motorcar was coming towards him.

"Best not attract attention!" he thought, and did not even turn his head when the vehicle came opposite where he stood.

But then, what a startling sight met his eyes! In the car sat a woman alone by herself, at the wheel. And lo! suddenly, as she was on the point of passing the young man, she leaned over and hailed him in a stealthy whisper, without ever stopping the car.

"Fandor!... Fandor!... He is alive! He is alive, I say! Save him!... Save him!..."

Then the noise of the engine drowned her voice. The car had darted on again, driven at full speed. Before Fandor had recovered from his surprise, before he had time to turn around and look after it, the car was far away, fast disappearing in the distance.

"Lady Beltham!... Lady Beltham!..." cried the journalist. Then he collapsed, overcome by emotion, intoxicated with joy, his ears still ringing with the words of kindly pity that had been graciously vouchsafed him:

"He is alive!... He is alive!..."

13. In One Second

An hour or so later Fandor found himself, without very well knowing how precisely he had come to be there, seated on a bench in the Boulevard Exelmans alongside the railway arches of the Chemin de fer Ceinture. He had indeed a clear recollection of his collapse, of the efforts he had made to master his weakness, of the difficulty he had experienced in dragging himself to a safe distance out of the reach of the police, and of the stupor that had seized him as he sank half-unconscious on the bench. What need to know more? So now, without giving a thought to what might have been his adventures in the interval, he drew his hand across his brow, struggling against the apathy that still oppressed him, while he told himself:

"He is alive!… Juve is alive!… Lady Beltham said so!"—and in one second, as if the words had galvanized him to new life, he was himself again—clear-headed, alert, ready for action.

"Bah!" he growled, "I think I must have had 'the vapors' like some silly woman!" He broke into a laugh, and declared: "But that's all over and done with!… Very good! Now I've only got to decide what's next to be done."

Only, while it was easy enough to say that, it was by no means so easy to fix definitely what course of action must be adopted.

"In one word, what have I learned of importance?" the young man asked himself—and he felt bound to reply that the one thing he knew most certainly was that he knew nothing… What, indeed, *had* he discovered fresh in the course of his highly dangerous expedition? That Lady Beltham was still with Fantômas? That Fantômas still hated Juve? That he professed to have murdered the police officer? A shrug of the shoulders was the only possible answer to these reflections. None of these "discoveries" afforded him any clue to follow up. Moreover every event of the night pointed clearly to the fact that from now on, knowing him to be on Juve's track, Fantômas was certain to focus his hostility directly on himself... Pulling a face that spoke volumes, the journalist resumed ironically:

"A great success, truly!—the net result being that, from beginning to end, I've been properly choused... The house-steward was of course Fantômas; I was a nincompoop not to guess as much. It was He... he and no one else, who played the part. Evidently he recognized me, chucked me out of doors and calmly took his precautions to throw me off the scent,"—and he gave a mocking laugh, a laugh of contempt at his own folly and failure. No! he was far from proud of himself at this moment.

"Yes! he has removed," he went on, "and I may rest assured I shall not see him again for some while in this quarter of the town, where, anyway, I shan't be so silly as to look for him... He has moved house, and made Lady Beltham do the same... How did he carry the thing out? No need to cudgel one's brains overmuch to guess that! The partition I discovered must communicate with the next house. The latter no doubt has two exits, one in the Rue Michel-Ange, the other on some other street. While I was keeping watch on one side, Fantômas left by the other. It's as certain as two and two make four! No matter! What to conclude from it all?"

The young man extracted a cigarette from his pocket and lit it. Then he laughed to show he was quite his own man again. After which he soliloquized:

"What to conclude? Well, here we are... I don't know where Juve is, but I do know now he is in danger. I don't know where Fantômas is, but I do know he is giving battle to Juve. I don't know where Lady Beltham is, but I do know now she is still, as she always has been, horrified at the scoundrel's monstrous villainies, and ready and willing to save any of his victims she can protect."

Then suddenly he broke off his monologue, raising his head and gazing at the clouds like a man startled by a new idea.

"True, all the same," he reflected again, "the unhappy woman, for all her passionate love for her husband, is shocked at his crimes; true, she refuses to betray him, but she feels compelled to save those he threatens. Oh! if only I could find her, question her, force her to put me on the track of my friend,"—and he heaved a sigh, for well he knew this scheme was unrealizable. If Lady Beltham, loving Fantômas as she did, would not betray him to justice, but did what she could to palliate his crimes, it was no less certain that Fantômas, on his side, had no illusions regarding his mistress's doings. It was surely because he too loved her that he took no measures to avenge her treachery, or what amounted almost to treachery, against himself. But his affection did not make him blind. He was a man very sure to keep a watch on her actions, to prevent her robbing him of the victims he had resolved to strike down.

"True! only too true!" the journalist growled. "It all comes to this—I don't know what to try next…"

Yet, hardly had he said the words in a tone of discouragement and bitter chagrin when, next instant, he sprang to his feet.

"Idiot!" he cried, "I am an idiot!… and a lunatic, if ever there was one!"

It was a strange and a hard thing to say of himself, but the journalist seemed in a veritable passion of irritation at his own folly and forgetfulness.

"Poor devil!" he exclaimed, "I must own he has every right to spring at my throat! A whole day long he has been waiting and a whole night long! He must be mad with rage by this time!"—and off he started at a run, making for the industrial districts of Auteuil, where he soon found a bakery the basement of which was lighted up, showing the men were still at work.

"You can let me have a four pound loaf?" he asked. "I'll pay for it handsomely,"—and he found no difficulty in getting what he wanted.

"There!" he said to himself, "that will put fresh hope in poor old Bouzille… So, quick now, a taxi…"

Then he broke into a chuckle:

"After all, no need for overmuch hurry! Hunger's a thing that makes people easier to manage. Ho, ho! but that's a feature of the case not unworthy of consideration!"

He hailed a taxi in the Place du Marché. Doubtless he was thinking of going as quick as might be to Rueil to release Bouzille who must surely be finding the time long. Nevertheless it was quite a different address Fandor gave his driver: "Rue Tardieu, No. 1," he ordered. It was to Juve's residence he was to be driven first.

*   *   *   *   *

Imprisoned in the tunnel or culvert where Fandor had left him to his own devices, Bouzille was, indeed, beginning to bewail his predicament in fine style. His wrists confined in the handcuffs which the young man had clapped on without the smallest compunction, his ankles tied together, the poor wretch thought himself abandoned by gods and men and was giving vent to his rancor in the most savage terms:

"There's no sense, there ain't, in such tricks!" he groaned. "I'm always the one to be put upon! Today, M'sieur Fandor… Tomorrow, M'sieur Juve… Day after tomorrow, Fantômas!… I'm fed up with trying to please everybody, that I be!… I'm fed up with helping first one lot, and then the other—and no way to satisfy any one of them!… God's truth! it's a sickening job being every man's friend, that it is!"—and heaving a deep sigh, the old fellow tried to turn over—and gave a sharp cry of pain.

"Oh Lord! my rheumatics! Fact is, with that there brook, the place is so damp I'm wringing wet… And poor me, who's so sensitive to cold!… God's truth! I shan't forget this job in a hurry… And I've got the toothache into the bargain, toothache and the pip!"

Then the old tramp fell silent for a bit, and shutting his eyes, tried to get to sleep and forget his woes. Alas! sleep refused to come. How could the wretch sleep, forced to lie flat on his back with jagged points of rock boring into his shoulder blades?

"I shall lodge a complaint!" he declared. "I don't quite know who to, but I shall! It's too bad altogether, to treat folks this fashion! It's an abuse of power, it is!… Oh, dear! oh, dear!"

This pitiful exclamation came from the fact that the old

scamp had just made another attempt, for the twentieth time perhaps, to get his handcuffs off. All he succeeded in doing was to force the steel a little deeper into the flesh.

"And, gracious heavens! the fellow's never coming back!" Bouzille resumed in a mournful voice. "He'll have been enjoying of hisself, traveling about and having larks, and I don't know what all... God's truth! it's all one to the brute whether I croak or not of hunger and thirst..."

The real fact was that, all the time, the old vagabond was not suffering too atrociously. Well used to lying hard and breakfasting on the chance fare his casual business enterprises provided, he was not the sort of man to trouble his head overmuch about a trifle of this sort. But now, to make up, little by little, to his physical annoyances was added a very real mental torture. He was thinking:

"And after all, what is there to show that Fantômas hasn't murdered M'sieur Fandor?"—and he shuddered with apprehension. We may be sure that at any other time the journalist's fate would not have been a matter of pure indifference to the old man, for if Fandor had a weakness for the tramp, the latter undoubtedly felt a genuine admiration for the reporter. Yet, at the present moment, if Bouzille, despite his grievance against him, was disquieted about the fate of Juve's friend, the feeling arose less from any pity for him than from anxiety regarding *his own* precarious position.

"God's truth! that would be a pretty go!" he thought. "Supposing M'sieur Fandor 'done in,' who would ever know I'm here?"—and the poor fellow's teeth chattered with the horror of the idea. Left helpless as he was in this subterranean prison, in an underground hiding hole that nobody knew of, the unfortunate wretch had good reason to tremble. If Fandor were dead, it was pretty obvious he ran a good chance of perishing of hunger and thirst.

"How can I tell?" Bouzille asked himself. "If he *is* dead, o' course I could shout for help... Somebody might hear me perhaps..."

Such was his anxiety by this time that he was sorely tempted to try the experiment there and then. Was not anything better than the present intolerable state of affairs?

"Hmm!" thought the old fellow, "it's no time to be after doing things without thinking matters well over first... If only I knew what time it is. Maybe it's the middle o' the night for all I know..." In fact, in the utter darkness he had been in ever since Fandor's departure, he had had no means of measuring the flight of time. It seemed indeed many days and nights he had been a prisoner, but he told himself this could hardly be the case.

"A pretty business!" he groaned again… "Not only..."

But the world was never to know what the poor man was going to say this time, for the words froze on his lips and the sentence was never completed.

"Oh, good God!" he screamed… "Good God A'mighty!"— and sheer panic terror found expression in the words, a terror that was fully justified by the appalling sight which suddenly met his eyes. Who that beheld the dread apparition would not have shared the old man's horror?

In the black darkness of the tunnel, the tramp, looking round, had seen a gleam of light. At first it was only the wavering light of a lantern, and Bouzille—with what a shock of delight!—had supposed it was Fandor coming back for him. Alas! he was quickly undeceived. As the light came nearer, of a sudden the old man had discerned the most nerve-shattering spectacle. A man was advancing upon him—a man whose face was hidden under the flying folds of a black hood, a man clad in a suit of black that clung close to his body, displaying the strong, supple lines of the figure, shod with felt-soled shoes that made his footsteps noiseless, black gloved, the grim form was unmistakable, like no other in the world!

"Fantômas!… It is Fantômas!" screamed Bouzille… Then, next moment, he forced a laugh. He was no hero, the old tramp. He was making no pretense to a courage he did not possess… It was Fandor he was expecting. It was Fantômas coming towards him. After all, what was the odds to him? The only thing that really mattered was that he should be released. Now, as always, the old scamp was ready to do what seemed best in his own interests.

Without a sound, meantime, the dreadful apparition had again advanced. Then Bouzille hailed it with a cry of:

"Master! Your devoted servant greets you!... Quick! Help! I'm sick and tired of snoring here on my back..."

But never an answer came.

"Master!" repeated the old man, "d'you hear what I say? See here, it was Fandor put me in this pickle—the brute!"

Again silence was his only answer.

"It was Fandor," reiterated Bouzille. "You understand, don't you, he wanted me to tell him your secrets? O' course. I refused... You know me, eh?"

But yet again Fantômas declined to open his mouth. "You know me?" Bouzille again demanded. "I am fidelity itself. But why won't you speak?... Answer, answer!... You don't surely accuse me of having blabbed? It's proof enough I've told nothing, the state you find me in..."

His voice betrayed the old man's growing anxiety. This obstinate silence of Fantômas began to terrify him worse than ever. Then, losing his head, as cowards always do, he gave himself away by the most unwise speech he could well have made:

"Oh! I can see how it is! You're actually telling yourself I'm a chattering fool. You think I've not been able to hold my tongue? Well, you think wrong; what I told Fandor was o' no sort of importance..."

A pause followed. Then a short, sharp click there was no mistaking sounded in the vaulted tunnel—and the tramp started off again breathlessly:

"Good God in heaven! You're cocking your revolver? But they've been telling you lies then? They've been slandering me?... No, no! don't shoot! I didn't tell Fandor nothing—or very little... Certain sure, if I did blab about Lady Beltham, you don't mind that, seeing as how she ain't true to you..."

But Bouzille got no further. Bending over him, still without a word, the man clapped his Browning to the old vagabond's temple. Words cannot describe the poor wretch's abject terror at that moment . Making a supreme effort, in a hoarse, choked voice, he panted desperately:

"But that's all I said! I swear that was all!... Fantômas! you're never going to kill me?... I never said a word of the Cemetery at Montellon, not one blessed word!... I never said that Lady Beltham... that you yourself... God's truth! don't shoot! Fandor don't know nothing!—The cellar... the grave No. 530... Don't fire! don't!"

The miserable man was half mad with fear. His concluding words were barely intelligible. Then he fell silent, incapable of uttering one other word, one single prayer to beg his life.

But at this moment a roar of laughter escaped the lips of the grim, hooded figure:

"You idiot! you old humbug! Eat, I tell you, and hold your tongue. Look here! I've brought you a four pound loaf... and pie... Now, what have you to complain of?"—and throwing off his hood, Fandor—for Fandor it was—made haste to free the astounded Bouzille from the handcuffs that he still wore.

"Eat!" he repeated. "Fall to!... And then, off with you!... You see how it is, I imagine... You don't?... Listen to me then. That was just the very thing I wanted to know about—the grave to which you brought flowers. It was my only chance of recovering trace of Lady Beltham. Oh, ho! man! I was convinced you'd speak, once you thought you were facing Fantômas. So, mind you, I never hesitated. I borrowed this costume from Juve's wardrobe... Good! you're getting your wits back, eh? you old coward?"

Yes! Bouzille *was* collecting his thoughts at last. A free man, delivered from the haunting terror that had tortured him, he staggered to his feet, still trembling a little, stretching himself, looking utterly bewildered. Presently Fandor continued:

"Of course it was a bit cruel to frighten you like that, but I had no choice of means! To save Juve's life, you understand, I was not going to let any empty scruples stop me."

"M'sieur Fandor, it's... it's..."

"It's just whatever you like, Bouzille! But, first and foremost, it's been a success! Anyway, to make up for your sorry treatment, I tell you this, I'm going to let you go free to get yourself hanged some other where—when you've completed your confidences. So eat, man, and speak!"

But the tramp shook his head, not yet quite recovered from his terrors.

"Speak about what?" he stammered.

"About the Cemetery of Montellon! About the grave 530! What's doing in that quarter?"

For the moment Fandor put on an air of something like indifference, while he stripped off his black tights, changed his shoes and generally resumed his everyday appearance. But, alas! what grief and suspense was torturing him all the while. A while before, in Paris, when he had applied the same epithet of "idiot" to himself, it was because he had suddenly remembered he still possessed a means of finding Lady Beltham and through her discovery Fantômas' whereabouts and perhaps saving Juve's life. He had told himself:

"Why, yes! Bouzille knows the woman visits a certain cemetery… that she is concerned with a certain grave. He is the one I must force to speak out. Will he speak out clearly, our friend Bouzille?"

"M'sieur Fandor," the tramp declared, "certain sure, at bottom, it's you I'd best like to help… Fantômas, you know yourself, he ain't no pal o' mine!… Only, I can't tell you what I don't know!…"

"Well, what is it you do know?"

"What I told you afore—and nothing more!… Lady Beltham, you see—I've a notion in my head it was Lady Beltham—she ordered me to take flowers to Montellon and lay 'em on grave 530, and to look about me in the Cemetery, to see if I noticed anything out of the way… But I never saw nothing… So…"

But first the old fellow cut a big slice of bread and helped himself to an enormous piece of pie, before he finished his sentence.

"So," he went on at last, "if so be you're hoping to make me speak to earn it, you may just as well give it me now straight away. I give you my oath you may."

"What do you mean by 'it'?" questioned the journalist.

"Wine, o' course! You've brought me a good bottle o' that, eh? It was well worth your while, I reckon."

But, as a matter of fact, Fandor had forgotten to lay in the needful liquid supplies.

"There," he said, handing his companion a twenty franc note, "drink that at the first tavern you come across. It's four o'clock in the morning by now, so the wineshops will be opening... So, get out!... vanish!... disappear!"—and five minutes afterwards he was moving off too, on the way to Montellon, desiring to pay a visit to this little suburban Cemetery, where Bouzille had been directed to watch "if anything happened out of the way..."

But his heart was very heavy. Something very like despair weighed on the young man's spirits. In spite of all the miracles he had performed, in spite of all his energy and adroitness, it seemed so vague, so inconclusive, this fresh clue he was about to follow up!...

*   *   *   *   *

While, with unflagging patience, and determination, Fandor was devoting himself to the task of discovering Juve's whereabouts, what *had* become of the police officer and the unfortunate Manager of the Crédit International?

Juve had heard without a tremor Fantômas' order to his accomplices to bring the winding sheets.

"Good and well!" he thought. "Now's the time to own up. I always said this business would end badly."

But this was different; he had shuddered in spite of himself on hearing the Lord of Terror add:

"The beeves, I suppose, are come?"

For all his astuteness as a detective, he was bound for once to admit he had not the faintest notion what Fantômas meant by the words. They were going to kill him, him and his companion M. Merandol, so much was certain. It struck him as no less certain that "beeves" had nothing whatever to do with the matter. "Perhaps a password?" he queried. "Perhaps by 'beeves' Fantômas means to signify something I am not to know?"

A trifle nervous, yes! but in no way terrified—for so many years had the police officer trained himself to face death that the thought had no terror for him—Juve, yielding to an odd whim, turned sharply round to look at his comrade in misfortune. The straitjacket still impeding his movements, Juve found some little difficulty in doing this, but presently succeeded.

"Possibly M. Merandol understood?" he asked himself. But alas! it was quite certain the financier had done nothing of the sort for the very good reason that he had fainted.

"Stupid that!" Juve did not hesitate to say. "The two of us together, we might have encouraged one another."

But then he corrected himself: "After all, no!"—it's very fortunate. Best for the poor fellow not to see the preparations making for his murder. Hardly an amusing game to watch one's own death agonies. Calmer than ever, in fact, without his heart going one beat the faster, Juve was actually preparing to do that very thing. Events were moving fast. With another wave of the hand Fantômas summoned two of his men, who hurried into the room.

"Merandol is to go first," he ordered them. "Carry him away now. I prefer to accompany Juve… The biggest of the beeves of course will be for him."

"The biggest of the beasts, eh? Much obliged for the preference!" growled the police officer to himself. "But devil take me if I understand… "No time was left him for further reflection. The two men who had come in at Fantômas' summons had seized the financier by legs and shoulders and without more ado were carrying him out of the house.

"To pitch him in the river?" Juve asked himself. "But no! they've promised us beeves… So let's wait for the animals."

Simultaneously two other men entered the little salon of the Romanesque villa.

"Come, quick's the word!" ordered Fantômas. "We're behind time. The meat must be there by now…"

"The meat?" Juve repeated the word. "Ah! the beef perhaps. My word, I'm further than ever from solving the riddle." He forgot that, in any case, death was the sure end of the journey he was making. Meantime, no sooner were the men, who had hoisted him roughly on their shoulders, outside the house than Juve shivered. The night, as it grew later, had turned frosty, and a chilly mist was rising from the water.

"I'm going to catch cold!" thought Juve. "St. Peter will refuse me admittance into paradise… And the beeves too? They'll be coughing!"

"Go by the pathway," Fantômas shouted after his men, "and take care not to slip into the river."

A new surprise for the detective! If the fellows were to be careful not to fall into the Seine, it was plain they had no orders to throw the men they carried in. But, in that case, where were they taking them?

Thinking back, Juve reflected:

"No! I can't be mistaken. This pathway runs along the bank of the Ile de Croissy, goes under the railway bridge and finally reaches the Bridge of Chatou. Now, there's always folk on the bridge, always! They can't be taking us there; that would be reckless folly… No! it's somewhere else they're bound for… But, where?…"

He remembered that the island was almost uninhabited. True, there was a farmhouse near the bridge, but was it occupied in the winter?

"And besides, I know the farmer's no accomplice of Fantômas," thought the police officer. "Last time, when the scoundrel escaped us, Fandor and me, he helped us. It follows…"

But Juve never drew his conclusion. He was gagged, but able to see, for the band that muffled his lips did not come up as high as the eyes—and what he saw utterly upset his composure. In the large open field forming the middle of the island five or six men were stationed, their figures so nearly lost in the foggy darkness that twenty yards away their presence could not have been discerned. At their feet, in the long grass, lay two enormous carcasses, like those one sees hanging in butchers' shops."

"Oh, ho!" Juve asked himself, "the beeves, I suppose? The deuce, they're big enough! But what on earth can Fantômas be thinking of doing with them?"

The detective had not long to wait for an answer to the question.

"Very good!" observed the Lord of Terror approvingly! "Make up the packages!"

At the same moment a smothered cry of pain escaped the police officer. With callous brutality the men who carried him had tossed him to the ground, where, still in a dead faint, lay the unfortunate financier, M. Merandol. Thereupon followed the most horrid scene that had ever perhaps troubled the peace of this calm and silent corner of the country. Without Juve's being able to strike one blow in self-defense, without M. Merandol knowing aught of what was happening, Fantômas' men dragged their two prisoners up to the carcasses. These they proceeded to open and slide the two men inside. Between the ribs of the beasts, eviscerated and prepared for the market, Juve and M. Merandol almost disappeared.

"Tie up the packages!" ordered Fantômas, and Juve at last understood the tragicomedy of this foul device which the brain of the Lord of Terror had hit upon. Who but He would ever have contrived such a stratagem? Who but Fantômas would ever have imagined such a ruse?

"It's to conceal our bodies!" Juve reflected. Passersby seeing the cart they're going to load us on will simply suppose it to be some butcher's wagon,"—and in this he was quite right.

"Up with them!" was Fantômas' next order. "And look sharp! The night's getting on,"—and the detective felt himself lifted from the ground. Half stifled, indeed, as he was inside the carcass that imprisoned him, he was to some extent losing track of events. He was suffocating, but still eager to know what was occurring.

"They're taking us somewhere," he muttered vaguely to himself. "Yes! but where?"

Then he gathered that the men who carried him were climbing a steep ascent of sorts, panting under the load.

"The slope leading up to the bridge, I suppose?" he guessed.

Then they pitched him into a cart.

"Pell-mell with the others, that's the way!" came in Fantômas' voice. The cart, in fact, was one of those big open vans butchers use, which you see go by piled up with great joints of meat wrapped in bloodstained strips of muslin.

"Where are they taking us to?" Juve asked himself again, as the vehicle got underway. After jolting a long time over a rough road, it suddenly came to a standstill.

"Anything to declare?" demanded a voice.

"No! nothing."

"Drive on to the weigh-bridge... Oh, ho! you're mighty heavy. You're not hiding anything in your 'rattletrap' by any chance?"

In spite of himself Juve shuddered with mingled hope and fear. If the *octroi* officer thought fit to sound the butchers'-meat with his pointed rod, he might easily, without meaning it, run through one or other of the prisoners and kill him. But, on the other hand, he might discover the unhappy captives!

"There's a lot o' bone. That's what makes the weight!" announced the wagoner.

"Drive on then!" answered the officer, and the van started off again. By the time it finally came to a stop, Juve was sick and giddy. The strong penetrating smell of the fresh meat raised his gorge, and strong and determined as he was, he felt prostrated physically. When at last his extraordinary prison was unloaded and its contents pitched out on the ground and so a little fresh air reached him, it was with keen delight he inhaled the icy breath of early morning. Then, presently, he found they were disinterring him from the carcass that had been his place of concealment, and he gazed about him curiously.

"Ah!" he exclaimed. "Our tomb, by God!"—and indeed no doubt was possible. In the half-light that goes before the actual dawn, he could see Fantômas' men busily engaged in raising the flagstone covering a kind of well or shaft of unknown depth. And, as if to make the spot yet more sad and sinister, a short way off, beyond a low wall, showed rows of crosses and funeral chapels, evidently those of a burial ground.

"Our tomb!" Juve groaned again. He could cherish no illusion on the point. The place they had brought him to was a large open space all overgrown with rushes and weeds. One guessed it to be some abandoned plot of ground—abandoned perhaps because of the near neighborhood of the graveyard— the garden of some ruined house. Could Fantômas have found a better locality for the disposal of the victims of his crimes? Was it not plainly enough into this well, a veritable cavern, he was going to hurl them?

"All together!" panted the men, straining every muscle. Then, at last, the heavy stone covering the well was dragged from its bed, and a puff of poisonous air followed it.

"Pitch the beeves down to begin with!" ordered Fantômas.

Presently, with a struggle, Juve managed to turn on his side, and saw that the villainous Master of Terror no longer bore the outward appearance he had assumed of Georges Merandol. The wretch had resumed for this criminal adventure his usual aspect, his livery of death and midnight murder. Under the black hood, in the black tights, shod and gloved in black, he seemed some fantastic horror risen from the nether pit, that unknown realm which, it may be, prolongs the life of human beings after death. Juve shuddered as he watched this Torturer's accomplices haul the two carcasses that had served their purpose of concealing him and M. Merandol to the edge of the gaping hole, into which a push sent them rolling. Some seconds, and then a dull crash showed they had reached the bottom. The well was evidently dry and of considerable depth.

"Now the men!" ordered Fantômas, and involuntarily, despite the impassivity it was his boast to preserve under all circumstances, Juve felt cold drops of sweat bead his brow. Abominable, the crime Fantômas was bent on—literally to bury his unhappy victims alive! He was choosing for his prisoners the most hideous of all deaths.

"Merandol first!" he ordered.

Juve looked on at the atrocity. In the gloomy enclosure, so close beside the graveyard where generations of the dead slept, the villainy was consummated. Noiselessly, pitilessly, while Fantômas stood with folded arms by the lip of the yawning pit, his accomplices, hauling him by the feet, dragged M. Merandol, still unconscious, to the edge.

"Unhappy man!" thought Juve, forgetting his own impending fate. "If only he does not wake"—and he shut his eyes, waiting with shuddering limbs for the dull thud announcing the end.

"Now the other!" came the next command, and the police officer drew himself up and opened his eyes, resolved to face his murderer with looks of proud defiance. Then the ruffians returned for the second victim and carried him to the fatal well. Juve could feel on his face a breath of the cold, clammy air that rises from an open grave.

"Now!" cried Fantômas... "Farewell, Juve! May you find eternal peace!"

Solemnly the parting words echoed in the silence, as Fantômas bowed low in a last ironical salute.

Then a push, a giddy plunge, and Juve sank down, down to the realm of darkness and the dead.

*   *   *   *   *

"What I'm doing is sheer folly, and can come to nothing! Yet, what better is there to try, what more profitable to attempt?"

So Fandor was telling himself despairingly a few days after he had extracted from Bouzille the information about the grave that Lady Beltham had charged him to decorate every day with flowers. A suburban train, jolting slowly on its way, had brought him to the neighborhood of Montellon. Now he was making for the cemetery. Yet what chance was there of his discovering any useful indication, any clue enabling him to renew his investigations?

"Juve, poor dear old Juve, shall I ever see you again?" the journalist was asking himself in a mournful voice. "How strange, how unhappy," he was thinking, "the infatuation of this great lady who loves Fantômas so fondly she can condone his worst crimes and leave him free to continue his life of villainy! She told me: 'He is alive!' *But* does she know? She besought me: 'Save him!' *But* does she believe I can?"

Out in the country now, Fandor hurried on, easily finding his way by inquiries from passersby, and soon, his heart beating fast in excited anticipation, reached the gate of the little grave-yard he had come to visit.

"Pray Heaven I don't leave the place in despair!" he mur-mured, and entered the cemetery, quite deserted at the moment. Gleaming white and flower-decked under the winter sky, the crowded graves wore almost a cheerful aspect. They seemed to suggest nothing more sinister than the deep peace of death, the eternal sleep, dreamless and unbroken, that never ends. After following divers paths in quest of the tomb No. 530 Bouzille had spoken of, he suddenly caught sight of it. It lay close under a low wall above which could be seen the greenery of an adjacent enclosure overgrown with weeds, in the center of which the flagstone covering the mouth of a well showed up. The tomb was of red granite that glittered in the sun. It bore no name. One word only stood out in letters of gold, a short and consolatory epitaph: "SPES," "Hope"!

"I shall find nothing here," groaned Fandor... "Who sleeps beneath this stone?... Who, I wonder..." Despite himself, his thoughts still dwelled on Helene, Fantômas' daughter, the woman who had loved him, and whom he had adored. Was it here, poor lily broken by the horrors that loaded her father's name with infamy, she rested at last? Yielding to feelings he could hardly analyze, the young man fell to his knees. The thought of Helene, the thought of Juve, mingled in his heart. Was not all he loved on earth summed up in those two names? Kneeling there, he surrendered himself to his dreams, mourn-ful, but at peace. It was a brief moment of calm in the young man's feverish life, a moment of self-communing, as he stood, his eyes fixed on the gold lettering of the word that spoke to him of the supreme law of life, the law that gives the strength to struggle—to hope, to hope on, come what may!

...And, without knowing it, without a suspicion of the truth, never perhaps had Jerome Fandor been in more mortal peril than at that moment!

* * * * *

With savage brutality Juve had been hurled to the bottom of the well in which it was Fantômas' ferocious will to bury his enemy alive. While he was falling—a few short seconds that seemed an eternity—the unhappy man had again and again been dashed against the walls of the shaft, bruising himself painfully, and the final shock as he reached the bottom well nigh robbed him of what little life was left. He lay where he fell, motionless, bleeding, incapable of uttering a sound. He had fainted, but he still breathed. He was covered with wounds, but none of them was mortal. Once released from the dreadful place, he might yet survive.

When at last Juve regained consciousness, when he realized where he was and recovered a clear memory of the last moments that had preceded his swooning away, the first question he asked himself was what period of time had elapsed since then. But in the black darkness of his prison what means had he of measuring the length, whether of hours or days. He thought vaguely: "I must have been here a long time." But a strange torpor still oppressed him. He could reason in a way, yet it was with difficulty he could follow up any connected train of thought. The heavy air he breathed left him still half-stifled, only half-awake.

"Long time or short," he reflected, "what matters it? I am here forever!… I am going to die… Hunger, thirst, the loss of blood… I am a man condemned to death!…"—and, strange to say, he broke into a laugh. Was he going mad?

Suddenly, involuntarily, he stirred, straightened himself, sat up. He was lying on something soft, something that gave to his movements… and it smelled like meat, fresh meat.

"Ah!" he told himself, "the carcasses of the beeves!"

And then, coming more fully to his senses, he gave a start of surprise.

"But, but," he ejaculated, "I am free, I am no longer bound?"

He had raised an arm, to find the straps of the straitjacket offered no hindrance.

"Free! I am free!" Juve cried in tones that echoed dully from the walls of the well. "As I fell the straps must have torn away and the straitjacket ripped up."

He tried to stand up, but his ankles were still fettered.

"Free!" he repeated, and added with a savage laugh, as he delivered himself from his last remaining bonds: "Yes! free, in my grave!"

Then he gave a stifled cry of dismay and horror, as he suddenly remembered his unhappy companion, M. Merandol, the sharer of his death agonies.

"Dead no doubt?" he sighed, and groping in the darkness, he searched for the financier's corpse. The bottom of the well, which had long been dry, was much wider than the mouth. M. Merandol had rolled some distance away. Juve felt his face. It was still warm.

"He is alive!" he cried. "Oh! better for him if he had died! But he will not revive to consciousness, I think."

Yet hardly had he said the words when the other heaved a sigh, gave a groan of pain. As Juve's hand touched him, he shuddered. Then suddenly, with a gasp:

"Where am I?... Where am I?" the wretched man panted.

Alas! what answer was there to make? But Juve had the courage, the courage of despair, the courage to lie! A dying man, he took pity on his dying companion, who lay there at his side in mortal terror in the black dark.

"Never fear!" he told him in a confident voice. "We are in an underground chamber. Fantômas, when he threw us down here, thought we should be killed by the fall, but the carcasses of the beeves broke our fall and saved our lives. Courage, I say! We shall get out of here..."

"We shall get out?"

"For sure we shall! I promise you that... Only have patience. I am going to untie your bonds, and you must try to go to sleep again. Meanwhile, I will prepare for our escape..."

"Our escape?... But... but..."

"Assuredly... we shall see the light of day again"—and Juve gave a smothered laugh. A fresh fainting fit had overtaken the financier, and he could feel the man's body sink together and weigh heavier in his arms... He could only envy his compan-

ion's relapse into unconsciousness. For the detective cherished
no illusions, felt no hope. He was thirty feet underground. No
cry or appeal of his could reach human ears, and how climb up
alone, unaided, without rope or ladder, from such a pit as this?

"We shall get out!" he repeated in bitter irony. "We shall
escape! Why, yes! by forestalling a lingering death, perhaps, by
managing to kill ourselves here and now!… Not otherwise!"—
and he laughed again. A hellish idea shone in his eyes, already
clouded by the signs of incipient madness.

It was at that same moment Fandor was passing the gate of
the adjacent cemetery.

*   *   *   *   *

Very certainly Juve was incapable of doing a cowardly act.
Many a time he had declared to Fandor that under no circumstances did he approve of suicide, because suicide was always a
mode of escape in face of the cruel hardships of life. Nevertheless, at this crisis, he confessed to himself that the most positive
convictions are bound in certain cases to admit of exceptions.

"Buried in this tomb," he reflected, "we are doomed, Merandol and I, to a hideous death, without the faintest chance of
escape being left us. Therefore, to kill ourselves is no cowardice,
it is simply behaving sensibly, to avoid unnecessary tortures.
Under these conditions, I hold I may take action without any
scruples of conscience."

Cool and collected, his mind made up, Juve rose to his feet.
Fantômas, when taking him prisoner by surprise, had appro-
priated his revolver, but had not searched him further, so sure
he was of having his prisoner entirely at his mercy, of murder-
ing him at his own time and pleasure.

"A lucky thing!" thought the police officer. "But anyhow,
my cigarettes would hardly have excited his suspicions, I
imagine,"—and so saying, he took from his trousers pocket the
case in which he always carefully stored the wherewithal for a
smoke.

"So," he went on, "I may very well treat myself to a last pleasure. A few puffs of good *caporal* will do me no harm"—and

he picked out a cigarette, struck a light and calmly began to smoke.

"Yes!" he proceeded. "It's very enjoyable... In fact, it's the condemned felon's cigarette they give him before stepping on the scaffold... Oh! if only Fandor were here..."

His voice shook. For the first time Juve's courage showed signs of failing. The thought of his dear comrade, whom he loved like a son, sapped his moral vigor. But he quickly added:

"Pooh! Fandor is *not* here!... And then, he is young... he will find consolation... In any case, he will avenge me!"

In the darkness Juve's eyes flashed. Yes! Vengeance! How he longed for it! Nor was it merely for himself he craved it. It was for all who, like him, had perished under the blows of the abominable Fantômas, the villain whose atrocities threatened all Humanity.

"He will avenge me," he continued. "He will avenge Merandol!... There, my cigarette is done? Shall I have another?... My God!..."

A moment's hesitation, and then:

"No!" Juve told himself. "No! What I am doing is cowardly. Merandol may wake up again. Better for me to kill him in his sleep. That will spare him all pain."

The police officer stood up. Again taking his cigarette case from his pocket, he felt over with his sensitive fingers the different little rolls of tobacco that filled it.

"Here we are!" he exclaimed. "An excellent precaution of mine to have these always about me! One would swear these four were just ordinary cigarettes... And yet, they contain enough 'cheddite' to blow us all up to rights... The results will be quite complete and satisfactory. The explosion will reduce us to powder, Merandol and me—and then bring the shaft crashing down. We shall be killed and buried at one and the same time... Come, to work!"—and with a hand that never trembled Juve set about preparing his own death. The four bogus cigarettes—four charges of the most powerful explosive known—he laid on the ground close under one wall of the well. One of them had a slow-match attached. This he unrolled and straightened out so that it should burn readily.

"That's all right!" he then remarked. "In two seconds it will all be over!"

Again he struck a light and set fire to the slow match. The flame crept swiftly towards the explosive.

"In one second!" muttered Juve… "The explosion will be terrific. Pooh! The place is quite deserted, I think? I don't risk killing innocent folks…"

Alas! What would the police officer have said, had he known that at that moment, a few yards from where he stood, his dear comrade, Fandor, stood lost in a fond reverie whose subject was himself.

"In one second!" he repeated. The flame, in fact, was actually, licking the "cheddite" cartridges.

But suddenly Juve started violently.

"God's mercy!" he cried. "One would think…" With a blow of the fist he extinguished the flame.

"Not yet!" he muttered. "Someone is coming! It is Fantômas! I hear a footstep!… Ah, ha! he will be blown up along with us!…"

It was Fandor's step as a matter of fact. The young man was patrolling the enclosure, looking about him for a clue. Through the ground, a good conductor of sound, the noise of his footfalls echoed and reached Juve's ears, where Juve stood motionless, a lighted match in his hand, ready to make the final, fatal movement.

He was thinking, in feverish excitement:

"Fantômas! It is Fantômas coming to watch our death agonies—perhaps to mock them!… Oh! for him to come nearer, a little nearer—and I kill him in killing ourselves!… I rid the world of him!"

14. A Compassionate Jailer

Jerome Fandor could have no suspicion of the danger that menaced him. Far from imagining that only a few yards separated him from the pit in which his poor friend Juve was at hand-grips with a hideous death, he was calmly walking to and fro in the pretty little Cemetery, now bathed in sunlight lighting up the flower-decked graves, that looked pleasant and peaceful under the clear January sky. His sole object was to discover some indication that might put him on the track of the comrade he hoped to save or of the scoundrel he was resolved to punish. Carefully the journalist had examined the tomb numbered 530, on which lay a half withered bouquet resembling those he had seen Bouzille make up. As a fact, he felt no doubt that this was indeed the grave in which the great lady, Lady Beltham, to the best of his belief, was interested. But alas! the tomb kept its secret inviolate—if, in truth, it had any mysterious secret to keep. Similar to all the rest—except only for its unique inscription, the one word "Hope," which Fandor had noted—it had nothing characteristic about it to hold the young man's attention…

"Oh! I am wasting my time!" thought the journalist. "Here, doubtless, reposes someone who was dear to Fantômas' wife… But that is all! It is not here I can find a clue worth following up."

And already Fandor was thinking of moving away and going back to Paris, once more disappointed in his hopes, when he decided to explore the immediate neighborhood. Could he indeed neglect any possibility? Did he not know that Fantômas was of the sort to have deceived him even about Lady Beltham? It was quite possible the unhappy woman might be tending this grave while all the while some other tomb alone merited her attention. He had made the round of the graveyard, laboriously

196 THE LORD OF TERROR

spelling out names and epitaphs—but without result.

Perhaps it was somewhere in the neighborhood he was likely to discover something. Accordingly he left the Cemetery, and proceeded to the piece of ground overgrown with weeds whose savage uncultivated aspect he had noticed on first arriving. There he saw the well in whose depths Juve lay dying—and never a suspicion entered his head! And he passed on. But, strangely enough, the young man could *not* make up his mind to leave the locality. Some vague presentiment compelled him to prolong his stay. Yet, how trust to such premonitions? How fathom the mystery of these uncertain warnings that at times obsess the mind? A second time Fandor crossed the open space, then went back again to the graveyard.

"No!" he told himself, "I have nothing to do here… The only thing left to try is a visit to Havard and another to Fuselier. One or the other, perhaps, has unearthed some fresh fact…"

But he was but trying to hoodwink himself. Where *he* had found nothing, he who was heart and soul in the investigation, was it likely those half-hearted officials should have lighted on any important clue?

"Best be going!" he thought, and he was already moving away when he came to a sudden halt, even darting aside to the shelter of a tree… On the adjacent road, the familiar tuff-tuff of a motor engine had reached his ears. A conveyance was drawing up at the Cemetery gate.

"A visitor?" he exclaimed in surprise. "A visitor at this early hour?"—and he stood on tiptoe to look over the wall, waiting eagerly to discover who this was, performing a pious pilgrimage so early in the day.

Then, next moment, he felt his heart thumping hard in his chest. The visitor was—a woman! From the distance at which he stood, Fandor could only indistinctly see the figure that was advancing with slow, weary steps. He could not make out the face, which he only saw in profile. But he thought to himself:

"A lady of fashion… a person of distinction… the carriage of a Queen!"—and suddenly his brain seemed to stop working, such a wild notion had flashed across his mind. The unknown had quickened her pace. She was following a path that led to a funeral chapel and turning a corner she reached grave 530—the tomb Bouzille had told of...

"By God!" panted the journalist, "it must be she!"—and he pronounced a name—the name that was bound infallibly to come to his lips:

"Lady Beltham! Lady Beltham!"

But, an instant later, he checked himself. "No, no! It is not she! It cannot be! Lady Beltham had lovely fair hair. This woman is dark... But still, a wig? A dye?..."

The mysterious lady had dropped swiftly to her knees. Then, standing up, she was now gazing about her on all sides, as if questioning the horizon, seeking to behold some sight invisible to mortal eyes. Sad? Nay! She was more than sad, this poor woman! Something about her spoke of a dull despair, an ineffable terror!

"It is she!... It is!" thought Fandor. Then yet again, he checked himself:

"No, no! I'm crazy!"—and then, without more thought, without a second's pause, he acted. The unknown had suddenly wrung her hands in a gesture of utter self-abandonment—and then with a last supreme effort of will to drag herself from the spot, was making for the entrance. Casting aside all further hesitation, Fandor leapt the wall and ran after the retreating figure, calling: "Madam!... Madam!..."

It was an audacious step to take, destined to lead to the most amazing of surprises. The stranger had wheeled about with an angry frown. Then, pressing her hands to her bosom in a gesture that betrayed her alarm, she turned deadly pale. She uttered no cry, and it was in a whisper almost, in a low, choking voice, that she stammered hoarsely:

"Fandor!... You!... You!..."

She knew him then? Was it Lady Beltham then, in very deed? A second time the journalist found no time to think. The unknown, flashing a quick look at him, had laid a finger on her lips as she stepped towards him, trembling, on the point of falling.

"Not a word!" she whispered in almost inaudible tones. "Come with me. But it must seem as if I was threatening you... forcing you to come!"

Fandor was fain to ask himself if he had really heard the indistinctly spoken words. What did the thing mean? But the woman was now by his side. Snatching a revolver from the pocket of her fur cloak:

"Look!" she said. "It is all playacting? But it has to be done!"—and with her slim fingers she opened the magazine of her weapon and emptied out the cartridges on the ground.

"Not a word!" she begged again, in a breathless whisper. "You must trust to me... You must appear terrified,"—and the empty pistol was leveled at the young man's head. A childish threat! An incomprehensible action—which Fandor never-theless understood... So surprising was it all that the journal-ist had no power of resistance left. He could only surrender himself to circumstances, submit to the unknown's ascendancy, follow where she led. Had she not told him: "You must appear terrified"?

"Come now," she ordered. "Come! But not a word! Not a word!"

Her revolver pointed at his head—the weapon she had a moment before unloaded—the mysterious lady took a step forward, again repeating:

"Come! Come, I say! I am risking my life—and *you* are risking yours!... Come with me, Jerome Fandor!"

As pale as she, pale and shuddering, Fandor decided to obey, and moving like one in a trance, like a sleepwalker, he started to leave the Cemetery. Who was the woman? What did she want? Where was she taking him? He had ceased to ask an answer to these questions. As if drawn by a magnet, passively he followed his guide, who, crossing the Cemetery, hurried to the gate.

"Not a word if you value your life!" she reiterated by way of final warning. At the gate of the graveyard a motorcar stood waiting. The chauffeur had left his box, and was holding his hands on the radiator to warm them. Turning round, the man gave a start of alarm, and with an oath, pointed his revolver at

Fandor's head. Did he mean to attack the journalist? Had the woman enticed him here that her accomplice might help her to master him?

"Say nothing!" she cried imperiously. "This only concerns the Master. It is I must hand over this young man to him!"

Then, as the chauffeur still hesitated, she gave the order:

"Drive on!... To the house... Don't stop for the octroi!"

Thereupon, amazed, bewildered, still doubtful if he was wise in submitting so tamely, Fandor took his seat in the car. The woman followed, and the door was banged to behind her. Next instant the vehicle was off full speed ahead.

But Fandor had by this time recovered some degree of coolness. Now he too could speak, could whisper a question, could demand an answer of the enigmatic creature who seemed to be carrying him off by main force. He opened his lips, but no sound left them. On his arm he felt the touch of his companion's gloved hand, while her flashing eye dictated the same behest of silence as before.

"Oh! this is foolishness!" thought the young man. "Here in this closed carriage none could hear a word I say." He was on the point of disregarding the order and speaking when, taking a card from her handbag, the unknown, with trembling fingers, traced a line which she held out for him to read:

"Not a word yet!... At my house, you shall know all!... There is a microphone under the seat. The chauffeur would hear us... Pity! have pity... in the name of the man we must save..."

And Fandor held his peace. The words he had just read, those words that spoke of saving life left him panting with a wild hope.

"The man we must save." Ah! that was Juve surely? His beloved Juve? For a moment he sat incapable of thought, unable to believe, unable even to doubt! His brain reeled, but a swift revulsion of feeling brought him to a stand. Was it conceivable he should let himself be carried off in this fashion by he knew not whom? This woman, who talked to him of saving *someone's* life, this mysterious being who called him by his name, who seemed to know his secrets, was she, could she be Lady

Beltham?

Jerome Fandor took, snatched rather, the card from his companion's hand. In his firm, determined handwriting he now wrote:

"I wish to know the truth? Who are you?"

But the unknown only shrugged, refusing to take the proffered pencil.

"Whose life are we going to save?" Fandor wrote once more. But again no answer was vouchsafed. Indeed the provoking creature barely suffered her eyes to glance a moment at the words he had traced.

Yet at last he forced her to break her strange silence. Tearing the paper by the nervous vigor with which he wielded his pencil, Fandor wrote, playing a last desperate stake:

"I know you! Confess! You are Lady Beltham!" But there by his side, no longer heeding him, no longer threatening him with her harmless weapon, the woman had closed her eyes.

"I'm going mad! It's all a dream, a nightmare!" thought the young man. "To stay longer in the car is sheer insanity! It is a trap they are drawing me into... I ought to leap out surely..."

But he did not move! He felt it was entirely within his power to escape. Nothing could be easier. And this very knowledge in some sort constrained him to remain where he was. Still traveling at top speed, the car was now nearing Paris. It traversed the Bois de Boulogne, shot like a bombshell, before the astonished eyes of the octroi officers in charge, through the Auteuil barrier, without a thought of stopping for the customary declaration of petrol, then turned in the direction of the Rue Michel-Ange.

Surely it could not be to the house to which he had paid his nocturnal visit that Fandor was being driven. Surely it was not possible the occupants of this mysterious abode could have the effrontery to return after the investigations he had attempted there. His throat parched with agonized suspense, the journalist nevertheless realized that the car was actually making in that direction. But, in that case, it was to Fantômas' house they were taking him!

Again he tore the card from his companion's hand, and

wrote, shaking with ill-suppressed fury:

"Whom are we going to save? Is it Juve?... Who are you? Mme. Rosemonde? Answer me! I insist!"

And at last, the car already slowing down and on the point of stopping at the door of No. 106, Fandor felt that the strange woman sitting beside him was about to break her obstinate silence. He felt her tremble, he saw her hand seize the pencil. He could guess the doubt, the hesitation, the terror that filled her mind.

Finally she wrote—but the words told nothing, served but to multiply his perplexities:

"We are going to save an innocent man. I am naught but an unhappy woman, and a compassionate jailer!"

*   *   *   *   *

Nor was this the end of the nightmare—for a veritable nightmare it seemed to Fandor, this grim, fantastic adventure. Now the brakes were applied and the car slowed down, then drawing up to the curb, came to a standstill before the door of the building that recalled to the journalist's memory such tragic happenings. The car door opened and the woman sprang lightly to the ground.

"Shall I come in with Madam?" asked the chauffeur, casting a look at the young man that spoke eloquently of his feelings.

"No!" replied the unknown curtly. Her eyes gleamed brighter than ever as they threw a burning glance at her companion, while she explained to the man:

"There is no need!... The gentleman understands."

Understands what? That he must obey? So many thoughts jostled each other in Fandor's head, so many contradictory facts clamored for belief simultaneously that the young man found not a moment for reflection. This woman—Lady Beltham, he felt convinced—appeared to fear her own servant. Could the man be charged with her surveillance? Was it to rid herself of his presence she had declared that her companion "understood"? Was it said to convince the man he would make no attempt to escape. Instinctively the journalist intervened, to say in a tone of perfect confidence: "Well, Madam, shall we go upstairs?"

"Yes!"—and his companion led the way. Quickly crossing the entrance hall, she reached the lift and stepped in.

"Are you coming, sir?"

"Certainly,"—and on the way they spoke only of ordinary, indifferent topics of the day. Any other occupant of the house overhearing them would never have suspected the grim secrets that lay behind, the wild thoughts that agitated their minds. But all the while the journalist was thinking to himself:

"Madame Rosemonde! It is Madame Rosemonde!… And Lady Beltham at the same time!… And He, He, Fantômas must be up there!… Is she going to deliver me up into his hands?… *Or*, is it he she proposes to betray?"

Glancing at his companion, he saw she was deadly pale, that she seemed on the verge of fainting, and:

"Courage!" he whispered. But instantly her eyes flashed, she was herself again, as she said:

"Fandor! Not a word! Take pity on me!… I will not have him kill you!… Is he upstairs yonder?… I do not know… Oh! you understand? You understand?"

Her words, her voice betrayed the extremity of her terror, but they had a not less startling effect on her auditor.

To whom was the woman alluding? To Him? To Fantômas? He was not sure. He wanted to know for certain.

"Madam," urged the journalist, "do you not know that it is your duty…?"

"My duty is to save whom I can!… My duty is not to betray any one whatsoever…"

"Madam, Juve…"

"Come with me! But, for God's sake, do not speak!… He may hear!… He may come!… You would ruin both of us!… For me, no matter! *I* count for nothing!…"

As the lift, with a slight shock, came to a stop, Fandor caught a look from his companion, a dumb prayer, that once more claimed his silence. Could he fail to grant her desperate appeal? He reflected, his thoughts still whirling wildly:

"Lady Beltham wants to help me save Juve's life!... She calls herself a jailer... Am I not bound to agree to what she proposes with such tactful vagueness?... Only let her give my friend back to me, and I renounce any idea of searching the premises, of hunting out Fantômas there... For that is what terrifies her— the notion of seeing me fly at her lover's throat, that is what makes her shudder..."

There his reflections stopped dead. So deeply was he absorbed by what ensued he could look on without an attempt to comprehend the meaning of the things he saw. Each succeeding second was so weighted with horror he had no time to think... Mme. Rosemonde? but surely it was Lady Beltham really, for all the cunning tricks of makeup that rendered her unrecognizable—had inserted a key in the lock of the flat. The door opened noiselessly, and: "Come!" she invited the journalist in another stealthy whisper. He could feel her cold, trembling and fall on his arm, and unresisting, he followed his guide into the vestibule.

A door, another door, a corridor... Then with a start the young man saw where he was—in the same working room he had visited when playing the part of a house-servant, in the room separated from the salon by the hollow partition that had so stirred his curiosity. Was he about to solve the mystery of the hiding place? Was it veritably Juve, his best friend, he was going to set free? He hoped so with all his heart and soul.

His companion, meantime, was tiptoeing towards the partition, and with pointing finger drew Fandor's attention to a projection on a molding.

"Push there!" she directed in a nearly inaudible whisper. "I am not strong enough."

The words were barely spoken before Fandor was doing as she bade him. The next few seconds seemed an eternity! But presently he heard a click, the sound of cogs and pinions working followed, and suddenly the panel yielded.

"Ju..." the young man began. But the name that had instinctively sprung to his lips hung uncompleted. The panel, pushed right back, had revealed a narrow cell, a sort of dark cupboard, and in this, pinioned, gagged, half dead, a man lay huddled.

But it was not Juve! It was an unknown stranger…

"Who? Who is it?" panted the journalist. He guessed, rather than heard the answer:

"Georges Merandol!… A hostage!… A poor madman! Save him!… Take him away with you…"

"But Juve?… What of Juve?"

"I do not know where Juve is!"

"A falsehood!"

"I am saving those I can! Kill me if you don't believe me! Kill me! Oh! it would be sweet to die!"

The woman was tottering, ready to fall, so deathly pale that Fandor was filled with a sudden pity for the unhappy creature. But, distraught and desperate, he made a last agonized appeal.

"Lady Beltham, for pity's sake," he besought her, "save Juve! You *cannot* let him be murdered…"

Yet, for all her weakness, what a force of will the woman possessed. She regained mastery of herself, a new flame of energy flashing in her burning eyes:

"Jerome Fandor," she cried proudly, "if you see in me Lady Beltham, you cannot but know this, that Lady Beltham is incapable of cowardice or falsehood!… Jerome Fandor, I give you my oath I do not know where Juve is… If I did, I would give my life to have him spared…"

And then, pointing to the poor lunatic, who seemed to understand nothing of the terrible scene enacting before his eyes, she added in despairing tones:

"Go! Go, I say! Save this unhappy creature! He too is an innocent victim! Will you abandon him to his fate?"

The burning words stirred Jerome Fandor to the bottom of his soul. He saw where his duty lay, and bowing low:

"You are right, Madam!" he declared. "I will save him!"

He stooped and in his strong arms lifted the madman, who offered no resistance. Then he made for the door, ready to quit this ill-omened room, Lady Beltham leading the way.

15. Suspicions

Such is the tragic intensity of some conversations they seem to concentrate in themselves all conceivable horror, leaving the interlocutors breathless, bewildered, sorely wounded. The words Jerome Fandor had exchanged with Lady Beltham—it was indeed that great lady; implicitly she had herself admitted it—were of so grave, so weighty an import that the journalist felt himself for the moment incapable of breaking the heavy silence that had fallen between him and the baffling creature who was the Arch-Criminal's wife. He was convinced she was speaking only the truth. A despairing, sorrowful sincerity sounded in her voice; all doubt was at an end.

"She loves Fantômas!" he kept telling himself. "She loves him, but she abominates his crimes. That is why, at the risk of her life, she lets me save this unfortunate young man... That is why she told me no falsehood when she declared she knew nothing of Juve's whereabouts." But this ignorance of hers plunged the young man in the depths of despair, extinguishing the last gleam of hope in his mind. Fondly he had hoped to find Juve, thanks to this very woman, convinced that Lady Beltham could never by her silence become an accomplice in the police officer's murder. And lo! she knew nothing! Distrusting his mistress's good faith, Fantômas had kept from her the secret of his crimes!

Carrying the madman in his arms, Fandor moved heavily to the door. He was thinking:

"A few more moments and I shall be leaving this house, and I shall have no notion what to do or what to think... Doubtless Lady Beltham will never cross my path again—and I have gathered no clue from her! And I *can* gather none! She knows nothing, can tell me nothing."

Heedless of the risks he was still running perhaps, Jerome

Fandor in these moments of disappointment, was lost in thought. Doubtless he was filled with delight at the idea of robbing the Master of one of his victims. No doubt he was overjoyed at the rescue of Georges Merandol. But it was Juve he loved—and Juve, the evidence all pointed that way, Juve was lost!

"This way!" came in a low voice from Lady Beltham. She had her hand on the handle of the room door, and was going to show her companion the way through the flat to the staircase that would be his means of escape... Her task was ended. Everything was done and completed.

"This way!... Listen!"—and slowly she opened the door. Plainly enough a fresh access of panic fear had seized her. Did she foresee some new danger? Slowly, softly her hand turned the knob, and the door fell open—to reveal an appalling, a blood-curdling vision.

Outside the door, one glance showed Fandor, motionless, with folded arms, grim and terrible, a figure—waiting for him. Instantly he knew it, its name of horror rang in his ears.

The face hidden under the black hood, the body swathed in the black, close-fitting suit of tights, the ill-omened uniform of his crimes that made recognition impossible, shod and gloved in black, it was Fantômas who stood there!

But already the wretch had abandoned his pose of grim immobility. At the sight Lady Beltham uttered a scream of terror, an inarticulate cry for mercy, and tried to rush back into the room.

She had not taken one step before Fantômas was upon her, a mocking laugh on his lips.

"You!" he vociferated. "You betray me!"—and he raised his arm to strike. The blow fell, and stunned and dizzy, the unhappy woman reeled, then with a hoarse cry, a choking sob, crashed to the floor.

But Fandor was ready for the fray. The same instant he had caught sight of his enemy and realized he was here and now to face the dread Lord of Terror, a tide of exultation, a flood of proud defiance sent the hot blood coursing through Jerome

Fandor's veins. To fight the Torturer! To come to grips with the Enemy of Mankind! To fall beneath his blows, or perhaps to master him! What better could the gallant young man wish for? Was it not the consummation, above all else, he had prayed for—a combat on equal terms, where each would be fighting for his life?

"Between us two, Fantômas!" yelled the journalist—and, leaping back, deposited the madman he carried in an armchair. Next instant, he had returned, and crouching for a spring, every muscle taut, he was ready to hurl himself at the head of the villain, the man who had forfeited all claim to be called a man.

Jerome Fandor indeed was unarmed, while Fantômas, on his side, was bound to have some weapon on him, dagger or life-preserver, implements of crime that kill without a sound. But may not the gallantry of the one side equalize the chances of victory in a battle where the other combatant has but malice and cowardice to help him?

"Between us two, Fantômas!" Fandor reiterated his defiance. He had only his fists, his bare hands… But his fists might strike down the Monster! His fingers might grip the scoundrel's throat! He might be killed? Yes! no doubt of that! But he would kill his adversary before he died! If, next day, some police raid should discover in the room two corpses tightly enlaced in the ferocious grip of their death agony, would it not still be a victory for the intrepid journalist?

"Between us two, Fantômas!"—and Fandor was making to spring at the other's throat, when he saw the brigand, cooler, more confident than ever, step back a pace.

"You are mad, Fandor!" he mocked.

Then, he lifted his hand, and with the swift, unhesitating action of a man who feels absolutely master of himself, he pressed an electric button.

With a yell of fury, a scream of agony, Fandor fell stunned to the ground, his forehead cut open, bleeding from a deep wound. Yet again, this foul trick played by the Arch-Criminal bore witness how the scoundrel, here as everywhere, held himself ready to defend himself against all possible opponents.

The switch he had opened actuated the catch of a terrible mechanism, a fearful engine of destruction. Moved by a powerful spring, a veritable catapult, the heavy wooden bar forming the back of the great bench that was part of the furniture of the salon, pivoting on one extremity, had swept the whole room at the height of a man's head, and this with such tremendous force no obstacle could withstand it. Keeping close to the wall, Fantômas of course had not been struck, while Fandor, where he stood ready to make his spring, received the terrific blow full in the face. All this without a sound—save the brief cry that had escaped the victim, a cry of pain and rage and anguish. Not a sound! This catapult of sorts, this devastating bar of timber, had done its fell work silently and well.

In the room Lady Beltham was stretched lifeless on the floor, while Fandor lay motionless, a trickle of blood that flowed slowly from the wound in his forehead staining the light-colored carpet red.

"So fall those who defy me!" sneered Fantômas. "Juve first! Fandor next! Oh! I am master of the world!"

Then he gave a start. Fandor's eyes were fixed on him, aflame with hate and menace, all the poor remains of life left in him concentrated in their gaze.

"What now?" cried Fantômas, "the skull fractured, and he is still alive? Well, the worse for him! I never strike twice; another shall be his executioner."

The wretch took a step forward to the armchair where with staring eyes and white face, yet seeming hardly to understand what was happening, lay Georges Merandol, and seizing him by the shoulders, dragged him from the room. With a monstrous callousness, heedless of Lady Beltham who still lay in a dead faint, no less heedless of Fandor, who seemed dying, he went out, carrying the lunatic with him. What, indeed, had he to fear? Was it not obvious the journalist was incapable of moving a limb, of uttering a single word?

Nevertheless the young man was conscious of his surroundings. Strange to say—a fact of which Science affords an explanation—Jerome Fandor felt little pain at that moment. Even his mind was perfectly clear. But his body was for the time being completely paralyzed—to his hideous anguish. To speak one word, to make one movement, was a sheer impossibility. His brain was unclouded, but his will had lost all command of his muscles. And what a storm of impotent fury raged in his breast!

"Captured! Fantômas' prisoner!" he thought, his breath coming in quick gasps. "Yet another victory for the villain! Oh, to die! to die!"

In the torment of his mental suffering he called for death as the sole and only solace! Yet presently, he found his weakness was not increasing. On the contrary, little by little, slowly, progressively, life seemed to reanimate his body. The blood ran freely in his veins. The torpor of his senses diminished. He felt he would soon regain the power to move.

"Stunned! the blow stunned me!" he reflected. "Yes! I know, the blow must have produced some sort of congestion of the brain… But wounds in the head that do not kill on the spot rarely prove fatal afterwards. The congestion is growing less… Very soon I shall be able to get up…"—and, despite his extreme weakness, he found himself quivering with newborn hope. If only Fantômas should put off his return a few seconds longer, the fight would begin again.

"Oh! that I could move!" he sighed, "that I might drag myself as far as the door… When he comes back, I will throw myself upon him… He will not shake off my death grip!"

But he still lay incapable of the slightest movement—truly a hideous torture, an agony beyond belief! He was there, thinking, reasoning, his soul aflame for action, while the body, the network of the muscles, obstinately refused to obey the mandate of his will.

"I will… I will get up!" he said to himself with desperate iteration, but legs and loins and arms still remained inert. And time was passing fast! And Fantômas would surely soon come back to the room where two of his victims lay…

"I will… I will get up!" Fandor told himself peremptorily. With a superhuman effort that overpassed the extremest bounds of mortal energy, he forced his numbed limbs to obey him.

Jerome Fandor rose to his knees on the floor, almost stood up, was all but on his feet...

Too late! A step drew near. Fantômas had come back. He faced his victim. He fell upon him like a wild beast ravening for the prey it means to annihilate...

*   *   *   *   *

Whatever Fandor's gallantry at this terrible crisis, whatever the fury that possessed him, it was evident the combat could not last more than a second or two.

The dastardly Lord of Terror had only to give a push and the journalist must fall again, so weak that he was incapable of anything but the faintest resistance. At this, the mocking, insulting laugh of his enemy came again:

"What! We still want to show fight, Jerome Fandor? Really you don't deserve the merciful death I am arranging for you!"

For the moment Fandor felt himself able to retort. The rage that boiled within him seemed to give him back the power to speak. His fury had driven away the dreadful torpor his wound had caused. But he clenched his teeth, he forced himself to silence.

"To let Fantômas gloat over my defeat, to show him I hear his gibes, that I am conscious of his victory, to condescend to address him! No! Never will I do that!"—and his silence, scornful and complete, was the deadliest insult to his foe. What indeed *could* he do? Did not his fate depend simply and solely on the caprice of the Torturer? Was he in a state to battle with him? Was he not as weak as a child?

"Jerome Fandor, you refuse to answer me?" demanded Fantômas. "Yet I think you hear what I say... Be it so! You are within your rights... Say nothing, if you choose. I respect every caprice of a dying man!"—and again the brigand broke into an ugly laugh. Then, bending, a hideous figure black-hooded and black clad, over the unhappy man he had just felled to the ground, he seized him by the shoulders and quietly, but with herculean strength, dragged him noiselessly from the room over the carpeted floors.

"You have nothing to complain of!" he began again in jeering tones. "Fantômas in person is arbiter of your fate. It is an honor you should be proud of… There, look! There is the place where you are to die…"

Fandor bit his lips hard to stifle a cry of horror. The "place" was a sort of narrow closet, the very look of which was terrifying. Floor, walls, ceiling, door, every part was covered with a lining of heavy, quilted padding, thick enough to drown the most heart-rending screams, the most agonized appeals for mercy. A closet? No! The chamber merited another, a more sinister name. It was a madman's cell, the prison where maniacs are confined, who, in their fits of fury, are liable to injure themselves by dashing against the walls, if these, and floor and even ceiling, are not thus protected.

"You will find this a first-rate place to die in!" scoffed Fantômas. "Besides, I have had a happy thought you will surely appreciate. You are greatly interested in Georges Merandol, are you not? You must be, seeing you want to save him. Very well, I am going to shut you in along with him… Oh! a charming youth!… Suffers from the mania of persecution, for one thing!… D'you see? I'm leaving a dagger within his reach… Oh! and that's not all. He is child enough still to like playing with fire. Very dangerous of course! But there, I don't want to disappoint your friend… See here, Fandor, I place here a lighted lamp. If it amuses him to set on fire the tow of the padding he can easily gratify his whim. Ah, ha!"—and once more Fantômas broke into the grim chuckle with which it was his habit to mock his dying victims. Then he resumed:

"As for you, of course I am going to tie you up. I don't choose you should take a fancy to balk the poor lad's caprices. No! You must be rendered incapable of making the slightest movement. By God! it's on the cards he may roast you alive… or else stab you—just for fun. There are always these little risks to run… Anyway, you won't be long in knowing if they materialize… In three hour's time I shall be back. If you are still alive, I shall think about getting rid of you some other way. For instance,

I have a very fierce mastiff I'm training to eat human flesh…
Well, we shall see… Good night, Fandor! Till we meet—or is it
farewell forever?… Now I'm going to settle accounts with Lady
Beltham…"

With the same jeering laugh, the wretch stepped back to
leave the death chamber. As the door was closing, Fandor
shouted after him:

"Goodbye, Fantômas! But remember this: you are beaten all
the same! I know it!"

It was a last defiance, that should trouble the scoundrel's
complacency a little, a pinprick to his self-confidence to make
him know what fear was. But as like as not he had not even
heard the words.

Pinioned tightly as he now was, Fandor managed, with a
twist of the body, to turn partly round on the padded floor.
For certain his fate was sealed; for certain he was going to die
a fearful death. Was he to perish by a dagger thrust, or by fire?
Or was he to be devoured alive by the savage dog Fantômas had
spoken of?

He looked about him for the madman, about whose mental
condition he entertained no illusions. Afflicted with the mania
of persecution, no doubt wildly excited by the tragic scenes he
had witnessed, he would surely throw himself upon his fellow
prisoner and murder him.

"A hideous fate, but there is no escaping it," thought the journalist. "What use then trying to avoid it?"—and he scrutinized
the four corners of the darkling chamber in search of Georges
Merandol. The madman was free to move and had now with-
drawn into one corner of the cell. Crouching with his back to
the wall, he was watching the journalist curiously. The eyes of
the two, the lunatic and the sane man, met in a questioning
glance.

"Poor boy!" Fandor was thinking meantime. "If he sets the
place on fire, he will be burned to death himself. Indeed, that
is what Fantômas most likely wants… Yes! but if I put out the
lamp, a fool could see we shall be in the dark. Now, I would
rather not be left in the dark with this madman,"—and next

moment, a striking proof of his calm self-possession, he added:

"Anyway, there's another question calls for answer—before considering if I *ought* to extinguish the light, it would be well to know if I *can*."

But Fandor was not the man to hesitate for long. His strength was returning. Certainly his head was still painful, but he felt new life circulating through his veins.

"It is my duty to put it out," he told himself. "After all, Fantômas has no motive for killing this poor madman. Besides, if the boy does fire the place, he will roast with me. Anything rather than that! So much the worse, if he stabs me with the dagger—or so much the better! It strikes me as more desirable than providing a meal for a savage dog!"

Encouraged by this reflection, Fandor gave another twist of the body and tried to wriggle towards the lamp burning on the floor.

"I upset it," he calculated. "Then I roll on top of it… Naturally I burn myself, but I put it out…"

But hardly had he begun to move when Georges Merandol, the madman, gave a jump.

"What are you after?" he demanded.

"Hang it all!" thought Fandor, "that's woke the fellow up!… Provoking!…"

"Nothing!" he declared. "I'm only shifting my place."

"What for?"

"Oh! but he's mighty inquisitive!" the journalist thought again, and added:

"I'm not very comfortable, you know."

Then, with another effort, he drew near the lamp. "You're going to set things on fire," said the madman.

"No! I'm trying to prevent it," answered the journalist.

"Who are you?" questioned the madman.

"Oh! the deuce!" growled the journalist to himself. "I have always heard say that, when madmen once start talking to one, a crisis of acute mania is imminent. A charming prospect truly!"—and he made no reply. But with the obstinacy that is characteristic of the insane, Georges Merandol at once repeated his question: "Who are you?"

"One of your friends."

"My friends?"

"Why, certainly!"

"I don't believe you."

"You are wrong…"

Fandor durst not stir any more. Courageous as he was, well prepared to die as he felt, he could not but try to postpone the fatal moment when the madman should attack him.

"Upon my word," he thought, "this poor devil is a bit trying. He's going to tell me now I am one of his enemies—and fly at me. By the Lord! he's actually got his eyes on the dagger!"—and he repeated earnestly:

"I am one of your friends."

"No! I have no friends. You are an accomplice of Fantômas… That man is really Fantômas, is he not?"

"Undoubtedly… But I am not an accomplice of his."

"Then why are you in his house?"

"To find Juve…"

"Juve? Who is he?"

"Another of your friends… But never trouble your head about that… See here, suppose we get to sleep, eh?… Suppose you blow out the lamp?"

"I'm not sleepy."

"But *I* am…"

"You cannot want to sleep, any more than I do… You understood what Fantômas said?"

At this, Fandor could not help looking curiously at his companion. He was ignorant of the fact that madmen often have lucid intervals, during which their reason works almost normally. All the same, he was struck by the cruel irony implied in the question put to him. A lunatic was asking him if he had understood the threats directed against himself.

"I understood perfectly well!" he declared.

"You gathered then that the villain thought I should kill you?"

"Hmm! Yes!… In fact… My word! what an ugly turn the

conversation is taking!" the journalist reflected. "If the fellow goes on exciting himself like this, things won't be long coming to a head…"

But, calmly and quietly, Georges Merandol went on:

"Fantômas believed I should set fire to the place with that lamp."

"No, no! nothing of the kind!"

"Yes, he did!… Or that I should stab you with that dagger…"

"Pooh! pooh! You're not so bad as that!… Besides, I'm one of your friends."

"You are one of his accomplices…"

"Never in this world! Haven't I already told you the contrary… If I was his accomplice, why should he wish you to… hmm! hmm!… to… to… in fact, want me to die?"

"I don't know…"

"You must see…"

"Perhaps you have betrayed him?"

"Oh! come, come! Don't insult me, my dear fellow…"—and Fandor tried to laugh. All the time he was thinking of the possibility of a sudden attack of furious mania. He blamed himself for putting off the fatal moment, but instinctively he did what he could to quiet the madman with soothing speeches.

"Accomplice or not," resumed the latter, "you ought to kill him."

"Kill whom?…"

"Why, Fantômas!"

"If only I could!"

"One can always kill one's enemies…"

Again Fandor found no answer to make. He was thinking:

"The deuce! the deuce! Now we're in for it!"

"Yes! One can kill one's enemies," repeated the madman. "I am weak, but *you,* you are strong…"

"That's plain enough. But I am bound hand and foot… Ah! don't you touch that…"

Georges Merandol had stooped and picked up the dagger Fantômas had left. He was feeling the point and cutting edge with an absorbed look…

"You are afraid?" he asked.

"Not I!… Only…"

"Listen! I want to tell you something."

"Well, say on."

"I am not mad any longer!"

"Oh!… But you've never been mad, come!"

Fandor felt a cold sweat beading his forehead. Every madman, he knew, professes he is not mad; every one of them says so, will have it so… And that is just the most convincing proof of incurable insanity. Patients suffering only some temporary derangement of intellect admit the fact. Those beyond all possible cure invariably deny it!

"If I contradict him," the young man reflected, that means he'll go raving mad straight away."

"You are mistaken!" resumed Georges Merandol. "For my part, I believe I *have* been mad! Yes, I have a vague recollection of being insane, and that is why I am afraid to act for myself…"

"To act for yourself?"

"Yes, to take the dagger and stab Fantômas, when he comes in."

"So you think to…"

"I will kill you too—if you are his accomplice…"

"But I am not… I am his victim…"

"If only I could believe that!… See here, listen. When he kidnapped me… Oh, yes! I know he kidnapped me! The woman who acted as my jailer told me so…"

"God's truth! you surprise me! Come, tell me more!… This woman—she was called…?"

"Lady Beltham, I think… It was she cured me. Yes! It was she! When they brought me here, I had a fearful attack of fury—and she cried… I saw her crying… That was the first gleam of reason, of sanity, I had."

"The first gleam of sanity?"

"Listen, I tell you… Afterwards I felt better… In secret, she nursed me. I had ice on my head… The attack had brought my complaint to a head… She used to tell me to *hope,* one day you will be rescued! She could not open my prison; she was not strong enough… But she wanted to get help to set me free…"

"Whose help?… Speak out…"

"No! If you are an accomplice of Fantômas', I don't want to let you know the name of the man she wished to help in my rescue… Presently, when the monster comes back, you would tell him, to make him spare your life.

"But, I swear I am not… Now hear me! I am called Fandor, Jerome Fandor!… Lady Beltham must have…"

"Fandor! You?… It was you?…"—and the journalist was to have the surprise of his life. With one bound Georges Merandol was by his side. "Fandor! You are Fandor? Why, it was you Lady Beltham wanted to call upon for help! It was you who were to save me…"

Then, on his knees beside his companion, the lunatic—was he still insane, the poor boy?—went on:

"Give me proof you are not telling a lie!"

"Hmm! not easy that!… But yes! it is! Read the name on my watchcase. It is in my pocket. Take it and look!"

"Fandor!… Fandor!… You are Fandor… Wait a moment! I'm going to set you free… I… I… Oh, God! my head, my head!… I…"

It was a moment at once of keen disappointment and of agonizing suspense for Fandor! Under the stress of sudden joy, Georges Merandol was staggering, tottering on his feet. He had not the strength yet, poor boy, to bear such a shock. No doubt he was recovering his reason, but it was still weak and ill-balanced. Repeatedly, indeed, he had heard Fantômas address Fandor by his name, yet he had only grasped the meaning of that name when Fandor himself uttered it.

"Great God Almighty!" swore the journalist in spite of himself. "It was all going so well!"

He had good reason to be bitterly chagrined. All of a sudden Georges Merandol had sunk on the padded floor, prostrated by a violent fit of giddiness.

"And the lamp!" screamed Fandor. As he fell, the poor fellow had upset it. Already the flame was licking the padding of the walls, which was catching alight. Oh! the hideous ill-luck of it—the fire breaking out at the very moment Fandor was perhaps going to be saved by the madman or in any case have his bonds cut.

"Curses on it!" he vociferated anew. "The poor devil's body stops me, so that I cannot drag myself so far." And so it was; half-paralyzed by his bonds, Fandor found it impossible to roll to where the fire was starting. Georges Merandol's body blocked the way.

"Am I to perish then like a rat in a trap? No, never!"—and he strained every muscle, stiffening all his body, in a frantic effort to break the cords that held him. Alas! did he really suppose it possible for any man to burst free when Fantômas had tied the knots?

Already clouds of acrid smoke began to fill the narrow chamber, while the flames, getting a ready hold on the padding, were running along the walls in rivulets of fire.

"Lost! Done for!" groaned the young man, writhing and fighting against his bonds. Then he caught the sound of a mocking voice outside the door, shouting a last insult:

"Goodbye, Fandor!… I can hear the roaring of the flames!… Goodbye! Oh! I have no fear of your escaping! I have taken my precautions. In the walls are fixed iron bars. You are in a cage impossible to break out of… And I have soaked all the rooms with gasoline. The whole building will be burned to the ground!… Goodbye!… Goodbye forever!"

"Fantômas!" yelled Fandor, though he was already choking.

But the flames were making headway. Suddenly they reached Georges Merandol's body, and the pain roused him from his swoon.

"Fire! fire!" he screamed, springing to his feet.

"Fire it is!" Fandor shouted back… "Quick, cut me free!"

But the unhappy lad did not so much as hear him. His face distorted with terror, he was now rolling on the floor, trying to smother the flames that were beginning to burn his clothes…

…And then it was that Fandor conceived the heroic notion that was to set him free, suffer him at least to meet his doom standing and look death in the face.

Crawling to the blaze, he plunged his arms in the stream of fire. What mattered the pain? With his flesh, the ropes that held him prisoner were burned.

"Free!" he cried exultantly, tearing off the cords now reduced to ashes… "Free!"—and he sprang forward and hurled himself against the walls, a madman too in his frenzy, furiously shouldering the burning panels that now showed in places the solid iron bars they had hitherto concealed, bars that indeed formed a horrible cage, wherein Fandor and Georges Merandol were to be burned alive—as everything went to show.

*   *   *   *   *

"Don't move, my dear man! No! Don't try to sit up!… You are in the Boucicault Hospital… There is nothing to be afraid of! You are not even in danger!… Now, go to sleep!"

But Fandor only struggled the harder.

"Go to sleep!" repeated the same kindly voice. "If you are in great pain, we will give you an injection… Come, be good!… Good heavens! don't tear off the bandage on your forehead!"

And this time Fandor kept perfectly quiet and good—as still as a graven image! At that moment the memory of late events had come back to him. He had suddenly recovered contact with life, after an interval of dreamy semiconsciousness due no doubt to some drug administered by the doctors.

"Yes! yes!" he told himself. "I threw myself against the door… I thought it was locked, and it was not!… It was Lady Beltham, without a doubt, who found means to turn the key and so let me free."

Then he shuddered where he lay in his bed. Undaunted in face of danger, he felt like to faint at the bare recollection of those awful minutes. Outside this door, which he had found so miraculously unfastened, he beheld a veritable sea of fire. Fantômas had indeed told the truth! Big cans filled with gasoline stood there, set alight by the flames carried thither by the draft. Yes! the villain was very sure nobody could escape from the flat he himself was leaving in frantic haste.

In spite of everything, the journalist broke into a smile.

He was safe at any rate! And Georges Merandol was safe too!
With the greatest clearness he recalled the tragic moments he
had just passed, seemed to be living them again. He had leapt
back, seized the youth in his arms; then, insane himself—for
his courage was that of a madman—he had plunged into the
flames, dashed through them, darting across the apartments,
reaching the stairs, where he fell staggering into the arms of
one of those gallant lifesavers, the Paris firemen. "But after that,
by God! I don't know what became of me," thought the sick
man... "It got a bit *too* hot, I suppose—and I must have lost
my coolness!"—and he grinned at his little joke. Surely a well
plucked one, this Jerome Fandor, who just arrived in hospital
after a series of the most abominable adventures, was still able
to laugh at his own play upon words!

Presently he raised himself in bed a little more. "All the
same," he muttered, "I'm in a fine state, no doubt about that!"

"Get back again under the bedclothes," ordered a voice...
"You're not in excessive pain, are you?"—and in reply the
patient uttered an inarticulate groan, that might mean whatever you chose; then lay down again with perfect docility.

"In a fine state," he went on to himself. "My forehead cut
open; that accounts for the bandage round my head... My arms
are burned; that's why they're all swathed in wrappings like
this!... And I'm bound to have a few little burns and bruises
here and there besides... It hurts like the devil when I move."

All the same Jerome Fandor was no mollycoddle. If he consented to stay still, it was only because he did not very well see
what better he could do for the moment than lie quiet and let
himself be nursed. His brain was clear enough, no doubt, but
his ideas were not marshaled as yet in perfect order.

"Suppose I run over what I have gathered?" he said to
himself—and calmly and quietly he explored his recollections:

"Georges Merandol is saved—that is beyond a doubt... Lady
Beltham, for her part, must have opened my cage—without
daring to let it be seen, for Fantômas would likely be following
close at her heels... One for her!... But Juve? what of Juve?" As
life revived within him his anguished suspense grew more and

more intense. What mattered his own personal safety? His one thought was to find Juve and rescue him from the Monster's clutches, and with him, it was quite possible, Georges Merandol's father as well.

"And I am here, lying on my back, forbidden to stir, treated like a sick child... I will not have it!"—and he partly raised himself again. But suddenly a voice—he could not see the speaker for the bandage that covered his eyes—repeated:

"Come, now, you're not to move!"

"The tyrant!" thought Fandor rebelliously. "But I've got to obey,"—and he lay down once more.

"Yes!" he went on soliloquizing, "I am out of the wood, but not so Juve. Oh! if only I knew what is happening, what Havard is doing, what..."

At that point he paused. A new notion had flashed across his mind.

"Suppose I ask to see Dupont de l'Eure? The Chief is bound to be in the know of what folks are saying..."—and he stammered out: "I should like them to send for Monsieur..."

"Hush! hush!" said the peremptory voice. "Don't excite yourself! You can't see anyone. You are under special confinement..."

"Special confinement?... Eh! what's that you say?"

"By order of the Police!..."

"The police. But, good Lord!"

This time the patient had sprung half out of bed. Sitting up, he panted:

"The police haven't arrested me, surely?"

"Listen here!" ordered the voice. "If you are not good, I shall go and tell the house surgeon..."

"Do as you please, only answer my question! I've been arrested?"

"Hmm! I don't know... I can tell you nothing!... Tomorrow, if there's no fever then, the Examining Magistrate..."

"Tomorrow? Tomorrow? No! now at once, by heavens! Let them go fetch him right away."

He heard a chair scrape on the boards and knew that someone was leaving the room. Was the nurse going to inform the "proper authority" of his demands? For the moment he kept quite still. He was thinking:

"By God! that's just the sort of thing the police *would* do! They find me in company with Georges Merandol, so they accuse me of having kidnapped him from the Asylum!... They see me rush from a house on fire, so they conclude I am an incendiary! Why, they're born fools, these people! Arguing that fashion, the Humane Society's men who haul a drowned man out of the river deserve to be clapped in jail as murderers."

Then, all of a sudden, he stopped dead. A wild idea had occurred to him:

"Was he actually, really and truly, in hospital? He could not surely have fallen into Fantômas' hands again?"—and he swore under his breath: "By God! that would be the climax!"

But his was not a nature to endure doubt for long, and the journalist had no sooner asked himself these questions than he was taking measures to answer them. The bandage was over his eyes; well, all he had to do was to take it off. Painfully, for the slightest movement of his arms hurt horribly, he unwound the dressing that encircled his head. The light dazzled his eyes, and he could see nothing, but quickly he recovered the power of vision. "We shall soon find out!" he muttered, and leaping out of bed, he crossed the room, a sort of prison cell, and looked out of window...

"Oh, yes, it is!" he exclaimed, glancing down into the courtyard below. "It is really the Boucicault... So much the better!... And my forehead? cut right open?"

There was a mirror on the wall, and he scrutinized himself in it. From temple to temple a great jagged wound disfigured his forehead. In fact, while he lay unconscious, a surgeon had had to put in several stitches.

"Bah!" said Fandor, "a mere scratch!"

He shrugged his shoulders, and added:

"If only my arms aren't any worse damaged?" For a moment or two he hesitated, but here again his habitual bravery asserted itself.

"Come, let's have a look, anyway!"—and he undid the wrappings. This time, he could hardly speak of a "mere scratch." Both arms were fearfully burnt, and the injuries, smothered in picric acid, which alleviates the pain of burns in such a marvelous way, were all swollen and inflamed.

"Oh!" cried Fandor. "But my hands are none the worse—or very little…"

Then he stopped speaking, stood a moment to listen, and with one bound leapt back into bed.

"We're going to have some fun!" he chuckled. He had caught the sound of footsteps—two people's footsteps—approaching. Before the door opened, his head was buried in his pillow, he had gathered the bedclothes about his shoulders and lay as if fast asleep.

"Well, what's all this yarn you're telling me?" came in a rough voice… "The fellow's asleep…"

"Yes! doctor, now… But…"

"Enough!… Go into the passage and stay there within hearing if he wants anything. You are all the same, you women! You go talking to the patients, and then you beg for morphia for them… The instant you've left their bedside, they drop off and sleep like the dead!…"

Next moment the door was re-closed—and Fandor was once more alone.

"So there we are!" he grinned, popping a smiling face from under the clothes. "It's my poor nurse who'll catch it… So much the worse for her, that's all! It can't be helped."

So saying, he got noiselessly out of bed. "Well, I *am* in luck's way!" he cried, as he looked round and saw, lying on a chair, a parcel wrapped in a cloth and labeled "For disinfection."

"My duds!" he opined. "No doubt the fire has played the deuce with them… Hmm! the trousers are wearable… As for the coat, *non est!* Must have been burnt! Oh, well! It's not an indispensable article, a coat."

In two twos he was dressed. Now and again a grimace had betrayed how painful the operation was, but he had completed his toilet notwithstanding.

"My collar? Hmm, collar gone west!… Hello! my boots—no

laces left! Bah! we can do without 'em!… So now, let's be off…"

He tiptoed again across the room—one of the isolation wards in a surgical block. Being on the ground floor and giving on a small courtyard laid out as a garden, it was admirably adapted to facilitate an escape.

"So," concluded Fandor, after an exploratory look round, let us thank Providence, the ruling factor in my holiday jaunts, and—make a bolt of it."

He mounted the window sill and dropped lightly into the garden. But the main difficulty was not there. The fact is, if the young man, under police arrest as he was, had not been subjected to more careful surveillance, this was simply because it had been deemed impossible for him to stand up or walk. Indeed the surgeon's mistake was perfectly natural, for they did not know the amazing reserves of energy possessed by their patient. All the same, the journalist was hardly outside before he felt everything turning round inside him and all about him!

"Oh, Lord!" he growled, "am I going to faint? No! that would be too silly, simply idiotic!… Courage! Courage, man!"—and he made a fresh appeal to his nervous energy. But, after all, it was just this giddy fit that was to serve his purpose. He was well acquainted with the general plan of the hospital buildings. He knew quite well that, to leave the premises, he must make for the gate in the Rue d'Alesia, which always stands open. He was likewise aware that it would be difficult for him to get away by this gate, at which a porter is always on guard, without attracting attention, especially in his present rig. But, as luck would have it, bewildered by his giddy condition, he turned to the left instead of to the right, so wandering away towards the block devoted to the lying-in department. For the moment, only one idea was in his head—not to faint right off, to keep a hold on himself and carry on.

He was simply following his nose, hardly conscious where he was going. Suddenly he caught sight of a side gate used for coal carts to drive in by, and made straight for it.

"Hi! You there," a voice shouted. "No way out this road!"

He answered at random: "Lord's sake! Let me pass… I live

just yonder!… It's a shortcut…"

"But it's against the rules, my man," declared a male nurse, running up.

"May be!" retorted Fandor, who felt ready to fall. "I tell you, I've just been to have my hurts dressed, but they won't let me stop… I can barely keep on my feet,"—and so evident was it he was quite exhausted that the man took pity on him.

"Well, well! Away with you!" he consented. "But be quick about it. If they saw you, I'm the one would get into trouble…"

"Thank you!" was all he could say, as he dragged himself through the gate, without even hearing the other's exclamation.

"Poor devil!" the man was saying as he looked after him pityingly.

No sooner out in the street, however, than Fandor began to feel better. He walked a few steps, then leaned against a wall to rest…

"There, there!… Pull yourself together… In a few minutes, I shall be able to walk on."

Again a voice hailed him:

"Hi! wish me to take you along? You don't look much like making headway!"

A prowling taxi pulled up at the curb. Like a good fellow, the driver, noticing the young man's exhausted look, was offering his services:

"Come on, mate! Get in! Must always help the wounded, you know…"—and Fandor climbed into the cab.

"Where am I to drive you to?" asked the chauffeur.

"Office of *La Capitale* newspaper."

"Fandor's shop, eh? Righto!… So you belong there?"

At first the journalist had not the strength to answer; he was panting for breath. But before long, sitting at his ease and feeling the fresh air blowing in his face, he began to revive. Oh! he was not going to waste his time much longer! Presently the taxi stopped at the door of the newspaper office.

"Here we are, my man," the driver announced. "But you do look awful pale! Shall I go and tell your wife? You live here?… You're caretaker, eh?"

A sumptuous automobile was standing at the curb. Fandor gazed at it as if spellbound...

"Ah!" he cried. "What a piece of luck!"

At the same moment a man was crossing the pavement, making for the car.

"Run after that gentleman!" stammered Fandor... "Stop him!... Tell him..."

The driver was off his box in an instant. The good fellow pitied his fare and asked nothing better than to be useful. In three steps he had overtaken the "gentleman" the latter had pointed to.

"If you please," he began. "It's along of a wounded comrade..."

"What say?"

"He would like to speak to you... See, there, in my cab!"

"Bless my soul! It's Fandor!"—and Dupont de l'Eure—it was no other—the Editor-in-Chief of *La Capitale,* leaving the driver standing stock-still in bewilderment, made a dart for his valued reporter.

"You, old man? And in such a state?... Why, wherever do you spring from?..."

"From the devil of a tight place, Chief!"

"And you are wounded?"

"Bah! Mere scratches... But, if *you* don't want any more of my 'copy,' I could still offer some first-rate stuff to your rival..."

"Fandor... my good old Fandor!... Why, what is wrong with you? Rest on me... Come, get out!"

"Hmm! I will directly!... But first, what news have you about Juve?"

"I know nothing of Juve!" said Dupont de l'Eure. "We thought you were with him, in hiding. Havard told me so only last night... 'Both of them must'..."

"He said that, did he?... The simpleton!... I'm just come from getting myself roasted!"

"Roasted?"

"In a fire..."

"Impossible!... And I, who was positively on my way to see a woman, injured in a fire, she too..."

"I've no monopoly, you know!" laughed Fandor. Then he asked, in spite of himself:

"A woman burned in the fire in the Rue Michel-Ange, Chief?"

"I don't know... She's a friend of mine... I heard about it by accident... And besides... see here! it was with her I wanted to find you a job as Secretary... Irene Beauchamp... She was an acquaintance of yours."

"She was an... Oh! heavens! Great heavens!"—and suddenly Fandor sprang up, as if electrified by a startling and unexpected shock of emotion.

"Irene Beauchamp!... She wanted to give me work... Oh! it is she! it is she!"

"She? Who, Fandor?"

"No need for you to know that!... Hold me up!... Quick! I'm in torment... Take me to your car... We are going to see her... now at once!... Yes, now at once!"

Fandor was under the empire of intense, feverish excitement. Scarcely needing the other's supporting arm, barely master of his actions, he was running to his Chief's sumptuous limousine...

"Quick! quick!" he kept repeating... "Oh! I don't wish to force you, but, a hundred francs for that good fellow, who drove me here... And now, away! Hurry, hurry, I say!... It is Juve, Juve we are going to save!"

"At Irene Beauchamp's?"

"Perhaps..."

"You're crazy, Fandor!"

"Not I! No, the brain-box is sound enough, sir! Come, trust me!"

So confident was the tone in which Fandor spoke that the millionaire could not resist his reporter's urgency.

"Very well then," he agreed and ordered his chauffeur to drive to Mme. Beauchamp's. Then, turning to his companion, he asked anxiously:

"But you are quite done up, my dear fellow... Shall we stop at a chemist's? Do you think a pick-me-up...?"

"Bah! mere scratches!" returned the journalist. "All the same, I wouldn't refuse…"

"What?"

"Two things… A cigar, to begin with. That's the remedy I need… And next, a revolver—and that's the medicine for somebody else!"—and Jerome Fandor gave a big laugh, seeing the scared look on his Chief's face.

16. Enemies!

Hearing Fandor's strange demand, seeing him in peals of laughter, when the minute before he seemed barely able to stand on his feet, M. Dupont de l'Eure manifestly felt a renewal of his anxiety. He well knew his reporter's high abilities, and no longer embarrassed by political intrigues since Didier Maujean's fall, he asked nothing better than to give him his entire confidence once more. Yet, all the same, he thought the journalist was pushing eccentricity a bit too far! Besides, was it not on the cards the young fellow was gone crazy?

"You want to smoke?" he questioned… "Really and truly?"

"As true as Gospel!…"

"And you demand a revolver?"

"I should much prefer to have one!"

"But we are going to see Mme. Beauchamp—one of my friends…"

"I know that…"

"Then?"

"Then, no matter. *You* are armed, sir?"

"Yes… but I cannot see…"

"Well, that only proves you are near-sighted! Let things take their course! You'll see all right directly. Your sight will improve!"—and grabbing a cigar from the case his chief handed him, Fandor relapsed into a long silence, only interrupted when the car pulled up at the door of a fine mansion in the Avenue Malakoff.

"Two words of warning, Chief," Fandor then observed.

"Speak out."

"It is indispensable—you understand, in-dis-pens-able!—that this lady should receive us… So, insist on seeing her!…"

"But I don't suppose she'll refuse."

"Very good! Now, I have excellent reasons for asking, don't

give my name when you tell them to announce us!"

"So you know her?"

"I have never seen her, Madame Beauchamp," replied Fandor shortly. "But it is possible that *she* knows *me*..."

"Still, if you..."

"Oh! Chief, don't let's waste time! I do assure you it's quite certain you'll understand in a minute..."

"So be it! Let's go then... You are able to walk?"

"I am always all right when something has got to be done!"— and the young man's voice had a ring of perfect self-confidence in it. The Editor of the *La Capitale* looked at him curiously. Then he gave a sudden start:

"Only, your costume..."

"Yes, that's true. But Irene Beauchamp herself, you told me, had just been hurt in a fire... She will excuse me..."

"You think so?"

"I am sure of it!"

Under the bewildered eye of the concierge, who stared in amazement at the young man in shirtsleeves walking arm in arm with the wealthy Senator, owner of *La Capitale,* the two entered the vestibule and reached the lift...

"First floor?" asked Fandor.

"Yes, first floor."

"Then here we are... Shall I ring?"

"Yes, do!"

Dupont de l'Eure was in a mood of childlike docility. He was too sagacious, in fact, and too keen a journalist, not to realize perfectly well that Fandor was leading him into some startling adventure. But what could it be? Having no inkling of this, he was resolved to let his subordinate act as guide in everything.

Meantime, in answer to the journalist's ring, a footman had opened the door. He too, on seeing Fandor, gave signs of lively surprise. However, recognizing Dupont de l'Eure at the same moment, he contented himself with asking in the tones of a well-trained servant:

"What names shall I give?"

"Only mine, Jean!" the Senator, a friend of the house, told

him. "But make a point of Madame's seeing us. She does not know this gentleman and I want to give her a surprise in meeting him…"

"Monsieur may depend on me… Madame, in fact, is in the small drawing room… I will show you gentlemen straight in," and a moment later the man opened a door and announced in the solemn voice customary on such occasions:

"Monsieur le Sénateur Dupont de l'Eure!"

"Oh! Come in. I am glad to see you!" said a welcoming voice. Before the fire where two logs were crackling cheerfully, at once a pretty sight and an effective addition to the heat of the stove, sat a very beautiful woman. Her fair hair, shot with gleams of pure gold, was half unbound and strayed over a white, shapely neck—a disordered toilet easily accounted for by a light surgical bandage that covered her brow. She rose quickly, holding out her hand and stepping forward to greet Dupont de l'Eure.

Then amazement nailed her to the spot. "Jerome Fandor!" she stammered.

The journalist bowed. "Madam," he said at once, "you will not think me unduly importunate, if I ask for a few minutes' talk with you,"—and as pale as she, the young man motioned Dupont de l'Eure to an armchair, adding:

"You will excuse me, Chief? Madame and I desire a few moments' private conversation together. Will you allow us to move away a step or two?"

Fandor went up to Irene Beauchamp and offered her his arm.

"May I lead you to the boudoir I see there through the half-open door?"

"No!" came the great lady's answer in a hoarse cry that was almost a groan.

"Madam, it must be!"

"But if I refuse to listen to you?"

"Madame, I shall beseech you in that case to grant my prayer in the name of him whose life you saved!"

"But you are mistaken… But it is not true!… But…"

"Madam, we have but half-a-dozen necessary words to exchange. My highest respect is due to 'Lady Beltham'... Will you dare to say that your pity is accorded only to the living, and that you forget the dying?"

"The dying?"

"Juve, Madam."

"Oh! hush! hush!"

So pale she seemed on the point of collapsing, yet refusing the support Fandor offered her, Lady Beltham—for it was indeed she—passed into the boudoir.

"What do you want of me?" she demanded, sinking on to a couch, prostrated by emotion. Fandor bent over her where she lay.

"Nothing that can hurt your conscience," he declared. "Everything your horror of certain abominations can urge you to say."

"I have done what I could!"

"You! You have saved my life. You have saved Georges Merandol's. I know that. But Fantômas..."

"I love him! Do you think I can betray him?"

"I do not ask you to!... I am not a policeman. Accomplice or not of this Torturer, it is no officer of justice stands before you."

"Still, we are enemies!"

"No, Madam! I am not the enemy of those who suffer. But I love Juve. I would rescue him from Fantômas' hands..."

"I would give my life to help you save him... I do not know where he is... if already..."

Fandor too felt himself grow pale.

"Oh, hush! it is my turn to bid *you* hush," he cried angrily. "I will not believe it!... No, no! He is alive! Something tells me so..."

"Jerome Fandor, I wish so too... But I can do nothing for him!"

"But yes! you can do everything,"—and Fandor's eyes were fixed on Lady Beltham's. "You can do everything," he repeated. "You love Fantômas. But Fantômas loves you in return. Well, I seize your person! I take you as a hostage... Let him release Juve, and I will release you... Think—I am here to propose this pact with you. Write to him. I will carry your letter to him myself... I give you my oath not to lay a trap..."

"Jerome Fandor, I have myself sworn never to second your plans..."

"Well, such an oath is not binding. It is Juve's life you can save..."

"It is another's life I am safeguarding by keeping true..."

The woman, ever mysterious, pronounced no name... Fandor, almost fainting, could only whisper the question: "Helene?"

"I do not know!"

Oh! to what grievous straits was this noble lady constrained, so dominated by the love of Fantômas that Fandor felt ready for any sacrifice rather than compromise it, expose it! The young man said nothing for a moment. Then, by a supreme and painful effort he mastered his agitation and resumed:

"Lady Beltham, I know that you keep a watch on the Cemetery of Montellon. Is it because..."—but his question remained unasked. She had broken in with an agonized whisper:

"Oh! on your honor," she besought him, "say no more. I could not speak, if you said one word more!"

She seemed to be thinking, absorbed in a bitter, painful reverie. At last she admitted:

"In the Cemetery of Montellon, yes, perhaps, there should be some indication to be discovered there as to Juve's fate. But what? what? Yes! go there, go there and search. I am already betraying secrets in telling you so much!"

Her beautiful, dreamy eyes were filling with tears. Fandor declared sternly:

"Madam, I *will* go there—and I will search... Shall I find anything?... But from now till then, you are my prisoner..."— and he called out:

"Monsieur Dupont, on your life, you must not lose sight of Madame, *no!* not for one second... on your life!"

"But..."

"No! say nothing! Listen to me. I am in command today. You must guard her as you would the most dangerous criminal. Oh!

I am not mad! One word will tell you why... You know her as Irene Beauchamp! I, *I* call her Lady Beltham!"

"Lady Beltham!" cried the Senator in a startled voice.

"Yes! Lady Beltham... And now, till we meet. Draw your revolver. Never take it off the unhappy woman... Oh! she is not the one I fear. No! it is someone else who might come, but who will not come if he knows that at the first step he took, she would fall dead..."

"Fantômas? You speak of Fantômas?" stammered the Senator. He was a brave man, but his face had blanched.

"Perhaps!" was all the journalist deigned to answer. Stern in his determination, Fandor stepped to the door. His hand was already on the latch when in two steps Lady Beltham was by his side.

"One word more!" she besought him, "a word that shows my cowardice!... I would ask you a favor..."

"I will do the impossible, Madam, to prove my gratitude."

"Very well, sir, I am in horrid pain... Ah! I am ashamed to say it..."—in her beautiful eyes was a look of painful embarrassment as she added:

"I was struck in the face, sir, and the savage blow has broken a tooth... I think the pain is driving me mad. When you came, I was just going down to see a dentist..."

"A dentist, downstairs?"

"Yes! here, on the ground floor a dentist lives. Will you allow me to have him see to me?... In your presence, if you so wish..."

Fandor felt himself turn red with shame. He hated this odious surveillance he was obliged to practice with a woman—and a woman he knew to be unhappy. Yet was he not bound to make proof of sternness? Did he not know that Lady Beltham's devotion to Fantômas might lead her to some act of treachery? He thought desperately:

"She has sent me to Montellon. She has admitted there is something there to be discovered... May she not regret her avowals? May she not decide to warn Fantômas of the imprudence she has been guilty of?"

He would fain have left her at liberty, he would have wished to rely on her word of honor. But he felt it his duty to be more uncompromising.

"Madam," he announced, "I will come with you, as you say..."

"Thank you!"—and she threw over her disordered coiffure a Spanish net. Then without another word she led the way downstairs. A minute or two later Fandor found himself with Lady Beltham in the dentist's parlor. The latter came forward to receive his distinguished visitor with eager politeness.

"I am in great agony with this tooth," she explained. "I am not good at bearing pain. Will you draw it for me, please. This gentleman, an old friend, did not like me to come all by myself to face this little operation."

She was speaking in evident agitation. But the dentist, accustomed as he was to find his patients frightened, did not appear to guess the real cause of her emotion.

"I give you my word you will suffer no pain," he informed her with a smile. "A prick with the cocaine needle and... There, Madam, it's over already!"—and holding out his forceps, he exhibited the tooth he had just extracted shining like a pearl...

"Thank you, sir."

Fandor and his prisoner returned to the room where Dupont de l'Eure was waiting for them.

"So here you are!" muttered the great man, who was plainly anxious and upset.

"Yes, here we are!" Fandor replied slowly and deliberately. "My dear sir, do you remember what I said? That your surveillance must be strict, rigorous to the last degree... Anyway, I don't suppose it will be for long. I am going to Montellon. It is my duty. Alas! I have searched there already without noting anything of importance. If I find nothing now, I will come back with all dispatch. After that, all that remains will be to await the offer Fantômas will make to ransom our prisoner..."—and he took his departure, leaving his Editor and Lady Beltham together.

He was thinking how, by holding the last named to ransom, he was at last in possession of a means to force the Lord of

Terror to make terms. But was Juve still alive? Was there yet time to save him?

The young man set off at a run. Three steps at a time he tore down the stairs, and found Dupont de l'Eure's car waiting at the door.

"Quick," he ordered the chauffeur. "Take the Vésinet road. At Chatou you'll turn to the right, for Carrières… After that I will show you the way. Quick! quick!"

He had no sense of weakness left now, fully convinced he was embarked on the decisive battle, the supreme struggle on which might well depend the fate of the man he loved as a son loves his father. Oh! it *could* not be too late! The horror of the thought was beyond bearing! The chauffeur, meantime, well accustomed to hold himself at the disposition of the staff of the *La Capitale* and an old acquaintance and, like all his fellows, an admirer of Fandor's, had observed the young man's impatience, and started the swift and powerful car at top speed. The vehicle seemed to devour the road. In a flash the hill of La Défence was surmounted. Then a giddy rush downhill to the crossroads at La Boule. A quick turn, a rapid swerve and they were on the Rueil road.

"To the right!" yelled Fandor, "make for the Chatou bridge…"

A few minutes more and he would be there. Now all weakness, all feebleness, was gone. In his excitement, in his agonized suspense, he had clean forgotten his wounds and exhaustion. Would he again find nothing in this graveyard he had already visited in vain, this spot that was evidently a haunt of the Arch-Criminal, the Lord of Terror?

The instant the car drew up at the cemetery, Fandor leapt out and hurried to the gates.

"Wait for me! And be ready to start away again at a moment's notice!" he shouted to the chauffeur.

And it was only then, as he passed through the entrance, that he remembered—with a careless shrug—that he was unarmed.

*   *   *   *   *

Thus finding himself weaponless at the very time he knew

he might at any moment encounter the monster so well des-
ignated the Lord of Terror, Jerome Fandor should surely have
beaten a retreat! The most elementary prudence told him so.
But it was never Fandor's habit to hearken to the counsels of
prudence. Then, was he not sacrificing himself to save Juve's
life—the "good old" Juve he held so dear? Was not this a sufficient motive, an all-sufficient motive to induce him to run any
and every risk?

Result, the journalist calmly pursued his way. Now, indeed,
as on his previous visit, the little Cemetery seemed deserted
and peaceful as ever. Strange how human beings often seem
afraid of such quiet spots where the dead sleep their last sleep!
There was nothing terrifying here. The graveyard lay all bright
and fragrant with its rows of white tombstones and the masses
of flowers decorating the graves.

"Oh! if only I could see something, discover something!"
thought Fandor.

But next moment he felt how impossible was any such discovery as Lady Beltham had spoken of, and had suggested his
searching for. What indeed was he to look for? What seemingly
insignificant detail was to arrest his attention? Was this or that
arrangement, the position of such or such a wreath a special
signal? Did the inscription on such or such a garland hide an
indication? Slackening his pace, he went to the grave 530, the
one in which he knew Lady Beltham was interested. But it was
still the same, like any of the others. There was nothing there to
draw his notice!

"And yet," the journalist groaned, "I know now that Lady
Beltham suspects some secret here! Ought I to have this tomb
opened? Ah! but my mind revolts at such a useless profanation!"

He knelt down, then lay at length on the grass, listening, his
ear to the ground. Nothing, not a sound! Then he made the
circuit of the grave, closely examining the red granite of which
the monument was made.

"I can see nothing!" he muttered... "But *is* there anything to
see? Lady Beltham herself found nothing!..."—and he was on
the point of abandoning the search when suddenly he halted,

bending down over the stone, gazing at it with startled eyes.

"Heavens!" he cried, "am I going mad?"

What he had caught sight of was all but indiscernible. There, on one corner of the monument, only just above the surface of the soil, cut in the granite as it were with a graver's tool, was a shallow marking, so small it occupied barely an eighth of an inch square—tiny hollows, projections, flat surfaces.

"I must be mistaken!" stammered Fandor. "It can't be true, it can't be real!... And, if it were, what meaning could it have?"

But next instant he doubted no longer, he could not doubt.

"But yes, it is!... I guess the riddle!... It is... Ah! the wretched, wicked woman!"—and his face grew ghastly pale...

Yet, after all, was he making a silly, stupid mistake? Carved in the solid stone, hollowed out of its substance, he could not conjecture by what process, Jerome Fandor thought he recognized the imprint of a tooth—a human tooth! At first glance he had refused to believe his eyes. Could a tooth have bitten into this close-grained stone that defies the slow attrition of centuries? And then, what could this carving signify?

But suddenly, startlingly, the truth flashed across his brain... A tooth was imprinted on this tomb? Ah! but had not Lady Beltham, held as hostage, begged to be taken to see a dentist? Had she not, this pretty woman, this lady of fashion, as she was, had one of her teeth extracted? Yes! a strange coincidence!—a coincidence that could *not* be the result of mere chance. Mere chances such as this do not exist for those who day by day bend their minds to the precise elucidation of the mysteries incident to police investigations.

"The wretched, wicked creature!" Fandor repeated... In a flash of thought he had divined an infamous trick played by the beautiful Lady Beltham. She had let him know this much, that he should visit the Cemetery of Montellon, yes! but afterwards she had regretted her indiscretion? Was it not for this reason, and this only, she had asked to be taken to a dentist's, had allowed herself to be disfigured?...

"I cannot make it out!" pondered the journalist, who nevertheless felt himself momentarily growing more furiously angry.

Yes! he was beginning to understand, he thought he did understand, that he had been cajoled… What this extraordinary mark indicated he could not imagine. But he had a firm conviction that Lady Beltham must know, and that she had deceived him, seized with remorse directly she had sent him on this wild goose chase.

"Ah! but I will make her confess! I will force her to tell me the exact truth!"

His eyes still fixed on the strange carving, he was thinking hard, his thoughts straying into the wildest, the most fantastic fancies. Was the tooth that marked the granite the one Lady Beltham had had drawn? But to what end?… And, besides, the dentist had not kept it, surely? No doubt had thrown the tooth away… And he broke into an involuntary laugh. Was he not going crazy? What next would he suppose? He exclaimed, unconsciously to himself speaking out loud:

"She told me: 'We are enemies!'—and she spoke truly! What I see is real, actual. I am *not* dreaming!…"

Then he turned around to go. Was he not wasting precious time, lingering in this graveyard? There was a riddle to be solved—and he would never solve it unaided. He swore to himself:

"Lady Beltham must speak out! She must and shall! No more pity! No more compunction! It is Juve I am fighting for! It is Juve whose life is at stake!…"

His face convulsed with rage, ready for any violence, out of his senses it may be, he set off running, hurrying back to the car that stood, with engine slowed down, waiting at the gate.

"Quick! quick as you can go! Avenue Malakoff!"—and the car shot off at a mad speed.

17. A Woman's Heart

While Fandor was on his way to the Cemetery of Montellon, Dupont de l'Eure had found the greatest difficulty in convincing himself that he was not the sport of a mad dream. Seated on an eighteenth-century couch—one of those exquisite pieces of furniture that show the consummate mastery of technique possessed by the cabinet-makers of former days and a perfection of artistic feeling equal to that of the greatest painters and sculptors—the Senator, revolver in hand, was gazing at the hostage committed to his care, the woman he had always known as Irene Beauchamp, but whom he had just learned to be actually Lady Beltham. Well accustomed though he was to the surprises incident to police investigations, familiar as he was, thanks to Jerome Fandor, his colleague at *La Capitale*, with all the sinister details connected with the name of Fantômas, yet he could not rid himself of a sense of intense bewilderment.

The room was luxuriously appointed, peaceful and quiet to the last degree. On the walls hung choice prints from Fragonard, Moreau, Boily; glass cabinets were full of priceless china—delicate Dresden ware, old Sèvres; everywhere dainty knickknacks such as call up associations of bygone centuries, miracles of grace and charm—pumice boxes, work boxes, dressing cases, vases, fans, hand mirrors once owned by fair ladies of the Court. Was this a fitting scene for the tragic drama in which he was playing a part? He recalled the days when he had known Irene Beauchamp, how she had first appeared in Parisian Society on the occasion of a Charity Ball of which she was a Patroness, a ball she was giving for the benefit of the wounded in the Great War, how from that time on she had begun to gather together in her salon the choicest elite of all Paris.

"And she is Lady Beltham!" he thought distractedly. "So that name of Irene Beauchamp was fictitious! and, of nights, when her guests were gone, she would lurk back to Fantômas—the hideous scoundrel Fantômas!"

Presently, a look of admiration crossed his face. How had Fandor come to divine, beneath the mask, the wretched wife of the Lord of Terror? Had he trusted simply to the coincidence of Irene Beauchamp's having been slightly burned at the same moment that a fire was raging at this other flat where Mme. Rosemonde lived?

"No! no!" the Senator assured himself. "There was something more than that... Irene Beauchamp, learning I was cashiering Fandor by order of the Minister, wished to take him on as Secretary. Yes! that is what must have struck Fandor! She wanted to entice him into a trap. She was acting under Fantômas' directions..."—and at the thought a feeling of boundless admiration possessed him for his colleague, who, wounded and worn out, had had this intuition, this flash of genius that had led to the surveillance he was at that moment exercising.

An easy task indeed! Ever since the journalist's departure Lady Beltham had sat motionless and speechless, half reclining on an ottoman, her face to the wall, in an attitude of dejection and despair. Alas! what agonies of mind must she be suffering!

"Unhappy woman!" the Senator thought involuntarily, looking at her askance, the very sight of her suffering cutting him to the quick, as he realized how fearful the penalty she was paying, how dreadful the tortures his prisoner was at that moment enduring. To curse Fantômas, and yet to love him! To wish, as she surely did, for Fandor's triumph and Juve's deliverance, yet to dread for Fantômas the snare in which he would eventually be taken! How appalling the dilemma, how her mind must be distracted, torn in these several directions. Whichever way she turned, all was pain and misery—the punishment of the dastardly affection she gave this monster, the man who had lost every right to be called a man, who one day would end his foul career forever on the scaffold!

But now the Senator gave a sudden start. Springing swiftly to her feet, Lady Beltham faced her jailer, her two hands clasping her breast, panting, scarce able to breathe:

"Good Lord!" thought Dupont de l'Eure, "a fit of hysterics!"—and he got up too.

"Madam… Irene… Lady Beltham… You are in pain?"

A hoarse groan was the answer:

"I am choking! choking!"

He ran to the window, shouting:

"Air! more air! Control yourself, I beg you!"

But, with staggering steps, the brigand's wife was tottering across the room, clinging for support to chairs and tables…

Then, in a moment, Dupont de l'Eure gave a gasp. Was it all a trick, this choking fit? Had not Fandor warned him to be suspicious? Was not anything and everything to be apprehended on the part of this companion of a scoundrel and a villain? Leaving the window, he darted to the door, barring it with outstretched arms.

"Where are you going?… You cannot leave the room…"

His tone was rough and harsh, though all his gallantry as a man rose in protest against the brutal attitude he had to assume with a woman. Lady Beltham, in fact, as she faced him, was trembling, cut to the quick, it seemed, by the coarse suspicion of which she was the object.

"Oh! the shame of it!" she faltered, "the cruelty of the penalty I must pay!"—and she was going back to her couch, to sink again into the same posture of despair, when a fresh spasm of pain contorted her lovely face.

"Oh! I am in pain!" she panted.

"Is there anything I can get you? Shall I call for help?" Dupont de l'Eure asked, beginning to lose his head. With a haughty gesture she waved him from before the door.

"There," she sighed out, "in that little cabinet, my salts… Oh! believe me, I was never thinking of escaping…"

The great man felt bitterly ashamed. Criminal as she was in her monstrous infatuation, surely Lady Beltham still deserved to be treated as a woman of honor. As a hostage, was it to be believed she would try to escape by feigning illness, pretending to faint? He longed to make amends for his brutality. Quick as lightning, he sprang to the cabinet the poor woman pointed to, and raised the rosewood top.

"Here! here it is!" he cried, catching sight in a pigeonhole of two cut-glass bottles. He took one, removed the stopper, made to hand it to Lady Beltham… and, in an instant, overmastered by the fumes that rose from it, fell to the floor, without a cry, his body lying stiff and stark across the floor of the salon.

At the sight, Lady Beltham started back, so ghastly pale she looked more dead than alive.

"Oh, God!" she stammered with white lips. "Was it Fate decided his choice? There were two bottles… He took that one…"

A wild laugh, then a choking sob, and she repeated:

"Yes! he took that one—and I am free, free!…"

Still holding by the furniture, the unhappy woman, more unfortunate surely than wicked, stepped up to the little cabinet, still standing open, and taking a second bottle from it, inhaled a deep breath of the restorative it contained. Then, refreshed and strengthened, she returned to where Dupont de l'Eure lay and bent over the Senator's lifeless form, kicking aside the vial he had let slip from his hand as he fell.

"He is asleep," she told herself. "He is merely asleep! Yes! Fantômas gave me his word the drug was only a harmless soporific. Moreover, I have tried it on myself to make sure I might use it without fear of consequences… Yes! he is simply asleep. In a few hours he will awake fit and well… And I shall be far away… *We* shall be far away… I shall be with my lover again. Now I have saved him, shall I win him to consent to give up his dreadful trade?…"

She seemed half distraught, hardly knowing what she was doing, scarce conscious of the words that escaped her trembling lips.

"Yes! I must fly and go to him!" she stammered. "He *must* have understood! I cannot hesitate now!"

Then, casting a last look around this room where she had gathered about her so many beautiful things, such a wealth of charming and delightful treasures:

"To leave it all!" she went on. "To become a vagabond... To take to flight and forsake everything!"

But soon her mind was made up. Proud and unfaltering under the spur of a desperate resolve, Lady Beltham crossed the room, reached the corridor outside and stood at the door of the flat.

"He will wake presently and go away," she reflected. "I need feel no anxiety on his account. In any case Fandor will be coming back and see to his safety. I have no call to trouble. Dupont de l'Eure runs no risk."

Opening the door, the wretched woman quitted her home, a fugitive. Bareheaded, she descended the stairs and reached the dentist's rooms, which, a short while before, she had visited in Fandor's company to have a tooth extracted. There she stopped, and listened intently:

"No! not a sound! He is gone! He has abandoned me to my fate!... But no! I am unjust; he knew very well I ran no risk. He was very sure he could trust to Fandor's honor and that Fandor, no matter what he may have said, would never have given me up to justice."

Therewith, she took a key from her pocket. Unhesitatingly, like one who is sure of acting rightly, she opened the dentist's door and made her way into his apartments, shutting it behind her.

"Nobody!" she repeated, and with a firm, determined step, she traversed a corridor and marched into the dentist's parlor. Evidently its owner was not there, obviously there was not a soul left in the flat—and Lady Beltham knew it, for she took no precautions whatever to avoid interference. She went straight to the desk, on which lay a writing pad. Opening this, she found a paper inside, and carried it to the window to read. It was typewritten and contained only these few lines:

> Thank you!... What you have done induces me to forgive you for saving Fandor's life, which I guess to have been your doing. May you never regret having suffered one of my worst enemies to live!

"Oh, God!" groaned the unhappy woman. "To hinder a crime, must this always mean to expose him, my lover, to peril? By rescuing Fandor, have I indeed betrayed Fantômas?"

Then she resumed her reading:

> When I saw you come in accompanied by that man, when I re-alized that you wished to give me a last, timely warning of the risks my most precious treasure ran, I felt rejoiced that I could now forgive you, happy to be no longer compelled to hate you!
>
> Ah! Lady Beltham! Lady Beltham! how I could love you, were you really and indeed my partner!

"His partner!" the great lady repeated the words in a tone of horror. "The partner of his crimes! Oh! never!... never!..."— and the letter shook in her trembling hand. But, with a forced calmness she continued reading:

> The tooth is hidden where you know. Take it. I have its match with me and have no need of that one. Who knows, indeed, if I am not to fall in my turn! I cannot say if you have betrayed me in other ways, or no... But what matter? Yes! take back this tooth, the real use of which you hardly know. If I die, directions will be given you. You would go to the spot, and you would be absolute mistress of whatsoever you found there.
>
> But this is wild talking! Goodbye, or rather, till we meet again!... Lady Beltham, in a few hours we shall be together once more.
>
> Our masks are torn off us perhaps. It matters nothing! I am not alarmed! I fear nothing!
>
> Never forget this: happen what may, they cannot arrest, and they cannot kill...   FANTÔMAS.

Then, the letter read, this letter signed with the terrifying name of the Lord of Terror, Lady Beltham shivered as if in a fever fit.

"Yes! he knows I saved Fandor's life!" she sighed. "Perhaps he suspects I told him of the grave at Montellon. Oh, God! is it my fate then to ruin those I love, those I would fain save, even at the price of my own life?"

The tears streaming from her eyes, she faltered on:

"Juve! Is the noble Juve dead? And Fandor? Have Fandor and 'He' met?... 'He' is bound to have hurried yonder—and Fandor was there! Oh! do what I will, is it always calamity my efforts bring about?"

Then, recovering herself by a supreme effort of will, reflected in the flash of her eyes, mastering the emotion that left her nerveless, she rose and went straight to the mantelpiece. There, under a glass shade, dentures were ranged—as they naturally would be in a dentist's parlor. And Lady Beltham counted: "The third set... the seventh tooth... that one..."—and picking out the tooth she had identified, she looked at it with a haggard gaze.

"Fandor may perhaps have found Juve?... and if he has found him, this puts him on the track... Can he yet be saved?"

But again she shivered.

"I must go! I must!... I am going to dress..."—and she took a step forward. Doubtless, in these rooms, which were of a certainty where Fantômas lived—passing here for a dentist, just as in the Rue Michel-Ange he played the part of a major-domo promoted to the office of House Steward—Lady Beltham would have at her disposal a traveling outfit for the flight she meditated.

But suddenly she stopped dead. Sharp and shrill, the bell of the outer door of the flat had sounded an urgent summons.

"Oh! who can that be coming?" she cried. Then lowering her voice, she added under her breath:

"One of his infamous accomplices perhaps? It is here he sees them, under pretense of their being his patients..."

But already a second ring sounded.

"No, no!" Lady Beltham thought. "An accomplice would never insist like that."

But yet she began to tremble. In the silence of the empty rooms, this loud, repeated ringing had an alarming, a threatening note.

"I *must* know!" she muttered. "They are surely getting impatient."

Then, gliding across the floor, her face livid, but with eyes

that burned feverishly, she moved to the door, at which the bell
was now ringing a continuous peal.

"Oh! the shame of it! But it must be!" she groaned. "For me
to do such a thing! To lower myself to such a meanness!"

Reaching the door, she stooped, gluing her eye to the keyhole,
trying to see this impatient visitor. Next moment she staggered
back, terrified, losing her head. Tired of ringing without elicit-
ing an answer and firmly resolved to get in, Jerome Fandor, for
it was in fact he who stood outside the door, was applying his
shoulder to the panels, trying to force the hinges…

"Lost! I am lost!" panted Lady Beltham. If the journalist was
there, was she not assured that this time he would show her no
pity? She would be forced to account for her presence, alone,
on these premises! She would be forced to lead him to where
Dupont de l'Eure still lay unconscious in her salon!…

"Lost! I am lost, undone!" she reiterated. "And if he *is* here,
if he has come hurrying back here, it is because he has found
yonder…"

But she broke off suddenly. A grating, scratching sound
had caught her ear. Failing to force the door, the journalist was
surely picking the lock.

Frantic, desperate, tracked down, trapped, Lady Beltham
thought wildly:

"Escape by a window? But a few yards off is a constable on
point duty! I should be arrested!"

The lock was yielding; a sharp crack showed that in another
two seconds the game would be up. The wretched woman
straightened herself, and disguising her voice:

"Who is there?" she demanded. "Wait! I am going to open.
Just a moment to fetch the keys!…"

*   *   *   *   *

No sooner had Lady Beltham declared "she was going to
get the keys to open the door" than she seemed to have gone
demented. She had realized that the direst catastrophes were
imminent. Once Fandor was inside and saw her, he would infallibly guess what must have happened to his Chief and would

at once take measures for her arrest. Moreover, finding her in these rooms which he had visited with her under pretense of having her attended to, would he not inevitably suspect the real motives that had taken her there? Would he not search her? Would he not force her to give up this object, evidently precious, which she had recovered?

"I am lost!" she reiterated, "I am undone!" She felt weak as water, hopeless, incapable of further resistance to fate. Yes! to have returned so soon, Fandor must have discovered in the cemetery of Montellon some damning truth. Was he coming to avenge Juve's death?

A second passed… another… and another…

"I *must* do something!" she faltered.

A mere door—thin and fragile, the sort of door usual in a Paris flat—separated her from Fandor. She could hear the young man's restless movements, and she guessed his fierce impatience. If she did not open, was he going to start again picking the lock?

"I must! I *must* do it!" Lady Beltham told herself. "It is my lover I have to save!"—and she sprang to her feet. The very extremity of her anguish gave her strength to dare a last desperate effort. Hurrying along the passage, she ran to a sort of store closet where cast-off clothes hung.

"To take an overall," she muttered… "pretend to be a nurse… an assistant… and then make my escape!"

As she spoke, she caught sight of one of those long white overalls dentists of repute and their assistants wear, to give themselves something more the look of real surgeons. In a moment she had donned the garment, which was long enough to hide her dress. She snatched off her hat, and a second or two more sufficed for her to conceal under a white coif the masses of her golden hair.

"There!" she said, "no one should know me now."

In the badly lighted entrance passage the electric light was burning, and she switched this off. Finally, frantic and determined at one and the same time, she turned the key in the lock and opened the door. Outside stood Fandor, dancing with impatience, but very far from suspecting he was to be confronted with Lady Beltham, who had gone back to the dentist's with no other object than to recover the tooth.

The door open, the young man asked:

"Anyone here still, is there?"

"No, sir!… Everybody gone!"

This in a voice she found the utmost difficulty in disguising. No less distressing the effort to keep her face concealed, to shun the light, to avoid recognition.

"The dentist has gone out, has he? I want badly to see him."

"But, sir, it is after hours."

"I know that. But it's on a matter of grave importance!"

"Still…"

"I have urgent reasons for insisting… If he is not here, I shall be obliged to call in the police to make a search…"

"Oh, sir!"

Up to this point Lady Beltham had still hoped to discourage the young man, to put him off to the next day. A short respite would enable her to carry through her project. But Fandor went on inexorably:

"And I shall be obliged in that case to beckon to the constable on point duty yonder, a few yards away."

At last she realized the impossibility of getting rid of the visitor, and clasping her hands in a wild gesture of fear, but which Fandor not unnaturally mistook for a mere expression of surprise and annoyance, she replied:

"Well, sir, I will take a message… I will ask if they will still see you…"

"They *will* see me… Give my name, Jerome Fandor."

"Very good, sir… Will you come with me?"—and she turned to precede the young man along the passage, adding in a shaking voice—Fandor noted this, but set it down to mere nervousness:

"Take care… It is rather dark… We were just leaving, the shutters are up and the electric current cut off at the meter."

"No matter for that."

"Please go in,"—and as she spoke the words, Lady Beltham

threw open a door and stepped aside to let her companion pass.

Facing him, Fandor saw a room in utter, absolute darkness.

"Well!" he exclaimed, "now I can't see anything, not a blessed thing!"

"No!… But I'm going to light up… Just go in…"

He took a step forward. Then he understood—and was struck momentarily dumb with horror and rage… The door had banged shut behind him, and a key turned noisily in the lock.

"Damnation!" he yelled. "Caught!"

He had his "smoker's companion" out in an instant and struck a light, to find he was in a sort of store closet, a poor, narrow cupboard with clothes hanging in it. Next minute he saw a hat lying on the floor, a hat he recognized. He had seen it on Mme. Rosemonde's—Lady Beltham's—head when he encountered her at the cemetery…

"Caught!" he repeated… "Fooled!… Ah! the wretch!"—and he hurled himself at the door. It was strong and solid, *this* door, but soon even it began to give way, splitting and caving in under his vigorous onslaught. He never even felt the cruel pain his fierce exertions provoked in his injured arms.

"So!" he panted, "free at last… the nurse can't be gone far, surely?"

Drunk with fury, he ran to the outer door of the flat, and tried to open it. It was screwed up!

"Well then, by the window!"

Still at a run, he dashed along the passage and into the first room he came to, one that must evidently give on the street front of the building. As chance would have it, this was the dentist's parlor. He caught sight of the open glass case, and saw the dentures thrown about in disorder.

"By the Lord!" he ejaculated. "Too late! I'm too late!"

But now he was tearing open the shutters and mounting the window sill…

"Hi there!" came a voice, and he beheld a constable hurrying up.

"Where d'you come from? Got to account for yourself, you

have!..."

"Just so!" retorted the journalist. "See here! you come in quick, my man... and search the house. Dupont de l'Eure, the Senator, must be inside somewhere... drugged or murdered..."—finishing up with a big oath, nearly choked by the rage and excitement that consumed him.

All the same, this time Fandor was in luck's way. Many a policeman, hearing these confused explanations of his would simply have refused to listen to the rigmarole. Most representatives of law and order would have forthwith arrested him and haled him off to the nearest police station. On the contrary the constable in question exclaimed in tones of admiring surprise:

"What! M. Fandor! Beg pardon, sir!... Yes, I know you. Once upon a time I used to be on duty with M. Havard... I've often seen you with M. Juve..."

"Then do what I tell you!... Search the house! So long!... Oh! by-the-bye, give the alert, eh? Ask for assistance!... Perhaps Fantômas is there..."—and, paying no heed to the involuntary start of alarm that escaped the worthy man, evidently far from anxious to encounter the Lord of Terror, Fandor sprang into the street, and started off at breakneck speed...

"No! she can't be gone far!" he told himself again. "I could swear it was she... yes, Lady Beltham..."

He caught sight of a milk boy coming down the Avenue Malakoff, whistling the Russian National anthem with might and main.

"Hi! youngster, you haven't seen a nurse go by?"

"A nurse?"

"A lady in a white overall?... You understand?"

"Oh! yes!... Course I did, sir!... Not two minutes ago!... She was legging it so fast I couldn't help noticing her..."

"Very good! and thank you!"

Now where could Lady Beltham be going? "Why, to the nearest cabstand, for sure!" he thought.

Tearing on, he reached the Place Victor Hugo, and gripping the terrified keeper of the shelter by the wrist, he gasped:

"Matter of Police duty!... A nurse has just taken a cab from here?"

"A nurse? Upon my word, no!… And anyhow, who are you?"

"You're making a mistake, I tell you!… Didn't a cab go off two minutes ago?"

"Yes, it did. But the passenger wasn't a nurse…"

"Oh! but she might have taken off her overall, bless my soul!… Where was she off to, this woman? Can't you answer?"

"But I don't know, not I!… And what's this to-do about, anyhow?"

Leaving the old man without another word, Fandor dashed up to a taxi-man who was standing on the rank beside his cab and appeared to be listening to the young man's questions.

"You must have heard… Think, man! You don't remember the address given?"

"My certy, sir! I know this much, the lady was out of breath…"

"That's it! that's it!… And what else d'you know?"

"That she said: 'I'll tell you the place to drive to, after Rueil…'"

"By the Lord! I've got her!" cried the journalist triumphantly. "She's going to Montellon,"—and he sprang onto the box, seized the wheel in his own hands in spite of the driver's protests.

"Off we go! Get up! Matter of Police duty! Don't you worry! A hundred francs for yourself!"—and he jammed in the clutch, and away at a mad pace. Little cared Fandor, this time, for the rules of the road. He whizzed past the refuges on the wrong side, while policemen yelled and passersby shook their fists at him. By his side, the driver, scared for the moment, soon entered into the spirit of the thing.

"Bravo!" he cried. "God A'mighty, what a pace!… Look out, sir!… Why, this beats cockfighting! You're the devil of a chap!… Neck or nothing, but we'll get there, anyhow!… By God! I thought we were into 'em that time!"

But Fandor's luck held out, and he reached the Porte Maillot with unbroken limbs. There he pulled up short at the octroi barrier, and next moment:

"There she is!" he ejaculated.

Leaning out of the window of a taxi to give directions to

her driver, who had just stopped for the customary checking of gasoline, a woman was speaking excitedly evidently impatient to get on.

"There she is!" reiterated the journalist. "It's Lady Beltham, for sure. No fear now but I've got her safe!"

"Yes! I've got her this time!" he chuckled, "and I'm not going to spare her! She shall save Juve, or be handed over to the Police."

At the same time, not to let her know she was being shadowed, he felt bound to allow the other cab to go on ahead. Indeed, there was no risk now of losing her altogether, for he knew where she was going.

"We must set about it cautiously," the journalist warned himself. "This time we play to win or lose the game once for all..."—and he sprang out on the pavement, and darting behind his taxi to avoid being seen, he took a notebook from his pocket. Tearing out a leaf, he scrawled hurriedly:

"I am tracking down Lady Beltham, who is on her way to Montellon, to the cemetery, where everything leads me to believe she is going to meet Fantômas. I do not know where Juve is, but she can save him. Come and bring Inspectors with you. Come quick!"

"There!" he concluded. "I may be killed... But Havard will come on the scene with fifty police. Once put on the track, he will follow up the quest!"—and he slipped his missive into an envelope which he addressed:

"Monsieur Havard, Chief of the Criminal Investigation Bureau—Urgent!"

"And now," he went on, "to dispatch an Inspector with this. There is always an Inspector stationed at the main octroi barriers, and I know them nearly all..."

The journalist found what he expected and quickly caught sight of the officer on duty.

"My man," he accosted the latter, "take this to its address at once. The matter is urgent, of the gravest importance... You may be sure I shouldn't interrupt your duties if it were not so... You will please see the Chief personally... And tell him to make the journey by car… Off with you—and thank you…"

Well known as he was to the Force by reason of his intimacy with Juve and his own celebrity, Fandor could rely on his missive being duly delivered.

"Now," he said to himself, "to work! The game is afoot! Shall I win the rubber?"—and he restarted his taxi on the road to Montellon in hot pursuit of Lady Beltham.

*   *   *   *   *

In the well, that hideous death trap, into which Fantômas had thrown him, with M. Merandol to share his fate, Juve, the indomitable Juve, was still alive. For how long a time had he been there? This he could not tell. Buried in this underground cavern, where a lingering death threatened him inexorably, he yet fought the oncoming madness that menaced him with superhuman willpower…

"Kill myself?" he debated. "Yes! I have a right to… But only when a man has satisfied his obligations… Now I am under an obligation, I have a duty, that deprives me of the right to kill myself—and that duty is to vanquish Fantômas."

Manifestly Juve was in full possession of his faculties thus to be able to think even now of battling on against this monstrous enemy. He felt in his pocket, where he had put them back to save them from contact with the damp earth, the cigarettes with the cheddite cartridges concealed among them. If he did not kill himself and put an end to the horrid tortures he suffered, it was because he was still watching for Fantômas' coming, because he wished by means of this desperate weapon to annihilate his foe along with himself.

"He knows I am here," he reflected, "and he knows my determined character. He must be hungering and thirsting to be rid of me. I am convinced he will come, sooner or later, to see my corpse. The great thing is for me to be still alive when he does come. Yes! I shall kill him then, if only I can last a while longer than he counts on!"

It was a relentless struggle against death, albeit death would have delivered him from a long and lingering agony, a hideous and protracted torture. Hope he had none left. He had no smallest doubt that in the explosion that should slay Fantômas he would surely perish himself. But would he not at any rate have won the victory? Would he not at any rate have accomplished his duty?

"Fandor will search," he thought, "and Fandor will find out the truth. Juve, struck off the rolls of the Department, will be justified, his good name restored! That is my heart's desire!"—and patiently he waited on, unflinching.

By his side, meantime, M. Merandol was dying. Long periods of somnolence were succeeded at intervals by wild fits of delirium. The fear of imminent death had provoked in a man of his age a kind of fever of the brain, and it was an added horror for Juve to hear the wretch's inarticulate moans forever ringing in his ears.

"Unhappy man!" he murmured compassionately. "And yet, I cannot murder him? No man has the right to kill another, to destroy life!... Yet how he suffers!"

For many hours, indeed, M. Merandol seemed to be in intolerable anguish. Then he had grown somewhat calmer, as his weakness increased. Now he was only groaning feebly from time to time: "Water! water!"

To quench the thirst of his companion—a burning thirst he himself shared—Juve possessed only the feeble resource of pressing to his lips the few drops of water he managed to sponge up with his handkerchief, the drippings from the damp walls. Still he held out. Doubtless he would rather, much rather, have died forthwith. But he was no man to trifle with the duties his conscience approved.

"Let us wait!" he told himself again. "Yes, wait and watch!"

From time to time he would eagerly put his ear to the sides of their living tomb, and once or twice he seemed to catch a far-off sound. Once or twice he even felt a gleam of hope, but a cruel disappointment invariably followed. No! nobody was coming. He was alone, alone and abandoned to his doom, alone with his delirious companion—and death that loomed nearer and nearer:

Little by little he felt himself weakening. No matter how courageous, a man cannot forever fight against an agony too long protracted. The human brain is but a machine, and like any other machine, is liable to be thrown out of gear. Presently he began to feel dazed and dazzled and his eyes to play him false. Painful hallucination bewildered his senses, setting him shuddering and shaking in a way that made him ashamed. He heard voices! He seemed to catch strange noises!

"God help me!" he faltered, "am I going mad?"—and he fought long and hard to regain his self-control.

At one particular moment he thought for certain his wits were leaving him. Distinctly he seemed to hear an odd buzzing, rasping sound, a noise as if a drill were boring into the stone-work. But the thing was impossible! It was at his own level, and consequently at the bottom of the well, that his ear detected the sound!

"No! no!" he warned himself, after listening involuntarily. "I am not going to put faith in this illusion of the senses. I can hear nothing where I am! There is nothing here! It is only the blood pulsing in my ears. It is only exhaustion makes me think…"

But the noise still went on. Still the tool seemed to be biting into the walls of the death chamber.

"What! delirious now, am I?" Juve asked, and with iron determination:

"Keep calm!" he ordered himself. "Take no notice! Stay where you are!"

But he could not help but listen, and in the silence of the pit that was his tomb, Juve heard the same creaking, grinding sound going steadily on and on, growing louder and louder…

"Ah!" he ejaculated suddenly. "Suppose it was Fandor!"

18. Tit For Tat

Juve had spoken in a dreamy voice, as if barely conscious of the words he uttered. What he said was, in fact, nonsensical, and a dreadful thing to think of, at the very same moment he conceived this wild hope, he was fully convinced how baseless the hope was.

"Fandor?" he repeated. "No, no! Fandor would never be coming this way!"—and the thing was self-evident. It *was* just possible that the journalist—whom Juve conjectured to be well started on his quest—might have found out how the police officer and M. Merandol were in durance vile in the well and doomed to perish there of hunger and thirst and exhaustion; but what motive could have led him to bore into the stonework of their living tomb with the object of delivering the captives? How, indeed, *could* he have done it? The prisoners, for their part, could not escape, because they were at the bottom of the well, without any means of mounting to the top; but Fandor would only have had to raise the flags covering the mouth of the shaft, take a ladder, or a rope, and hasten to the rescue of the unhappy pair.

"No!" it is not Fandor! It cannot be Fandor!" Juve assured himself... "No! it is nobody at all!" he concluded. "I am deluding myself!... That's all about it!"...

But, all the same, the noise went on! The more he forced himself not to heed it, the more obstinate his conviction grew, the more the sound beat in his ears, unceasing, insistent...

"Perhaps it is an animal... a mole... a dormouse?"

But he could not well put faith in any such supposition. Moles and dormice, hibernating creatures, lie fast asleep through the winter. Beside which, they never penetrate the earth to such depths.

"Well then, it is nothing! just nothing whatever!" was his

final word. But now he heard so distinctly that he was simply bound to protest against the belief his reason forced upon him. It could *not* be anything—that was the truth; but nevertheless there was something he heard—and that was no less a certainty!

"Very good!" Juve told himself next moment. "Quite right to keep one's head, but no need to be *pig*-headed. I *do* hear something. So now to find out what it is I hear,"—and by a final effort of will he compelled himself to get slowly to his feet. Then, stepping over M. Merandol's body, he staggered to the side of the wall from which the noise came, and laid his ear against the wall.

But then, in an instant, he found himself trembling, for now no further doubt was possible. Someone was boring a hole; some tool, drill or center bit, was working its way through the soil and the stonework lining the shaft. Nor could the implement be far from the surface now, for he could feel the vibration by laying his hand on the wall.

"Who?" he asked himself, and anxiously, eagerly, frantic with renewed hope, he waited, his mind so distraught it could frame no precise idea.

A friend? But a friend could only be Fandor—and Fandor would not have come underground.

An enemy? But an enemy could only be Fantômas, and Fantômas had no motive to act like this.

"I am dreaming, without a doubt!" Juve told himself again, and the old dread, the hideous dread of madness, came over him once more. Men who die in the desert or in mines of exhaustion have these strange hallucinations, so those who have escaped tell us. This Juve knew, and the horror of falling victim to his own delusions was a hideous torment. To doubt the testimony of one's own senses is to feel madness close at hand.

"Come! come!" he chided himself. "If it was Fandor, he would knock on the wall, as miners do on the rock they are piercing to rescue their buried comrades… Therefore…"

But suddenly he stopped, his face paling with excitement. His palm laid flat against the wall had felt a prick. The point of the drill must have just touched it.

Juve gave a cry. This time hope surged up again in his breast. Here was life, new life, come to visit him in the kingdom of death, where he had lain despairing for so many long hours. And seizing his knife, he set to work too. The gritty stone of the well was comparatively soft and friable, and the hole quickly grew bigger. Soon he put his lips to it, and shouted loudly:

"Fandor! Fandor! Is it you?"

"Juve, it is Fantômas!" answered a far-off voice, faint, but unmistakable...

Horror-struck, Juve started back speechless... He had hoped for rescue, for life. Now, what new torture was preparing?

The voice went on in clear-cut tones:

"Juve, my friend, I am coming to kill you... Yes, I am!... Oh! it is Fandor you should curse. He it is who cuts short your span of life... The fool is on my track. I have to fly... You understand? I do not choose to fly leaving you alive behind me!"

Paying no attention to the words he heard, Juve stepped back deliberately to the wall. Was this not the moment so ardently desired—the moment when he could fire the explosion that should annihilate the Lord of Terror and by the same act deliver his two victims by death? Juve glued his eye to the enlarged orifice piercing the stonework of the well.

But suddenly a scream of rage and disappointment escaped him. The hole drilled by Fantômas by mean of a long-shafted boring tool, such as well-sinkers use, was at the least six feet in length, and this meant an immense thickness of earth between the brigand and his prisoner. The cheddite cartridges would never have power enough to throw down such an obstacle.

"No hope!" he groaned in despair... "*We* can die. I cannot kill *him*..."

But Fantômas was speaking again:

"Under these circumstances, Juve, I have decided to rid myself of you by a sure method, sure and comparatively speedy... Uncover the well and open fire on you? Hmm! too dangerous! Who knows if the cemetery is not kept under watch?... So, look you! I have thought of a better way. I have here a receptacle filled with asphyxiating gases, the same sort the Police authorities occasionally use to capture a formidable gang of criminals... You take me, I presume?"

Juve did not deign to answer, but very surely he understood only too well. By this hole bored through the ground Fantômas was simply going to drive the death dealing vapors into the well. No possibility of defense against such an attack ! Slowly but surely death would come... Fantômas need not ever stay there. Once a tube was fitted to the hole he had bored, he had only to turn a stop-cock and walk away. The deadly work would go on fatally and inevitably.

"You hear what I say, Juve?" demanded Fantômas. "Say your prayers, my friend!"

The police officer ground his teeth. At last he had every right to end it all. It would be no act of cowardice now to fire the explosive that should free them from their sufferings once for all. To anticipate a death that is slow indeed but certain, this is no suicide. And then, was it not well to show Fantômas that his threats, appalling as they were, failed to terrify his victims?

Juve took out the fatal cigarettes, and with a firm hand struck a light. Meantime a sickening smell was filling the confined space. A heavy, poisonous gas was filtering through the hole, the deadly gas that made the bravest tremble in the trenches in the days of the Great War... Yes! the game was up! the last stake was played—and lost!

Juve stood ready, match in hand... Another second, and all would be over... But a cry made him pause momentarily:

"Juve... Juve! What voice is that?"

The detective looked round, to see a sight that set him trembling still more, forced the fatal decision yet more urgently upon him. Roused from his sick torpor, M. Merandol had half risen to his feet. By the flickering light of the match he held Juve could see his face red with fever, livid and haggard, contorted in anguish.

"Juve, who is there?" he panted.

The police officer reflected for a moment... Had he any right to kill this man along with himself, without so much as a word to warn him of his purpose? Could he, in common honesty, steal a march on him in this fashion? Then he spoke, hesitatingly:

"Monsieur Merandol... it is... it is Fantômas!"

"Fantômas?"

"Yes!... And he is poisoning us with gas!... A slow and painful death... So, if you wish it, I have cheddite cartridges here... I am going to..."

"Oh, no! no! I do not wish you to! Have some pity on me! Let me kill myself!"

Juve could not understand it. M. Merandol was asking him to take pity on him? He wanted to kill himself? But, in that case, he had only to fire the explosive? He brought the lighted match closer yet.

"No! no! We may not be killed outright. We run the risk of being buried alive!... A ball from a revolver is better!"

"A ball from... But I have no revolver!"

Weird indeed this argument between the two doomed men!... But now, under the stress of his dying agony M. Merandol seemed to be in full possession of his faculties. He said in a steady voice:

"I have my weapon, Juve... *I* have my revolver!"—and already he was feeling in his pocket for the Browning with which he was really armed, but which Fantômas, when he felled him with a sudden, unexpected blow, had given him no time to use.

"I would rather..." he began again. But in a twinkling Juve had sprung at him.

"Great God!" he screamed. "Give me that..."

"But I want..."

"Give it up!"

Brutal for once in his fierce insistence, the detective almost tore the weapon from the financier's hand.

"If it is not too late," he cried, "I can kill him!"—and he dashed to the wall, leaned against it and pushed the barrel of the pistol halfway into the hole from which the deadly vapors were pouring.

And six times, at random, he let fly.

So quick the detonations followed one another he could catch no cry to show if his balls had met their mark.

*   *   *   *   *

On nearing the village of Montellon, Fandor stopped his car, thinking it best not to risk a further pursuit of Lady Beltham's vehicle. She might look behind and see him…

"I will make a shortcut across the fields," he thought to himself. "That way I can reach the wall of the Cemetery without her ever suspecting my presence. Then I shall intervene when needful…"—and leaving the driver in charge of the car, Fandor started off across country. Soon, panting and breathless, but his heart beating merrily, the young man was within two yards of the Cemetery. Behind him, as good as under his very feet, was the well in which Juve was condemned to endure such tragic and agonizing moments. Jerome Fandor, alas, was thinking only of Lady Beltham…

"She is not here yet!" he told himself. "I have outdistanced her…"

Then, next minute: "Ah! there she is!" he corrected himself, and at sight of her his agitation and excitement were redoubled.

Lady Beltham was pale as a corpse. A look of madness glittered in her eyes. She moved like an automaton, a woman in a trance.

"Surely she is going to faint," thought the young man. But he miscalculated the hardihood of Fantômas' comrade. Great as was Lady Beltham's terror, she fought her womanly weakness and mastered it.

"Grave 530, yes! It is indeed to grave 530 she is going!" thought Fandor. "What can she mean to do there?"—and then, his eyes wide with wonder, he saw a strange, an amazing sight. Before the flower-decked tomb Lady Beltham had dropped to her knees, and, with a swift furtive look, was gazing fearfully about her. Quickly reassured that no one could see her—she had not caught sight of Fandor—she put out her hand and began feeling over one corner of the funeral slab.

"The tooth!" muttered Fandor. "She is searching for the

impress of the tooth!"

But there he stopped, and only with an effort checked himself from dashing forward. Lady Beltham had started back sharply. Suddenly the ponderous stone, evidently moved by some secret mechanism, tilted up, pivoting on one of its edges, opening like the lid of a box!...

"Good God!" groaned Fandor... "So, it's not a real tomb at all? Those flowers were only there to put folks off the scent?"

But to reason, to reflect was impossible. His whole soul was in his eyes. Standing before the half-open tomb, Lady Beltham was calling:

"Fantômas!... Fantômas!... Beware!... Fandor knows that..."

But there she stopped, and with a sudden cry of terror, anguish, grief and despair, clasping her hands on her bosom, lifting her head as though suffocating, the wretched woman whirled about and fell—fell on the edge of the gaping grave. A spasm shook her graceful body, then she slipped and rolled over into the interior of the hollow space.

"Dead? She is surely dead?" thought Fandor, and he sprang forward. The act was purely instinctive—the natural instinct of brave men who rush, never heeding the risk, to the rescue of those in danger. The journalist scrambled over the Cemetery wall, jumped swiftly to the ground, sped along the pathways and bent over the yawning cavity.

"Oh! poor creature!" he groaned. No! it was no tomb. It was simply a cellar of sorts or underground chamber, a chamber all of polished marble—walls and floor. Lady Beltham had rolled to the bottom, where she lay prostrate, motionless save for the heaving of her bosom panting for breath.

"She is dying!" repeated Fandor. "But is she hurt, wounded?"

He could not understand the cause of her fall. But what matter? Instinct drove him on. Striding to the edge, he leapt down into the pit beside the unfortunate woman.

But before he had time to stoop and try to raise her, a prostrating weakness all but brought him to the ground himself... He strove vainly to recover his breath, felt a horrid giddiness seizing him, more pronounced at each inhalation.

"Poison gas!" he told himself again. He too was on the point of collapsing on the floor—and this meant death!

But now, recalling the past with a wonderful clearness of memory:

"She saved my life," he thought. "I am bound to save her!... I *must* save her!"

Stiffening his muscles, barely able to stand himself, yet resolved to rescue his companion, he grasped Lady Beltham by the shoulders, and eyes shut and teeth clenched in an effort that claimed the impossible of his exhausted strength, he lifted her in his arms.

"I *will* save her!" he panted, and with extended arms, as a man hoists a heavy burden he wants to heave over some obstacle, he managed to raise Lady Beltham to the edge of the cavity and cast her on the ground above.

"Help!" he gasped, all but unconscious now, no particle of strength left in him. Vainly he clawed at the cement of the coping. His fingers lost hold, his muscles refused to act.

"I will!... I will!" he gasped. All else was gone, his will alone remained unbroken. With closed eyes, clinging desperately to the edge, staggering and tottering, he still fought for life...

"Done for?... So I am done for?"

With a last spasmodic effort he made a final attempt to climb out. But at that same moment a hideous stab of pain drew a scream of agony from him, and with fingers crushed and bleeding, Fandor fell back on the floor of his underground prison, lifeless.

Above him, slowly, inexorably, the ponderous slab of stone, obeying the automatic action of its mechanism, had closed down.

The accursed irony of fate!

Fandor was entombed... Lady Beltham was safe, lying unconscious but alive, in a pathway of the Cemetery...

19. Brought to Bay!

"I assure you, Sir, it was a revolver!"

"Nothing of the sort!... An explosion perhaps..."

"No, no! It was a volley..."

"You're crazy! It went off under our feet!... It was in the Cemetery!..."

"But how should anything go off in a Cemetery?"

"Forward, I say! Forward! We'll argue it out later on..."

The posse of Inspectors grouped round M. Havard, who had cut across country, just as Fandor had done, to surround the graveyard, had come to a halt, startled by the sound of a succession of detonations, as to the precise nature of which they were far from agreed... While some maintained it was an explosion—and M. Havard was of the number—others were more inclined to deem it a volley of shots from a gun or pistol.

However, at their Chief's suggestion, all now resumed their advance. M. Havard himself was the first to reach the scene of action, and no sooner did he catch sight of the woman's face, the woman he believed to be dead, than he recognized her instantly:

"Mercy on us!" he gasped. "It is Lady Beltham!"—adding next moment: "But she is alive!... Her heart still beats!... Come, help me, someone! Has anybody a case of instruments? a bottle of salts?"

Of course nobody had anything of the kind.

"Cold water then," added M. Havard. "Someone steep a handkerchief in water."

Then, while two Inspectors rushed to a ditch by the roadside where they had noticed a little stagnant water, the Head of the Criminal Department stood up and forming a speaking-trumpet with his hands:

"Fandor!... Fandor, I say!" he shouted with all the strength of his lungs. But only echo answered.

"He is here, all the same... Or he was here... He must have fired at her."

M. Havard seemed beside himself with vexation. He felt sure a tragedy had just been enacted, and he had arrived too late to witness its grim conclusion... But at his side Inspector Louis was objecting:

"Fandor would never have fired at a woman, Sir..."

"Why, didn't you hear? Those revolver shots, eh?"

"It was not at Lady Beltham Fandor must have fired..."

"Well, have it your own way!... In any case it is she who was hit!..."

"You think so, Sir... I don't!"

M. Havard fell silent, blushing slightly. Had he, in fact, any good ground for believing that the unfortunate woman had fallen under Fandor's fire? It was often his failing to imagine over soon that he had fathomed the mysteries of police investigations, with the result that his Inspectors, of a more circumspect turn of mind, were able sometimes by one quiet observation to make him see the mistakes he was committing.

"Sir," pursued the officer calmly, "if it was a shot that wounded the lady, where the devil is the wound? She is not bleeding..."—and this was precisely what M. Havard had just noticed for himself.

"Well, we shall see later on," he declared. "What matters now is to bring her round... How now, no water to be found? You go and look, Henri!"

"Very good, sir!"—and the Inspector hurried off. "The rest of you, meanwhile," the Chief went on, "search the Cemetery! One has to tell you everything!"

Then he issued another order:

"You stay with me, Louis!"

"Aye, aye! sir!"

But suddenly Inspector Louis, whom his Chief's order kept near Lady Beltham, gave a cry of surprise:

"Look, in her hand... Upon my soul!"

"Why, what now?"

"She is holding something..."

"Poison, I wager?"

"Not a bit of it, sir!... a tooth!"

"A tooth?"

"Yes! a tooth!... A human tooth! Look for yourself, sir!"

Forcibly unclasping the poor woman's clenched fingers, the Inspector had dragged out of Lady Beltham's hand the tooth she gripped with an instinctive clutch.

"It's enough to send a man crazy!" groaned M. Havard. Then, meditatively turning the tooth over and over between his fingers, he soliloquized:

"It was Fandor summoned us here—and it is Lady Beltham we find!... It was for him to fire at Fantômas—and it is Lady Beltham falls under his fire!... She is struck by a ball—and she never bleeds!... Everything points to her having taken poison—and it is a tooth she has in her hand!..."

Then suddenly he gave a startled cry: "Listen! Listen!"

Inspector Henri's voice could be heard shouting urgently for help; whereupon, leaving Lady Beltham to her fate, all dashed off again. The officer's cry came from the adjacent enclosure, and thither Havard and his men rushed.

"Great God! they have killed him!" gasped M. Havard, and he pointed to his colleague stretched full length on the ground.

But at that moment the Inspector jumped up.

"God's truth! But they're calling out down in there!" he vociferated...

"Where? What d'you mean?" stammered M. Havard...

"Down in there!" reiterated the man... Someone's shouting!... It was from there the revolver shots came! I was sure of that! For heaven's sake, help me!"—and he began tearing with bleeding fingers at one of the stone slabs that covered in the disused well in his frantic efforts to lift it off.

"Fandor! It is Fandor, by God!" swore M. Havard, and now all were elbowing one another in their haste to raise the stone, which all of a sudden fetched away, revealing a dark, yawning, evil-smelling aperture...

"Courage!" yelled the Chief. "We are here! Is that you,

Fandor?"

A weak voice, but quite distinct came up from the depths: "No Fandor here!"

"Who are you then?"

"Juve, oh God!..." stammered M. Havard, and crazed with astonishment, he fell back, tottering on his feet.

*   *   *   *   *

Only a few minutes later, however, and while two officers were conveying M. Merandol to the village to send him from there to some hospital where he would be properly looked after and nursed back to health, a diverting scene of tragicomedy was enacting between Juve and M. Havard.

Barely out of his living tomb indeed, Juve seemed to recover all his habitual self-possession.

"Good day, Chief!" he addressed his erstwhile superior. "I may still give you that title?"

But M. Havard had quite other things to think of.

"Juve!" he demanded, in a breathless voice, "it was you who fired?"

"Yes! twice over. The last time when I heard your steps. My voice did not reach you, but I made sure my shots would attract your attention. Luckily I still had a clip of revolver cartridges in my pocket… But I will explain it all to you later on…"

"Good! You fired another time, you say?"

"Certainly!… Three-quarters of a hour or so before…"

"At Lady Beltham?"

"Eh! what?… So they've found her?…"

"Yes!… You had recognized her?"

"Recognized her?… But I've never set eyes on her!"

"But… if you took aim at her?"

"Why, bless my soul! It was not at her I fired!"

"Who at then?"

"At Fantômas!"

"He was there, then?"

"Obviously!"

"But where?… In the well?…"

"Where?… I don't know where!… Oh, no! not in the well!…
Further away than that…"

"But, Fandor?"

"Fandor?"

"Yes! You have seen *him*…"

Juve's face suddenly clouded.

"Come!" he exclaimed, "don't let us play at riddles! I don't
know where Fandor is. Why do you mention him?"

"Because it was he invited us to meet him here!"

"And he's not here?"

"No, Juve! It was Lady Beltham, I repeat, we found…"

"I don't like it! No! I don't like the look of it!" growled the
detective. He was still ghastly pale and hardly able to stand. No
matter for that! The mere mention of Fandor's name seemed to
inspire him with renewed vigor.

"He must be saved!" he said emphatically. "Where is Lady
Beltham? She will speak. She will tell us…"

"There!… over there!… Come!"—and once again, Juve and
M. Havard leading, the posse of police climbed the cemetery
wall. Thereupon a simultaneous cry of amazement escaped all
who had, only a few moments before, seen Lady Beltham lying
senseless on the ground. On the spot where they had left her to
hurry off in answer to Inspector Henri's cries not a soul was to
be seen!

"Gone!" faltered M. Havard.

"Bolted!" Juve corrected… "I expected as much!" Then, next
moment: "But… but, look there…"

There, in the sand of the pathway, Fantômas' ally with the tip
of her finger had traced an arrow.

"It's enough to drive one crazy!" M. Havard stammered for
the second time. "It's a nightmare! What did she…"

But he got no further. Juve had just dropped to his knees.
With his keen eyes he was examining the gravestone at the spot
to which the arrow pointed.

"A tooth!" he announced. "The mark of a tooth!"

"And I found a tooth in her fingers!" broke in M. Havard.

"And you… Oh! give it here! Give it to me!"

Juve seemed to have suddenly gone mad, ejaculating frantically:

"Fantômas was on a level with the bottom of the well… therefore under the ground! Therefore… By God! the thing's plain as a pikestaff, as simple as A B C!"—and, with all his might, he pressed the tooth found in Lady Beltham's hand against the impress carved in the stone. Then came a click… and lo! the wheels of some mechanism set in motion by an electric contact effected by this extraordinary master key, a tooth, began to revolve. Slowly the ponderous slab swung over—just as it had a few moments before in obedience to Lady Beltham's performance of the same maneuver.

"Revolvers ready!" commanded M. Havard. But Juve was already craning over the cavity.

"Fandor!… It is Fandor in there!"

There was no checking him. While two officers held up the granite block and prevented it from closing again, he leapt into the hollow.

"Fandor!" he gasped… "Fandor, my dear lad…"

Then a yell of fury: "Poison gas!… By God! the poison gases have choked him!…"

No force could have torn his dear burden from Juve's arms. Regaining all his vigor under stress of the feverish excitement of the moment, with a bound he was out of the villainous chamber again.

"Fandor!… Fandor, do you hear?"

In the fresh air the young man seemed to be recovering. Presently he opened his eyes:

"Juve!… My dear old Juve!" he said faintly. "Don't speak!" ordered the police officer, contradicting himself in his agitation. "How do you feel? You're not wounded?"

"I feel…" came Fandor's answer. "…I feel, hmm, well, annoyed!"

"Annoyed?… Annoyed!"

"By God, yes!… I wanted to save you! And it is you…"

"Why, no! No! that's not true! But for you, I should still be at the bottom of the well… It was you brought the police here!…

It was you..."

"And Fantômas, Juve?"

"Ah! that's true! You are right!... Oh! no need to be anxious about you any more!... And as for him..."

Juve sprang to his feet. After days and days of long-drawn agony, he could still indulge his wit.

"Chief!" he laughed ironically, "do you authorize me—albeit no longer a member of your staff..."

"You're talking nonsense, Juve!" Havard interrupted him. "The Minister has fallen... I restore you to office... But what authorization is it you wish?"

"Authority to arrest Fantômas!"—and while M. Havard stood there dumb with bewilderment, Juve turned to Fandor:

"So now, you feel better, eh? Will you help me?... It's you and I must take him!"

The detective stooped and helped Fandor, who was still tottering, to keep his feet, and supporting his faltering steps as he walked, led him up to the tomb 530, which still remained open.

"We are going down into it again," he explained... Oh! there's no danger now! The air has been changed!... And I am quite sure... But you shall know everything later on!... My shots hit the mark, by God!... Otherwise, the gases would have filled the well instead of escaping this way... I must have holed the receptacle... I must have wounded him into the bargain—killed him, perhaps!..."

Juve leapt into the yawning pit, and helped down Fandor after him. Then, while they all bent over, eagerly watching his every movement, asking themselves if he were not mad, he moved his hand slowly over the smooth surface of the marble forming the walls.

"Ah!" he exclaimed presently, "there it is!"—and they saw him take the tooth and press again, as before.

"So there is another imprint?" observed M. Havard...

"Yes! evidently."

The same rumbling noise that had signalized the opening of the tomb followed. Then next instant the wall fell apart... Beyond the first chamber—where Fandor had lain in a swoon after rescuing Lady Beltham—another chamber was revealed...

A cunning hiding place in good sooth! In this quiet cemetery, concealed beneath this flower-decked tomb, who but Juve
would ever have suspected what now all present could see?...
Scattered over the floor, a fabulous deluge of wealth recalling
the glittering caves of the fairy tales, gold pieces lay in heaps...

"Fantômas' treasure," cried Juve... "The millions of the
Crédit International must be there..."

He took a step forward, scornfully, nonchalantly, trampling
all this wealth underfoot...

"Fantômas, surrender!" he shouted.

Then, from a dark corner, crawled a darkling shadow—a
shape but too well known, a man whose face was hidden under
a black hood, whose body was molded in a close-fitting suit of
black tights, who was gloved and shod in black...

"Fantômas!" gasped the astounded officers.

Still crawling on his knees, a woeful spectacle, he came
nearer... In the dim, diffused daylight he seemed a part of the
darkness...

"Show a light!" ordered Havard... "Quick! It may be only
a ruse"—and a dozen electric torches flashed out. But it was
no ruse! In the strong light the grim figure was at last clearly
visible. It was splashed with bloodstains... Wounded in head
and chest and arms, the Genius of Evil seemed on the point of
death.

"Fantômas! you surrender?" reiterated Juve.

"To you and to Fandor, yes!"—answered the Lord of Terror.

He came another step forward, a miracle of hardihood, an
almost dying man!

Suddenly they saw him lift his head, and from under the
hideous mask came a hoarse gasp, a sob of anguish:

"Yes! I surrender to you two, Juve and Fandor... To you,
Juve, first and foremost! You have well earned your triumph!
You have won your victory at last!"

His breath whistled in his throat. Striving desperately to
speak again—a last spasm of proud defiance and undying
hatred:

"This is your day of victory, Juve!" he gasped... "Yes! but a momentary triumph!... Only momentary!... No more than that!..."

Underneath his grim black hood, the scoundrel seemed to be laughing—a laugh of deadly irony!

THE END

THE FANTÔMAS SERIES #1–7
NOW AVAILABLE FROM ANTIPODES PRESS

#1 Fantômas
Originally published as *Fantômas* in 1911.
Paperback: 310 pages. ISBN 978-0-9882026-1-0.

#2 The Exploits of Juve
Originally published as *Juve contre Fantômas* in 1911.
Paperback: 196 pages. ISBN 978-0-9882026-2-7.

#3 Messengers of Evil
Originally published as *Le Mort qui Tue* in 1911.
Paperback: 298 pages. ISBN 978-0-9882026-3-4.

#4 A Nest of Spies
Originally published as *L'Agent Secret* in 1911.
Paperback: 336 pages. ISBN 978-0-9882026-4-1.

#5 A Royal Prisoner
Originally published as *Un Roi Prisonnier de Fantômas* in 1911.
Paperback: 184 pages. ISBN 978-0-9882026-5-8.

#6 The Long Arm of Fantômas
Originally published as *Le Policier Apache* in 1911.
Paperback: 336 pages. ISBN 978-0-9966599-1-8.

#7 Slippery As Sin
Originally published as *Le Pendu de Londres* in 1911.
Paperback: 238 pages. ISBN 978-0-9966599-2-5.

Printed in Poland
by Amazon Fulfillment
Poland Sp. z o.o., Wrocław